Mississippi Blues

D'Ann Lindun

author of *Wild Horses*, *Shot Through the Heart*,
Desert Heat, and *Cooper's Redemption*

CRIMSON
ROMANCE
F+W Media, Inc.

This edition published by
Crimson Romance
an imprint of F+W Media, Inc.
10151 Carver Road, Suite 200
Blue Ash, Ohio 45242
www.crimsonromance.com

ISBN 10: 1-4405-6139-7
ISBN 13: 978-1-4405-6139-9
eISBN 10: 1-4405-6140-0
eISBN 13: 978-1-4405-6140-5

Dedicated first and foremost to my daughter, Brandi, who loves this book as much as I do. I'll never forget her perfect southern accent and "how's your mama" as long as I live!

Second, I'd like to mention a very special lady—my aunt, Ruth Burlison—whose faith in me has never wavered.

Third, this book was rejected a million times before I held my breath one last time and mailed it to my wonderful editor, Jennifer Lawler, who said yes!

Thank you all!

Chapter One

Something tangible sizzled in the air, an undercurrent of high tension.

Jace Hill shot a glance around. All the other cons seemed normal, so he pinched his lips together. The last thing he needed was to draw any attention to himself. Angola guards were quick to use their clubs first and slow to ask questions later. Most were overly eager to put anyone in the hole who looked at them the wrong way.

Jace figured out a long time ago it was safest to keep his head down and his mouth shut. After five years behind the prison's unforgiving walls, he'd learned the art of living an invisible life. Like a ghost, he moved about praying no one saw him. Keeping low was how he'd survived so far and how he planned to keep on surviving. To the guards, the cons, anyone on the inside, he had no name, no identity beyond the number stenciled across the back of his orange jumpsuit—20010.

Someone yelled, and the driver tromped on the gas shooting the bus forward. Whether from its unusual speed, or the deep ruts, the vehicle whipped from side to side. One tire dropped into the shallow ditch lining the road, tipping the bus still rolling on two wheels. Shackled to a steel pole, Jace's arms screamed a protest when the movement jerked him sideways. His limbs stretched so hard he feared them being pulled out of their sockets. The floor seemed as if it were going to fall from under his feet. Shouts and curses filled the air.

For a moment, it felt as if the bus would right itself. But instead, it flipped, sliding down an incline. The chains anchoring Jace to the pole broke in half, and he flew like a basketball. Someone's fist or foot hit him in the face, his ribs slammed into metal. He grabbed for something solid, but caught only air. The squeals of tearing tin sounded like a dying animal. Or maybe he heard his own cries mingling with the others.

His head crashed into the ceiling and the world went black.

...

Jace's left cheek rested against cool Louisiana dirt, and he tasted blood, dirt, and gasoline. Gradually, the world came back into focus. When he gingerly touched the back of his skull, his fingers came away clean. By some miracle, he didn't have a bashed-in brain. His head hurt worse than the time a guard hit him with a shovel for mouthing off about the shitty food.

One at a time, he tested his fingers, arms, and legs.

All worked, though he hurt like hell.

He pushed up to a sitting position. His wrists and ankles still wore iron bands, but the force of the wreck had broken the chains. He turned his aching head and saw the other men laying in bloody tangles of flesh and clothing. Snake Wilson lay a few feet away, his sightless eyes staring at the blue sky. *Lucky bastard.* Jace wished they could trade places.

The driver hung half in and half out of the shattered front window. Easing his pounding head the other way, Jace looked for the two guards. One lay sprawled in a twisted heap a few feet away, but there was no sign of the other man. Maybe he'd been squashed under the bus. Jace couldn't muster up any sympathy.

Completing his perusal of the area, Jace saw something that made his pulse jump. The wreck sheared the razor sharp fence surrounding the perimeter of Angola.

A chance to escape. Already the alarms began to scream a shrill warning, and the hounds bayed with blood lust. If the dogs picked up his scent, there'd be no second chances. If they caught him running, though, there'd be no telling how he would end up. Hanging from a tree, maybe.

He almost jumped out of his skin when somebody grabbed his arm. Handy Graves, an enormous black man, said, "Come on. Let's get the hell out of here."

With a groan, Jace pushed to his feet and staggered toward the woods. With a jolt of adrenaline, he thrust himself over the barbed wire and into his unexpected shot at freedom.

• • •

After an hour of steady jogging, they found a cove of magnolia trees and collapsed in the middle of them. Covered in sweat, out of breath, too tired to move, they weighed their options. "We need to split up," Jace gasped. "Our odds are better that way."

Handy nodded. "Where you gonna go, man?"

He had no idea. For the last five years, he'd dreamed of walking into Mama's kitchen and sitting down to a meal of ham and cornbread. But he couldn't now. Not like this. "I don't know. I guess I'll figure it out later." He spat. "We gotta move. The guards'll be on us like flies on honey." The baying hounds sounded closer.

Handy held out his hand. "Good luck."

"You, too." They shook and left in opposite directions.

Like a homing pigeon, Jace turned toward Mississippi.

• • •

The silver Greyhound, destination Juliet, Mississippi, squealed to a stop in front of the Jackson bus station blowing a cloud of noxious smoke behind it. Trey Bouché watched the driver throw his duffle bag into the bus's underbelly then followed the surly man aboard.

He chose the cleanest seat he could find, one toward the back. Only two other passengers rode this route—an old black man snored loudly in the furthest corner and a young woman wrestling with a squirming baby claimed a center seat. Ignoring Trey, she unbuttoned her blouse and offered the fussy infant a nipple. The baby settled down, suckling contentedly. Finally, the woman covered the child's head and her bare breast.

Trey looked away. After five years in the marines, most spent in Afghanistan where a woman could be stoned to death for showing her face in public, he sometimes found American women amazingly free. He settled in the seat with not enough legroom, intending to snack on a Snickers and Coke he'd bought from vending machines in the station. Instead, he set them on the empty seat next to him. The combination of the bumpy ride and the scents of stale popcorn and unwashed bodies turned his stomach.

He stared out the window. Magnolia trees were in bloom, their pink blossoms hanging like lace veils over the road. The bomb-weary streets of Kabul just didn't compare to springtime at home. Nowhere came close. He'd never been to a place he loved more than Juliet, Mississippi.

The city streets of Jackson passed, and soon the flat, pine-covered land of the delta rolled by. A wave of nostalgia washed over him. For five endless years, he'd longed for the sights and sounds of home.

And for one woman.

He could've come back sooner, but he'd not been wanted by his family…or Summer. Lifting his hip, he reached in the back pocket of his Levi's and pulled out a crumpled envelope. Inside was a card. He knew the words by heart —

Miss Salinda Samantha Bouché

*requests the honor of
your presence at her
high school commencement…*

He refolded the card and stuffed it back in his pocket as a heavy sigh escaped him. At least one member of his family wanted to see him. He doubted anyone else cared if he ever showed his face in Juliet again. Before ugly history could grab him and drag back into the past, he slammed his mind closed.

There would be plenty of time for facing his demons once he reached *LeFleur.*

• • •

Lightning streaked across the sky, promising a storm.

Summer Hill patted dark soil firmly around the roots of the very last candy-striped petunia and leaned back, satisfied with the results of her hard work. The garden was a little late this year, but would soon be overflowing with vegetables. Although exhausted, she'd taken time to add flowers down one edge of the vegetable garden. Thankfully, she'd gotten all the plants in before the incoming rain hit.

"Supper's on," Mama called from the safety of the porch.

"Okay. I'm finished." Summer stood and brushed off her dirty knees. Her lower back ached and she rubbed it. Although only twenty-seven, today she felt more like forty. Peeling off her gardening gloves she admired her handiwork. The dark earth would soon be alive with baby veggies and flowers. She glanced at the falling sun as a drop of rain hit her nose.

Mama's voice raised a notch. "Summer, you comin'? It's goin' to rain."

"Yes, Mama. Won't you please come out and see my petunias? They're still your favorites, right?" Even as Summer pleaded, she knew it was useless. No matter how many flowers she planted her mama would sooner die than step one foot beyond the porch.

"I can see them from here." Mama backed away from the door. "Get cleaned up now and I'll bring supper out."

Summer rinsed her hands and face in the hose then climbed the steps, taking care to lock the screen door carefully behind her. It had taken months of scrimping every penny to buy supplies for the porch, and several more months before she could afford to have it built. The entire time the workers had been here Mama hid inside. Summer talked Mama into sewing brightly colored tablecloths and cushions for the old wicker furniture she'd dug out of the shed.

Proud of their work, Summer nearly despaired when Mama refused to step foot on the newly constructed project. After days of gentle coaxing, she finally gave in and did as Summer asked. But she insisted upon a lock on the screen door, never mind someone could put their fist through it.

Summer hated to think what it would take to get her mama out in the yard and garden. Hopeless. She would never do it.

Reaching up, Summer switched off the overhead fan. They wouldn't need it. The wind scattered the muggy May heat. A red sunset cast a soft, pink glow on the side of the old house making it appear as if it had gotten a recent paint job. She smiled grimly. The walls hadn't seen paint in many years and wouldn't again anytime soon.

Mama came out carrying two platters. "I didn't make anything fancy. Just soup and sandwiches."

"Sounds good." Summer darted through the door. "I need to change first."

"Hurry," Mama fretted. "I want to finish before it rains."

"Looks real good."

After washing up and pulling on a loose sundress, Summer joined Mama on the porch and settled into the opposite chair. Just like every other Sunday, Mama was dressed as if she'd just come from church. She wore her favorite dress, matching heels, even nylons, and her nearly gray hair was clipped up in a loose bun. Large, midnight blue eyes dominated the delicate bone structure of her face. Only when she turned her head, and the puckered red scar cutting across her right cheek and mouth showed, did her perfectly put-together image shatter. Summer and her mother looked enough alike to be twins. Well, they had once—before Mama had been beaten, raped, and left for dead in a rain-soaked alley.

She set the last bowl on the table. "It's not much of a Sunday supper. But there's lemon cake for dessert."

"This is perfect." Summer popped a cherry tomato into her mouth and savored the sweet taste. Mama had all the time in the world to plan meals. Tonight there were slices of turkey, bacon, home baked bread, bean soup, and sweet tea.

She prepared food as if Jace still lived at home.

Summer forced away the unwelcome thought. She would not dwell on the injustice done to her brother tonight.

They ate in companionable silence until the first drops of rain hit the screen. Mama immediately jumped up and began clearing dishes.

"Just relax," Summer urged. "It's only a summer rain. I'll help you in a minute."

"I have it. It's no trouble," Mama said. "You worked so hard today you deserve to rest." She disappeared inside, and in a minute the sounds of running water and a Frank Sinatra tune floated over the evening air.

Knowing it was useless to fret about it, Summer sank down in the oversized chair she'd found at a yard sale. Mama had good reason to hate the rain. The night she'd been attacked, she'd huddled on wet, cold ground for hours until someone finally came along and rescued her. Wishing things were different for all of her family, Summer pulled a knitted afghan over her shoulders, curled up and closed her eyes as a few soft raindrops blew through the screen and cooled her sunburned face.

•••

Lindy Bouché stared at her plate, fighting tears.

Today should've been one of the best days of her life—her high school graduation. When Trey graduated, there had been a party with most of Juliet's population in attendance. Although not the best student in school, she still thought there'd at least be balloons, cards—hell, something. Not just sitting in the kitchen eating an ordinary fried chicken dinner. Their housekeeper made her special vanilla-champagne cake, but that was the extent of Lindy's graduation party.

Turning her arm, she admired the ruby bracelet Trey brought her from Afghanistan. With no warning, he'd come to the football field and seen her walk with her class. A shock since he hadn't been home once in five years. Not since he joined the Marines. He explained he received an unexpected graduation announcement and decided to surprise her. Lindy knew Mother must have mailed him the invitation without telling anyone.

She darted another glance at Trey. Five years had changed him a lot. Always taller than her by several inches, he'd gained twenty pounds of pure muscle. Lindy sensed the changes were more than physical. He was an adult now, not the kid he'd been when he left. Still drop dead gorgeous with dark hair and skin, her friends would be all over him again. Chasing him probably wouldn't do them any more good than before. He had eyes only for Summer Hill, although she always ignored him like the pesky kid he'd been back then.

He reached for another piece of chicken and winked at her. "Is Mother awake? I'm anxious to see her."

"No. She usually drifts off about six or so." The Chief heaped a third portion of mashed potatoes and gravy on his plate. Without further comment, he dove into the pile of food. He had barely spoken since Trey arrived. If she didn't know better, Lindy would think their father didn't want his son home.

She pushed the pile of mashed potatoes around on her plate. She didn't have any appetite. Their family was a joke. Trey halfway across the world. The Chief consumed by his job. And the stupid doctors who said they couldn't do anything for Mother. They couldn't even give her enough painkillers so she could come to Lindy's graduation. No one seemed to give a damn Mother was fading like a summer rose right under their noses.

The Chief broke into Lindy's glum thoughts. "What are you going to do tomorrow?"

She stirred her green beans without interest. "I dunno. Nothing."

"How about looking for a job? You could help out at the station, do some filing." He waved a chicken leg at her. "Or there's summer school. Mrs. Knight said you could get your marks up enough to get into Vanderbilt for the spring term."

"Yeah, right. Like I have a chance of that happening." Her mood grew murderous. Why couldn't he just get off her back? She'd sooner sell herself on the street corner than be stuck in the police station where the Chief could keep his eye on her. She didn't know what she wanted to do, but one thing was for sure—getting into Vanderbilt or any other college ranked last on her list.

"Maybe you could at least apply to junior college." He continued to point the chicken at her. "It's not your mother's wish, but it's something."

"I don't want to go to school. Not Community and not Vanderbilt. Especially not Ole Miss." Attending the University of Mississippi had always been Trey's dream, not hers. Lindy narrowed her eyes at the Chief. She was so sick of hearing about her mother's dream she could throw up. Just because Miss Emily Devereaux had been the belle of the ball at college, everyone expected Lindy to follow in Mother's high heels. Her mother wouldn't care what Lindy would be doing because Mother wouldn't be here in the fall. She'd be in the family crypt.

Without warning, the Chief slammed his fist on the table. China and crystal jumped, food spilled. "Stop this nonsense, Lindy. Your mother's fondest dream is for you to go to college. You're going. That's the end of it."

"Trey didn't go to college and the world didn't stop turning." She curled her fingers into her palms. "He wanted to go to Ole Miss to play football. Yet, you didn't mind when he gave up his scholarship to join the military. Why wasn't that the end of the world? It won't kill Mother if I don't go to college." Realizing what she'd said in the heavy silence following her outburst, she jumped up and shoved her plate halfway across the table. Her chest filled with an ache nothing could heal. "I'm out of here."

Before anyone else could react, the doorbell pealed.

Lindy called over her shoulder, "I'll get it on my way out. I'm going to see my friends."

The Chief picked up his coffee cup. "If it's for me, send them in here. My appetite's ruined now."

Still fuming, she stalked to the front door and opened it to Jody Marvell, one of the Chief's police officers. Once a college football star, Jody lost his chance to go pro when he blew his knee his first season with the Ole Miss Rebels. As the first black man on the police force in Juliet's history, he wore his shiny blue uniform with pride. He and Trey had been friends and teammates since the third grade. She lowered her eyes and flashed a sly smile at him. "Hey, Jody. Guess who's here?"

He ruffled her hair like she was still ten. "I don't know. Who?"

Annoyed he couldn't see her for the adult she was, she shrugged. "Go into the kitchen and see for yourself."

"Thanks, Lindy. Congrats on your big day, by the way." He grinned at her and her pulse sped up. He was a good-looking man. Too bad he was head over heels in love with Lilah Desmarteau. "What are you going to do with your cute self now?"

She rolled her eyes. "If you say anything about me working at the station or going to college so help me I'll scream so loud…"

"Whatever you say, kiddo." He gave her a mock salute and headed toward the kitchen, but before he reached it he shot over his shoulder, "It's up to you if you want to waste your life."

She stuck her tongue out at his broad back. Damn, why couldn't everyone just get off her case? Burning with curiosity to find out what brought Jody out in the rain, she followed him and stood out of sight just beyond the doorway. Jody wouldn't show up at *LeFleur* without a good reason. Maybe something interesting was happening in boring old Juliet. Mrs. Lewis probably fell and broke her hip at the five and dime. Or maybe one of the farm boys got good and fired up after today's ceremony, climbed the water tower, and painted his girl's name across it.

Lindy risked a peek around the doorway.

"Hey, man," Jody was saying to Trey, "When did you get back in town?"

"Jody, hi." Trey jumped up and the two men embraced, thumping one another's backs. "I got home just today."

"What is it, officer?" the Chief asked impatiently.

"I'll leave you alone." Trey moved toward the door. "Let's get together and have a beer. We can catch up then."

"You got a deal," Jody agreed.

"Sit down, finish your supper," the Chief ordered before turning to Jody. "Officer, what's on your mind?"

With a nod, Trey obeyed.

"Sir, I've got some bad news." Jody paused, shuffling from foot to foot. "Jace Hill escaped today."

Lindy covered her mouth with both hands to keep from crying out.

"What?" The Chief jumped to his feet, sending his chair crashing to the floor. "When?"

"Round 'bout six A.M. this morning, sir. A bus carrying prisoners overturned en route to the fields. The warden thinks the driver tipped the bus on purpose."

"Why?" the Chief demanded.

"Because the trustee who drove was in a gang, most on the bus." Jody fidgeted with his hat. "Fourteen men killed, two prisoners survived and both made a run for it. Jace Hill and another man named—" he glanced at his note "—Handy Jones. Neither has been caught yet. They've got the hounds on them, but they lost their scent on the highway. Looks like someone picked them up."

A shudder ripped down Lindy's spine. Angola prison guards were notorious for what they did to escapees. No mercy allowed. If the hounds caught the runners, the guards might not have anything but pieces to take back to Angola. She closed her eyes and mouthed a silent prayer. "Be safe, Jace."

Her eyes jerked open. What was she doing? Jace Hill was a dangerous convict, a murderer. An enemy to the Bouchés. No matter how much she once liked him, he'd become a felon.

The Chief shot orders at Jody. "Get out to the Hills' place and see if his mama and sister have heard the news. Maybe he's already contacted them. I'll go to the station and keep an eye on developments from there."

As Jody hesitated, the Chief barked, "Well, get on it."

"Yes, sir."

Lindy turned and fled. Wait 'til she filled Candy in on this one. This was big, really big. Trey back; Jace escaped. Two shattered families about to collide…again.

Chapter Two

For a long minute, Trey felt like he just missed stepping on a land mine. He couldn't breathe as the room spun. He had every intention of looking his demons in the face now he was home, but he hadn't expected them to jump him the first day he got back. Here was his chance to wrestle a big devil. "I'm riding along," he told Jody.

"The hell you are." The Chief's eyes glittered like blue diamonds and a muscle jerked along his jaw. "This is a police matter. Hill has been making threats since day one, promising revenge. You'd be his first target.

"Yes, sir. I know." Trey blew out a ragged breath. "But I'm still going."

"Let this bad dog lie." If possible, the Chief's eyes grew even colder. "Poke it and it's going to bite you in the ass."

"I can't sit idle and do nothing, sir." Trey planted his feet. He met the Chief's angry stare and refused to blink. "If Jace wants to make me pay, then I'm going to face him head-on. I know he killed Soloman. I found him over the body."

The Chief snorted. "What makes you think MiLann will let you on the premises? Much less talk to you? She isn't about to invite you in for tea and a nice piece of jam cake."

"I won't know if I don't try, sir."

"Jace Hill's been in Angola for five years and who knows what tricks he might've learned there. Those animals know games you can't even imagine," the Chief declared.

"Sir, the Marine Corp has prepared me pretty well to deal with most anything. Including prisoners." He straightened his shoulders. "If Jace is on the hunt for me I'm better off knowing where he is."

"I'll keep you posted," the Chief insisted. "The last place you need to be is in the middle of this dust up. Sticking your nose into things that were none of your business is what got you in trouble the last time Hill decided to break the law." Used to being instantly obeyed, the Chief turned his attention to Jody. "Use your brains, Marvell. This guy's a hothead. If he is out at his mama's place and you think he's going to blow, call me ASAP. I'll have everyone on alert."

"Sir," Trey interrupted doggedly, "maybe Jace'll listen to me. I can reason with him. He was my best friend. Maybe I can get through."

The Chief glared at him, his face turning deep red. "That was before your testimony sent him to Angola for life, son. It's unlikely Hill has anything but real deep hatred for you now. I think I've made it pretty clear how I feel."

Their eyes locked.

All Trey's life he'd deferred to his father. But no more.

He was a grown man with his own mind. What happened between him and Jace still ate at his gut even though Trey knew he'd done the right thing. If he'd kept silent, he would have been just as guilty as Jace. Trey needed to see Jace again, to look him in the eye and tell him so.

The Chief looked away first. "Go then. But if there's any sign of Hill, you radio me instantly." He ordered Jody, "Don't try to bring in the prisoner until I can get you some backup. Be on the lookout for Lindy, too. She needs to stick close to home with Hill running loose. I wouldn't put it past him to hurt her for some kind of twisted revenge plot."

"Understood, Chief." Jody glanced at Trey. "Let's go, buddy."

Trey followed Jody out to the patrol car, his thoughts jumping around everything that happened to MiLann, Jace, but mostly Summer.

Turning his unmarked car into the driving rain, Jody said, "You should listen to your old man. Who knows what Hill will do? Now I gotta look out for your butt as well as my own."

"I can look out for myself. I've been in tight spots in Afghanistan that would make your skin crawl." Trey drew a deep breath. "What happened to MiLann Hill is partly my fault, too. They have every reason in the world to hate me. But I'm not afraid of Jace."

"That's crazy talk and you know it." Jody's dark eyes met his. "Jace sent himself to Angola by what he did to Soloman. You're holding on to guilt that isn't yours to own and it's tearing you up inside. You can't keep it up, or guilt will eat you alive. You gotta let it rest."

"Yeah, I know." Trey stared out into the rain-drenched night. The twisting road seemed endless. There wasn't anything out here but copperheads, cotton, and cornfields. If it was only so easy to forgive himself. If Summer hadn't been hurt in the process, he might find it simpler to find some peace.

Summer. He'd been in love with her since before he knew exactly how strongly a man could feel about a woman. From the seventh grade on, he fantasized about making love to her. No other woman would do. Summer Hill was the only one for him.

As if Jody could read his mind he asked, "You feeling that old feeling again?"

"What do you mean?"

Jody quirked an eyebrow at him. "Come on, man. No matter how many honeys threw themselves at you, you were too hung up on Summer to notice. Too bad she didn't know you were alive."

Jody's words rang true. Trey spent most of his life consumed by Summer Hill, much to the dismay of girls who couldn't catch his interest, and to the delight of his friends who loved ridiculing him. He'd never told anyone the doors of heaven swung open for one brief moment before they slammed shut in his face.

• • •

LeFleur had looked like a movie set with the five acre yard mowed golfing green short, white tents billowing in the evening breeze, and flickering candles softly lighting it all. A live band played everything from Nat King Cole to Springsteen. Trey wandered among friends and family, accepting congratulations with a smile. Trying not to be obvious, he scanned the crowd, looking for Summer. She would be here. He didn't doubt it, but he hadn't seen her yet.

Finally he spotted Jace and his mama at the buffet table. They chatted with his mother as they filled their plates. Trey kissed MiLann's cheek, then sidled up to Jace and nudged him. "It's about time you showed up."

Jace grinned and elbowed him back. "Summer took forever getting ready."

"Where is she?" Trey hoped he sounded nonchalant.

With a knowing grin, Jace pointed toward the house. "She went inside for something."

"I'm going to say hi," Trey said. "I'll see you around."

"Yeah, yeah." Jace waved him off, already moving off to talk to Mavis Annette Brewer.

Trey couldn't find Summer anywhere in the house and disappointment coursed through him. Maybe she'd gone back outside to mingle with the crowd. He went out the back door, and just as he was about to turn the corner, something caught his eye. Turning, he saw her. In a flowing, white dress, she stood with her back to him looking into the pool.

Trey walked up behind her and stopped. "What are you doing out here all by yourself?"

She shrugged. "Waiting for you."

Someone played Etta James's "At Last" on a record while the band took a break. His heart jumped. "I like this one," he said, fighting for calm. She'd never sought him out before. "Care to dance?" Without waiting for an answer, he took her in his arms and they swayed slowly. Summer tucked her head into his shoulder and the soft vanilla scent of her shampoo tickled his senses.

In all the years he'd wanted her, Trey never risked their friendship. Having part of her was better than nothing at all. But being her kid brother's friend wasn't enough anymore. Dancing her behind a pillar, he cupped her face and looked into her surprised eyes. Then he kissed her. Expecting a slap or at least an angry withdrawal, he couldn't believe it when she opened her mouth to his. Instead of pushing away, she clung to him. When neither of them could breathe, he broke the kiss. He smoothed a tendril of hair out of her face. "I want you."

She lowered her eyes and a rosy blush climbed her cheeks. "I know."

"Make love to me."

She nodded shyly. "Yes."

For a moment, Trey stood frozen. Then reality hit. Taking her hand, he led her toward the guesthouse.

• • •

Jody spoke, breaking the memory. "You might give it another shot. Summer hasn't hooked up with anybody I've heard of."

Trey ignored the jolt of joy that ripped through him. She hadn't married. Did she still care for him? Could she? He turned off those dangerous thoughts. "It's better I don't cause her any more pain."

"What happened wasn't your fault, man. She has to know deep down inside Jace is responsible for what he did to Soloman. You did what you had to do." Jody's tone was somber as an undertaker's. Jace had been his friend, too.

"Yeah. I've never had a second's doubt Jace killed Soloman for what he did to MiLann." Trey's resolve held fast. Why did he feel so crappy? He'd 'done the right thing' and destroyed the person's life he cared most about in the process. When he'd left Mississippi, there'd been no chance to fix what happened between him and Summer. After he testified at Jace's trial, none of the Hills wanted anything to do with him. He didn't blame them. But the cost had been high.

"You'd do it again," Jody said, conviction in his voice.

Yeah, but nothing could prepare him for the asking price. If he had to do it all over, knowing the fee, would he stand up in court and testify? Or would he turn a blind eye to the obvious? Although he knew telling the truth at the trial would be the hardest thing he had ever done, he faced it head on like a man. He learned at a young age things were rarely black and white. That sometimes the choices weren't clear-cut and you made a decision and stuck with it.

Since that fateful night, Trey hadn't spoken to any member of the Hill family. God knew he tried, but the door had been repeatedly slammed in face. Within days after Jace's arrest, the Chief had packed up Trey, taken him to a Marine recruiter, and forced him sign on the dotted line. Nobody told the old man no.

Trey hadn't been able to stand up to him back then, giving up Summer, football at Ole Miss, and everything else in the blink of his father's eye. Six months later, after the trial, he'd gone overseas and hadn't been back on U.S. soil until today.

Jody turned into the driveway leading to the Hill home and parked. Trey's gaze took in the deserted Nichols' farm. He couldn't believe anyone lived here. The steps were crooked, falling down. A few boards at the side of the house had ripped loose and no one had nailed them back. When a burst of lightning lit up the sky, he noticed a new porch along the side of the house. The Hills used to live near his family's place down by the river. He expected them to move away from there, but he hadn't anticipated them to be living in poverty. Familiar guilt grabbed Trey's gut and twisted it.

Before her illness, his mother had written him about MiLann Hill going crazy after Jace's trial. She wouldn't leave her house, became a recluse. Regret lay just under his skin like an itch he couldn't reach.

Jody pounded on the front door while the storm beat at their backs. Finally, a light came on and a woman opened the door a crack. "Who's there?"

Trey's heart stopped, then jump-started, racing furiously.

Summer.

The girl he'd dreamed about for years. The girl he'd worshiped his entire life. The girl he'd lost his virginity with. His blood thickened, raced low. Would he ever quit wanting her? Would he ever stop regretting losing her?

"It's Jody Marvell. I need to speak to you on official business." Jody pulled a notepad from his pocket and tapped it with his fingers.

Trey held back a groan. Jody sounded like Sergeant Malloy, one of the tough interrogators in his unit. Jody would never get anywhere with Summer starting off like a hard-ass.

"Jody. What on earth are you doing out in this kind of weather?" She opened the door another inch. She sounded warm and friendly. Then she narrowed her eyes at him. "Why are you being so formal? I've known you since grammar school for crying out loud. And who's there with you?"

Trey stepped under the bright overhead light. "It's me."

For an instant their gazes met and held.

Her eyes widened with shock, then darkened with fury.

• • •

Summer recognized Trey at once. No one else sounded like him. God gave him a voice that sounded like it had to crawl across gravel to get out of his throat. She blinked the rain out of her eyes. Maybe she was seeing things. What was he doing on her doorstep in the middle of a rainy night? Of all the places she'd expected him to reappear, this wasn't it. All the days and months she'd waited for him to show up and explain why he'd turned his back on Jace—*and her*—and he'd never bothered. Then she heard through the grapevine he joined the marines and took off for parts unknown.

Now he was here? Five years too late? Her ears rang and her knees threatened to buckle. She grabbed the door for support and held on until her knuckles turned white. When Trey reached for her she shook her head. "Don't you dare touch me."

Jody's lips moved, but no sound came out. She forced herself to focus on him.

"Summer? May we come in? You look a little shaky."

"I can't let Mama see…him." Glancing over her shoulder she was relieved to see Mama still intent on her TV program. Apparently, she hadn't heard the knock on the door or the subsequent conversation.

The stairs didn't seem big enough for all of them. Jody Marvell was enormous—well over six feet tall and weighing more than two hundred pounds. He was famous in Juliet, but he seemed to disappear next to Trey. Although not as heavy, and a bit taller than Jody, Trey seemed to suck up all of her air.

Her breath rushed out of her lungs, making it hard to focus. Every cell in her body tingled with awareness of him. Telling herself he was nothing more than a memory, she tried to calm down.

He'd changed, but yet not at all. He'd always seemed so unaware of his effect on her. As a child and a teen, he'd been beautiful, but even she had no idea how stunning he would become as an adult. Wherever he'd been it had sculpted his face into defined, angular planes. His short haircut showed off dark eyes that seared her soul and a full-lipped mouth that could kiss like sin itself. And what he could do with his hands ...

Summer mentally shook herself. Was she drooling? She resisted the urge to wipe her mouth with the back of her hand. "What brings you out here?" she finally rasped. Her voice sounded as rough as his.

The clouds opened up and rain poured out of them but no one moved.

"It's about your brother," Jody responded. "He…"

"Something's happened to Jace?" Her breaths came in short, fast gasps. Had someone harmed him? Angola was one of the worst prisons in the country. The warden held the men's lives in his hands like he was God. He hadn't approved her for visitation because she complained about the conditions in which her brother was housed. She shot Trey a venomous look. The last person she wished to discuss this with was him.

"The Chief sent me out here to tell you your brother escaped from Angola today. A bus overturned carrying prisoners—Jace among them. He and another man are still on the run." Jody wore a cop expression. Serious, subdued. He wiped his rain soaked face with one big hand. "Have you heard from him?"

She couldn't focus on him. "No, I didn't know. We haven't heard…I don't understand."

Lightning cracked again, lighting up the three of them like scarecrows. Drenched by the downpour, Trey looked like some kind of sex god. Clothes molding to his body, outlining every impressive muscle. Even though heat shot through her like a body slam, she refused to be moved.

"Has Jace come here?" Jody pressed.

She glared at him, willing herself to stand up to his questions. "You mean my brother, the boy you both went to school with, the one you both played football with for longer than I can remember? No, I haven't seen Jace since the day he was taken away in handcuffs."

Trey looked at her with something like guilt or remorse flickering in his eyes. "We think Jace is probably headed this way. The Chief wanted us to check and see if Jace has come home."

"Why should I care what the Chief wants?" She folded her arms over her chest and stared him down. "Your father doesn't give a tinker's damn about us. No one ought to know better than you."

She had the satisfaction of seeing him flinch. Good. Score. Trey Bouché and his incompetent father were the reason her baby brother spent the last five years behind barbed wire and brick walls with no way out but in the back of a coroner's wagon.

"The Chief does care." Trey looked as sick as she felt. "He's also worried Jace may do something stupid. If you think that might happen…"

"It won't." She cut him off. "I'm going inside."

"Just a minute," Jody insisted. "We assume Jace is headed here. Be on the alert."

Summer's head swam. She couldn't focus. All she could take in was her brother somehow broke out of Angola and might show up here. And Trey was home. The combination was too much to process.

"Summer," Trey warned, "just be careful."

She stared at him through narrowed eyes and tight lips. "Stay out of my family's problems. We're none of your business."

"I just wanted you and your mama to know about Jace so you weren't frightened if he shows up." He reached for her again and she dodged his hand.

"I said don't." *Mama*. What this news might do to her was unthinkable. "If I see Jace, I'll welcome him with open arms." She wiped the rain off her face with shaking hands and reached for the doorknob. "Please just go."

Jody stepped off the stoop. "Fair enough. I'll be in touch. Remember one thing, though. Aiding and abetting is a crime."

As Trey turned to follow Jody, he paused. "If I can help—"

Summer laughed, if the noise coming out of her throat could be called laughter. It was more like a strangled gasp. The sound grated on her ears. "Help me? Or Jace? Like you helped us last time? No, thanks. I don't think we need your kind of assistance." She dared him to argue.

"Your brother killed a man in cold blood. I saw the evidence dripping off his hands with my own eyes. What did you want me to do?" His lips turned down and his voice went icy. "Lie?"

Yes. No. Why couldn't you just keep your mouth shut? She wanted to rail at him, but instead she fixed a stone-cold glare on him. "All the help you can give me is to leave me and my brother alone."

"I can't do that." Rain ran down his face in rivulets, but he seemed unaware of it. "I'm going to prove once and for all your brother killed Soloman. Then you'll have to face the fact Jace is where he belongs no matter how much we both hate it." He turned and walked away, joining Jody in the car.

Once they were gone, she collapsed on the step in the soaking rain. Her body shook with shock.

Jace free.

Trey back.

She didn't know which one was more upsetting. One was almost as crazy as the other. Jace escaped from behind the fences of the most notorious prison in Louisiana, the country. After five long years of silence, Trey showed up on her doorstep as if it were yesterday. Offering his help, even. The nerve. Why did her traitorous heart beat just a little faster at the thought of him back in Juliet?

Mama opened the door. "Why are you out in the rain? It's almost nine and our TV program is about to start."

Remorse gripped Summer as she looked up into her mother's scarred face. Even though she had done nothing wrong, she felt terrible every time she made her mother worry or become nervous. The weight wore heavy on her shoulders at times. She stood. "I'm sorry, Mama. I lost track of time."

She hated lying to her mother, but she hated the consequences of telling her the truth even more. She stood, stepped inside and closed the door.

Mama instantly locked it. "I don't like you out in the rain." Her gaze darted around the familiar room. "I'm afraid of what could happen."

"Nothing's wrong. I promise. Let's get a drink of water so you can take your medicine." With a firm, gentle grasp, Summer herded Mama through the spotless front room, into the kitchen. The dishes were done, the floor swept clean. Mama's *problem*—agoraphobia—kept her locked prisoner inside. With little to do, she kept the house immaculate. Summer sighed deeply. She longed for the old days when Mama laughed and played freely. At times, she even left the dinner dishes on the table and raced outside with her children to catch lightning bugs in canning jars or go down to the creek to fish for crawdads.

Keeping her head turned away in case Mama could read her face, Summer filled a glass with water and unscrewed the cap on the medicine bottle.

"What's going on?" Mama plucked at the sleeve of Summer's wet shirt.

"Nothing." She kept her gaze down. It wouldn't do to frighten her. "Why do you think something's the matter?"

Mama peered over Summer's shoulder into the dark window. "I thought I heard a car drive up a few minutes ago. It's got me rattled." With each word her voice raised a notch. "Who came here?"

"Nobody for you to worry about." Reluctantly, she turned and faced her mother. The signs of an oncoming fit were apparent. Mama's face tightened, her lips pinched, her eyes squinted tight. Fear had taken control. "Mama, please calm down. I stayed outside a little longer than I meant to is all."

The worry didn't fade from her eyes, but her tone lowered. "I'm sorry. I just don't like it when you're out on a night like this."

"I know," Summer murmured. When Mama got upset, the best thing to do was stay as calm as possible. "But nothing happened. See? I'm just a little damp."

She never lied to her mother, but in the space of two minutes she'd told three whoppers. She couldn't continue this charade. "Mama, sit down, please."

"What is it?" She perched on the edge of a chair, wringing her hands.

"Jody Marvell came out here tonight." Mama wasn't going to take this well. There was no easy way around it either. Summer dragged in a deep breath. "He was with Trey Bouché."

Instantly, wounded disbelief clouded Mama's eyes. Summer rushed on. "They came to tell us something. You need to hear it, too."

"No." She shook her head from side to side and clutched it with both hands. "You can't mean it. Not a Bouché. You know what they have done to this family. To Jace. To me."

Summer knelt beside Mama, pulling her hands into her own. Then she pleaded on deaf ears. "Trey isn't the Chief…" They never, ever spoke of the past. Or of the people who changed their lives forever. All dead subjects. Speaking their names now was a sacrilege.

Mama stumbled to her feet, knocked over her chair, and rushed out of the room with her hands over her ears, howling like a wounded animal.

Summer ran after her and found Mama facedown across her bed, shoulders heaving.

"No, no, no."

Sinking down on the bed, Summer stroked her mama's back with gentle strokes and murmured soft words of comfort.

Finally, Mama rolled over. Her scarred face twisted grotesquely—her mouth an angry slash, eyes swollen and tear-stained, and hair splayed wildly about her head. She looked like she belonged in an asylum.

No. Mama's mind was sick, but she wasn't crazy.

Summer feared telling her the rest of it. That Jace escaped. If Mama caught even a glimmer of the truth—that Chief Samuel Bouché was once again going to arrest her son, her mind might permanently snap.

Summer wasn't so sure she might not have a breakdown herself.

Chapter Three

Summer worried about Mama all night.

If Jace showed up out of the blue, she'd likely flip out. But if he didn't come back, and she got her hopes up for nothing, that could also destroy her. With her stomach in knots, Summer decided to tell Mama the truth.

When she came downstairs, she appeared normal—as normal as she could be anyway. Her hair was done in a French twist and she wore a flowery dress and sandals. "Mornin', darlin'."

"Good morning, Mama." Summer poured them each a cup of coffee and pulled out a chair. Her nerves played cat and mouse. "Please sit down. I need to talk to you."

Her blue eyes clouded. "No more talk of that…family."

"This is about our family." Summer waited until her mother was seated. Taking a deep breath, she tried to steady herself. "I have some bad news." Mama's eyes began to cloud and Summer blurted out the rest. "Jace escaped from prison yesterday."

For a moment, Mama didn't react. Then her eyes brightened. "My boy is out of that horrible place?"

Summer reached across the table and squeezed her hand. "Yes, but not legally. Apparently, he was on a bus transporting prisoners and it overturned. Two men escaped, Jace is one of them."

Mama gave a small cry and twisted her fingers together until they turned white. "Oh, my Lord. What's going to happen to him?"

Summer circled the table and folded her mother in her arms. Her body shook with uncontrollable tremors. "I don't know, Mama. The police think he's going to come home."

"I hope he does," she sobbed. "I'd give anything to see him."

"Mama, that isn't likely to happen." Summer patted Mama's back until she calmed. After a few minutes her tears dried, but her body still shook. Summer reluctantly released her. "Are you going to be okay?"

"Yes." She wiped her face with a corner of her apron. She looked around. "Oh, heavens. I have so much to do. Cleaning, cooking. Yes, cooking. I'll make stuffed pork chops, my boy's favorite. Oh, and an apple-cinnamon cake with vanilla ice cream. He loves that."

Summer's heart lurched. She chose her words carefully. "Jace can't stay here. You understand, right?"

Mama's lips tightened, making her scar stand out in stark relief against her pale face. "He can if no one knows."

Summer stood up. She'd have to make Mama understand later. "I have to go to work. I'll call you as soon as I have a break. Love you."

"Love you, sugar." Mama got up and began rummaging through a drawer. "Where'd I leave my recipe for orange-cranberry glaze?" Her mind was on her meal preparations and Summer let it go. If she pressed the issue, Mama might have another fit. Better to leave her halfway happy in her own world.

Summer got ready to leave, still troubled. If Jace came back, he would probably wait for dark. She'd be home by then. A regular client had an appointment at ten and Summer couldn't just not show up. During high school, she had taken enough courses at the vocational school to certify as a hairdresser. Luckily, she'd found a job at a salon. Doing hair wasn't her dream job, but at least she could keep her mother at home.

Living in Juliet was hard, but nowhere else would be any easier.

• • •

Summer's old car sputtered to a stop in front of the Curl Up and Dye. As she turned it off, the beast backfired loud enough to send the robins in a nearby tree off in flight. One of these days, the Escort was just going to croak on the spot, forcing Summer to walk or peddle her old bike to work. She couldn't afford a new vehicle right now. As she gathered her bag from the backseat, a shadow fell across her window. She looked up, startled. Galen Franks stood there smirking at her with his gap-tooth grin.

"Mornin', Miss Summer." He leaned over and she tried not to gag at his awful odor.

"Hello, Galen."

Already running late, she didn't have time to chat today. He waited for her outside the shop nearly every morning, and she usually took a minute or two to visit with him. Weighing well over three hundred pounds, he rarely wore a shirt and the sides of his grease stained overalls gaped open. They had gone to school together and she always tried to be kind to him. Others often weren't. They made fun of him because he weighed a lot and he wasn't overly bright.

He moved in front of her, bouncing up and down on the balls of his feet. "I can fix it."

"Oh, that's not necessary. I'll take it over to the mechanic later." She slowed, not completely halting. She didn't want to be beholden to him, and besides she couldn't pay him anything right now.

"Your car is going to die." His little pig eyes and down turned lips looked as solemn as if he were headed to a funeral. "You will be stranded. That's dangerous."

She hesitated for a moment; hand on the doorknob. Rick over at the local garage was reasonable and did a good job, but he was out of her budget. Galen fixed cars, but most people didn't trust him because he was a little slow-minded. "Could you do it today? Repair this old thing in one day, I mean?"

He nodded, pumping his head like a piston. "Yeah. I can do it."

"Well, all right then." She opened the door. "Thank you, Galen."

His head continued to bob. "I can do it."

"I'm sure you can." Praying she was right, she hustled inside.

As she dashed through the salon's door, Glory Lavery looked up from her station with a frown. "You're late."

"I know, I know." Summer hung her purse on the coat stand behind the door. "Sorry."

"Lucky for you, Mrs. Simpson cancelled." Glory took a bobby pin out of her mouth and placed it in the thinning hair of Viola Krebbs. "Said she's not feeling well."

"Oh my. I'll have to call her," Viola said. "Did Evelyn say what was wrong?"

"No, ma'am." Glory shook her head slightly and her short, spiked hair danced like a cockscomb. The color and style was similar to a male bird's, but her short, plump body reminded Summer more of a little red hen.

Summer owed Glory a great deal. She moved to Juliet after Mama's rape and Jace's trial and if she heard about the whole nasty scandal, she didn't pry. When Summer couldn't find a job, Glory gave her one.

"I'm sorry Mrs. Simpson isn't feeling well. I could sure use the money, but it doesn't hurt my feelings to have a few minutes to catch my breath. I didn't sleep well last night." Summer checked her supplies. Everything looked good to go.

Viola's eyes sharpened. "What's the problem, young lady?"

Summer knew there wasn't anything Viola liked better than a piece of gossip to share with her ladies' sewing circle. Her heart must be broken today because her fellow rumormonger wasn't here to spread more stories. Summer busied herself moving combs around on her workstation. "Nothing, ma'am. Just a lot on my mind."

"Your mama okay?" Viola barely kept the venom out of her voice. It wasn't even concealed well, riding just under the surface.

"Yes, ma'am. Mama's fine." Summer kept her face averted so the woman couldn't see her face. Mrs. Krebbs and her crowd didn't care about Mama. All the busybody wanted was a juicy tidbit to dissect with her friends. Her bunch showed how much they cared about MiLann when they whispered a divorced Yankee who wore her skirts too short got what she had coming.

Viola smiled like a little yippy dog about to bite. "Give her my regards."

"Will do." Summer had no intention of doing any such thing.

"All's not lost. Check the book. You have another appointment. Someone called and I gave him Mrs. Simpson's spot." Glory grinned. "It's not a perm, but a client is a client, right?"

"Absolutely." Summer didn't care whose hair she cut just so they paid. "A man? Who is it?"

"Don't know. Didn't get his name." Glory shrugged. "He hung up before I could ask for it. This fellow asked if you had any openings this morning and to put him with you."

"Me? Why?" Summer figured her surprised expression matched Mrs. Krebbs's. Although not unheard of, they didn't get many men in the Curl Up and Dye. Most of Juliet's middle-to-older male population hung out at Leroy Eaton's place on Main whether they needed a haircut or not. And the younger kids went to one of the fancier salons down in Jackson.

"Couldn't say," Glory said around a mouthful of bobby pins.

Mrs. Krebbs dangled her hand at the wrist and gave it a few little shakes. "Must be a funny boy."

Glory shoved another bobby pin in the meddler's head and she gave a little yelp.

"Sorry," Glory mumbled, promptly digging in another pin.

Before anyone could respond, the bell over the door chimed. All heads turned, Mrs. Krebbs rubbing hers. All mouths dropped as Trey Bouché walked in.

"I have a ten o'clock appointment," he announced casually. Nothing in his demeanor suggested he didn't walk into a women's salon every day.

Summer's stomach did a few rollovers. She didn't know what to do. The vow she'd made to her mama ran through her head. She'd promised not to see Trey again, and here he stood not even twenty-four hours later. If she treated him coldly, she'd be in trouble with Glory. Worse, Viola would be watching like a hawk just waiting for any tiny tidbit to spread over town before her curls dried.

Summer forced a casual tone. "What would you like? A haircut?"

He grinned and ran a hand through his already short style. "Yeah, I'm getting a little long."

What a liar. Although a bit longer than most military men wore, it was still short by most standards. She bet he'd cut his hair less than a week ago. "Do you want your head shaved?"

His smile faded. "No. Not that. Just take a little off the top."

"That'll take about a minute." Summer motioned to her booth. "Sit here."

He settled his big frame in the delicate chair. She tied a dark brown apron around his neck, taking great care not to touch him as she tied the strings. Her fingers stilled for a second as she remembered tasting his neck and the way he'd trembled. She jerked the knot tight and their eyes met in the mirror.

His dark and unreadable, hers angry.

She dropped her gaze to his gold-tipped locks. "A trim?"

"Yeah." His voice grated on her nerves like a nail file dragging across a counter. She tried not to shiver.

Hesitantly, she ran her fingers through his hair, just as she did every client who came through the door. This was different, though, and they both knew it. A dark red burn crept across her face as she thought about the last time she'd touched his hair. His mouth had been at her naked breast, her fingers splayed at the back of his head inviting him closer.

She leaned across him and reached for a pair of scissors, her breast brushing his shoulder. Her hands seemed to grow ten thumbs and the lid from the disinfectant jar fell to the floor, rolling across it. In the silent room the lid ricocheted like a firecracker. Viola and Glory both turned their attention her way. Ignoring their curious glances, she dashed after the lid, caught it and returned it to its rightful place. She needed to get a grip before this got embarrassing.

Scissors safely in hand, she went to work, concentrating only on the task in front of her until out of the corner of her eye she saw Glory leading Mrs. Krebbs to the sink. As soon as the water came on she hissed, "What are you doing here?"

"I came by to see if you were okay," he answered in a low tone.

"I'm as fine as can be expected." *Oops.* She snipped a bit too much. She'd have to smooth out the rough spot.

"Have you heard from Jace?"

"No." She glanced around to make sure no one was listening. Another tiny thread of his woodsy-smelling hair fell to the floor. "And if I did, you'd be the last person I'd tell."

"You'll see him." He sounded positive. Almost like he knew something she didn't.

Startled by his so-sure tone she faced his reflection. "How do you know? And keep your voice down."

"Because he's got nowhere else to go." His dark eyes bore into hers. She looked away first. "He'll be changed, Summer. Not the same person you remember.

"No thanks to you." With quick, sure movements she moussed his hair with her palms, her thoughts focused on her brother. Jace might not be the same innocent boy he'd been, but he was still her brother. Blood ran thicker than water. "Jace wouldn't hurt me or Mama."

"Jace is a convicted murderer because he stabbed a man to death. Not because of anything I did. You know that." He ran a hand over the back of his neck. "I'm not worried about him hurting you physically. Emotionally is another story."

He sounded so protective, she weakened for a moment. Then she stiffened her spine. "You don't need to worry about anything to do with me. Especially if it concerns my brother, who you helped frame."

His features froze. "I'm just trying to lend a hand."

"Don't." Summer hardened her heart. "Stay out of my life. I don't want anything to do with you."

"Are you ever going to face the truth?" His tone matched hers. "Or continue to live in denial forever?"

"Are you going to admit you're wrong about Jace?" She glared at him, glad her scissors were out of reach. Stubborn, pig-headed ox. Why couldn't he just admit there might be a perfectly logical reason Jace had blood on his hands? Like maybe he tried to save Soloman's life, not end it.

He stood and pulled a twenty out of his pocket. "This ought to cover it. I don't care if you want me around or not; I'm sticking close until Jace is found. There's nothing I can do about the past, but I can make sure another tragedy doesn't happen."

She wanted to laugh, but it hurt too much. "Don't hold your breath."

Leaving the bill on the counter, he left.

The minute Trey went out the door, Summer hurried in the back room and called home. On the third ring, Mama picked up. "Hello? Jace? Is that you?"

"No, Mama. It's me." Summer relaxed a fraction. Jace hadn't returned.

"Hi, darlin'. I keep looking outside every few minutes, but I haven't seen anyone. I thought this might be Jace calling." Apparently picking up on her anxiety, Mama's voice rose. "Is something wrong? Have those people done something bad to him?"

Summer closed her eyes. She could see her mother, fingers plucking at the collar of her floral dress, gaze darting about looking for monsters in the air. "No, Mama. Everything's fine. I'm just checking to see if you need anything from the Piggly-Wiggly."

"You scared me there for a minute. No, I don't think so. Well maybe a pint of cream. I could make some whipped cream to go on the cake…"

Tuning her out, Summer breathed a sigh of relief. This conversation was similar to the one she had with her mother every day. She finally said, "Okay, Mama. I've got to go. Just cream? Anything else?"

"No, darlin'. I'll see you tonight. Hurry home, please. We've got to make certain your brother's first night home is a special one."

Instead of arguing, Summer hung up hoping Trey was wrong. Maybe Jace would run the other direction; maybe he'd go to the Gulf of Mexico and disappear on one of the many unnamed islands out there. The more distance he put between him and this town, the better.

As soon as Glory finished Viola's perm, took her money, and ushered her out the front door, she settled onto a stool. "Spill it. What's going on?"

Summer evaded Glory's sharp gaze. She went in the back room and poured two glasses of sweet tea. Faking nonchalance, she came back out. "What makes you think something's going on?"

Glory shrugged and took her tea. "Oh, I don't know. Maybe because when that tall drink of water came strolling in here, you tensed up like a bird with one foot on a hot wire. I got a strong feeling he meant a bit more to you than just a customer looking for a cut and style."

Knowing Glory wouldn't give up until she knew what made her so nervous, Summer sipped her tea trying to decide how much to divulge. "That was Trey Bouché."

For a moment, Glory didn't react. Then her mouth formed a perfect O. Snapping it shut she said, "Oh my gosh. No wonder you froze up like a cherry popsicle."

"Yeah." Glory moved here after the scandal and Summer hadn't talked about it much, but Juliet was a small town. Gossip traveled faster than trash on a windy day. Summer preferred not to discuss her involvement with Trey. She'd been dumb enough to sleep with him once. She didn't want to share her humiliation with anyone. Not even one of her best friends.

"Why on earth would he come here?" Glory studied her over the rim of her glass, her emerald-green gaze sharp as cut glass. "If I didn't know better, I'd think he was looking for you."

Before Summer could reply, the doorbell chimed. Both women looked toward the new arrival. Lilah Desmarteau, the third stylist at the shop, came bursting in. Her coffee-with-cream skin, almond shaped eyes, and ample curves often caused men to fight for her affection, but Jody Marvell held her heart.

"Summer. My goodness gracious, honey. Are you all right?"

Summer sighed. She should've known Jody couldn't resist Lilah's charms. "What'd Jody tell you?"

"Not a thing. I heard some news on his little ole police scanner." She wiggled her raven's wing eyebrows a few times. "Baby doesn't know I listen sometimes just for fun. What he doesn't know won't hurt him, right?"

"What are you going on about?" Glory demanded. "You're not making a lick of sense."

"Well, really." Lilah wiggled over to her empty booth and settled into her chair. She picked up a comb and studied it as if she'd never seen one before. "I guess you don't want me to catch you up on all the newest developments. I don't know all that much anyway. Summer's got the big scoop."

"What! What!" Glory looked ready to explode with curiosity.

Trapped, Summer reluctantly shared her secret. "My brother escaped from a bus wreck near Angola yesterday. Chief Bouché believes Jace is headed home with revenge on his mind. Jody came out last night to warn me."

"This gets stranger by the minute," Glory commented to Lilah. "Guess who was here, looking for a haircut? Trey Bouché himself."

Lilah opened and closed her mouth a few times. "No way. Jody told me Trey was back in town, but I haven't seen him yet. He showed up here? Why?"

"Trey came to see me," Summer said. "Last night, he was with Jody. Today, he said he was checking up on us. He said he's going to keep anything bad from happening to Mama or me."

Lilah recovered her power of speech first. "Well, there's worse things in life than being protected by a big ole hunk of man like that."

"Oh, for pity's sake." Glory jumped up, placing her hands on her hips, ready to argue. In her opinion, a woman didn't need a man for much more than recreation. Certainly not for protection. Lilah's helpless act around Jody made Glory nuts.

Summer held up her hand. "Please, you two, not the man, no-man argument again."

Glory, puffed up, slowly pulled in her feathers. "Fine."

"Okay." Lilah leaned forward. "How does Trey look? What did he say? Is he still one fine piece of man cake? Tell, girlfriend, tell."

"He looked good." Glory licked her bright red lips. "Real good."

"I don't want him anywhere around me." Summer refused to admit exactly how great Trey looked. Time hadn't hurt him any. "If Mama finds out he was here today, she might go off the deep end for good. I had to tell her he showed up last night and it took forever to calm her down. I didn't even get around to telling her about Jace because she was so upset about Trey. I finally got the chance this morning. She took the news okay. Better than I thought she would."

Both women stared at her waiting for more details.

"She completely lost it last night," Summer said, "and she made me promise not to have anything to do with Trey ever again. Of course I agreed."

"That was a bad move." Glory sipped her tea.

"What?" Summer spun her styling chair around and stared at her friend. "Why?"

"Because if the heat sizzling between you two today is any indication of how you feel, then steering clear isn't going to be easy." She fished a piece of ice out of her glass and held it toward Summer. "Here, hon, you'll need this."

"Heat? Are you kidding? I loathe him," Summer sputtered. Trey Bouché and his father are the reason my brother has been rotting in jail and my mama won't leave her own front porch. The only heat you thought you saw was my suppressed rage. I don't want to see him, I don't want to talk to him, and I don't feel anything for him but hatred."

"You keep telling yourself that. You might eventually believe it." Glory reached over and touched Summer's knee with the ice cube. "But I judge differently. Me thinks thee protests too much."

"Oh, for crying gypsies!" Summer jumped up, and without a backward look, stomped into the laundry room. Fuming, she threw a stack of dirty towels in the washing machine and turned it on. For a moment, she stared into the washer. Glory didn't have a clue what she was talking about. Of course she had been tense when Trey strolled into the shop like he had every right to be there. He betrayed her brother. She held absolutely nothing in her heart for him now. There wasn't room for the risk.

•••

As he left the shop, Trey noticed the hood of Summer's car up and someone bent over, head hidden underneath. Curious, he walked over to see who it was. As he approached, the man looked up with an expression of pure terror. Galen Franks. Trey wondered about his fear. He never harmed any of the Franks, although he knew they took a lot of abuse. Maybe this one had a run-in with the Chief.

"Hey. What's up?" He kept his voice soft, using a tone one would use with a frightened hunting dog.

The big man cocked his head. "Nothin'." Almost reluctantly, the other man held out his hand. "My name is Galen W. Franks."

Trey shook hands. "I'm Trey. Good to know you." He indicated Summer's car with a tip of his head. "What's wrong with the car? I'm pretty good with engines. Maybe I can help."

The obese man wiped his hands on his ample rear. "It don't run good. Miss Summer needs it fixed."

"Do you have any idea what's wrong?" Trey bent over the engine. The whole car needed to be junked. But obviously Summer couldn't afford something better.

The man gestured toward the spark plugs. "Needs new ones."

"I see. Do you have some?" He lifted one corroded battery wire and snorted. The battery needed to be replaced too.

"Yeah." Galen nodded toward his truck. "In the back."

"Get them, and I'll help you put them in." Trey didn't know what made him decide to help, but he didn't want to leave until he made sure Summer's car was running. He glanced at his cherry red mustang, and a wave of nostalgia washed over him. Restoring the old car with Jace and Jody had been some of the best times of his life.

Galen came back with the new plugs and they changed the parts in a matter of minutes.

"That'll make Summer happy." Trey slammed the hood shut. "I'm going to buy her a battery and cables. She needs them. She's going to find herself stranded somewhere."

Wiping his greasy hands on his filthy overalls, Galen said, "Miss Summer don't like you no more."

"Not much." Trey wondered how the big guy knew this.

"She used to like you a bunch." Galen giggled, high-pitched, almost girlish. "You were boyfriend-girlfriend. Sitting in a tree. K-I-S-S-I-N-G."

"How do you know? Did she say something to you?" Trey couldn't imagine Summer sharing anything intimate with this strange man. Had he spied on them five years ago? The guy was mentally challenged; no need worrying about him.

Galen shrugged.

Seeing he wasn't going to get any more information out of him, Trey let it go. "I guess that's it. See you around."

With a nod, Galen lumbered off.

Shaking his head, Trey went to his own car and drove away.

The Chief pulled alongside as he turned out of the Curl Up and Dye parking lot and motioned him over. Trey turned into the Piggly-Wiggly lot, parked, and slid out of his car. He walked over to the Chief's big Cadillac, placed his palms on the roof, and peered inside. "Am I under arrest, sir?"

His father didn't smile. "What were you doing with the Hill girl?"

"Just checking to see if her brother has come home." Why did the Chief care what he and Summer had to talk about?

"Did anyone see you there?" the Chief pressed.

Trey shrugged. "Her boss. Buford Krebbs's wife, Violet. No, Viola."

The Chief's frown deepened. "Surely you realize if anyone spots the two of you together all the old rumors and speculations will rise up like an old dog beggin' for one last hunt. Months went by before this town went back to normal after the trial and the conviction. I don't want all that old garbage coming up again. You sniffing around the Hill girl will fuel the fire faster than anything."

"You can't keep people from talking, sir. Or thinking what they will," Trey said.

"No." The Chief glared at him. "But you don't have to stir up the gossips either."

"If people in this town don't have anything better to do than talk about me getting a haircut from a pretty girl then I'm sorry for them." Trey met his father's eyes. Why was he making such a big deal out of this? Surely he knew there was no way to keep people from thinking what they wanted to. "Or is there another reason you don't want me to see Summer?"

The vein in the Chief's head began to throb. "You're asking for more heartache, son. I don't want to see you go through it all again."

"Thanks for your concern, sir, but it's my heart," he said.

"I'll not tell you again to stay away from that girl." The Chief's face flushed dark red and the vein in his forehead picked up tempo. He tapped his fingers on the car door. "She's too old for you."

"I have to disagree. I'm twenty-three, Summer's only four years older." Trey kept his tone respectful, but he wasn't going to bend. Didn't matter that Summer didn't want anything to do with him. Not the point. "We're both adults, able to make our own choices."

"Nothing good can come from this. When Hill is caught and sent back to Angola, all the old anger is going to resurface. You might think you can strike up your old friendship. Hell, I know how you felt about that girl. Maybe you even thought you were in love with her, but you can't erase that you were the one whose testimony sent her brother to prison. Do you think that's just going to disappear because you wish it would?"

"Did the talk stop when you sent me away?" Bitterness edged Trey's voice.

"I did what was best," the Chief shot back, ignoring the question.

"Best for who, sir? Me? Or you? What was best about being shipped halfway around the world to fight in wars no one cares about? I think that may not have been the best thing for me. But once I was out of sight, this whole mess could be put out of your mind."

Without warning, the Chief's hand flashed out and grabbed Trey's T-shirt, twisting it tight. "Boy, you might be a mite bigger than when you left, but I'm still your daddy. You do as you're told. I have my reasons for what I do. I don't have to explain them to you or anyone else. Now steer clear of that girl."

Trey twisted out of the Chief's grasp. "No, sir. Not for you or anyone else."

Chapter Four

Being the Chief's daughter was a pain in the ass.

Lindy popped her gum and checked her look in the Jeep's mirror one last time. Even a heavy layer of cheap makeup and pitch black hair couldn't disguise the fact she wasn't twenty-one. Although she carried a fake ID, it wasn't any good in Juliet. Everyone knew who she was. Luckily, Jimmy Ray Hunt liked following rules as much as she did, and looked the other way when Lindy and her friends partied in his bar.

She climbed out of the Jeep, tugged her skintight Lycra mini down over her hips and struggled on six-inch heels toward the door of Mugs-n-Jugs. Her life sure had changed in the last year. When she was little she had been the perfect child. Blue-eyed, blonde, sweet, polite. But the older she got, the more she resented all the boundaries placed on her. The Chief was the law, her mother the last word in Juliet's society. *Lindy,* they lectured, *follow in our footsteps. Do all the right things. Be a lady. Take ballet, riding and art classes, and most important of all, keep your reputation spotless.*

Last year, when her mother began to slip away, Lindy quit going to dance, then art. She dyed her blonde hair pitch-black and threw away all her proper, oh-so-perfect clothes. Courtesy of the Salvation Army, she found an entire new wardrobe. Finally, she ditched all her Clinique and Estée Lauder products, and replaced them with the cheapest brands of black eyeliner and dark red lipstick Juliet's drugstore had to offer.

She took a breath and opened the door. Excitement buzzed through her. Anything could happen tonight. The bar was packed, she could barely see through the curtain of heavy black smoke. She inhaled the stench of cigarettes, booze, and too many sweaty bodies packed together. Heavy metal blasted her eardrums. A short, dark-haired girl standing near the bar spotted her and motioned wildly.

Lindy fought her way through the crush of bodies until she reached her friend. "Hey, Candy. Guess what?"

"What? You ready to fly? I've already hooked up with a guy who wants to party later." Candy giggled. "He's hot, too."

"Great. Hey, I've to tell you something big." Lindy couldn't wait to talk about Jace. Maybe Candy would understand the fascination he held for her.

"What do you think of my new outfit?" Candy did a spin, her arms held out. The gold hoop in her nose glittered in the low light.

Frustrated by her friend's lack of interest in her big news, Lindy gave a thumbs-up for Candy's simple black dress with a half dozen chains wrapped around her waist, fishnet stockings, and spike heels. She had on more makeup than Lindy did and her jet-black hair glimmered under the mirrored ball.

The kids Lindy would've considered losers her freshman year were now her crowd. The thing she liked most about her new group was they weren't afraid of what anyone thought, and they went out of their way to prove it. Annoying the Chief was high on their list of priorities. Drinking, and getting high when anyone could come up with weed was another favorite activity. School and work didn't matter to them.

Jimmy Ray hung over the bar. "What're ya havin' tonight, babe?"

Skinny, wearing a wifebeater undershirt that showed off his overlapping tattoos, a nickel-studded belt that didn't hold up his jeans, and heavy silver rings on every finger, he reminded her of Keith Richards. At least she thought he looked like the Rolling Stone before Richards got old and wrinkly and ugly.

"Rum and Coke." She angled her shoulders so he could get a good look down her shirt. As long as she let him look, he let her party.

"Coming right up." He placed the drink in front of her with a wink. When she dug in her purse he said, "On me."

"Thanks." Lindy wrinkled her nose and took a big gulp of the drink. She didn't really like the bitter taste, but she'd found the more she drank the easier it went down and the better she felt. When she got plastered, she didn't have to think about anything. Especially her dying mother, her stoic dad, and her exiled brother.

She still couldn't believe Trey showed up out of the blue. What did he want? More than to wish her a happy graduation, that's for sure.

She turned and leaned against the bar. Candy was on the dance floor gyrating her hips against some guy. Probably the one she just met. Lindy wondered where the rest of their friends were. Probably already at the quarry getting high. No one here interested her. Most everyone else was ancient—thirty, at least. She downed her drink and ordered another. Swallowing half of it, she mumbled, "This bites."

"What's the matter, Lil Sugar?" Jimmy Ray sounded less than interested as he dried a glass.

"I'm bored." She wasn't, not really. Her insides ached like they were crumbling in on themselves. Being here with these losers was a hell of a lot better than staying home and watching her mother waste away. And watching the Chief ignore them all.

"Is that a fact?" He put away the glass and rested his elbows on the bar.

She pouted, finishing her rum and Coke in two quick gulps. "Give me another one."

"Coming right up, Lil Sugar." He made a gun out of his fist, thumb and index finger and pointed it at her, making a clicking sound with his mouth.

She held out her empty tumbler. "Stop calling me that and pour."

He shrugged and fixed her a drink. "Bottoms up, baby."

An hour later, a couple more drinks, and Lindy no longer dwelled on things she couldn't change. She spun around the dance floor with anyone who asked, and some who didn't. Spying an empty table, she climbed up on a chair and stepped onto the tabletop. Someone whistled and she moved her hips in a seductive arc. Who needed ballet? Who needed approval? Shaking her ass in front of this crowd was much more fulfilling.

Inspired, she did a pirouette. One of her heels caught in the middle of the table and she toppled like a doll, landing on the floor in a heap. Her Lycra skirt slid up to her waist, exposing her red thong. One bra strap slid off her shoulder, dangling down her arm. As she struggled to stand, no one offered a hand, only made a few nasty suggestions.

Lindy giggled, pushing to her hands and knees. "Where's Candy?"

"Here I am." The other girl wound her way forward and held out her hand. After two or three attempts, they entwined fingers and Lindy managed to get on her feet. She tugged her skirt down and fumbled with her bra, but it wouldn't stay in place so she let it be.

"Boy, can you dance," Candy said. "Wish I could do that."

"Ballet lessons." Lindy staggered toward the bar. "I need a drink."

"I'm gonna find my date," Candy mumbled.

"The bar's closed," Jimmy Ray told her when she asked for a refill. "Last call was thirty minutes ago. You missed it. You were kinda busy giving lap dances."

"Jealous?" she taunted. "Maybe you wish you could have one. In fact, I think you want in my panties."

"I get into them, you won't ever forget it." He reached across the bar and dragged a thumb under her bra strap, sliding it back in place. His fingers lingered for a moment.

She shivered. He was different from anyone she'd ever met. Dangerous. Edgy. Someone who would really piss off her mother and the Chief. "You're a big talker."

"I'm big in a lot more ways than talk. Try me, and I'll show you." He kissed two of his fingers then brushed them across her cheek.

Candy wandered up beside her, arms wrapped around the waist of her new boyfriend. "Can you find a ride home? I'm going with Ralphie."

"I have my Jeep." She heard the Chief's voice in her head warning her to never drink and drive. Sober was a long ways behind her. She glanced at the man behind the bar. "Jimmy Ray can take me home."

"Yeah, and other places." He smirked. "Like Heaven."

"Cool. I'll call you tomorrow." Before Lindy could change her mind, Candy left with her latest chance at love.

"Let's get out of here." Lindy slung her bag over her shoulder and handed Jimmy Ray her car keys. "You drive."

"Cool." He tossed the keys in the air catching them in his palm. "Let's ride."

• • •

He drove like a man possessed. Even loaded, Lindy worried they might wreck. She hung onto the roll bar for dear life. Her stomach pitched, threatening to boil over. "Slow down."

"No way, baby. I don't do anything half speed." He tromped on the gas, sending the Jeep into a fishtail.

"Where are we going?" she mumbled, tightening her hold.

He reached over and slid his hand up her thigh. "Somewhere we can be alone."

Her skin crawled. Shouldn't she be looking forward to being with him? When the Chief found out, he'd blow his stack. "I just wanna lay down." Lindy's head felt as though it might explode. She thought she might feel better if it did.

"Oh, you'll go down, Lil Sugar." Jimmy Ray licked his lips and leered at her. "And so will I."

Suddenly, the last thing Lindy wanted was this toad's hands on her. Her skin under his hand felt dirty. There were other ways she could piss off the Chief. "I've changed my mind. I need to go home."

He shook his head. "No way. We're gonna see this through. Tonight."

Although her brain felt like scrambled eggs, she tried to think how she could get out of this mess. Maybe she could get away from him when he stopped the Jeep. Pretend to have to pee or something then run. She stroked his hand with her nails. "I know. Let's go to the lake."

"That's good thinking. No one will be there." He squeezed her knee and her stomach did a somersault. What had she gotten herself into? Jimmy Ray wasn't a high school boy she could tease then laugh in his face.

"Just us." Her mind raced as she tried to come up with a plan.

He floored the accelerator so hard the Jeep seemed to jump ahead like a spurred horse.

Through her soggy brain, Lindy tried to find a logical way out of this one. She'd really done it this time. The last thing she wanted was to have sex with Jimmy Ray, but if she just came out and said so, he might hurt her. Her plan to make the Chief and Mother worry seemed kinda stupid right now. No one but Candy had a clue where she'd gone. Probably getting busy with her date, Candy wouldn't worry about Lindy until tomorrow—if then.

• • •

She let him kiss her.

Surprisingly, he was good, using his tongue like a weapon. He tasted like mint chewing gum, not alcohol as she expected. His hair and body stunk like smoke and booze, though, making her stomach do a back flip, and she had to force herself not to hurl all over him. When he slid his hand under her shirt and undid her bra, she moaned a protest. He fondled her breasts with rough hands, squeezing hard and pinching her nipples.

She struggled, but he tightened his hold on her and yanked the strap of her top off her shoulder working it toward her waist. Dipping his head, he nipped her neck and collarbone. She squirmed, trying to get away, but he made his way to her breasts biting so hard he drew blood on one. She shoved at his head and cried, "Stop it. You're hurting me."

He slobbered against her. "I don't think so. You've taunted me long enough. I'm hard as a rock." For emphasis, he grabbed her hand and placed it on his crotch. His erection strained against his leather pants.

"I said no." She struggled to get free, but he held her palm against him. Grossed out, she didn't want to admit she'd never done it before. She put on a good show, but the truth was she had never gone all the way. And she didn't want her first time to be with someone sleazy like Jimmy Ray Hunt. All of the guys she messed with before had stopped when she said to. None had ever dared to push when she called a halt to the games.

"You teasing little bitch. You've been swishing your cute ass in front of me for the last year knowing how bad I want you, and now you're saying no? I don't think so, babe." He let go of her long enough to unzip his pants. Then he reached under her skirt, the seam giving way, tearing up her thigh. He ripped one side of her panties and crammed two fingers into her unwilling, dry body.

She screamed and writhed, clawing at his face and digging her heels into his legs but nothing she did discouraged him. Her actions only seemed to excite him more. When he rose above her, she screamed again and aimed her foot at his nuts.

•••

Jace hid in the galley of *The Emily*.

He felt like a punching bag.

Unsure what else to do, he'd headed for Juliet. He had a half-baked idea he could retrace Soloman's steps and prove he hadn't killed the scum. But before he got to the Mississippi state line, he realized he didn't have a chance in hell of proving his innocence after all these years. He couldn't just march up to anyone involved and demand answers. They'd laugh in his face before sending him straight back to Angola.

Then he remembered a place that might be deserted, where he could hide out and make plans. Chief Bouché's fishing boat anchored at Mystic Lake, a few miles from Juliet.

A perfect plan.

No one would think he'd have big enough balls to hide in plain sight.

He heard the motor before he saw the headlights. How had they found him so soon? Diving off the couch, he slipped outside into the dark. He jumped off the deck and fell with a grunt. Righting himself, he forced himself to run up the dock, disappearing into the trees at the shoreline. Moving far enough away from the boat to feel safe, he hid and watched. The vehicle didn't go to the boats, but instead turned down a road a few yards before the dock lane. Then it stopped. Not cops. Just to be certain, he moved a few yards closer. He spotted two people silhouetted in the open-topped Jeep.

Relief flooded him. Just a couple parking.

In the clear night air, a girl screamed.

It'd been awhile, but he didn't think the cry was one of passion. Someone was in trouble. He turned away. Not his problem. The girl's cries raked across his conscience. No one had helped Mama. "Shit."

A shriek rent the air again.

He hesitated. Staying out of it would be the best thing to do. No way could he stand here while someone raped a woman. He edged through the trees until he could get a clear view. If all the couple was doing was engaging in rough sex, he'd feel pretty stupid. On the other hand, if this were a crime against a helpless woman, he couldn't walk away.

"Get off me!"

A definite call for aid.

Shaking off his doubts, Jace streaked across the meadow. He had to save the girl. He picked up a heavy stick and advanced. Before he got close enough to help, she somehow managed to get the guy off her, jumped out of a Jeep and ran past Jace, swerving like a scared rabbit. The would-be rapist stumbled out of the vehicle and hobbled after her, one hand on his crotch. Had she racked him? Good for her.

Jace faded into the darkness, waiting until the man grew even with him, then he reached out a foot and tripped the chaser who sprawled in a heap at Jace's feet. Before he thought it out, Jace hit him on the head with the branch. The guy went limp. Jace kicked him hard in the ribs until the guy groaned.

Reality grabbed him before he killed the guy. This wasn't the creep who raped Mama.

The last time Jace went after a rapist, he found himself convicted of murder. Shit. Had he killed this moron? Leaning down, he reached to feel for a pulse. Halfway there he stopped. He couldn't risk leaving evidence of any kind. While he debated, the guy groaned and stirred. He had a knot on his forehead and a trickle of blood coming out of the corner of his mouth, but he'd live.

Jace had to get out of here before the guy came to and reported him. He'd find himself back in Angola before dawn. Where was the girl? He looked around, but she'd disappeared like mist. Where had she run to? The boat? Double damn. He'd eaten and changed out of his prison-issue outfit into some clothes he'd found on the boat, but the jumpsuit and candy wrappers were still on the floor. Anyone with half a brain could tell he'd been there.

He sidled up to the Jeep and took the keys from the ignition, then slipping through the nighttime forest, approached *The Emily*. Reaching the boat, he slowed. Silent as death, he made his way along the dock. At the ladder, he paused. Nothing made a sound, but the hair on the back of his neck stood up. He sensed a trap. With all his senses on alert, he turned and scaled the ladder. Nothing.

Easing the door open, he moved inside.

A small whimper from the corner let him know he wasn't alone. Again he froze. She had beat him here. He waited for his vision to clear before he moved again. Gradually, his eyes adjusted to the dark, and he spotted her curled up on the corner of the couch, trying to hide. He stepped further inside, closing the door behind him. She made another small noise.

"Who are you?" He couldn't believe how soft he was being. He ought to pick her up and toss her overboard. The cons in the yard would laugh themselves silly if they could see him playing hero.

She made a sound low in her throat.

Turning the lamp on low, he stood by the door. She curled up in a fetal position and whimpered again. Moving beside her, he knelt and reached for her scratched, bloody arm. At the last second, he jerked his hand back. There was no way he would touch her, leave DNA and incriminate himself in this crime. "Look, you've got to get out of here. I've got your keys."

Sobs wracked her body. He realized she was crying so hard her body shook. He had his own problems. Frightened she was going to bring the cops down on him, he lost patience. "Are you hurt? If not, you've got to get up and get the hell out of here."

She curled up tighter as if she hadn't heard.

"You've got to go." His desperation built. He'd already spent way too much time with her. She had to pull herself together and go home. Her skirt had ripped all the way up, scrunched under her, just a piece of tattered material. Even though her smooth, bare legs were scratched and blood streaked he couldn't help checking out her shapely thighs and the tiny scrap of red material covering the enticing V where they met. Five years behind prison walls was a long time to be without a woman, but no way would he ever touch someone who was afraid of him.

She coughed and lifted her head.

Their eyes met and held. Dark rings of mascara ran down her red, blotchy face, but her enormous honey-brown eyes mesmerized him. He couldn't look away. He gave himself a mental shake. He had been in prison too long if he found anything about this bedraggled, scared creature appealing.

She sniffed and wiped her nose with the back of her hand.

Encouraged, he squatted and waited.

"You're Jace." Her voice came out ragged.

Shit. He'd been made. For a millisecond, he thought about jumping up and running. Then he sighed. There wasn't any point in denying it. "Yeah."

"You look different." Her gaze roamed his face and body with curious abandon. Her eyes lingered on the raw, red marks on his wrists where he'd beat at the iron with a hammer he'd found on the boat.

"Most likely." So this was someone who knew him. Yeah, he'd changed. Entering Angola, he'd been eighteen years old, thin and naive. He'd grown two inches, gained weight, and learned more about men in cages than he'd ever wanted to. He studied the girl, but couldn't place her. She seemed familiar, but he'd been gone five years. "Are you hurt?"

She shook her head.

He made an impatient noise in his throat. "Can you stand?"

She shook her head again.

"Why not, if you're not hurt?" Fear gnawed at his gut. She had to get out here now. Why was she playing games? He just wanted her out of his hair.

"I just can't." Her cheeks turned bright red. She shifted and a rose-tipped breast was exposed for a half second before she snatched the edges of her ripped shirt over it. His cock stirred and he turned away. No way would he allow himself to be turned on by this girl and lose his focus. All he wanted to do was get rid of her and get out of here before he was discovered. Climbing to his feet, he went to the bunk and took off a blanket. He handed it to her then turned his back. "Here."

He heard her scramble to her feet and the soft swish of the material as it covered her. "I'm decent."

He faced her. She stood huddled in the blanket like a pole in a tent. Only her head showed. "C'mon, I'll take you back to your Jeep."

"No." She shook her head. "I want to stay here."

"You can't. I haven't got time for this." He forced himself to stay calm. After what she'd been through, she wasn't rational. His mama lost her mind after being violated.

She narrowed her eyes and lips. "You don't have anything to say about it."

"Pretty big talk coming from a little girl who got herself assaulted tonight. You looking for round two?" Jace chose his cruel words deliberately, hoping he sounded mean enough to make her leave.

"You wouldn't do that." She sounded positive. "And I wasn't raped, thanks to you."

"Relief filled him at her words. True, he'd never lay a hand on any woman but he wanted her out, now. Oh yeah? What makes you so sure?"

"Because after what happened to your mama, you would never do the same thing to someone. Especially after what you did to the man who hurt her." Her big eyes looked as trusting as Bambi's.

"You don't know anything about me or my mother." Rage filled him. How dare she judge him? "So just shut the fuck up."

"I know all about you and your family." She went on as if he hadn't just spoke to her like she was a bad dog. Hardened men on the inside had backed down from his tone of voice.

"How? From the newspaper? Because I sure the hell don't know you." He racked his brain, trying to place her, but nothing came to mind.

"I know you." Her big brown eyes filled with tears. "It's so sad."

"Who's your daddy? Another Lookie-Lou with an opinion about me? Probably just someone shooting off at the mouth." Bitterness filled him as he remembered all the people who crowded into the courthouse during his trial, most there for the entertainment of seeing him go down.

"Don't you recognize me?" She lifted her head and their gazes locked. "I'm Lindy Bouché."

"No way. You're lying." Incredulous, he remembered the little girl who'd followed on his heels like a stray pup. She had been a twig. He'd only caught a glimpse of her spectacular tits, but this girl was all grown up. Damn. Time had sure changed her. "You're what, sixteen—seventeen now? You were just a kid when I left."

"I'm eighteen, not a kid anymore." She moved to open the blanket. "Need me to prove it?"

His ripple of disbelief quickly turned to rage. He grabbed her arm through the blanket and jerked her toward him. He wouldn't hurt her physically, but he could cut her with his mouth. "No, I don't want to see your itty-bitty titties."

A moment of fear filled her eyes, replaced by anger matching his. "You bastard."

"You got that right." He dropped her arm like it was diseased. If she only knew how bad his cock was calling her name, she'd run away faster than a bullet, screaming all the way. "Get out of here. I'm sure you can't wait to run to your daddy and tell him where I am. Well, you can walk back to town. That'll give you a good long time to think up an excuse for being out in the woods with some guy who had only a fast lay on his mind."

"I won't tell the Chief anything." Her eyes flashed fire and her cheeks blazed an angry red. She moved away from him, drawing her blanket tight.

"Yeah, right." He chuckled without humor. "Forgive me if I don't believe you. The last time I trusted a Bouché to keep their mouth shut, I found myself doing time for life."

"I'm not Trey, and the Chief doesn't talk to me. He's not interested in anything I have to say. Even if I marched in there tonight and said 'guess what, I have Jace Hill outside,' no one would notice."

"I think he might want to hear you've found out where I am. What a great way to get Daddy's attention, huh?" He resisted the urge to shake her. Spoiled rotten brat had ruined everything. Now he had nowhere to hide and form a plan.

"I won't say anything. I promise." The fire in her big eyes was replaced with something he couldn't place. Pleading?

He refused to soften. "You're lying. You'll start blabbing the minute you get home." He pointed to the door. "Leave."

"I won't." She jutted out her chin daring him to touch her. "You can't make me."

"You'll go if I have to throw you overboard."

"You wouldn't." Her words were brave, but there was a shadow of doubt in her eyes.

Had Angola made him into such a prick that he'd rescue a girl only to scare her to death? Shit, why wouldn't she just go away? "There are clothes in the closet. Put something on," he ordered.

He reached for the blanket and she dodged away, the blanket catching on the edge of the door. Unprepared to catch it, the material fell to the floor. Lifting her chin, she stared defiantly at him. God help him, he should've looked away, but his eyes refused to obey. She stood nearly nude before him, her hands at her sides. Her bra was twisted around her waist, her panties and skirt hung from her hips. Red welts and scratches covered her pale skin and dried blood covered her right breast.

Jace's stomach rolled and bile rose in his throat at the sight.

He should've killed the motherfucker who did this to her.

When he caught up to the bastard who raped his mother, he gave him a beating the guy deserved, but he hadn't killed him. Jace's resolve to find out who had murdered Deke Soloman grew. Although the bastard deserved to die, Jace hadn't done it. He couldn't stand to look at Lindy another second.

"Put something on." She refused to move until he advanced another inch with a steely glare. "Move."

She dove by him and did as he told her.

While she dressed, he gathered his jumpsuit and the remnants of the chains he'd filed off and crammed them in a cooler and secured it with a bungee cord. With a quick look over his shoulder, he slipped outside and tossed it overboard. He watched as it sank out of sight then went back inside and found matches, flashlight, a change of clothes, and all the food on the boat. All went in a pile. He grabbed the first aid kit and added it too. Gathering all, he stuffed it in a duffle bag. He pounded on the bathroom door. "Let's go."

Obviously reluctant, Lindy came out of the bedroom wearing a pair of baggy jeans and a man's T-shirt that hung past her hips. On her feet, she wore a pair of flip-flops that looked two sizes too big. "Happy? I look like a clown."

With huge clothing and dark rings of mascara rimming her eyes, she still looked good as Mama's cornbread smothered in honey to him. "You're not going to a beauty contest." He motioned toward the door. "Now haul your ass. You're going home and I'm going to find the killer who ruined my life."

She shuffled out the door holding her too-big pants up with both hands. "Not without me."

Chapter Five

Trey couldn't sleep.

He tossed and turned, unable to put a finger on exactly what was bugging him. Rolling over, he checked his watch. Two in the morning. The Chief seemed invincible, but Trey knew he worried about Jace's return. Plus, his wife's illness had to be wearing him down. Then there was Lindy. The Chief wanted her to stay in the house, but she had done what she pleased and left in a huff again.

Had she come home yet? Trey hadn't heard her come in. She had been gone over four hours, and no one including him, even worried about her. Suddenly wide awake, he got up and dressed in the dark. Sick at heart, he went to her room and knocked. She didn't answer. He eased open the door and looked inside. As he feared, she wasn't there. She was probably at someone's graduation party. They hadn't even eaten a slice of cake for her big day. Maybe he could make it up to her.

Slipping out of the house, he went to the garage and backed out the gleaming red Mustang. The car had been his pride and joy. He'd found her at an auction, bought her for a song and he, Jody, and Jace had restored her. A vintage '69, cherry red with a big block engine, she was any guy's fantasy.

He flipped on the radio, tuning it to a blues station. Ray Charles came on wailing the last few bars of "Georgia." Trey sang along when B.B. King took over with "How Blue Can You Get?"

He left his window down, the warm night air flowing over his left arm. Even at this late hour, the humidity hadn't faded. The night was lit with a million bright stars and an orange-pink quarter moon hung low in the sky. Evenings like this often reminded him of his sole night with Summer. As hard as he tried to forget, he couldn't get her out of his mind. He shook off his longing. She'd made it more than clear she didn't want him in her life.

She would never face the fact Jace deserved his prison sentence.

Trey cruised by Tango's, not expecting to find his sister there. When he had been a kid, the proprietor had been a go-by-the book kind of guy. Not very likely to allow underage drinkers in his place. Especially the Chief's daughter. Trey briefly considered Mugs-n-Jugs, but quickly discounted the idea. The bar was a known hangout for toughs and lowlifes. Lindy was too young to be admitted there.

That left Daisy's. He seriously doubted Lindy would be let in there either, but he decided to check anyway. There wasn't any sign of her bright yellow Jeep in the parking lot, but Jody's dark green SUV sat there. Trey pulled along the big car, parked, and went inside.

He walked to the bar and ordered a beer from a petite girl with curly dark hair wearing a low-cut top that showed off breasts pushed so high they nearly touched her chin. As she handed him a longneck, deliberately letting her fingers brush his, she winked.

"Thanks." Ignoring her come-on, he laid a five on the bar, turned and leaned against the counter and did a quick perusal of the room. Several couples swayed to a band playing a country tune. No sign of Lindy.

He recognized a few other people. A guy he'd gone to school with, a young woman who looked familiar but he couldn't place her. No one he wanted to talk to right now. Maybe later when he had more time and less on his mind.

He turned and spotted Jody across the room. He wore civilian clothes, not his police uniform. Trey took a deep swig of his beer then headed that direction when the song came to an end.

Jody met him halfway. "Hey. What's up?"

"Why aren't you on the lookout for Jace?" Had the force gone to hell in a handbasket? It looked that way—if the officers were out partying when there was a convicted killer on the loose.

"The Chief wants to me to lay low and see if I hear anything. I thought I might pick up some interesting gossip in here." Jody took a sip of his Coke. "How about a beer? Catch up?"

Trey shook his head. "Thanks, I can't. I'm looking for Lindy. Have you seen her?"

"No. Not here. But Daisy's doesn't allow underage drinkers."

Trey shrugged. "Yeah, I figured this was a long shot. I just thought I'd check it out. She's not home, and with Jace on the loose, I'm worried."

"Try the quarry. That's where the kids party. You ought to know that, man. You haven't been gone that long, have you?" Jody tipped his glass and swallowed the last chunk of ice.

"Yeah, I'll try out there. Have you seen anything interesting tonight? Heard anything about Hill?"

Jody glanced around as if he might spot him lurking in the corner. "Jace?"

"Yeah. Who else?" Trey wondered if his old friend had been drinking.

"Just thought you might be thinking of his fine lookin' sister." Jody grinned and wiggled his eyebrows.

"Will you let it go?" Trey turned to let someone by and bumped into him. "Pardon me."

An attractive redhead reached out with a slim hand to brush his shirt where part of her drink had spilled on him. "I'm so sorry."

He glanced up from the dark, damp stain on his gray T-shirt into a pair of friendly blue eyes appraising him. He read the open invitation she was offering. He moved away from her caress. "No problem."

Taking the gentle brush-off, she gave him a smile full of regret and moved on.

Jody swirled his glass. "You can deny it all you want, but the lady was doing everything but climbing on top of you. All you could think of was a certain blonde. I saw it on your face."

Trey swallowed a wave of irritation. "You're the one who's obsessed with Summer. You bring her up every time I see you. Maybe you ought to take a shot."

Jody's shook his head. "No way. I'm with Lilah, and I ain't the kind to stray. Besides, vanilla isn't my flavor. I like hot chocolate better."

Trey smiled. "I'm not interested anymore, okay?"

Giving his head a shake Jody said, "Sure. You just proved my point. You got your back all up at the mention of the lady. What's holding you back from getting with her?"

Why wouldn't he let it go? Trey ran a hand across the back of his neck, wishing the knot there would go away. "Our history."

"History? What the hell's the past got to do with the way a man feels?" Jody looked at him like he'd lost his mind. "Listen to what your heart, your cock, or both are telling you. Go for it. History be damned."

"It's not that simple. I have no chance of overcoming what happened with MiLann, Jace, and everything in between. Even if Summer could get past all that, there's still the fact her brother was behind bars—where I helped put him—and she doesn't believe he should be there. Unless she faces the truth, there's no hope. And that's never going to happen."

Jody's mouth fell open. "From what I know of the case, it was open and shut. You ought to know that, seeing how you're the one who found Hill with bloody hands. Justice prevailed."

Trey didn't need reminding. "Yeah, I know."

"Then what is Summer hoping for? A miracle?" Jody held his arms wide, hands palms up like a roaming snake oil preacher. "Get real."

Realizing he'd already revealed too much, Trey shrugged. "She believes he was set up."

"By who? You? Jace was our best friend. Your old man? Why would the Chief do that? Summer's reaching for something she can't grab onto." Jody shook his head. "Man, that's just crazy. Maybe her mama isn't the only one who isn't firing on all cylinders."

"Summer's as sane as you or I, but she doesn't see the conviction the way we do." Trey wished he'd never said anything. He felt disloyal for talking about her.

His old friend slapped him on the back. "I'd tell her the same thing I told you before—let it go. There's no point holding onto a lot of old crap that can only make you feel bad. I need a beer."

Relieved Jody dropped the subject, Trey said, "Right now, the only thing that's making me feel rotten is my sister. Do you know she didn't even have a party? No presents. Nothing. I know the Chief is worried about Jace, and my mother's health is too bad to have a big celebration, but someone could've at least bought a few flowers or balloons. I think I'll get back on the hunt."

Placing his glass on the closest table, Jody asked, "Mind if I tag along? Two heads are better than one. There's nothing going on here."

Trey shrugged. "Suit yourself. But only if you knock off trying to get me and Summer together."

• • •

Too restless to go to bed, Summer sat on the dark porch, sipping sweet tea. She wondered where Jace could be. Why hadn't he called? Surely, he had to know she would be frantic. Of course, being on the run, he couldn't exactly walk up to a pay phone and call home. With a deep sigh, she rose and padded into the kitchen. Best get to bed. Tomorrow was Saturday and she had to work.

"Summer."

The voice was so low, she didn't think she'd heard it at first. There'd been so much trauma the last couple of days that her imagination had to be working overtime. Then it came again. The voice. "Summer."

She gasped. Turning, she tripped over the misplaced kitchen chair and landed on her stomach in the middle of the floor. Her breath rushed out of her in a long whoosh. "Ouch," she finally managed.

Strong arms lifted her and held her against a solid chest. Still out of breath, she couldn't struggle. The overpowering scent of a man's sweat stung her nostrils. He whispered in her ear, "Hold still. It's me."

Jace.

Her baby brother.

She stopped squirming.

"Don't turn on the light." He released her.

She spun around and touched his face with her fingertips. Day-old stubble scratched her fingertips. In the moonlight, she saw his black eyes and an ugly scratch across his right cheek. Emotions she couldn't even identify swirled through her. Her throat felt tight and raw, like she'd been breathing in a cotton mill for a month. "Thank God you're here. Are you okay?"

"Yeah. A few bruises, but nothing I can't handle." His voice had changed, grown deeper. He stood a good three or four inches taller than her own five-eight. He felt like solid rock where she touched him.

She didn't care how he'd changed. She wrapped her arms around his waist and hugged him tight as hot tears ran down her face. His body was as tense as a fence post. "I'm so glad to see you."

His arms circled her, reluctantly at first, then in a fierce hug. "Me, too."

She reluctantly pulled away, wiped her tears and studied his face. "Mama will want to know you're here. She went to bed about an hour ago."

"I don't want to scare her by waking her this late." He released her and went to the window. He moved the curtain aside and stared outside for a moment. Then he turned on the light over the stove. A dim glow lit the kitchen. "I can't stay long."

"Where are you going to go? What are you going to do?" She studied him, memorizing his features. His once round, babyish face had narrowed, hardened. But it was his dark blue eyes, so like hers, which had changed the most. They seemed to have no soul left in them. Her gaze roamed over his body. Rock hard, biceps bulging, he bore no resemblance to the gawky boy he'd been five years ago. He looked like a stranger. Like Trey, he'd become a man.

"I don't know for sure. If Chief Bouché finds out I'm here, I'll be back in prison before I can blink. When I saw my shot, I took it and ran away from that hell. I couldn't take any more." Savage anger colored his tone.

Her heart caught. "Is it too terrible?"

He laughed, low and harsh. "Think of a bunch of horny, hungry pit bulls in a cage, and you can imagine what it's like. Don't you see? I have to prove I didn't kill Soloman. It's my only chance to get out of there alive."

"I'm so sorry." She touched his arm. Whipcord muscles bunched under her hand. Because of Mama's condition, there had been no way to leave her, to travel to Angola to visit him, even before the warden banned her.

"How's Mama?" he asked as if reading her mind.

"Doin' good." She dropped her hand as if he could read the lie through her touch.

"I wish I could see her." A note of wistfulness colored his voice.

"Stay the night. See her in the morning. I'll go with you to see the Chief. We'll ask him to reopen the investigation." She knew he wouldn't even as she pleaded. But the alternative was too terrible to bear. If he ran, he would be hunted down and shot like a rabid dog.

He snorted. "You have a short memory. The last time we were stupid enough to trust a Bouché I ended up a guest of Angola. Something you must've forgotten."

She flinched at the image. "But, Jace—"

"No buts." He moved to the fridge and opened it. Without taking anything, he closed the door. "Do you have aspirin somewhere?"

"Yes." Fear for his safety again rushed over her. "Do you need medical attention?"

He paced to the window and looked out again. "Naw. It's just some scratches. Nothing to worry about. Do you have any cash?"

"My tip money." She moved by him and went to the strawberry shaped cookie jar she kept on the top shelf. Taking out the carefully rolled bills, she handed them to him. "This is all I have. There's only about a hundred and fifty."

He stuffed the money in his pocket without looking at it and without thanking her.

"Where are you going to go?" She knelt before the sink cabinet and removed a small tin. She stood and handed him a half-full bottle. "This is all the medicine I have on hand."

He wouldn't make eye contact. "Don't know."

It hurt he wouldn't tell her the truth. "Why won't you tell me?"

"Can't." His features closed down, shutting her out.

"Why not?" she pressed.

"You might let something slip."

She could see there was no arguing with him, but still said, "That's not fair. I wouldn't say anything."

"Not even if Trey comes around, putting on the sweet talk? You might just lay down for him. Before you can say hot damn, he knows where I'm at."

"No!" Appalled by the idea, she stared at him mortified. What had made him say that? The kind of things that people had always said about their mother. That she was wild and easy to bed. Why on earth would Jace throw that kind of accusation at her? Her eyes teared and she blinked furiously.

"You might." He looked around and curled his lip. "Old Trey with all his money probably looks pretty tempting."

"No." Her fingers bent around the edge of the sink until they turned white. Jace was out of line with his insinuations. Prison had turned her funny, polite brother into a stranger. One she didn't think she liked.

"Liar." Jace's voice was soft. The word was not.

"What do you mean?" Why was he doing this? Saying these things to her?

"You know what I mean. Trey Bouché has always been the one. Even after everything that's happened, you still believe his sweet talk." He twisted open the bottle and swallowed four tablets without water.

"Jace...please." Her voice shook. "That's not true. I haven't seen Trey in years. All of a sudden he's back in town."

He stepped to the door. "He always had a hard-on for you. You thought he was just a pesky kid, but you were his wet dream. Don't be too surprised to see him coming round again."

"He showed up here tonight," she admitted, fighting to ignore his crude comments. If Jace ever found out she'd slept with Trey... She shuddered thinking of it. "I told him to leave us alone and stay away from me."

"Sure." His voice held so much doubt she wanted to cry. What made him distrust his own family? They'd always believed in him, stood by him.

"I don't want to argue with you, Jace. I haven't seen you in five years. All I want to do is touch you, talk to you and make sure you're okay. I don't want to have anything to do with the Chief... or his son. Please believe me."

"Just don't get suckered into trusting them again. Never forget what they cost us. I'm going to prove my innocence, then I'm going to make old Chief Bouché pay for what he did." Jace stared at her with his cold eyes until a shiver ran down her back. "I gotta go."

Then he disappeared.

For a long moment, Summer stood in place, unable to move.

She stumbled to the door, but Jace had vanished like a shadow across the moon. Still reeling, she collapsed in a chair, her emotions a jumble. What a night. First Trey, then Jace. One truth stood out above all others. Her brother was in deep trouble.

* * *

Hidden in a copse of trees a few yards from the Hill home, Lindy huddled in the driver's seat of her Jeep. Lifting a numb hand for the spare set of keys in the glove box, she dropped it in her lap. Not sure why she waited, she stared at the dark house but didn't really see it. Her whole body trembled uncontrollably. The aftershocks of what happened with Jimmy Ray had caught up to her. She was lucky in more ways than one. After he was done with her, he probably would've dumped her body in a bayou somewhere, never to be found again.

She'd been brave in front of Jace, but now…now she was a mess. Some instinct told her she could trust him. He'd always treated her well, even when she'd been a kid in pigtails, tagging along when he worked on the Mustang with her brother. Trey would've preferred her to leave, but Jace never minded her hanging out with them. She'd always had trouble believing what he'd done to Soloman. Everyone else turned on him, but she had her doubts. No one listened to her protests then. She doubted they would now.

God only knew what Jace had in mind for her now.

Dump her off on *LeFleur's* doorstep like a sack of mail, most likely.

A tear dripped from her chin. She wished desperately for her legs to work. If only they would support her weight, she'd get out of the Jeep, start walking and disappear into the woods. She'd become a legend, a myth. They'd write folk songs and poems about her. Anything was better than what she was now, just a big screw up. She swiped at her damp cheeks. Nobody in the whole world would care if she never went home. The Chief only saw what she did wrong. She shuddered to think what he'd do to her when he found out what she'd done tonight. Would he send her off to the military like he had Trey?

Come to think of it, being dumped in a bayou held some appeal.

Jace appeared out of nowhere. He swung in beside her and dropped her keys in her lap. "Drive."

Automatically, she picked up the keys and switched on the ignition. "Why aren't you staying here? This is your home."

"Not anymore." His face was set in grim lines. Whatever had happened in there, it hadn't gone well. "I've got to get out of here before someone spots me."

"Where are we going?"

She shot him a glance as she pulled out of the Hill's driveway, her mind racing. An idea caught her imagination. Maybe she could go with him, start fresh. Kind of like Bonnie and Clyde. Her life as she knew it was over now. Once the Chief got word of what she'd done—deliberately encouraged Jimmy Ray Hunt— he'd disown her. She knew he would send her away at the very least. Hadn't he turned his back on Trey five years ago? And Trey hadn't even done anything wrong. Maybe she and Jace could put their heads together and prove his innocence.

"Let me go with you."

"No fucking way!" He glared at her. "Are you out of your mind?"

Cringing, she drove mindlessly. After a few minutes of uneasy silence, she tried again. Desperation filled her as they drew close to her home. "Listen, I could help you."

"I don't need your kind of help." He sounded so bitter she almost lost her nerve. "Bouché help is something I don't want or need. Just go home and forget you saw me tonight."

"Sure you do," she pleaded with him. "I even know a place we could stay. Someplace empty, somewhere nobody ever goes."

He seemed to consider her words for a minute. "No way. You're setting me up."

"No, I'm not. This is a great plan. It's perfect." She almost bounced in her seat. "I'm talking about Granny's farm."

He pounded his palm with his other fist. "Yeah, not bad. The old lady won't squeal."

"Granny died last October." Lindy swiped at her nose. "No one's been up to her place since. The old house is probably falling down by now."

"Even better. Maybe you could be useful. No one will think to look for me there." He glanced in the mirror. "If I can just get out there without getting caught."

"Probably not," Lindy agreed in her most scathing voice. After Granny died, they'd gone as a family and cleaned out her house of personal effects, but left the furniture with the intention of using it as a vacation home. Then Mother got sick and they'd never fulfilled their plans. Lindy almost shrugged. Who cared? Their family wasn't exactly close.

"Granny Bouché treated me right." Jace sounded almost nostalgic.

She waited, but he didn't elaborate. He didn't have to. Lindy remembered the times with Granny as well as he did. As children, Lindy, Trey, and their friends were welcomed at Granny's farm with open arms. They'd often spent a week or more with her, fishing, swimming, and making jam out of the wild berries they picked together. Lindy couldn't figure out how the Chief, who had been raised by Granny with a heart as big and wide as the mighty Mississippi River, could not have one of his own. She had more important things to worry about right now. Like convincing Jace to let her stay with him.

• • •

The lump in Lindy's throat grew as she drove up the long, twisty dirt road to Granny's place. Even in the moonlight, the two-story house looked weathered and lonely. The dozens of overgrown wild roses couldn't hide the peeling gray paint and leaning steps. Worst of all, Granny didn't come to the door like she always had—no matter what time of day or night—wearing her old-fashioned print dress and big, clunky shoes, waving a corner of her apron, calling them to come in and sit a spell and have a bite to tide them over 'til supper.

Stealing a glance at Jace's profile, Lindy wondered if he felt any sense of loss. She couldn't read him. His features were set like one of the cliffs down at the quarry. Didn't he have any feelings? Probably not. He was a convicted murderer, after all. Her mind elsewhere, she drove into one of the rose bushes, breaking off some of the branches.

"Hey! None of that." He grabbed her arm. "Park where no one can see the Jeep."

Doing as he instructed, she drove into the three-sided shed and turned off the motor.

"Are you going to let me stay?" She shored up her courage and took a deep breath. "Because if you don't, I'll tell the Chief where you are."

Their gazes collided.

He held out his hand. "Give me the keys. Spares, too. I'm not having you sneak out of here in the middle of the night to turn me in."

She let out the breath she'd been holding. "Is that a yes?"

"For now. Now give them to me. I don't want you changing your mind and go running off to squeal to your daddy."

"I don't have another set." Avoiding contact, she handed him her key ring with the fuzzy soccer ball and tiny, jeweled ballet slippers on it.

"Don't lie to me," he said in a soft voice that sent shivers scurrying down her back.

"In the glove box," she squeaked.

"That's better. Get out and let us inside." He took the spare set of keys and put them in his pocket.

She shot out of the Jeep and went to the empty flowerpot where Granny had stored her house key—she had never locked her doors—and retrieved the old-fashioned, rusty key and inserted it into the lock. With a groan, the door opened. With Jace at her back, Lindy stepped inside. A musty, unused scent greeted her. Wrinkling her nose at the unfamiliar odor, she stopped. This home had always smelled like fresh flowers, baking, and the rose water Granny wore religiously. Now the house seemed just as dead as her granny.

Jace gave her a push. "Go on. Get inside."

She stumbled a few feet forward. Recovering, she whirled around and faced him. "You don't have to be nasty."

"I have every right," he growled. "On top of everything else, I'll be facing kidnapping charges if your daddy finds out you're with me. How the hell could I explain this one away? I can't, that's how. You're a spoiled brat who needs a spanking. I'm stuck with you until I send you home. Hopefully without getting myself back in the pen."

The thought of him spanking her gave her a tingle she refused to acknowledge. Lindy placed her hands on her hips and glared at him. "I am not a spoiled brat. I'm eighteen years old. Plenty old enough to decide who I want to be with. You will not be facing kidnapping charges unless I press charges. Which I just might do if you don't quit being so mean."

He considered her for a long minute. "How can you be so dense? You don't have to be the one to press charges. Your dear old daddy can do it."

"I won't let him." She folded her arms over her chest and planted her feet. When she made up her mind, nobody changed it.

Seeing she wasn't going to back down, he looked around. "Are there lamps?" He paced around the front room, peering out the windows.

"In the kitchen, I think."

"Go see." He stopped and said, "I don't want much light, though."

She'd won round one. With a big sigh, she went into the kitchen. A cobweb stuck to her face and she shrieked, wiping furiously at her cheek. With a quick glance over her shoulder, she tiptoed to the back door and tried to push back the lock. The rusty metal squealed. Jumping away, she opened the pantry and found lanterns, lamp oil, and matches. Half expecting Jace to come yell at her, she took them all back in the living room.

He peered out of the window. "Where's the closest neighbor?"

"Old Jeremiah, down on the river." A smile played around her mouth as she thought of the bent, ancient man. He'd always had a tale for them when they wandered down to the riverbanks near his home to fish.

He turned to look at her. "He's still alive?"

"Last time we were here he was." A knot formed in her throat as she thought of the last time she'd seen him. Jeremiah had come to Granny's funeral, unashamed of his tears.

"Anyone else? No newcomers?" Jace turned away from the window and walked toward her.

"Not that I know of." This remote, forested area of Mississippi was basically deserted. Used mostly by deer hunters, nobody would be around this time of year.

He took one of the lamps and filled it, turning the wick down low. The light lit up the room just enough to cast it in an eerie glow. Even spookier was the furniture shrouded in blankets. He jerked an old quilt off the sagging sofa and dust flew, making her sneeze.

"Are the beds still here?"

"Yeah," she admitted reluctantly. Would he expect her to sleep with him? Her thighs trembled.

"Let's catch some Zs. I'm beat."

For the first time since they'd hooked up, she wanted to leave. What if he had more than sleep in mind? He had been in prison for more than five years, after all. Having sex was probably high on his list of things to do before he was caught. She wasn't ready for another go round like Jimmy Ray had put her through. A shudder ripped through her. "I'm not tired."

Jace advanced a step. "Quit stalling. Move. Now."

With a little yelp, she darted toward Granny's bedroom.

The wrought iron headboard and bare feather tick mattress brought another wave of memories. Snuggling next to Granny on rainy nights, eating popcorn in bed, telling and keeping secrets. "I'll get bedding. It'll be in the hope chest at the foot of the bed."

Jace leaned against the doorframe, arms and ankles crossed, his expression unreadable. With jerky, uncoordinated movements, she slipped on the sheets and Granny's familiar wedding ring quilt. Done, she stood by the bed unsure what to do next.

He motioned to the bed. "Get in."

Pulse pounding in her ears, Lindy shot a glance at his expression. The black circles around his eyes made his blue eyes even meaner. Trembling, she kicked her flip-flops under the edge of the bed. Leaving on her clothes, she climbed between the sheets. With the covers pulled to her chin, she stared at the ceiling. Jace's heavy work boots struck the floor; his jeans and shirt followed with a whisper.

Lindy lay rigid as a fishing line with a big old bass on it. Her heart sped up and her breathing came shallow and fast. She stared at the ceiling, trying to think of a reason he wouldn't want to have sex with her.

He pulled the covers back and slid in beside her.

His leg touched her thigh, and she jerked it away.

Suddenly, with the quickness of a cat, he flipped over on top of her. She gasped as his weight pressed her deep into the feather tick mattress. Too terrified to blink, she stared at his mouth. She thought he was going to kiss her. Bracing for his lips to slant across hers, she wouldn't admit a slight disappointment when he spoke.

"Let's get something straight. You don't run home and tell your daddy where I am until I figure out who set me up, nothing's gonna happen to you. I don't want to hurt you, and I won't, long as you do what you're told. Stop looking like a rabbit about to be stuffed in the stew pot and go to sleep."

She couldn't relax long after he rolled away from her. The tension didn't leave her body until he began to snore. Her mind raced, trying to come up with a way out of this mess, but nothing concrete came to her. Finally, bone weary, she closed her eyes.

Just for a moment.

Chapter Six

Lindy woke with a jolt.

For a moment, she forgot where she was. Her head felt like someone had hit her with a hammer. Booze was a great thing, but the hangovers were hard to take. She didn't even know where she'd slept. Rolling over, she realized she had spent the night in Granny's bed. Half expecting Granny to call her from the kitchen saying breakfast was on, come and get it, reality splashed over her like a cold shower. Granny wasn't here and Lindy had run away with Jace Hill. Where was he? Had he left her alone?

She got up to find out.

She cried out as her feet hit the ground. Her entire body felt like one big bruise. A wave of nausea crawled up her throat and she fell across the bed, too sick to care. Sharp pain pierced her heart. Had anyone at home noticed she was missing? Did they care? She doubted it. Most of the time, they didn't even know when she was around, much less not.

"You're finally awake?" Jace filled the doorway, a green canvas bag in his hand. There for a while I thought you'd died. It's late."

He hadn't abandoned her. She faced him, hoping he didn't see her relief. "Where'd you go? Shopping at the Piggly-Wiggly?"

"From your old man's galley, actually. There wasn't anything to drink there, and I wanted a soda. And a newspaper. So I went to the old store down at the crossing." He tossed her a package of peanut butter crackers.

"It's open? You just strolled in like a normal person?" Or, had he knocked off the old man who ran the little store for a coke?

"Naw." He pulled a twelve-pack of pop out of the bag. "No one was around to notice me, so I helped myself."

No one could say this man wasn't full of surprises. "Not beer? Or something stronger?"

"I've got to keep my wits. Besides, I never liked the stuff." He popped the top off one of the bottles and took several long swallows. "Unlike you. Bet your hangover is a bitch."

Lindy glared at him without answering. She wasn't going to justify herself to him. She had been thirteen when he was sent to Angola, but he stood in her memory as clearly as he stood before her now. But the boy in her recollections bore almost no resemblance to this man. Tall and skinny then, he had filled out, his arms and legs now heavily muscled. He reminded her of a lion with a mane of shaggy, blonde hair that fell past his collar, and blue eyes so dark they were nearly black. Or maybe it was just the bruising around them that made them seem so deep and mysterious.

More than the physical, though, his lack of humor struck her. He had been a crackup, always making everyone laugh. She loved to be around him back then. He treated her like a kid sister, but he hadn't been mean. However, he'd also had a hot head. Quick to anger, quicker to forget it and make a joke.

"What're you staring at?" he growled.

"You need a doctor. Your face looks awful."

"I'm fine. You're no prize yourself. Eat up. I need you to be strong so you can keep up with me. You're a scrawny thing. When are you going to fill out?" He tossed another pack of crackers at her. She let them fall to the floor.

"Some guys like skinny girls."

His gaze roamed over her face, then dropped to her chest. His eyes remained there. "Take off your shirt."

"What?" Had her big mouth gotten her into more than she could get out of this time? Her pulse and heart rate sped up as she looked desperately for an escape route. His big body blocked any way out.

"Take off your shirt." His gaze locked on her breasts.

Stalling, she followed his line of sight. A dark red stain colored her light blue tee, just a little below her bra line. "What on earth?"

"You're bleeding." Without waiting for her to act, he reached forward and lifted the hem of her shirt, tugging it over her head. As the shirt pulled free from her skin, it felt like a hot iron and she cried out.

She covered her breasts with her hands. "That hurts."

"Let me see." With surprisingly gentle fingers, he removed her hands then pushed the flimsy material aside. And stared. "Jesus."

Dropping her own gaze, she gasped. Blue and purple bruises, red welts and bite marks covered her right breast. The left one didn't look much better.

"Does the rest of you look this bad?" Jace's voice sounded as raspy as her brother's.

She refused to give into the desire to cry. She noticed her hands. Sore, the knuckles were bruised. Every one of her nails broken. She must've really fought hard to get Jimmy Ray off her. Where had he gone after she kneed him in the nuts? Hopefully, he crawled all the way back to town. "I don't know. I ache everywhere. I've never hurt this badly. Not even after hours of riding or dance lessons."

"Take your pants off. Let me see." His tone, sarcastic moments earlier, sounded almost gentle.

Lindy shook her head, embarrassed. "I'm okay. You must feel just as bad, maybe worse."

"You're not okay. Stand up." Without making any comment about his own battered body, he took her by the arms and lifted her to her feet. When he reached for the zipper of her borrowed jeans, she shook her head.

"I can do it." She reluctantly undid the snap and stepped out of the denim. She thanked God she'd replaced her torn panties with a pair of bikini bottoms she kept on the boat.

His gaze roamed her legs. "That bastard."

"Yeah." Not as bad as her top, ugly, bruises and jagged scratches crisscrossed the inside of her upper thighs. She hadn't realized how hard she had fought Jimmy Ray until she saw the evidence in the daylight.

"You said you weren't raped." His eyes met hers. He looked like the boy she remembered. Kind and sweet.

She struggled to find her tongue. "No."

"You telling me the truth?" His eyes resembled two lifeless blue stones. "Because if he did that to you, I'll—"

"What? Kill him?" She couldn't believe her own bravery, but the look in his eyes scared her. He seemed as if he could hunt down Jimmy Ray and beat him to death. She hastened to add, "I know what they say you did to Deke Soloman because of what he did to your mama."

His mouth twisted into a bitter line. "You don't know anything about my mama. Don't talk about things you don't understand."

She laughed a bitter chime. "Oh, I think I get it."

"You're together mentally. You'll survive without any scars. So don't compare yourself to my mother. Ever."

He hobbled out.

The breath she'd been holding whooshed out of her. She couldn't believe she'd said that about his mama, but in that moment she realized he wasn't going to do her bodily harm. His anger at Jimmy Ray surprised her. Why should he care what happened to her? As he'd pointed out, she'd asked for it by going with the creep last night.

Jace came back carrying the first aid kit he'd taken from the boat. "Sit down."

She did as he instructed watching him warily, still holding her borrowed shirt together with both hands.

"Let go."

Her eyes on his, she moved her hands, and the slip of material fell away. When she started to cover herself again, he put his hand over hers and shook his head. She lifted her chin and stared at him as he took a moist towelette from the package and unfolded it. Powerless, she sat as he wiped the cold square across her scratches. Her nipples peaked, and her belly tingled in a way she'd never felt before. Her pulse pounded like a river, whether from fear or shock she couldn't say.

Although she talked big, no male had ever seen her vulnerable like this before. At the eighth grade dance, Homer Bellafonte had put his hand on her breast, over her blue taffeta gown, and she had slapped him so hard he said his ears rang. Word got around and no one else had ever dared to go that far for a long time after. Since she'd run around with Candy, Lindy had made out with a few boys, but this felt different. Forbidden. Tantalizing.

Homer had grossed her out, but she wished Jace would keep ministering to her. Her breasts and stomach ached in a way that had nothing to do with her wounds.

Could he tell she wanted his hands on her? She stole a glance at him. His expression was neutral. A while ago, he had told her she needed to fill out. Did he find her appealing now that he saw her mostly nude? If he did, he didn't show it. Like a doctor, his movements were clinical, efficient. He didn't even seem to notice her bare breasts. She might not have the biggest boobs, like Charity Ann Clawson's fat old Ds, but hers were perky.

Lindy sniffed. Charity Ann couldn't wear a leotard like she could. Ryan Fairchild had played the prince in last year's ballet production of *Cinderella* and she'd seen him sneak a peak at her when they changed costumes between scenes. He hadn't seemed to think she was too small. Plus, she knew she had great legs and a flat belly from riding and dancing. When she'd gotten her bellybutton pierced last summer, the guy who'd done the job had commented how great she'd looked in her belly shirt.

•••

Jace concentrated with all his might. It took every ounce of self-control to keep his mind on the task at hand and not his throbbing groin. Lindy had been nearly raped last night. He didn't want to do anything to scare her. He knew what a woman who had been through that kind of trauma experienced because he'd seen his mama the day after she'd been raped and left for dead in the rain.

With her features battered, they'd barely recognized MiLann. Soloman not only violated her person, he'd beaten her to a pulp and cut open her beautiful face. The doctors hadn't expected her to live. When Jace saw his mother lying in a heap, tubes and needles sticking out of her, he lost it.

The Hills thought the Chief would have an arrest within hours. When he did, they rejoiced. But, for reasons no one ever made clear, Soloman was released within a day. Jace charged into the Chief's office, demanding answers. The policeman gave lip service about not enough evidence and having no choice but to release Soloman.

Stunned, Jace had made his fatal mistake. He raged at the Chief, promising to find Soloman and get a confession even if he had to beat it out of him.

Good to his word, he kept the promise.

He'd searched out Soloman to beat him half to death.

And sent himself straight to the bowels of hell. Angola Federal Prison.

He pulled another towelette from the package and dabbed at the dried blood where Lindy had been bitten. He brushed the cloth over the bite. "This has to sting."

She bit her lip as he cleaned the wounds. He ran the cloth over the scratches on her legs, then took a tube out of the kit and opened it. "This is antibiotic ointment. It should keep your cuts from getting infected."

With careful movements, he spread the medicine over her scrapes and bruises as gently as possible, although her legs shook. Then he replaced the cap. Wiping his fingers, he said, "There's a spare T-shirt in the stuff from the boat. I'll get it."

With her shoulder to him, she mumbled thanks when he tossed her the tee. She smiled when she saw the logo over the pocket. Juliet Police. He didn't smile back. Her expression turned serious as she faced him full on. "You've got to get out of here. Leave me. I won't tell the Chief where you went. I promise. But, you've got to go."

"Since when do you care what happens to me?" He couldn't allow himself to trust her. She hadn't been in her right mind last night. Soon she would be thinking clearer. Remember who she was—a Bouché. Duty-bound, she'd turn on him in a jumpin' jack flash.

She turned away and tugged the tee over her head. "I don't care. That doesn't mean I want to see you get killed."

"I'm not going to get killed 'cause I have you for insurance. Your daddy isn't going to hurt me as long as you're along. So until I figure out where I'm going, you're stuck with me." He forced his voice cold and mean. "You chose to put yourself this position. You're along for the ride now."

"No problem." Her tone matched his. "Where are we going?"

"Nowhere for awhile. I like it here. I can rest, think, come up with the perfect plan."

"There isn't any perfect plan. The Chief won't quit until he has you back behind bars." She didn't sound positive.

"I'm not worried about your old man." Jace stepped close and gripped her chin in his hand. "Know why? Cause he's nothing to me but a bad memory."

• • •

Trey was worried sick.

By noon he knew he should've kept searching for Lindy. She thought she was so grownup, so independent, but the truth was she was still a young girl. He hated to think of all the things that could happen to her. Half the women back in Afghanistan had been raped. Some by their own people, some by American soldiers.

Just for a moment, he allowed his mind to return to Katia, a young woman he'd known there.

• • •

His unit had come across a burned out village. In one still-standing, but badly used building a group of women and children huddled, terrified for their lives. One woman, about twenty, had stood up daring them to fire. He'd admired her spirit. All the guys had.

Reassuring her they meant her no harm, they'd taken the women and kids back to base for medical treatment and a safe haven for those who were physically well but had nowhere to go.

Katia recovered from her ordeal faster than most of the others. Her English improved every day and she found odd jobs around to make herself useful. In spite of his feelings for Summer, Trey found himself drawn to the little spitfire. Nothing like Summer, petite, with dark hair and eyes, Katia thawed the ice around his heart just a bit.

They spent a great deal of time together, healing.

The orders came down from brass that the women were to be moved to a refugee camp outside camp.

Trey was helpless to keep her from going.

He promised to find a way to bring her back.

When he didn't hear from her in a few weeks, knowing she wouldn't just disappear without a word, he tracked her to an unmarked grave on a hill overlooking the city. Grief-stricken and enraged, he didn't give up until the story came out.

Just as she had stood up to the American soldiers, Katia dared the Taliban to harm her.

Her bravery cost her life.

She'd been murdered, her throat slit.

• • •

Trey forced thoughts of Katia away. He had to focus on a woman he could help. Where to begin? First, who did Lindy hang out with? He didn't have a clue if she still ran around with the same kids he used to know. If she did, none of them had been at the quarry last night. He hadn't recognized any of them. Bothering his mother wasn't an option. Neither would the Chief have time for this right now. Who else would know anything?

Etta. The family's housekeeper. She was the pulse of the family, had been for as long as he could remember. She'd be home now from her visit with her daughter. She'd made Lindy's celebratory dinner, but hadn't stayed to serve it. He went to the kitchen to find her.

The old black woman was bent over the stove, removing a tray of fresh cinnamon pecan cookies. Seeing him, her eyes went wide and she let go of the tray. It clattered to the floor, scattering her cookies. "Mr. Trey. You came home. Oh, lordy, thanks be alive."

"Yes, ma'am." He enveloped the tiny woman in his arms. Her ice white hair tickled his nose. "All because of you. I couldn't stay away from my girl any longer."

"Pshaw." She wiggled out of his arms. "Never mind that. You've been gone too long."

"Yes." He knelt to reach for the cookies and she swatted his hand away. "I got it. Just you sit down at the table proper. You're in my kitchen now, not some camp on a mountain."

"Yes, ma'am." Obediently he sat at the table and poured a tall glass of orange juice. He took a sip and waited for her to pick up the crumbled cookies. Then he said casually, "Do you know who Lindy spends her time with nowadays?"

Etta's mouth puckered as if she'd swallowed something distasteful. "No, sirree, I don't. All Missy Lindy's friends used to come here. I haven't seen any of them in longer than a beaver's front teeth."

"Not even Becca? Or Mary-Gray?" He held the glass poised halfway between his mouth and the table. The three girls had been inseparable since the second grade.

"No, sirree. None of them." She turned away, but not before he saw the sadness on her face.

He stood up and put his hands on her shoulders, moving her toward him. "Miss Etta? What is it?"

She kept her gaze locked on his feet and dabbed at her eyes with the corner of her apron. He lifted her chin, and tried to read into the depths of her black eyes. "What's wrong?"

She shook her head. "I ain't gonna talk poorly of this family. No matter who done what."

"Just tell me what's troubling you so much," he urged. "I need every lead I can get to find Lindy."

She took a deep breath. "I'm worried."

"About what?" His pulse sped up.

She was obviously reluctant to talk. "Missy Lindy."

"Miss Etta, what about her?" He let go of her chin and placed his hands on her shoulders. "Tell me. I want to help, but I can't if I don't know what the problem is."

"Missy's gone, that's what." Tears filled her eyes again. "I just know something bad's happened to her."

Trey's heart lurched. His fears exactly. "How do you know that? She's probably just spent the night on someone's couch."

"I doubt that," Etta muttered. "You been gone for a long time, Mr. Trey. Missy Lindy isn't the girl you knew. She gone…bad. Real bad."

"What do you mean?" He kept a tight rein on the surge of fear that coursed through him. His version of bad and an old black woman's might be somewhat different.

"Missy is disrespectful to your mama and daddy, number one." She held up two bent fingers. "Number two, she runs with a rotten bunch of skunks. Lilah told me she saw my young miss at that trashy joint on the outside of town. And you know them kind that runs outta there."

"Lilah knows this for a fact?" His heart pinched into a painful crease. What was Lindy thinking?

Etta nodded. "Yes, sirree. My Lilah don't lie none."

"What else did Lilah say?" Trey planned to make sure Jimmy Ray got his ass kicked. He had no business allowing an underage drinker in his bar. Everything from illegal guns to drugs was rumored to be found there. A girl like Lindy would be an easy target for the scum who trolled around there.

"Nothin'." Etta held up a third crooked, arthritic finger. "Another thing. Most days I hear my missy come in about the time I get up. I might not be as young as I once was, but I still got ears and I still climb out of bed plenty early. Yes, sirree, I do."

All her life, Etta rose before the sun came up. Close to daybreak most mornings. In her opinion, the most productive hours were the earliest. Who in the hell was Lindy spending her nights with?

"What does the Chief say to her?"

"I ain't told on my missy." The housekeeper hung her head again and for the first time, He noticed how fragile she seemed. When had she shrunk so much? "Mr. Samuel's so tied about in knots about Miz Emily he can't stand it. I didn't want to burden him more."

"He hasn't noticed Lindy's actions?" The Chief had never been soft with his children. Why hadn't he put Lindy under restriction?

She twisted her perfectly pressed apron in her hands. "If he has, he hasn't said."

"You should've said something," Trey said gently.

"I couldn't." Etta studied her feet. "Because of what he'd do to her. Send her away. Same's he done to you."

Trey didn't have a response for that one. She was right. If the Chief found out his teenage daughter was running wild, no telling what he'd do to her. Whatever the punishment, it was bound to be severe. He had to be torn up bad by Emily's illness to let something like this slide. Trey knew he better run interference and find out what was going on, fast. He gave the top of Etta's head a light kiss and her thin shoulders a gentle squeeze. "Try not to worry anymore."

She wiped her wrinkled cheek with a corner of her wrinkled apron. "Go on now. Git. I gots chores to do."

"Yes, ma'am." Ducking her lightning fast slap, he grabbed two warm cookies off the tray. Licking frosting off his fingers, he went to find the Chief.

Finding Lindy was top priority.

Chapter Seven

Ida Baker sat behind her desk, in front of the Chief's office, guarding it like she had for the last twenty years. Nothing, from her cat eye glasses to the sensible shoes she'd always worn had changed.

Trey winked at her. "Hello, Miss Ida. May I go in?"

She blushed and gave him a look of mock anger. "Not just now. Someone's in there. When you do see the Chief, make it snappy, young man. He has a lot on his mind."

"Yes, ma'am." He grinned at her, and she fumbled with some papers on her desk.

A minute later, the door swung open and an attractive redhead came out. Without a glance at him or Ida, she hustled by them, slipping on sunglasses. Ida didn't look up, but sniffed. Trey hurried inside.

The Chief sat in his walnut colored leather chair, head in hands.

"Sir, what is it?" Alarmed, Trey hurried to his side. "Did that woman know something about Jace? Has something happened?"

The Chief looked up with bleary eyes. "Huh? Oh, her. No. Forget about that."

"Then what is it?"

"I said nothing. What is it?"

"Lindy didn't sleep at home last night," Trey said. "She never came back after she stormed out."

"You positive about that?"

"Yes, sir. I looked for her last night, but couldn't find her. I thought I saw her headed home, but she wasn't in her bed."

"Why didn't you wake me?" Accusation filled the Chief's voice.

Trey hesitated for a moment. "I thought she'd be home by this morning."

"Damn it," the Chief spat, "your sister is in big trouble."

"What kind of trouble?" Trey's mind raced with the possibilities. 'In trouble' in Juliet, Mississippi usually meant pregnant and unwed, but he didn't think that's what the Chief meant this time.

"Don't you see?" The Chief pounded his desk with his hand. "That Hill boy has got his hands on her."

"That's quite a jump, sir. Do you know for sure that he even came home?" Trey wondered at his father's mental stability for a moment. "Pardon my saying so, but Lindy seems a little flighty. Maybe she just spent the night with a friend."

"I should've seen this coming when I got the word that boy was on the loose." The Chief held his head again. He wasn't making sense.

"I'm not following," Trey said.

"This." With an explosive wave of his arm, the Chief scattered a pile of letters to the floor. "Threats, all of them. Jace Hill had promised to get even for years. Now, he's making good on his promise. He's paying me back."

"You're saying Jace has threatened you from prison?" Trey couldn't believe it. His former friend had sent promises of revenge through the mail? "Why didn't you tell the warden?"

The Chief's complexion was pale and a sheen of sweat covered his forehead. "I figured I was man enough to take a few nasty letters. A thing like this can get a prisoner in the hole for a good long time."

For a moment, Trey was speechless. This was the closest thing he'd ever heard to the Chief admitting he felt anything but good about Jace's conviction. "Sir, do you think there's any substance behind these threats? Do you believe Jace would come back here and harm one of us?"

"Hell yes, I do." He slammed his fist on the desk. "That's the last time I make a mistake where Hill's concerned. If he harms a hair on my daughter's head, I'll hunt him down and drag his cold, dead body back to Angola myself."

"There's no reason to think he has hurt Lindy, is there? I mean it's probably just coincidence she's not home." Trey tried to remain the voice of reason although his heart was sinking fast. None of this looked good for Lindy. Or Jace. "What are you going to do?"

"What I should've done sooner." He picked up the phone and bellowed into it. "Ida, get every available body here. We're going on a manhunt."

"I'm going to keep searching, too. Will you let me know if you find them?" Trey headed for the door. If he didn't beat the Chief to Jace, one of them might die.

• • •

Trey drove across town to Mary-Gray's place. She lived in the older part of town in a large antebellum mansion. Surprisingly, she answered the door herself. She wore tennis whites, her brunette hair pulled back in a sleek ponytail. "Trey! Hello! What are you doing here? I thought you were in Afghanistan."

"May I come in?"

"Of course. Please." She threw the door open and waved him in. "I was just having lunch on the patio. Won't you join me?"

He followed her to the flagged-rock patio and waited while she sat at a table under an enormous umbrella. The sweet scent of jasmine scented the air. As she poured him a glass of tea he didn't want, he studied her. Bearing no resemblance to the gawky thirteen-year-old he remembered, she had grown into a stunning young woman with a clear, smooth complexion, expertly made up eyes, and shiny hair. Her perfect smile and long legs would drive the boys at Ole Miss or Vanderbilt crazy. For him, she did nothing.

All he could think of was Summer. He forced his attention back to Mary-Gray when she spoke.

"When did you get home?"

"Night before last." He ached to jump all over with questions, but small talk was the polite, southern way. He forced a smile. "Not soon enough."

"I hadn't heard." She leaned over and gently tapped his forearm with a perfectly manicured hand. "Naughty of you not to come by and say hello sooner."

He watched her pink nails on his arm, wishing she'd remove them. "Actually, I'm trying to find out what Lindy's been up to. Naturally I thought of you. You ladies have been friends for forever and a day."

Her lovely face clouded. "Not anymore. For the last three or four months, since your mama got really sick, Lindy quit talking to me. Becca, too. Instead of turning to us so we could help her, she completely shut us out. We tried to help, but it finally got to the point we realized we weren't wanted. I don't know if she even plans on going to college. You know the kind of grades we've always had? Lindy's are in the toilet. Pardon me, but she seems to have just quit caring about everything. Even herself."

"Do you know who Lindy hangs around with now?"

"Not a clue." She took a delicate bite of lettuce then waved her fork. A sour look passed over her face. "I saw her with Candy-Can awhile back. No one I'd ever be seen with."

"Why's that? And why do you call her that?"

"Oh, you know. Candy can and will do anything any boy wants her to. She's just lowlife. A river rat. Lives in one of those shanties down on the banks of the river that no well-bred young lady is supposed to know about, but we all do." She made a clicking noise with her tongue. "I've heard her mama…well…does things no lady should for money."

Trey kept his silence. He'd almost forgotten how sharply the lines were drawn in this small town. Mary-Gray wouldn't think she had a mean bone in her body, but her ignorance of other people's troubles made him cringe. Maybe he had a clearer picture than most because his mother had crossed far over the social line to marry a poor police officer just beginning his career. Or maybe being a Marine had taught Trey early on that people often did things out of sheer desperation. He thought of Katia for a moment before he pushed back his chair and stood. "Thanks, Mary-Gray. I've got to be going."

"Don't be a stranger, okay?" She followed him to the door and saw him out. "Come by any time. Maybe we could have dinner, talk some more."

"Sure." He wouldn't be seeking her out again.

...

Pulling into the Curl Up and Dye's parking lot for the second time, Trey ignored the way his pulse sped up. Telling himself he'd come there to talk about Jace, he couldn't help but hope there was more.

Disappointment filled him as he entered the little beauty shop. Summer was nowhere in sight. Only Lilah at her station reading a novel. The radio played a pop tune he didn't know. "Hey, stranger."

With her face wreathed in smiles, she jumped up and hugged him. "Hey. It's been a long time."

"Too long." He stepped back a bit and looked at her. "You look good. Love agrees with you."

She laughed. "It sure does. What about you? Anyone special in your life?"

"No." He changed the subject. He glanced around, but saw nothing any different than on his last visit. The stench of perm solution was a little less pungent. "Summer not here?"

She shook her head. "No. She had to run some errands."

He leaned on her counter. "Got a minute?"

"Sure. What's up?" She twisted her engagement ring. Something was making her nervous.

"I'm trying to help Summer whether she believes it or not. The Chief is organizing a manhunt. If I don't find Jace first, he's going to get hurt or killed. Did Summer tell you if Jace made it home?"

"I haven't heard, Trey." Her slanted eyes met his straight on and he knew she spoke the truth. "Maybe he ran for the gulf."

"Anything's possible." He changed the subject. "I'm wondering if you know anything about a girl named Candy who runs with my sister. Some of the kids call her Candy-Can."

Lilah shrugged. "Not really. I was with Jody one night and we stopped in at Mugs-n-Jugs to look for some dude he wanted to talk to. I had a drink while I waited."

"And?" Trey prompted.

She played with the end of her corn rows. "I noticed two girls there who looked too young to hang out in that place. I mentioned it to Jody and he said he'd run them out. By the time he got around to it, they had disappeared. He said one was named Candy."

"And the other was?" He knew. Lindy.

Lilah confirmed his suspicions. "Your sister."

Horror filled Trey at the thought of his little sister in that kind of place. If she knew her way around a bar like that, she wasn't the sweet innocent she should've been.

"I didn't recognize Lindy at first. Her hair's real dark, a bad dye job. She also had on a ton of makeup and extremely tight clothes." This from the woman who didn't wear anything unless it was at least two sizes too small. He shuddered.

"Do you know anything about Candy?" He wondered what hold this girl had on Lindy. Why would his sister dump friends like Mary-Gray and Becca for someone like Candy?

Lilah studied her two-inch nails. "No. But I've heard her mama has one of those massage parlors down on the river. I wouldn't know for sure."

He hated to press her. Women in Juliet weren't supposed to know about the whores who lived on the riverbanks in a row of rundown shacks called Shantytown. A gentleman didn't bring them up in front of a lady. Somehow, they all seemed to know, however. "Do you know what her mother's last name is?"

"Jolene—no—Carlene, I think is her first. Jody might know more. Why all the questions?" She looked up from her hair.

"Lindy didn't come home last night. I'm worried about her. I think this Candy might have a lead." He smiled and she relaxed. "Thanks, Lilah. When will Summer be in?"

"Leave it alone, Trey. Her mama wigged out when she heard you were at their place. The past is over and done. Leave things where they fell."

"I'll keep your advice in mind." Idly, he lifted a hairbrush and studied it. He had no intention of trying to revive he and Summer's relationship. When the Chief caught Jace and sent him back to Angola, the Hill women would be angrier than ever with his family.

Lilah apparently didn't believe him. "What's the point in it? Stir up her mama and your daddy and everyone in between again? Surely you haven't forgotten how much hurt got spread around the last time your two families were together."

"I haven't forgotten." The past was going to bury him alive. He also remembered how good it had felt to make love to Summer.

Lilah reached out and squeezed his hand. "You'll both get hurt if you don't keep your distance."

"I plan on it. Tell her if she knows anything about her brother's whereabouts, she'd be smart to tell him to turn himself in. Right now, I've got to find my sister before she gets herself into something she can't get out of. I think I'll look up this Carlene and talk to her. Thanks for your help. Let's have dinner soon, okay?"

"It's a date. I'll even bring a friend and we'll double." She winked at him. "I know a lot of ladies who'd line up to go out with you."

"I'll call to make plans, but forget the blind date thing, okay?" Romance was the last thing on his mind. He just wasn't interested in anyone. Except the one woman who didn't want him.

She nodded, stretching up to kiss his cheek. "For now."

He went out the door knowing he'd turn down any woman she suggested.

•••

Summer came out of the supply room, feeling guilty. "Is Trey gone?"

"Yeah." Lilah gave her a long look. "I didn't like lying to him."

"I'm sorry. I take it his sister's not home?" Summer glanced at herself in one of the mirrors. "What's your schedule like? I'm thinking about some pink strands. They'd make me look younger."

"Pink? Not. He asked a lot of questions about that tramp down on the river and her kid." She turned to her booth and began disinfecting combs. "I couldn't tell him much."

"Lindy probably stayed at a friend's house." Summer picked up a broom and swept around her station. Her mind wasn't fully on the conversation. She couldn't get the image of Jace appearing in her house last night out of her mind. "Nothing about Jace?"

"Just told me to tell you if you know where he is to tell him to turn himself in." Lilah's eyes sharpened. "You don't, do you?"

Summer held her gaze. She'd lie to the devil himself to protect Jace. "No."

"Good. The Chief's organizing a manhunt. If you do know something, you better tell Jody. Jace might get hurt." Lilah's eyes filled with compassion. "Better prison than dead."

"Where'd Trey go?"

Lilah made an uncertain motion with her hands.

"I'll see you in the morning."

Not sure of her destination, Summer left the shop.

She spotted Trey's car at the little convenience store on the corner across from Miller's Feed. He came out of the store carrying a giant-sized coke and a paper bag. Wearing a simple gray T-shirt, Levi's, and Nikes he looked good, really good. She couldn't look away from him. As he came alongside, he noticed her. "Summer. What're you doing here?"

She said the first thing that came to mind. "I need to talk to you. It might be important."

"I'm kinda in a hurry. I'm still looking for Lindy." He hid his expression behind a pair of sunglasses marked Serengetti on the corner of the lenses. Expensive.

"Actually, that's what I wanted to talk to you about." She looked around. "But not here."

He motioned toward his car. "Jump in. Ride with me and tell me about it."

She hesitated a fraction of a second. What the heck? There were worse things than going for a short ride with Trey. She ignored the tiny flutters in her stomach. This was just a chance to ask about the Chief's plans, nothing more. "Okay. Let me pull around the side of the building and park out of the way."

When she jumped out of her own car, he stood beside the passenger side of the Mustang, holding the door open. With a quick glance around to see that no one saw her, she climbed in and he closed the door behind her. Trey came round and got in. Johnny Lang blared out of the radio. Trey's voice was deeper and raspier than the singer's. With a smile, he turned the sound low. "Sorry."

"I like that CD," she said, to cover her sudden confusion.

"You know it? All the guys back in Kabul listened to it."

"Uh-huh." She nodded. Her mind raced, trying to find a way to ask her questions. "We have it at the shop."

"I figured you more for a country music listener." He checked traffic and pulled out on the street heading out of town. "That's what you used to like. Reba, Garth, Vince."

"I love country," she said, "but I also like blues, old rock, a little pop."

"Did you find me to talk about music?" He glanced at her. "Although I like the subject well enough, I find it a bit odd that you told me to get lost, then look me up to discuss the merits of blues over rock. So what is it you really want?"

A little taken aback at his tone, Summer said, "I could care less what kind of music you like. It's not really important to me what you think of what I listen to on the radio. What I wanted to talk about has nothing to do with either. This is about Lindy. Kind of."

"What about her?" He shot a piercing look at her. "Did you hear from Jace?"

"No." Summer glanced out the window. They had left Juliet behind, entered the forest. A canopy of moss-covered oaks shaded the highway. During the day the road was dim, during the night it was frightening, stuff of *Sleepy Hollow* legend. She shivered a bit. Maybe the shadows would hide her face enough that he couldn't tell she was lying. "Nothing from Jace. I heard the Chief is going to send all his men on a manhunt. Is it true?"

"Is that what you had to ask me?" He sucked Coke through his straw.

"Yes," she admitted. "I knew you'd tell me the truth. There's no one else to ask…"

"And when you know the details will you contact Jace and warn him?" His gaze was sharp. And penetrating.

She took a deep breath. "I told you, I don't know where Jace is. But, yes, if I did I'd urge him to run away."

He didn't answer. "What does this have to do with Lindy?"

"That's just it. You tell me." Summer picked at her peeling manicure.

For a long moment, he didn't answer, Johnny Lang's words filling the car. "It's true. The Chief called for a full-scale search about an hour ago. We have substantial reason to believe Jace has Lindy."

"What?" Her head spun. "Are you insane?"

"It's true. I couldn't buy it either at first. But he's been writing threatening letters from prison. The coincidence is too great to ignore. He's out, she's missing." He sounded sad.

"I don't believe you." Summer stared straight ahead. If she as much as glanced his direction she would either punch him or burst into tears. She knew he hated Jace, but she hadn't known how much. Until now.

"I can hardly take it in myself, but I saw the letters with my own eyes." He wasn't lying. In her heart and in her gut she knew it. She'd seen how much her brother had changed with her own eyes. "Where are we going?" Dread filled her. If the posse found Jace and he didn't turn himself in, they'd shoot. She moaned.

"I'm trying to find Lindy before anyone else does. A woman named Carlene lives out here. Her daughter pals around with Lindy. Someone told me they live out here on the river. I have a general idea of the location, but not exact." He sounded as grim as she felt.

A tiny flicker of hope lit. Maybe they could stop the massacre she felt certain was coming. "Will they tell you anything?"

"I'm going to persuade them it would be in their best interest to fill me in."

She stole a glance at him. Noting his perfect profile, she thought most women would tell him anything he asked with minimum effort on his part. She amended her question. "With me along?"

"I don't know. Guess there's only one way to find out." He glanced at her, his gaze intense. "Lives are counting on it."

"I'll stay out of sight." She'd do anything to ensure her brother's safety.

"No. You're coming with me." He turned on a dirt road that led deep into the woods. Rough, deep ruts made driving nearly impossible. Pulling under a large pine tree, he turned off the car. "Guess we'll have to walk from here. I don't want to tear up my shocks."

"How far do you think we'll have to go?" She glanced around and shivered.

"I'm not sure. The river can't be far from here." He appraised her outfit, a plain white T-shirt, short jean skirt and thick-soled tennies. "I have some bug spray in the trunk. You'd better cover yourself with it."

Together, they got out and he locked the car. Then he opened the trunk and retrieved the promised spray. He held it up and said, "Turn around. I'll get your back."

Doing as he asked, Summer turned away, holding her hair up on her head.

• • •

Trey's gaze locked on her long, slender neck. He wondered what she'd do if instead of spraying her with the cold, sticky mist she expected, he touched her there with the tip of his tongue. Probably slap his face.

"Are you going to spray me or not?" she asked impatiently.

"Yeah." To his own ears, his voice sounded rough. He lifted the bottle. Just as his finger depressed the button, a blast rocked the air around them. He grabbed Summer around the waist and jerked her to the ground shielding her body with his.

As the sound died away, he looked around. A woman, wearing a man's fedora, with a shotgun in her hands stepped into the clearing.

"Who are you? And what the hell are you doing shooting that thing?" Trey's voice vibrated with anger. She seemed familiar, but he couldn't place her. Too worried, he didn't dwell on it.

"A better question is who are you and what're you doin' on my property?" The woman came closer and spat on the ground. "Never mind. I see what you're up to. If you want to screw, do it on your own time."

Trey rolled off Summer, stood, and helped her to her feet.

Summer, brushing off her clothes, hissed like an indignant kitten. "We were doing no such thing."

Trey took her hand and gave it a warning squeeze. "We actually came out here looking for someone. Do you know Carlene Carter?"

"Maybe." The woman gave his crotch a lewd stare and licked her full lips. "From the looks of what you're packing, I'd be glad to take care of you. If you're looking for a threesome, that could be arranged too. I help lots of young men fulfill their potential."

Out of the corner of his eye, Trey saw Summer's cheeks go bright red. He spoke before she lost her temper. "Thanks, but I just need to ask some questions. Are you Carlene?"

The woman settled on a large stump and lowered her gun. Her fedora tipped back on her head and a mass of curly red mane fell around a pretty face. She wore little makeup and fewer clothes. One strap of her silky, lime green negligee fell off her shoulder exposing most of a freckled breast. She made no move to pull up the offending strap. "Yep, but I ain't much for talkin'. What do you want to know? Prices vary dependin' on what ya want. The nastier ya get, the pricier I get. But if your girl just wanted to watch…"

Summer made a disgusted noise beside him.

He ignored the comment about money, hoping Carlene would tell him something if she thought he wanted more than information. Although Summer kind of foiled his plan. "I'm looking for a girl. Your daughter, I think. Candy?"

"What do you want with my kid? She's a bit young yet for anything kinky. Plus, I know a hell of a lot more than she does."

Carlene fiddled with the low neckline of the negligee, pulling it even lower exposing a large, dark brown nipple.

"That's disgusting," Summer muttered.

Trey squeezed her hand, warning her. He tensed, but kept his tone level. "I think my sister's in danger. Your daughter might know something that can help me."

Carlene waved her hand in a dismissive gesture, and made no move to cover herself. "Naw. Candy don't know nothin'."

He smiled at her. "Would you allow me to ask for myself?"

"You a narc?" She looked ready to jump and run like a deer.

"No. I'm Trey Bouché." Although he hated using his name to gain access, he knew his dad was aware of the river women and their camp. He left them alone as long as they kept a low profile and minded their own business.

"Chief Sam's kid? Hells bells. Never thought your daddy would let you and me come face-to-face. He's okay. Leaves us in peace anyway." Carlene stood up and motioned for them to follow her. She finally pulled her top over her bare breast. "All right. C'mon."

"This is crazy," Summer muttered as they trailed behind Carlene through the forest.

After several minutes of winding through the dense stand of trees, they came upon a row of small shacks on stilts partially submerged in the edge of the slow-moving river. A cluster of shanties sat together in a line along the banks. Carlene stopped and faced them. "Wait here. I'll send Candy out."

While they waited, Trey looked around. Summer studied the ground as if she wished it would swallow her whole. Like every red-blooded male in Juliet, Trey knew of the mysterious women who lived here. At present, none were in sight. All the huts seemed to be well maintained, none of the outsides were messy. A brightly colored quilt hung over the edge of one railing. Behind another, a clothesline held satiny underthings. A primitive village with no electricity or running water, the little town had a certain charm.

Like every boy over the edge of ten in Juliet, he'd heard the rumors, the stories, and the legends about the women here who made their living by selling sex. His senior year he'd passed on the annual tradition of spending the last night of school with one of them. He hadn't wanted anything to do with the sleazy ritual.

Maybe because he was the Chief's son, he knew the women made money the only way they knew how, that they survived the best they could—on their backs. Even then, he hadn't wanted to be part of it.

He was a normal all-American boy and he'd wanted sex as bad as the next guy, but the only woman he'd ever wanted stood beside him. From the time he figured out what sex was all about, she was the girl he dreamed about. No other girl ever caught and held his imagination the way she did.

A bottle blonde came out of one of the shacks when Carlene called for Candy. "She ain't here. She went to town."

"When?" Carlene stared at the other woman until she fidgeted.

"'Bout an hour or so ago."

"What for?"

The blonde shrugged. "Beats me. I ain't her keeper. Seems to me that's your job."

Carlene glared at her. "Watch your mouth, Drea."

Drea dropped her head and slipped back inside her cabin. Carlene glanced at them. "You heard her. I don't know where that kid of mine goes or what she does. I try to get her to do right, go to school, but she has a mind of her own. The way she's headed, she's going to end up right here like the rest of us."

"If you hear from her, could you have her come see me? Please?" Trey reached out and touched her arm. "It's important."

"Yeah, okay." Carlene nodded. "I'll try." She hesitated. "Go see Jimmy Ray Hunt."

"Thanks." Trey took Summer's hand and led her away.

Chapter Eight

Summer wanted nothing more than to go home and forget the whole dismal afternoon. She was sorry she had asked Trey to tell her the Chief's plans, she was sorry she had seen Shantytown with her own eyes and she was sorry Carlene had come along when she did and stopped Trey from kissing her. Summer had known he was going to try and she longed for him to try. In spite of everything, she wished he would kiss her until she couldn't think straight. Nobody affected her like Trey Bouché with his husky voice and handsome face and easy words.

No one ever had.

No one ever would.

"I need to get back to my car, please." She averted her face so he couldn't see the regret there. "This was a mistake. I shouldn't have come with you."

"Why did you?"

"I wanted to tell find out what your father has planned." She kept her gaze firmly out the side window.

"Keep telling yourself that, Summer, and maybe you'll believe it. I don't. I think you wanted a reason to talk to me. You found one." His smug tone grated on her nerves.

"What?" She turned and glared at him. "I don't give a fiddler's damn what you believe. In spite of everything, I don't want anything bad to happen to Lindy. But that doesn't mean I want anything more."

"I do." He met her eyes and she saw only honesty there.

"What?" Her jaw dropped. She snapped it shut.

"You heard me." The intensity of his emotion nearly seared her. "I've always wanted more. One short night five years ago wasn't enough. I've never stopped thinking about it."

"What's to say? I had too much to drink and we had…sex. End of story." She didn't want to do this. There wasn't any point in this conversation. Even if she did have feelings about him, there was no future for them now.

"There was more to it than that and you know it. Quit denying it. Stop hiding behind stuff that has nothing to do with you and me." His entire body tensed as if preparing for a body blow. She feared they might wreck.

She couldn't believe her ears. *Stuff that had nothing to do with you and me?'* Was he kidding? Mama had been hurt the night of his graduation party and everything fell apart between them. Between all of the Hills and Bouchés. After the trial, Trey left Juliet. Summer hadn't heard a word from him until now. What if she had borne his child? A shiver slipped through her. Would he have come back if he knew? She glared at him. "Hiding? I'm not the one who was kept under wraps then hustled out of town like a thief."

He didn't answer her at first. When he did, his voice went rough. "I did try to see you, but I couldn't get to you. I called and called, but you wouldn't return the favor. I did what the Chief told me to do. He and my mother thought it was best if I went to into the military and left the trial behind."

The sound that came out of her throat might've been called a laugh if it hadn't been so raw. He hadn't called once. She would've known. Even if he had, she couldn't have dealt with him. During the trial, and after, all she had been able to focus on was her mother. "Oh, I should've known. The mighty chief speaks and all the little Indians jump."

"He's my father."

"Yes. He was right. Sneaking you out of town was for the best. That way there was no chance of a repeat mistake between us. You were my brother's best friend. Too young for me. I was drunk." She crossed her arms over her chest and pressed her lips together.

"You didn't think I was too young that night," Trey said tightly. "And don't pretend you didn't participate. You wanted me. I wanted you. Alcohol had nothing to do with it."

She couldn't deny it. "I won't make that mistake again."

He didn't answer. He had wanted nothing more than to be with her. He had never gotten over her. If her mother hadn't been raped, and they hadn't been forced apart by that circumstance, he wouldn't have given up on Summer until she was his. That they had made love had only increased his desire for her. No other girl had ever filled the void she left in his life when she closed the door on him. Not even Katia. He hated that Summer blamed him for what had happened to Jace. But even though Trey felt he had done the right thing, his actions would stand between them forever.

He slammed on the brakes and skidded to the side of the road. "Making love wasn't a mistake," he declared. "I'm not going to let you ruin a great memory."

Jerking his seatbelt free, he leaned across the seat and without asking, covered her mouth with his. For a moment, she resisted, but he pried at the corner of her lips until she opened them.

He assaulted her tongue with his own. With his mouth, he tried to erase the pain. Desire flooded him, hardening him, as his fingers tangled in her hair. The silky strands rushed over and under his fingers like waves. He held her still, even though he didn't need to. She was responding, kissing him as fiercely as he kissed her. His spirit soared as he realized her hunger matched his.

Freeing one hand from her hair, he found her seatbelt button and pressed it. With the confining belt out of the way, he slid his hand under the hem of her tee, thrilling when a shudder ripped through her as his fingertips brushed over her ribs. Careful not to spook her, he cupped her breast under a lacy bra. Her hands fluttered in her lap. She wasn't immune to him; her nipple peaked against his palm. He flicked his thumb across it and she moaned into his mouth.

Her hands touched his abdomen, testing. His erection strained against his jeans. He wanted her fingers lower, wrapped around him. Now. But he could wait. For a minute.

His lips left hers to sample her neck. She tasted sweet like ice cream with caramel spilled over it. Maybe it was her vanilla scented hair. Whatever it was he liked the effect.

Working his hand under the slip of fabric covering her breast, he filled his palm with her. Letting go of her hair he used his free hand to lift the edge of her tee, wanting it off.

With a half sob she begged, "Stop. Please."

He closed his eyes and took a deep breath. Then he removed his hands from her body and sat up straight. He ran his palm over the back of his neck. "Just don't say you're sorry."

"I'm...not." She sounded breathless.

Frustration gripped him. He had wanted to make her remember, knowing full well that even if she did, he wasn't free to pursue a future. Not that she'd want him. When Jace was caught he would get more time tacked on his sentence at the least. And that was if he didn't get shot in the process.

She wouldn't ever forgive him. Stealing a glance at her, Trey was tempted to try and gain her permission. Pale blonde hair hung in disarray around her flushed face, pink lips were puffy and her short skirt exposed year-long legs. Without even knowing it, she screamed to be his. A far cry from her usual cool demeanor. His cock throbbed and he tore his gaze away. At this rate, he wouldn't be able to walk for a week.

She looked at him from the corner of her eye. "What?"

"You need to comb your hair." It was all he could manage.

"Oh, God," she moaned. Finding a brush in her bag, she dragged it through her hair. Then she pulled it into a severe ponytail. "If Mama even suspects we…I…well…I'll never hear the end of it."

If MiLann had any imagination at all, Trey figured she would take one look at Summer and instantly assume she'd been in his bed all day. He lied. "She won't."

Summer sniffed as she applied a sheer coat of lip-gloss that smelled like berries. "Ha. You don't know. Mama's got this sixth sense like radar."

His lips lifted a little at her tone. "Yeah. I kinda got that."

Her troubled gaze met his. "Trey, listen. I don't feel like what happened between us was a mistake. But we were lucky no one found out. You know how this town is. I don't want to be gossiped about…like Mama."

"I know…"

"Juliet hasn't changed. If people see us together all the ugly past will bubble up. I don't want to live through that again. You got to leave. I didn't." Her voice cracked a little and she raised her chin. So proud.

"You won't." A surge of protectiveness boiled through him. He would pound anyone who hurt her. He reached for her hand and she evaded him.

"I know you won't talk. You proved that once. It's the rest of the town that worries me."

He flinched. He wouldn't beg. "I get your message loud and clear. This won't happen again. I'll drop you off at your car."

She didn't answer.

"I need to check in and see if Lindy's come home." He took his cell phone from the cup holder and dialed. For a few seconds he spoke to the housekeeper then hung up.

"No word?" Summer's soft voice almost undid him.

"Nothing." He no longer doubted there was a problem with Lindy. She had to be found right now.

"I wonder where she could be? I won't believe she's with Jace." Steel laced Summer's voice.

"I'm going to find out." He sounded as determined as she did.

"What are you going to do?" Her eyes were troubled as she looked at him.

"Find Jimmy Ray and beat him until he tells me if something happened between him and my sister last night." Fury filled him when he thought of that slug doing anything to his little sister. If Jimmy Ray didn't come clean, Trey would welcome the chance to make him talk. He smiled thinking about it.

"Kind of like Jace did to Deke Soloman when he found out what he did to Mama?" Summer arched her brows at him and tipped her head a little. Clearly, she wanted him to recognize the parallel.

Trey started. He never doubted Soloman got what he had coming. If only he hadn't been the one to find Jace over the body, everything would be different. "I guess you could say that."

"I just hope I don't have to testify against you." She stared out the window.

"Me either," Trey said, heartfelt. No one should have to go through the agony of testifying against their best friend or loved one. The result left one hollow and empty. He wished he could tell her how much it hurt. "I'll take you back to your car. Then I'm going to go see the Chief and find out if there's anything new."

At the mention of his father, she frowned.

"As far as I know, Jace is safe," Trey told her.

"Until the Chief finds him and they tangle. Jace'll end up dead this time." She sounded as though the event had already happened. Grief stricken.

"No one's going to tangle." He prayed he was right. "All Jace has to do is turn himself in and nothing will happen to him."

"He won't trust your father." She didn't pull any punches. "He has no reason to."

"For his sake I hope you're wrong." Trey knew the tempers involved and if either one lost it…he wasn't going to go there. Jace would be fine.

"Jace was dead wrong the last time his life depended on the Chief," she shot back. Her accusation hung between them like a thick fog.

She meant him, too. Would she ever forgive him for what he had done?

"The Chief followed the law." Trey knew reasoning with her wasn't going to help. In the Hill family's mind, what they had done was a betrayal running so deep it would never heal. He changed the subject. "I pray my sister isn't lying dead in the woods somewhere."

"Me, too," she said. "We can agree on that. I need to get home to Mama."

Trey turned into the parking lot and watched Summer step into her car, but he was distracted. He hated to admit it, but his fear was growing. If this ended up being one of Lindy's stunts, he would wring her neck himself. But this felt different. Lindy was in danger.

•••

Summer, Glory, and Lilah sat on the porch chatting while Summer's mama prepared supper. She refused all offers of help. Both women had been at their house on occasion and MiLann trusted them.

Glory held up a paper bag and grinned. "I brought stuff to make drinks. Everybody want one of my specialties, a Morning Glory margarita? It's right here."

"Oh, I don't think I need a drink," Summer protested, although it did sound good. "Cola or iced tea would be better."

"Live a little," Glory insisted. "You need to relax."

Lilah nodded solemnly. "Yes, you do."

"What the hell? One drink isn't going to kill me." Summer gave a little wave. "Bring it on. Why do you call it a Morning Glory margarita?"

"Well, the glory part ought to be obvious." She smirked. "I added the morning part because after two or three of my special mix, it sometimes takes 'til the next morning to remember everything."

"Go easy on me," Summer pleaded.

When she tasted the perfect blend of peaches, strawberries, and tequila a few minutes later; she almost moaned out loud. This was good, really good. She could get used to Morning Glory margaritas. Never much of a drinker she hadn't had any drink since…she racked her brain. Nothing came to mind at first. Then the realization came to her. The boys' graduation party was the last time she'd had anything alcoholic. She'd sworn off after that night. Thinking about that event, she took a deep swallow. And choked.

Glory pounded her on the back. "You okay?"

Somehow Summer managed to breathe and nod at the same time. "Yeah."

Lilah lifted her half-empty glass and grinned. "Good, huh?"

"Yeah. Tasty." And extremely dangerous.

"So, friend," Glory leaned back and crossed her short legs, "Let's have us some girl talk."

"What about?" Summer was afraid she knew the answer.

Glory watched her over the rim of her glass. "Oh, Trey Bouché, for starters."

"Didn't we already cover this? There's nothing more to say." Summer glanced at the kitchen. "Don't let Mama hear you talking about him."

"Uh-huh." Lilah nodded wisely. "That's a can of worms that you oughta keep closed. No sense dragging up old news. Move on, I always say."

"Move on from what?" Glory pressed, although a little quieter. "I never did hear the whole story."

"Nothing to tell." Summer took a manageable sip this time. She took her time gathering her thoughts. "We were friends that's all. We're not now. End of story."

"I don't think so." Glory shook her head and her dark red hair shimmered in the evening light. "What exactly did Trey do to you again? I forget."

A long-buried pain near Summer's heart began to surface. She spoke harsher than she intended. "He betrayed my brother."

"Oh, lordy, you did it now." Lilah looked around. "Where is that pitcher? I have a powerful thirst for a refill. Glory? You need another? Summer, you?"

Glory leaned forward and studied her like a science experiment. "How did Trey sell out your brother, exactly?"

Lilah's eyes grew bigger. "I'm thirsty. You girls thirsty?"

Glory seemed intent on pressing the issue. "Maybe his treachery came from caring about you? Or did it go deeper? Something really heinous?"

Summer leveled her gaze on Glory. "Yes, it's awful. I can never forgive him. Trey doesn't care about me. If he did, he wouldn't have sat on that stand and said what he did. You're supposed to be my friend. Why are you sticking up for him?"

"I am your friend. You know that. But I guess I'm missing something. What did Trey do that was so wrong in your eyes? Didn't he find your brother standing over the beaten body with blood all over his hands?" Glory looked at her own hands and shuddered.

"Yes, that's true. But the final nail in Jace's coffin was that Trey testified Jace planned the murder." There. That's what had destroyed her trust in Trey. He shouldn't have shared that Jace swore to him he'd see the man who beat and raped Mama dead. Jace had trusted his best friend. Of course he'd say something crazy in front of him. Why hadn't Trey realized Jace was just blowing steam? She knew Jace hadn't killed Deke Soloman. Why didn't Trey trust him, too?

"He should've lied by omission?" Glory raised her over plucked eyebrows.

"Yes." Summer met her friend's eyes with a steady look. "I guess he should've, because it would've preserved Jace's freedom."

• • •

Trey sat with his mother on the wraparound porch of the big three-story mansion she'd inherited, *LeFleur*. They overlooked a rose garden, the sweet scent of the flowers rising to them. The sun hung onto the sky, refusing to fall. Etta had gone to see her new grandbaby and the Chief was hunting Jace. Trey took advantage of the chance to spend some time with his mother.

If Jace was headed to Juliet, Trey wasn't going to upset his mother with the news. Although warm outside, Emily Bouché shivered and snuggled under the homemade quilt she'd stitched herself. Trey reached over and smoothed the edge of the fabric. His mother's cancer was terminal. There wasn't anything he could do for her. Still, he asked. "Do you need anything?"

Leaving her eyes closed she said, "Just your company."

"I'm happy to provide that." They had once been close. Until the Chief and sent him away to the military and driven a wedge between them. Facing her now made his heart hurt. Once a dark-haired beauty queen, Emily had always protected her appearance. Now, she looked like a living skeleton. Heavy lines crisscrossed her face, her brown eyes had sunk deep into her skull and her once long, shiny hair was now a cap of gray. She looked twenty years older than her true age. There wasn't much time to mend old hurts.

"I'm glad you're here." Her fingers fluttered like a wounded butterfly.

"Me, too." He took her hand his, careful not to crush delicate bones. "Are you hungry? Etta left some chicken salad in the fridge."

"I don't want food. But I know you have to be starving. Go ahead." She slipped her hand from his.

"Will you be okay while I get some?" Reluctant to leave her side for even a second, he wasn't sure she'd still be here when he returned.

As is she'd read his thoughts a faint smile crossed her creased face. "Of course. I'm not going to die while you're fixing your supper."

Startled, he didn't know how to reply. Placing her hand in her lap, he went to the kitchen. He filled two glasses with tea, made three sandwiches, added chips and carried a tray back outside.

His mother slept. He set the glasses beside her elbow, the food on the table next to him. Sitting, he took a big bite of Etta's famous chicken salad and almost sighed. There were a lot of things he missed about home.

"It'd be a blessing if Jace Hill came here and put me out of my misery." Emily's voice was so low, he wasn't sure he'd heard right.

He swallowed a big hunk of sandwich without chewing. He faced her. "Ma'am?"

"Just because I'm dying, doesn't mean I'm deaf." Her voice was barely a whisper.

His appetite fled and he set the sandwich aside. "We didn't want to worry you."

"I'm carrying so much pain inside. Death will be a welcome relief." Her deep-set eyes didn't blink.

Trey forced down the lump in his throat. Marines didn't cry. "Can I get you some more morphine?"

Her chest rose and fell. "My sins weigh on me, not the disease."

"You don't have anything to feel sorry for." Watching her struggle to breathe was almost more than he could endure. His heart felt like it was collapsing. "Do you want me to get a priest?"

"A priest can't make it all right. What we did was so, so wrong." Her hand fluttered and he took it. "I hurt you, my own son. I deserve this and much worse."

He loved her no matter what she had done. He held her hand in both of his, praying to bring the right words to mind. "It doesn't matter now."

"We shouldn't have sent you away. We only wanted to protect you." Her eyes begged for forgiveness. She needed his absolution.

"I don't blame you. The Chief made me go into the Marines, not you." Forcing him out of the family had been the Chief's decision alone. Like Trey himself, she had been powerless back then to stop it.

Her gaze found his face. "No…no. I wanted you to go, too. You had to grow up so fast here. I'm…so…sorry." Her dry fingers curled around his for a moment.

Shock waves reverberated through him. All these years, he had thought it was only the Chief who wanted him sent away. He didn't know how to answer.

She touched his cheek for a moment. "Samuel loves you. He just doesn't know how to show it."

He didn't respond. Words wouldn't squeeze through his tight throat. This request was harder. The Chief had sent him halfway around the world with no more than a nod. "We're fine," he managed.

"MiLann…how is she?" Her weak voice held something—longing?

Why had she jumped from his father to MiLann? The drugs she took for pain must be messing with her mind. "She's doing okay."

Her breaths came in shallow gulps. "If only that terrible night had never happened."

"None of us can change it now." Regret filled him that his mother and MiLann couldn't repair their friendship in time for both of them.

Her chest heaved. "Find the truth. For me."

"What do you mean?" he asked carefully. What truth? His heart pounding in his ears made it hard to hear.

Her head lolled to the side and he feared she'd fainted. Heart racing, he took her pulse. The beat, faint and irregular, was there. She was asleep. Relieved, he picked her up and carried her into her makeshift hospital room. The medicinal smell reminded him of a hospital. Another scent, one of cancer and death, lingered there, too. Gently, he tucked her into bed, kissed her dry forehead, and then flipped off the light switch.

He walked into the kitchen, puzzling over his mother's words. What truth was he supposed to find? He shrugged it off. The drugs had to be talking.

The Chief sat in the breakfast nook eating his own share of Etta's chicken salad.

Trey spoke to him. "I didn't know you were here. Mother's asleep."

He nodded. "I'll check on her later. Did you have any luck locating your sister?"

"No. I went everywhere I could think of." Trey straddled a chair backwards. "I even went to Shantytown. Lindy's got a friend out there. But no dice."

"There's nothing out there but a bunch of sluts. No one this family would associate with any of them. Stay the hell away from there," the Chief ordered. "Talk to Mary-Gray and Becca. Those are Lindy's friends."

"Yes, sir. I already did. They don't run around with Lindy any longer." Trey wondered how the Chief could be so out of touch with his own daughter. Maybe Candy was back home. He would talk to her as soon as possible. "Have you heard anything about Lindy or Jace yet?"

"Not so far. So far, he's evading even the dogs." He took another bite and chewed.

Trey's mother's words rang in his head. "Did you ever think Jace might not have killed Soloman? That someone else might have been the culprit?" He watched his father carefully for signs of doubt or regret. If he showed anything but self-assurance, it would be the first time Trey could remember.

The Chief shook his head. "I can't think like that. Besides, you know what he did. You're the one who found him."

Trey bit his thumbnail. "I know Jace was crazy mad, but I still have a hard time believing he would kill Deke Soloman in cold blood. The person I knew wasn't capable of that kind of violence."

"His fingerprints were all over the weapon. Live long enough, boy, and you'll find out people have the capacity to do most anything." The Chief chewed thoughtfully. "Sometimes, folks still surprise even me."

"Then you believe Jace did murder Soloman? No doubts?" Trey knew the answer before the Chief gave it. But he wanted to hear it again.

"No doubts at all." He got up and placed his plate in the sink. His voice held steady. "I'm going to put that boy back where he belongs."

Chapter Nine

Trey dialed a number. "Yeah, Jody, listen. I need your help. Meet me in ten. I'll wait at the Dairy Queen. Okay, see you in a few minutes."

While he waited, he thought about the last two days. He never expected his life to go this way. He hadn't wanted to leave Juliet like a sneak in the night. That had been his parents' idea. Why? What had made them hustle him out of town in such a hurry? Yes, he had to testify against Jace, but he'd been old enough to understand the consequences of that action.

Had they somehow found out about Summer and wanted to separate them? Shipping him halfway round the world seemed a bit excessive. So what remained to make them send him away?

Now he wondered about the reason he'd left. What was so important he had been exiled from his family? From his home? A nagging hunch had begun to form in the back of his mind, but he didn't want to believe it. Maybe Jace hadn't really killed Deke Soloman. Did the Chief know who had really done it and he thought Trey did, too? The idea was too terrible to contemplate. If Trey had sent Summer's brother to prison, and he was innocent, she would harden her heart even more.

The idea was crazy. Jace had been standing over the body of Soloman with blood on his hands. The murder weapon had his prints on it. Trey had seen both with his own eyes. Who would the Chief be protecting? There hadn't been anyone else at the scene and no evidence to the contrary. Trey stirred his chocolate sundae, lost in thought.

Jody drove in and parked his patrol car. He got out, came inside, and slid across from Trey. "What's up?"

"Have you found out anything about Lindy? Or Jace?" Trey forced the words out. His heart felt like a chunk of lead and he had a hard time catching his breath. The chicken salad he'd consumed earlier felt like a pot of boiling sewage stewing in his stomach. "She's been gone more than twenty-four hours."

"I know. Your old man has every man and woman in the department looking for Jace. He's convinced he's holding Lindy prisoner. The Chief won't listen to any other possibility."

"Look, I want to help. If I can find them first maybe I can prevent another tragedy."

"What can you do?" Jody sounded dubious. "You're not a cop. Or a trained negotiator."

"Jace was my best friend. I can talk to him." Trey refused to acknowledge history was repeating itself.

"Do you think he's got something to do with Lindy's disappearance? You think he nabbed her?" Jody put on his cop face, all business. "Why?"

Trey forced himself to consider the evidence. There was none beyond a few letters. Just the Chief's suspicions. If he was right, Jace had changed more than any of them could've imagined. Trey dragged in a deep breath and held it for a moment. "All I know is that Lindy hasn't been home since late yesterday afternoon and Jace is on the loose. I've talked to a couple of her friends and they haven't seen her either."

"Which friends?" Jody reached for a pen and notebook in his pocket.

"Mary-Gray Bennet, for one."

Jody made a face. "Any others?"

"I've heard Lindy runs with Carlene Carter's daughter. I went to talk to her, but she wasn't at Shantytown." Trey took a bite of ice cream, but it slid over his tongue without him tasting it.

Jody whistled. "Oh, man. Your old man is gonna shit a brick when he finds out about this."

"I already told him, and he ordered me to stay away from Shantytown. He said no member of our family would be caught out there." Trey slapped the table. "That's it! I knew I saw that woman before. Carlene Carter was coming out of the Chief's office when I went in."

"The hooker?" Jody grinned, but didn't say more. "What was the Chief doing with her? Relieving stress?"

"I kind of doubt she was there on a business call. You can say what you like about my old man, but he loves my mother. Worships her would be a better definition." Whatever faults the Chief had with his children, he didn't have the same issues with his wife. Emily had always been the sun, the moon, and the stars in his world.

"Maybe a john got rough with one of the ladies," Jody suggested. "For some reason, no one in the department has ever been able to figure out why, but the Chief leaves Shantytown alone. They mind their business and he looks the other way."

"Yeah, I know." Trey changed the subject. "When the Chief finds out how wild Lindy's become he's going to hit the roof. He might even send her away…" *Like me.*

"He's going to come unwound when he finds out Lindy's running with white trash like that." Jody's dark eyes were troubled. "I don't want to be anywhere close when he finds out."

"If you'll help me, maybe we can find Lindy before he finds out." Trey pushed his melting sundae away.

"Let's go talk to Candy Carter and her mother and see what they'll tell me. If we can beat the Chief to Lindy and Jace, it'll all be good. If we don't it'll be my badge." Jody stood up. "So let's hustle."

Trey was already moving. "Quit standing around."

• • •

Carlene Carter smiled seductively and ran a finger along Trey's cheek. "You again? Change your mind about me? I see you got rid of the uptight blonde. I could tell you didn't want to play in front of her. This time you brought along such a handsome friend."

Trey ignored the look Jody shot him at the mention of Summer. He'd hoped not to bring her into it.

"I'd like to show you a good time." She continued to stroke his face. "But it'd be a little too close for comfort."

He was troubled by the way she touched him. He didn't like it, but didn't want to offend her. He nodded at Jody. "This is Officer Marvell, a friend of mine. He'd like to speak to Candy."

Jody nodded.

"Hells bells." Carlene sighed dropped her hand. "Never thought I'd see the day my kid was more popular than me."

"We'd just like to talk to her, ma'am." Trey didn't want to think about how easily this woman would sell her daughter to him or any other man who had enough cash.

She laughed, a harsh grating sound. "'Ma'am'? Honey, I'm not old enough for that particular term of endearment. I don't care to be called by that old lady name. Carlene'll do."

He gave her the most charming smile he could manage. "I'm sorry…Carlene. Is Candy here?"

She threw her head back and laughed. "I like the way my name sounds coming from you. Bet you only sound better when you're makin' love. Guess I'll just have to use my imagination. Yeah, my kid's home. I'll send her out. If you change your mind about getting to know someone a little more seasoned than your blonde, come on in. You won't regret it."

Trey shifted. Maybe her clients liked this kind of talk, but it made him feel dirty. He imagined Jody grinning beside him, probably waiting for a chance to rib him later. Were his feelings for Summer so transparent? He hoped not. He'd have to be more careful to mask his emotions. Any involvement between them could only cause them both heartache.

"Before you do that, ma'am, I'd like to ask you about the Chief." Jody pinned her with a cool stare. "You went to see him? Mind if I ask why?"

She paused for a moment. "That's between me and him. Wait here. I'll send you my kid."

Jody and Trey exchanged long looks.

Before they could discuss anything, a teenage girl, hair dyed pitch black, eyes rimmed a matching shade with kohl, sauntered up to them. She wore a slip and nothing else. Her dark nipples and areolas showed clearly through the thin material. "Yeah? Carlene said you wanted to talk to me. In spite of what she probably told you, I don't screw for money."

Jody gave her a kind smile. "We hoped only to ask you about Lindy Bouché."

"You wanna know somethin' about Lindy, ask her." Candy jutted out her chin and narrowed her eyes to a thick, black line. "I'm not going to rat her out to a cop."

Jody frowned and Trey spoke up. "I'm her brother. I would talk to her, only I don't know where she is. We just want to know if you have any idea where she went last night."

Candy studied him and he could almost see the debate going on in her head. Finally, she made up her mind. "She was talking with Jimmy Ray Hunt. That's all I know."

"Why, in God's name, would she go anywhere with that lowlife!" What had his sister been thinking to go anywhere with scum like Jimmy Ray Hunt? Everyone knew he was trash. Although he was known to run drugs, guns, and anything else illegal through his bar he'd never been caught.

Candy shrugged. "He wanted to take her home. She was drunk, she might've let him."

"And you just let her go? Are you crazy?" He wanted to shout, but kept his voice even.

"Trey." Jody's voice held a warning.

He trembled with rage. What kind of friend did something like that? He caught himself before he said anything else. He had sold out his best friend in the entire world. At least his motives had been honorable, if hurtful.

She stiffened then shrugged. "I'm not her mama or her keeper. I had my own hookup to worry about."

"My sister hasn't come home since last night." Trey's voice was raw. "If anything happens to her, I'm holding you personally responsible."

Jody moved so that he stood between them. "No one's accusing you of anything, Miss Carter. We're concerned for Lindy. An inmate named Jace Hill escaped a couple days ago from Angola. He hasn't come home yet, either. Has Lindy ever mentioned him to you?"

"Nope. Never heard of him." Candy shrugged again, seemingly unconcerned. "She's probably sleeping off a good night's lovin' somewhere."

For a moment, Trey was speechless. Then he realized who he looked at. In spite of Candy's protestation that she didn't sell sex for money, he guessed she'd probably been initiated to her mother's profession at about the age of twelve. The girl probably didn't have the first clue about morality. She couldn't be blamed, he supposed. There had been a lot of women in Afghanistan who had done things they never would in ordinary times.

Jody dug a card out of his back pocket and handed it to her. "For Lindy's sake, and that of Jimmy Ray Hunt, I hope you're right. If you hear from her, call me at this number."

"Sure thing." Candy stuffed the card between her breasts without looking at it first.

• • •

Jace paced like a caged animal.

Lindy watched him warily. He hadn't harmed her in any way, but tension radiated from him like heat waves off the sun. For several hours, he'd been surly and on edge. He'd left the house for a short time, and when he came back inside, he told her he'd lit the furnace and there would be hot water to bathe and the kitchen stove would work. He didn't want her to turn on the lights, though, and the only illumination came from the moon.

Every bone in her body ached and all she'd done most of the day was sleep on the lumpy sofa. Now her stomach grumbled and she wished Etta were here with her mountains of food. "Do you have any more peanut butter crackers?"

"Yeah. You want a Coke, too?" He stopped pacing long enough to look at her.

"Sure."

He tossed her a cold can of cola and a pack of crackers. "Ain't much of a meal."

"It's fine." She popped open the cola and drank deeply.

"Not like you'd have at home."

Why was he pressing her? "Not the same food, but I'd be eating alone."

"Why's that?"

"Because the Chief would be at work and Mother would be in bed." She fiddled with the pack of crackers, her appetite gone.

"I don't follow." He folded his arms across his chest.

"Things have changed since you've been…away." Tears formed at the corner of her eyes and she blinked them away.

"How?" He straddled the end of the couch and stared at her with a cool expression. A faint smile crossed his face. "Are the debs wearing blue instead of white this year?"

"Mother has ovarian cancer. The doctors can't do anything." Her throat tightened too much for more words to come out.

"I didn't know." He didn't sound sorry, but he didn't sound happy either.

The tears threatened to fall and she swallowed them. "Yeah."

"So why doesn't Trey keep you company?" His tone went hostile.

Now it was her turn to stare at him. She didn't think she would ever hear Trey's name out of his mouth again. "A lot changed when you left."

"You're telling me."

"With everyone." She was getting sick of his pity party. "Not just you."

"My heart's breaking."

"Trey went into the Marines, to Afghanistan. In fact, we haven't seen him since you left."

He didn't reply to that. "Do you ever see my mama or Summer?" Longing colored his voice.

"Not your mother. No one sees her. But Summer works at the Curl Up and Dye. I bump into her sometimes." She played with her crackers.

"Do you have her cut your hair?"

A test. She hesitated. There was no right way to answer this one. If she said yes—a lie—he'd think she had his sister wait on her. If she told the truth and said no, he'd think she thought she was too good. There was no way too win. "Not really."

"No, I didn't think so." Spinning on his heel, he went to the window and peered out.

"My friends and I usually go to the mall. Or do our own hair." There was no way to make this come out right.

He continued to stare out the window. "Yeah."

She had to make him understand. "Look. I don't have any problem with Summer. She seems really sweet, but my parents… they made Trey leave…"

The look on his face when he spun around was ugly. "What do you mean? Trey ran off the first chance he got."

Is that what he really thought? "Who told you that? Summer? You're both wrong. He never wanted to go away. But the Chief packed him up and took him to see the recruiter in Jackson. The next thing I knew, he was gone." She snapped her fingers. "Just like that."

"How'd your old man force Trey if he didn't want to go?" He sounded dubious.

"I don't know. The Chief said there were too many bad memories here and Trey needed a fresh start."

"He probably couldn't face what he did."

"Did you expect him to lie?" Lindy held his gaze, but he refused to back down. "You know he wouldn't."

"I expected him to be a friend."

"Even if that meant lying under oath?" Lindy couldn't believe her guts. She didn't know where her courage came from, but she wasn't going to sit here and let him feel sorry for himself any more. If he got a chance to start over, he was going to blow it.

Jace ran a hand through his long hair. "Hell, I don't know. All I know is I didn't kill Deke Soloman. I thought someone would listen to me."

"Your mama and sister believed in you." *So did I.* Back then she had been convinced Jace couldn't have done the crime. But she'd grown to realize there wasn't any other logical explanation.

"Yeah, but they didn't have any power to keep me from going to that hell hole called Angola." Bitterness oozed out of him so strong she could almost smell it.

"Neither did Trey or the Chief," she insisted. Trey wouldn't lie, and the Chief might be a hard-ass, but he wouldn't set anyone up to go to prison.

Her words hung between them. She held her breath until he spoke again.

"I didn't do it and I'm going to prove it." He jutted out his jaw in a fierce angle.

"So, let's do it." She arched her eyebrows at him. "How do you propose we go about it?"

He almost staggered. "What do you mean?"

"I mean," she said softly, "let's figure this out and set you free."

Under his frown she could see hope. "What's in it for you?"

"I'll help you." Right now, she wasn't going to examine her motives. If she could lend a hand and find the truth, maybe he'd forgive a little bit.

"I need to find out who had a motive to kill Soloman, for starters. I was somebody's flunky. But whose?"

"Who would want to kill him besides you for what he did to your mama?" She met his glare unflinchingly. "If we're going to figure this out, we need to look at all the evidence."

She got up, went into the kitchen and rummaged in a drawer until she found a piece of paper and a pencil. Coming back into the front room, she said, "Let's make a list of suspects."

"Don't you get it? There are no other suspects. That's why I took the heat. No one else had a motive to kill Soloman."

"If you didn't do it, then someone else had to have a reason." She bit the end of the pencil. "We just have to figure out who and why. Soloman was new in town, right?"

"Yeah. It came out at the trial that he got turned down for a job as a custodian at the school where Mama taught English the same week he…raped her." Jace looked like he might hurl.

Lindy made a note on her paper, speaking out loud as she did. "Soloman attacked MiLann for revenge?"

"That was her theory. But it doesn't add up. She didn't have anything to do with the school board's decision." He plunked down on the end of the sofa and looked over her shoulder.

"So, why pick her?" Lindy glanced up at him and their gazes held.

"I don't know," he said.

"Where was she found? I can't remember," Lindy admitted.

"Why would you? You were just a kid."

"That was then. Times change." She touched her dry lips with the tip of her tongue.

"Yeah." He looked away. "Mama was found outside the Blue Cat motel. In the alley. A maid spotted her and called the hospital."

Lindy tapped her pen against her notepad. "How did she get there?"

"Nobody knows. Mama can't remember. She blanked out everything after the party at *LeFleur*. They tried to make her remember at the trial, and it just made her freeze up worse." He heaved a sigh and stood, stuffing his hands in his pockets.

"So, after your mama was attacked, Soloman was released, right?" Lindy made another note.

"Yeah." He looked enraged. "The Chief said there wasn't enough evidence to hold him. Mama was so badly beaten she was still in the hospital and couldn't finger him in a lineup."

"What about physical evidence?"

"There is none."

"What?" The pen slipped out of her fingers, and Jace bent to pick it up.

"The rape kit was lost." He said it as flatly as if he said the wind was blowing.

"What? How? I don't understand," Lindy cried. "Who lost it?"

"You tell me," Jace muttered. "But it's gone. Disappeared. The nurse on duty had it and by the time it got to the police it was gone."

"My God." Lindy stared at him. "Are you saying what I think you're saying?"

He met her eyes. "Yeah."

"You can't mean to say that the Chief did something to the evidence?" She shook her head. "No way."

He didn't answer.

"He wouldn't do that," she protested.

Jace held his tongue.

"Why?" she cried.

"You tell me. If I knew the answer to that one, I wouldn't have been locked up like a dog in a pound."

"You're saying the evidence was lost by the Chief and he let Soloman go." Lindy took a deep breath. "Then what happened? How did you find out?"

He smiled bitterly. "Trey. He was down at the police station. He called and let me know."

"What did you do?" She reached for the pen. "I've heard the story, but you tell me in your own words."

"I lost my head." He paused and gathered his thoughts. "I left Mama's hospital bed and tore over to the Chief's office. It was late. Around nine-thirty. No one else was around and I told him he'd rot in hell. That I'd see to it." He met her wide-eyed gaze. "I told Trey I was going to kill the fucker who hurt Mama."

"Then what?" she whispered.

"I ran out."

She leaned forward, perched on the edge of the couch. "To go after Soloman?"

"Yeah." He looked lost in memories. "I went back to the Blue Cat on the hunch Soloman would go back to the scene of the crime. I was right. The door was unlocked and I went in. He was in his room."

"Alive?"

He shook his head. "No. Dead. He was on his stomach. I hauled him over intending to give him a beating. I wanted him to confess to me at least. But he was dead. He had a knife sticking out of his chest."

"You touched it? Why?" She breathed the word.

He whirled around. "I don't know."

"That's when Trey showed up?" Her question was more of a statement.

"Yeah." Jace laughed without humor. "He came to the rescue just in time to find me with a bloody knife in my hands. The rest, as they say, is history."

"Who else could've done it? Who had a motive? Your Mama was still in the hospital. What about Summer? What did she do?"

Jace snorted. "You're really reaching if you think Summer would kill anyone. Besides, she was with Mama."

"I didn't say she did it. I asked who had a motive, no matter how farfetched. If we're going to do this we need to be open to all the possibilities." She made another note.

"Fine. Summer was as mad as I was when your old man turned Soloman loose. But she isn't capable of killing anyone." He paced. "I can't think of anyone who would want him dead.

Lindy leaned on her fist. "Who else? We have to figure out who else was as upset as you and your sister. Like your mama's friends, for instance. Did she have any men friends?"

Jace bristled. "People talked trash about her, but she never even went out."

"Okay, okay," Lindy tried to soothe him. "What about colleagues?"

"No one she was close enough to that would kill on her behalf. Your mama was her best friend. Can you picture Miz Emily Bouché killing anyone? Not hardly." He continued to pace. "This is hopeless."

"No, it's not. We just have to keep thinking. Maybe we're going at this from the wrong direction. Maybe Soloman was killed for something that had nothing to do with your mother at all. Maybe it happened because he said the wrong thing to someone. It's a possibility he mouthed off to the wrong person and they did him in for it."

"Too much time has passed. No one would know now." He turned the other direction. "It came out at my trial that he had been seen drinking at Mugs-n-Jugs right before he was murdered. Maybe someone there would remember seeing him."

Lindy shivered. "That's a great idea."

He shook his head. "That's probably a dead lead. We're sure not going to stroll in there and start asking questions. But I might be able to get some information out of old Jimmy Ray."

"How?"

"If he's in the shape I think he is, a little gentle prodding might persuade him to open up." He stopped moving and grinned at her. "Give him a little of his own medicine."

"You can't hurt him." Horror crossed her face. "Surely you don't intend to use force, much as I'd like to see Jimmy Ray squirm."

"Why not?" His expression mocked her. "Change your mind about screwing him?"

She froze. Then her hand snaked out and slapped his face. "Let's get one thing straight, Mr. Hill. You don't speak to me like that. Ever. And another thing. I never did, nor do I now want to be with Jimmy Ray Hunt in any way. Have I made myself clear?"

"Clear as glass." He grinned. "You sure get riled up in a hurry."

"Don't forget it." Picking up her paper she asked, "What do you think he'll tell you?"

He shrugged. "I dunno. Probably less than nothing."

"What time is it?"

He shrugged. "I guess around six-thirty. Why?"

"This is a perfect time to go see him." She jumped up. "Let's go."

"No way. You're not going."

"You're not leaving me here alone."

Chapter Ten

Mugs-n-Jugs' parking lot stood empty save for one classic pickup. Trey pulled in alongside it and turned off his engine.

At the door, Jody said, "Let me do the talking."

Trey nodded and they stepped inside. A few early bird drinkers sat at the bar, but Jimmy Ray was nowhere in sight. A bleached blonde in a neon blue, skintight mini dress approached them and flashed a smile. Her upper teeth were crooked, but she was pretty in a harsh way. "What're you boys having?"

Jody flashed his badge. "Jimmy Ray around?"

Her eyes went cold. "In the back."

"Get him."

"He's busy."

"That's okay. I'll find him myself." Jody pushed by the blonde, Trey following. They walked into a room off the hallway marked private. Jody went through the door first, Trey on his heels. They both came to an abrupt halt. A man lay sprawled across a maroon sofa, his leather pants undone, a dark haired girl kneeling in front of him sucking his dick. He looked up, but didn't seem to be terribly affected by their presence. "Hey! Get out! This ain't the bar."

The girl jumped up and darted by them, pulling her top together.

"We're closed." The guy made no move to button his pants. His erection seemed to stare at them, mocking.

"Jimmy Ray Hunt?"

"Who wants to know?"

"I do." Trey wondered what Lindy saw in the guy. Skinny, with a pockmarked face, Jimmy Ray wouldn't attract a lot of girls on looks alone. The large purple knot he sported on his forehead and two black eyes didn't help his position. A ragged scratch ran down his right cheek.

"Zip your pants." Jody pulled a little notebook out of his shirt pocket. "I don't want to see that little bitty thing."

Jimmy Ray's face flushed. "Fuck you."

Trey fisted his hands. "I'll ask again. Are you Jimmy Ray Hunt?"

"Yeah." He tugged his pants together, but left the top button undone. He reached for a glass on the nearby table and poured himself a shot of tequila. Downing it in one quick motion, he poured another and stared at them belligerently. "Who wants to know?"

"What happened to your face?" Trey countered.

He shrugged. "Bar fight. I had to break it up."

"Can anyone corroborate that story?" Jody asked.

"Why do you want to know?" Jimmy Ray poured another drink and tossed it back like water. "Cops don't give a shit about my problems."

"Did you see a girl named Lindy Bouché in here last night?" Jody asked.

"I saw a lot of chicks last night. What's so special about this one?" Jimmy Ray downed yet another shot. "They come and they go…if you get my meaning."

"This girl we want to talk to you about is Lindy Bouché. Maybe you recognize the name?" Jody met the other man's eyes with a cold stare. "The police chief's teenage daughter. Too young to be in this place, too young to drink, and way too young to run with your kind."

"I don't know what you're talking about." Jimmy Ray's gaze darted around wildly.

Trey jumped in. "Give it up, Hunt. You know who she is. Apparently, you allow Lindy and her friends to hang out in here. An eyewitness told me you were with Lindy last night. So why don't you tell me what happened after you left here, and I won't go to the Chief and tell him about the teenage crowd that hangs out here?"

"You always have your daddy fix your problems? I heard you run when the going gets tough." Jimmy Ray grinned.

Trey leaned over and took hold of Jimmy Ray's wifebeater tank and twisted it until their noses nearly touched. "I can handle you if you prefer me instead of the Chief. I'll be gentle since it looks like you'll fall over if I breathe hard. From the looks of things, someone else didn't like your act either. Can you take another pounding? Cause I'm fixing to hand one out if you don't start talking."

"I'd suggest you listen to him. We can do it here, or we can go down to the station and you can look Chief Bouché in the face and tell him why his little girl didn't come home after she left here with you," Jody shrugged. "Your choice."

"Yeah, yeah." Jerking away so hard his stained tank ripped, Jimmy Ray glared at him. "She was all over me like white on rice so I offered to give her a ride on the old one-legged pony. We went to the lake to fu…"

"Watch your mouth," Trey warned. "My sister is eighteen years old. You're what? Thirty?"

"So? You always shag girls the same age as you?" Jimmy Ray smirked.

"Who Trey dates isn't the issue," Jody said, "but who you were with last night is."

Jimmy Ray reached for the half-empty bottle of tequila. Jody got to it first and moved the booze out of reach. "Quit stalling."

Jimmy Ray sat back and glared at him. "The little bitch has been in here every weekend for the last three-four months letting me see every way she can she wants to get to know me real well. Understand what I mean?"

Trey made a noise in his throat and Jody shot him a warning glance. "And?"

"I know underage when I see it, but last night I lost my mind and thought a little tangle with the kitten would be a sweet way to spend the night. We get out to the lake, we're halfway to the point of no return and the bitch changes her mind and runs off like she's never seen a dick before. She stranded me out in the woods. I had to walk all the way home with my balls achin' so bad I could hardly manage."

Trey dug his fingers into his palms until they hurt. Hearing his sister called a dirty name by this pond sucker was nearly more than he could stand. If he did it again, Trey figured he might have to teach him some manners. "Lindy did that to your face?"

Jimmy Ray touched the knot on his head and grimaced. "I guess it wasn't enough that she left me with blue balls, but she had to try and brain me too."

"I'll not ask you to watch your mouth again," Trey warned softly. Before Jimmy Ray could react, Trey moved and took him by the back of the neck and squeezed. "Please."

"I'm right sorry. The chick left me with aching nuts." Jimmy Ray grabbed his crotch and grinned at him. "Bet you know how that feels, don't you?"

"What'd you do to her to make her hit you?" Trey tightened his hold. This guy was pushing every button he had. "Maybe talk to her the way you're talking to me?"

Jody stood near the door and kept watch. "I was wondering that myself."

Trey shoved Jimmy Ray's forehead between his knees and held him there.

"Nothin'. I've told you everything." Jimmy Ray flailed around, but couldn't break free. "That chick's nutty in the head if you ask me. She don't know her own mind. For all I know, she's in Jackson or Memphis by now."

"Lindy is perfectly sane." Trey pushed a little harder. "I'll ask one more time. What did you do to her to make her scared enough to hit you? Did you harm my sister in any way? If you tried to force her you'll live to regret it." Trey's hands shook with effort not to throttle him.

"No, man." He struggled like a bass on a line. "I never touched her. I'm the one who's hurt. Just look at my face."

"You're claiming a tiny little girl gave you those shiners?" Jody asked in disbelief.

"That's right. Only because she used a stick." He put on an innocent tone. "I didn't do nothin'. When she ran off I followed her. Just wanted to go home and forget the whole thing ever happened, you know? But she hid behind a bush and waylaid me. When I came to I was alone, stranded."

Jody raised one eyebrow. "Where exactly did Lindy ditch you?"

"I don't know. I wasn't looking at the trees. The scenery inside the car appealed a lot more. You know what I mean? But, I guess it was out by the old blowout road. I got back on the highway at mile marker twenty-nine." He twisted in Trey's grasp.

"If Lindy was driving, she should've been home in less than half an hour. What time did you last see her?" Trey tightened his grip on Jimmy Ray, wanting to strangle him until the guy begged for mercy. He'd seen men broken like that and he longed to demonstrate the technique here.

Jimmy Ray panted. "I locked this place at two A.M. The drive took about twenty minutes, so I guess the last time I saw the chick was about three."

Jody kneeled close to Jimmy Ray's face. "One question remains, Hunt. Where is Lindy now? What's your explanation as to why she didn't come home last night?"

"How the hell should I know? I told you everything." For the first time Jimmy Ray sounded a little less sure of himself.

"How'd you get home again?" Jody prodded.

"I already told you. I walked, man. The whole way. I climbed in bed about five-thirty this morning." He pointed to his shoes. "Want to see my blisters?"

"That's okay." Jody made a few notes before he asked, "Anyone see you along the road or come into your place that can corroborate your story?"

"No. I'm dying here. Let me up."

"What happened to Lindy's Jeep?" Jody asked.

Jimmy Ray squirmed. "How would I know? She hit me, circled around and took off. She drove it home and parked, I guess."

"For the last time…she never got home," Trey said shortly. This guy was hiding something. He could feel it in his churning gut.

Jimmy Ray moaned. "I don't know nothin' else."

"Did you kill her?" Jody asked abruptly.

"What?" Jimmy Ray thrashed about. "Hell no!"

Jody went on as if he hadn't spoken. "You got a little trashed, took a girl too young for you out in the woods to have sex. She changed her mind, you got mad, tried to force her. She fought; you got rough and killed her. That's how you got that scratch across your cheek, right? You hid the Jeep and walked home. Sound about right?"

Shaking his head, Jimmy Ray touched his face and said, "No, man. Nothing like that. I didn't kill nobody. I didn't even drink last night."

"I hope you're telling me the truth," Jody said. "It'll go easier on you if you are, than if you're lying to me."

Trey felt sick at the images Jody's words conjured up. He knew all too well what dead bodies looked like. His little sister might be lying out in a swamp somewhere and this trash was responsible.

He resisted choking him to death. "If you know what's good for you, you better tell me now if you know where Lindy's at."

"I don't, man. I swear. I'm choking. Let me up."

"I don't believe you," Jody said bluntly. "I'm going to do a little checking and see if your story adds up. If not, count on seeing the inside of Angola for a good long time. Chief Bouché is pretty popular in these parts and that was his little girl you messed with. Nobody's going to go easy on you."

Trey let go. "You better pray Lindy comes home safely."

Jimmy Ray sat up and rubbed his neck.

Without another word, they left him sitting there to think about it.

In the parking lot, Jody stopped. "I'll talk to the Chief, then run Hunt's background."

"What do you think about his story?" Trey asked.

Jody met his eyes. "I think he's as guilty as an ant in a sugar bowl."

"Yeah." Trey exhaled a long breath. "Me, too."

• • •

Lindy and Jace stashed the Jeep in a cove of pine trees about a mile from the bar and walked up near the back door. They hid behind a row of bushes and checked out the half full parking lot. Loud music blasted from inside.

Lindy pointed to a classic pickup. "That's Jimmy Ray's truck. He's here."

Jace glanced around. "Do you think we can get in unseen?"

"Yeah," Lindy said. "If there are any girls here, they'll be busy up front. Jimmy Ray'll be in his office. He counts money at midnight. It must be close to that now. Look, the back door is propped open. We can slip in that way."

He took a deep breath. "Let's go."

Together, they scurried across the open lot and in through the open door. Inside, they paused to catch their breath. They stood at the end of a long, dimly lit hallway. Loud music poured down the hall from the front.

Lindy motioned toward a door. "In there." She led the way, stopping short in the middle of the room. "Oh my God."

Jace bumped into her back. "Oh, man."

Jimmy Ray, a bullet hole in the middle of his chest, lay sprawled across the couch with his arms and legs flung away from his body as if the force of the bullet had thrown him back. Blood had sprayed, coating every surface for several feet, including a pile of money on the table in front of him.

"Shit. I wonder who did this?" Jace asked.

Before Lindy could answer, they heard a woman's voice. "Jimmy Ray? We need you out front for a minute." Lindy recognized the voice of Stephanie, one of the barmaids.

"We have to get out of here," Jace whispered urgently. "Right now."

The door wasn't an option. Whoever was coming would walk through it in about a minute.

"In here." Lindy dashed through a door leading out of the office into a storage room filled with haphazardly stacked boxes of liquor. She squeezed herself into the farthest corner behind a leaning tower of empty cardboard boxes, dragging Jace with her. In the tiny space, crushed together, they tried not to breathe in dust particles dancing in the dry air, making it difficult not to sneeze or cough.

They both listened as the woman was called back to the front. Lindy, pressed against Jace, tried not to let his proximity affect her. Their bodies touched in every intimate place making her nervous in a way that had nothing to do with a dead body within a few feet of their hiding place.

Lindy whispered, "Whew. That was close."

"We're not out of the woods yet. There'll be cops all over the place before too long. Someone is bound to look back here and find us." Jace tightened his hold on her for a second.

"We've got to get out of here," Lindy urged.

"Yeah, I think we'd better make a run for it," Jace agreed. "Let's make a break while we can."

Freeing herself from his embrace, she took a deep breath then darted out of the storage room, Jace hot on her heels. Without looking at Jimmy Ray's body, they raced into the hall. No one was there and they bolted like a pair of racehorses on the straightaway for the back door. Slipping through it, they hurtled toward the Jeep.

Reaching it, they jumped in, and tore out of the parking lot.

Jace looked in the rearview mirror. "Slow down. We don't want to draw attention to ourselves."

"Oh my God! That was so close. I can't believe we didn't get caught," Lindy babbled. "Who killed Jimmy Ray?"

"We got lucky." He continued to watch the mirror. "I don't know."

Lindy shot Jace a wild glance. "Who the hell did that to him?"

He shrugged. "Somebody wanted to get even, or shut him up."

"This is crazy. We decide to go talk to the one person who might be able to help you and he's dead on arrival. Our arrival, that is. Weird." Her nerves were jumping like kangaroos, and she figured she wasn't making any sense.

"Yeah." He sounded resigned.

Lindy risked another glance at his profile. "What are you thinking?"

His gaze was bleak. "Nothing."

"Yes, you are. I can tell. What is it?" Was he giving up hope?

"Just what you said. As far as anyone knows, I skipped the country. They probably think I headed the opposite direction of Juliet. But what if whoever really killed Soloman that night suspects I'm back in town? What if they whacked Jimmy Ray to make sure he didn't let the cat out of the bag? Or we might be way off. Someone might've killed him just because he pissed them off in a bad drug deal."

"Who would go to those lengths if your first theory is right?"

"Someone even more desperate than me." Jace's features were grim.

"We're back to square one," Lindy wailed.

"We never even got out of the box," he corrected.

"Was there someone else who testified to Soloman's whereabouts before he was killed?" She swerved to miss a pothole.

Grabbing the roll bar, Jace shook his head. "I can't remember. It was five years ago."

"Try. This is important." She wanted to scream with frustration.

"You think I don't know that?" he snapped. "I think I do."

"Of course you do. We just have to think who else might've been at the bar. I don't think the waitresses are the same now as they were back then."

He pounded the dashboard. "That's it!"

"What?" Lindy swerved again as she looked to see what excited him so much.

"Watch the road."

"I am. What's 'it'?"

"I can't think of her name, but she was one of the women who lives down by the river. She was partying with Soloman at the bar." He hit the dashboard. "I can't remember her name." He hit the dash again. "Damn."

"I can find out." She looked away and the Jeep went toward the ditch.

"Watch out!" He held onto the roll bar with both hands. "How?"

"I'm best friends with Candy Carter. Her mom is one of those women." When he didn't immediately answer, she glanced at him and saw the amazed look he gave her. "What?"

"Someone like you hangs out with a hooker's kid?"

"I'm hanging out with you, aren't I? Some people might be amazed by that. Including me." Instantly, she regretted her words. "I'm sorry. Candy's okay. What her mom does isn't who Candy is."

He didn't react for a moment. "So, you're one of those rich chicks who gets off by running with trash? Think you can maybe reform one or two us lowlifes and feel all warm and fuzzy inside?"

"That's not true." Lindy blinked back the tears that threatened to overflow. How could he be so mean? Hadn't she proved to him that she was in his corner?

"Isn't it?" he taunted.

Suddenly furious, tears forgotten, she pulled to the shoulder of the road. "Get out."

"What?" His mouth gaped open.

"You heard me." She pointed. "I said get out. Now."

"You're not serious."

"Oh, yes I am. I don't have to be insulted by you." If she didn't make him start acting decent, he'd continue being a jerk. She'd had enough. She'd put her whole life on the line and he didn't even appreciate it.

A sudden smile crossed his face. "Okay. Hey, I didn't mean to get your dander up."

"Well you did big time," she said. "I don't judge people by what they do or who they are. I treat people the way they treat me."

To her utter amazement, he reached over and brushed her cheek. Butterflies went crazy in her stomach. "No harm meant."

She started the Jeep and drove back onto the road. "Just don't do it again."

After a mile or so, Jace spoke. "So, you think this Candy could find out which woman was all over Soloman the night he died?"

"Yeah. Candy'll find out if I ask her. The trick will be getting her alone. We don't want to tip anyone off that you're here." She frowned.

"We'll come up with a plan. Don't they say two heads are better than one?"

• • •

Trey and Jody stood in the Chief's office early Monday morning.

They brought him up to date.

"I'm going to bring Hunt in for further questioning," Jody said, "but I wanted the go ahead first."

"Go," the Chief ordered. "If that boy was the last one to see Lindy, I want to know about it."

They turned to go as Ida stuck her head in the door. "Chief, a 911 call just came in you might want to know about. A man's been killed out at Mugs-n-Jugs."

He stood. "Who is it?"

"Jimmy Ray Hunt, according to the caller," Ida said.

The Chief looked at Jody. "Looks like you stirred something up. Get out there and find out what. Fill me in as soon as you know what's going on. Another thing, officer…I want Jace Hill found. Yesterday."

"You still think he has Lindy?" Trey asked.

Chief Bouché nodded. "I figured that boy would come straight home to his mama and his sister. If he's taken a turn for the worse and done something to Lindy on some misguided revenge plot, he'll live to regret it. Angola will be welcoming him back with open arms."

Trey knew without a shadow of a doubt that his father meant what he said. If Jace had somehow taken Lindy hostage, he'd made a terrible mistake. Chief Bouché ran a hard line on any criminal, but when his family was involved, he would be even tougher. He hadn't allowed his feelings of friendship for the Hill family to come between him and his job before and he wouldn't now.

Trey wanted to talk to Summer, to tell her if her brother showed up she needed to warn him not to harm Lindy. But the logical side of him knew Summer didn't know where Jace was, and even if he showed himself to her he wouldn't admit to taking Lindy. Besides, this was all conjecture. There was no evidence that Jace had anything to do with Lindy being gone. It was more likely Jimmy Ray Hunt was the culprit. Still, the feeling nagged him.

"Do you think Lindy had anything to do with Hunt's death, sir?"

"Not a chance," the Chief said. "I'd stake my reputation on it."

"Will you let me know what you find out about her?" Trey asked.

The Chief nodded. "Yeah. I'd ask the same."

"Yes, sir." He moved to go.

"What are you going to do?" The Chief pinned him with a cool stare.

"I don't know," Trey said honestly. "Maybe drive around some more and look for her."

"I'd like it if you'd go check on your mother, too. I talked to Etta a bit earlier and she said Emily is having a bad day. I can't leave right now."

"Sure, I'll go right now."

"Thanks, son. Your mother and I appreciate your help."

Trey paused, surprised by the sentiment. His father rarely remembered to thank anyone. His heart ached at the prospect of his mother's imminent death and he knew his dad's heart was breaking, too. Although Trey didn't blame his dad for putting work first this time, he wished things could be different in these twilight hours of his mother's life. "I'll check in with you from home."

Trey left his father's office, intending to go home. Instead, he turned left on Main and drove out of town toward Mugs-n-Jugs. He wanted to satisfy his curiosity and see if Jody had found out anything about Jimmy Ray. Wherever Lindy was, it was far more likely that Jimmy Ray had a part in it than Jace.

Trey turned his Mustang off the highway into the parking lot. Jody's patrol car sat in front alongside an ambulance with flashing lights. Trey jumped out and headed for the open side door. He stepped inside and took a minute for his eyes to adjust. No one was in the bar, but he could hear voices coming from the back office. He headed that way.

The blonde he had spoken to yesterday and two other girls huddled in the hallway. One of them was crying. Jody was talking to them, making notes as he did. Trey leaned on the wall and waited to speak to him.

"None of you heard the shots?" the officer asked.

The blonde shook her head and not a hair moved. She'd probably used half a can of hairspray. "No. There was a huge crowd last night. We wouldn't have heard a cannon going off back here."

"None of you came back here to look for Jimmy Ray?" Jody pressed.

"We were cleaning and we had the jukebox really loud," Stephanie said.

Jody glanced at his notes. "The three of you were all out front all night?"

They nodded.

He graced the big-breasted brunette with a glance. "Did you go back to the office after I left here for the first time?"

A flush covered her cheeks and neck. "No. I had to help get ready for tonight. We always have a big turnout on Monday night. It's ladies night."

"Are we in trouble?" the crying girl asked.

"Did you kill Jimmy Ray?" Jody asked.

"No!"

"Then I can't see why you would be. Go on home, and if I have any more questions I'll find you there." As they left, Jody closed his notebook and stowed it in his shirt pocket. He spotted Trey. "What are you doing here?"

He stepped forward. "I just wanted to see if you have any theories as to what happened to our buddy here. Looks like he found some trouble, huh?"

"He's not going to give anyone any more grief that's for sure." Jody shifted slightly so Trey could see over his shoulder. Two EMTs were loading a body bag on a stretcher.

"Any idea what happened?" Trey didn't watch as they maneuvered the body through the door. He'd seen more bodies loaded onto stretchers than he could count.

Jody shrugged. "I'm not sure. Looks like a homicide. Someone shot him in the chest."

"I wonder who killed him?"

"Could be any number of people. He wasn't exactly popular and he ran drugs and guns out of here. Trouble was we knew it, just couldn't ever catch him in the act. I shouldn't say any more." Jody moved a few feet into the room where a female officer dusted for prints. She glanced at Trey with raised brows, but didn't comment. "I don't think there's going to be a lot of mourners at his funeral. Maybe a few hardcore drinkers who'll miss his booze. And don't forget your sister," Jody said. "Maybe this news will bring her out of hiding."

Two EMTs rolled the gurney carrying Jimmy Ray's body. When Trey glanced away, his gaze lit on something under the edge of the couch. "Hey, check it out."

Jody looked where he pointed. "What is that?"

"Looks like a necklace or bracelet. Probably one of those girls lost it in here."

Bending to retrieve it with a gloved hand, Jody examined it. "It is a bracelet. Apparently your sister's."

"What do you mean?" Trey demanded.

"Doesn't this belong to Lindy? Isn't it the one you gave her?" He held up a ruby bracelet.

"Yeah. It's the one I gave her for graduation." Trey's throat grew tight. He forced his next words out. "Do you think she murdered Jimmy Ray?"

Jody shot him a look. "I hope not. We know she was here night before last, so hopefully she lost her bracelet then. If I were a betting man, I'd say Jimmy Ray got himself killed in a bad drug deal. But I need to look at all the angles."

"Maybe Lindy came back here and shot him for what he did to her." He voiced his fears. "And lost that."

"I doubt it. My guess is that Lindy dropped it before she left," Jody said again.

"I hope you're right." Trey ran a hand over the back of his neck. "How long before you have something on prints?

"Not long, and you really do need to go so you don't contaminate the scene any worse." Jody stared at him until he backed up a step.

"Okay, okay. I'm going." Trey headed for the door. "I'm going to find my sister. It's more important than ever that I find out where she's hiding."

"You come up with any new ideas?"

"No. I'm going to go see Summer. Find out if she's heard anything from Jace yet." Trey kept his voice matter-of-fact. No sense letting anyone see how his heart sped up at the prospect.

"Do you think that's a good idea?"

Trey heaved a sigh. "Probably not."

Chapter Eleven

Summer sat in the kitchen watching Mama pace from the porch to the window to the stove. She stopped briefly and stirred her butterscotch pudding with a vengeance. "Where could Jace be?"

"I'm not sure, Mama." Summer swallowed her guilt. She wished now she'd told her mother about Jace's nocturnal visit. Because he hadn't stayed, Summer feared that would upset Mama more than not knowing where he was. Bracing herself, she said, "I need to tell you something."

"What is it, dear?" Mama tasted her pudding, frowned and added a drop of cream. "That's better. Jace likes it sweet."

"Mama, listen to me, please." Summer gathered her courage, taking a deep breath trying to prepare herself for what Mama might do.

She continued to stir. "I am listening, dear."

"It's about Jace."

Finally giving Summer her full attention, Mama set her dripping spoon on the stove. "What about him?"

Avoiding her mother's eyes, Summer said, "He called me today. From Biloxi. He went there instead of coming home. He said there's too much bad blood here."

"My baby isn't coming?" With a bewildered look, Mama sank into a kitchen chair. A tear slipped down her scarred cheek. She raised a hand and fluttered it in the air. "But I cooked all his favorites."

"Oh, Mama." Summer took her mother in her arms and held tight as her body shook with grief. She murmured words of comfort and stroked her back, but nothing seemed to help. "I'm sorry. I wish I had happier news." Guilt and regret filled Summer. In the last twenty-four hours, she'd lied to Mama more than she had her whole life. She prayed she made the right choices.

"Why doesn't Jace want to see me? I miss him so much." Mama wiped her red eyes with her apron.

"I'm sure he does," Summer managed around the catch in her throat. "But he's afraid to come here. When he feels safe, he'll come home and you'll have all the time in the world with him."

"I wish he wasn't afraid of those people," Mama whispered.

"I know," Summer said. "Me, too."

"Those people can't do any more to us." Bitterness filled Mama's voice. "We won't let them."

She meant the Bouchés. Summer's guilt grew a few notches. If her mama found out she'd spent yesterday afternoon in Trey's company, she'd flip out. "They can't hurt us anymore."

"If my boy calls again you tell him I said to come home." She stood and turned off the stove.

"I will, Mama. I promise." Summer's heart broke. If it were in her power, she'd put her family back together. She'd turn back the clock and all pain would just disappear like fog on a hot Mississippi morning.

Mama braved a smile. "There's pudding. Want some?"

"Yes, ma'am." Summer faked an appetite and dished a bowl. Together they carried their dessert to the porch and sat. A robin chirped at them from a nearby pine branch. Summer ate her butterscotch dessert without tasting it. Damn Jace anyway. Yes, he had been through a lot, but he should've stayed long enough to see Mama. She had been through hell, too, and she deserved some happiness.

"I'm tired this morning. I think I'll do the dishes, then take a little nap," Mama said.

"Go on and lay down, Mama. I'll clean up."

"You do too much already." She reached across the table, took Summer's hand and held it. "I've asked too much of you. This isn't fair for you to put your own life on hold. You're young. You should have a husband and children to take care of, not an old, useless woman."

"Stop it, Mama. First of all, you're not old, and second, you're far from useless." Summer's heart twisted painfully. Mama rarely waddled in self-pity. To hear her do so was frightening.

"What good am I to anyone stuck here in the house like I am?"

"I couldn't get along without you." Summer leaned forward and stared into her mother's troubled eyes, trying to make her see how much she meant her words. "I don't want to hear any more of this kind of talk. You're just overtired. Go on to bed now and I'll take care of things down here."

"I think I will. Thank you, darlin'."

Cleanup took only a few minutes, and then Summer went back outside to water her garden. The morning air felt wonderful, caressing her bare arms and legs. The humidity wasn't too bad, but it was going to be a scorcher later. The nearby pines loomed like an army of watchful sentinels.

Without Mama's income from teaching, they hadn't been able to afford the three-bedroom cottage they'd had near the Bouché estate. Living on Summer's limited income and Mama's teaching pension, they'd had to settle for much, much less. The old Nichols' farm had seemed perfect. Although falling down, it was far enough from town that Mama hadn't had to endure people's stares or whispers. The isolation was exactly what she needed.

Summer had never felt afraid here. She would hate to be out here in the middle of nowhere all the time, though, with no one to talk to. Like Mama. Her friends had given up on her a long time ago. Initially after the trial, a few had tried to keep their friendship going, but she hadn't been able to endure their questions, their pity.

After a time, she had begun to refuse visitors, then she would make excuses not to go to town. Before Summer realized what happened, Mama completely separated herself from her past. Rarely did anyone even ask after her anymore. It was as if she'd died.

Realizing she'd soaked a tomato plant too much, Summer shook off her painful memories. Laying the hose on the next row, she went to the porch and retrieved her glass of iced tea. Mama said Summer needed a husband and children. Trey's face came to mind. She fought the image. He was the last person who would fit the bill. Her mind skipped back to the kiss he'd planted on her. If things were different, she knew she wouldn't have stopped him.

He had the exact effect on her as the last time she'd seen him. He made her heart pound, her knees go weak, and her mind turn to mush. Why couldn't she feel like this about Scott Lewis at the bank? Or maybe Will Stone who'd she'd gone out with a time or two? Whatever the reason, they didn't make her lose all good sense like Trey did without even half trying. If she didn't keep her distance from him, he could do a lot of damage to Mama, to Jace, and most importantly, to herself.

Still deep in thought, she turned off the hose and rolled it up.

She didn't immediately notice the car in the driveway, or the quiet engine come to a stop. Not until the tall figure came around the corner did she become aware of him. Startled, she jumped and let out a little scream.

"Summer, it's me."

Trey.

What was he doing here? How many times did she have to tell him to stay away? "What do you want?"

"To talk to you."

"Why? What else is there to say? I thought we'd covered it all." She shot a glance at Mama's bedroom window. Thankfully, the shade was down. Grabbing his arm, she dragged him to the corner of the house where the magnolia would shield them from Mama's window, should she decide to look out.

He leaned against the wall and folded his arms over his chest. "This is about Jace."

His tone was so serious she panicked. "What about him? Has something happened to my brother?"

"No. No. Not that."

She resisted the urge to slug him for scaring her. "Then what?"

"I went back to Shantytown last night with Jody and we talked to Candy Carter. She told us Lindy was with Jimmy Ray Hunt. We then went and spoke to him. His face was all beat up. He claimed Lindy hit him." He waited a moment. "Summer, we went back again and he was dead. Somebody shot him at point-blank range. The Chief wants Jace found right now." Trey's gravelly voice sounded somber as if he'd been at a funeral. "And he's not going to be patient."

"So he can throw my brother back in prison for another murder he didn't commit?" Summer's fingers curled into her palms until they ached. "I can't believe you want to keep dragging my family through the mud. Why won't you and your dad just face the fact that my brother isn't here? You just said Jimmy Ray Hunt was the last person to see Lindy. Why don't you make his employees tell you what they know?"

"I wish they could. The Chief would if he had that much power."

She glared at him. "Why can't he?"

"None of them are talking."

"I suppose you think Jace had something to do with his death." Her nails dug into her palms until she feared she drew blood.

"Don't be ridiculous," Trey snapped.

"I'm not," she shot back. "You're the one who said this has something to do with Jace. If he's not under suspicion for Jimmy Ray's death, then what?"

"The Chief thinks there might be a link between Lindy's disappearance and Jace not showing up here."

"Why? That's a huge leap. She left a bar with another man, disappears, and it's my brother's fault? How? I know your daddy had it in for us, but this is taking it too far. I'm glad Jace decided not to…that he went elsewhere." Had he caught that slip? Oh, God.

He straightened. "What do you mean, Summer? Did he come home? Have you seen him? If you know where he is, you need to tell me. If he doesn't have anything to hide he has nothing to fear. Don't forget, Jace has been making threats of revenge from prison. It's not beyond the realm of possibility that he took Lindy to make us pay."

"He didn't." Realizing she'd almost slipped up and let it out that Jace had been here, she fought to regain her footing. Going on the offensive she said, "I don't know where my brother went. He didn't come home for obvious reasons. You and your daddy won't leave him alone. You should be focusing all your attention on Jimmy Ray. Jace has nothing to do with this."

No way on earth was she going to confess that Jace had been here.

"I hope you're right," Trey said. "Because if Jace did do something to Lindy the consequences aren't going to be pretty."

"I told you, I don't wish any harm on Lindy, but I'm not going to stand by and watch you and your daddy railroad my brother twice. There was nothing I could do but stand by and watch before." She poked him in the chest with a finger. "But I won't let it happen again."

"An innocent man doesn't have anything to hide." Trey grabbed her fingers and pulled her close.

Heart pounding, Summer snorted. "You dare to say that to me? After what you did? In this town there's no such thing as an innocent man. Your daddy decides who's guilty and who isn't and he makes that person fit the crime. With your help, of course."

"Now who's being ridiculous? Jace was found with a bloody knife in his hands, after all. I had no reason to testify against him if that hadn't been the case. He was my best friend. It about killed me to testify against him." He tugged her closer.

"Was he really your best friend, Trey? Or were you so eager for your daddy's approval you were willing to sell Jace out to gain it?" Summer picked her words carefully hoping for maximum effect. She wanted to hurt Trey like she had never hurt anyone in her life.

He dropped her hand like it burned him "That is the craziest thing I've ever heard."

"Is it?" Now Summer stepped close enough that their bodies touched. She looked into his dark eyes. "I've always known that your daddy's approving eye means everything to you."

"Yes, it once meant a lot. But not at the cost you're suggesting. To sell out Jace not once, but twice? No." His gaze didn't waver from hers.

She nodded. "Yes."

"This conversation is pointless. You're so twisted with resentment that there's no getting through to you." He sounded as bitter as she felt.

"I guess there isn't," she said, "because there's nothing you can say or do that's going to change my mind. In fact, by coming here to question Jace about something he has no link to only makes me certain I'm right."

"Then I guess you and I don't have anything else to talk about." Resignation—and something else, regret?—filled his voice.

"I guess not." She slipped by him before he could see the despair in her eyes.

• • •

Summer rifled through her closet not finding a thing she liked. Finally, she chose a floral print dress and white sandals. She loved the way the floaty, full skirt and fitted bodice made her feel extra feminine. Pulling her hair back in a high ponytail and adding a touch of makeup, she told herself none of it was for Trey.

"You look nice," Mama commented when she saw Summer.

"So do you." Like every Wednesday evening for the last five years, Mama had gotten dressed in her good blue suit, including her pearl necklace, nylons, and high heels. Her hair and makeup were done perfectly. If you didn't see her left side, for all the world she looked like any other woman off to church until she turned and the morning sun highlighted her scar. "You going to the late service with me today, Mama?"

"I'm thinking on it." She picked up a piece of apple and ate it in tiny, delicate bites.

"Glory's going to come by in about thirty minutes." Summer tried not to let her mother see how much she hoped for her to walk out the door a healed woman.

"Okay. I'll just wait in the front room." Mama wiped her fingers on a towel and went in the other room where she turned on a gospel album and began to sing along.

Summer didn't answer. As she cleaned, she hummed along to the tune on the stereo.

Soon, Glory knocked on the door then came in. Her bright red hair stood on end and clashed wildly with her sleeveless, short purple dress. "Ready?"

"Sure. Let me ask Mama if she's coming." Summer refused to allow herself to hope. Disappointment hurt too much. She steadied herself.

Glory arched her penciled brows. "You think today's the day?"

"No, but I keep hoping." Summer went in the living room where Mama was watching a TV program. "Glory's here," Summer said, "are you ready?"

"Oh, darlin', I've changed my mind. I think I'll stay here today. Jace just might change his mind and come home. What would he think if no one was here to meet him?" She stared at the TV, refusing to make eye contact. "I think I'll make a special supper."

Summer knew this ritual well. For a minute, she wanted to argue, to urge, to plead. But she knew none of it would do any good. She'd tried everything short of physical force in the past to get her mama to leave the house and nothing had ever worked. Doc Marlette didn't know what to do. He'd even consulted with a specialist in Jackson and that doctor suggested letting Mama decide when she was ready to come out. Summer forced a smile. "Okay, Mama. See you later tonight."

"Do you think she'll ever go outside again?" Glory asked as she made a U-turn in the driveway.

"I don't know." Summer closed her eyes and leaned back against the headrest. "She hasn't once in five years. The prospects don't look good. Now with Jace on the loose, all the things that upset her the most are staring her in the face."

Glory's quick glance was sharp. "Any sign of him?"

"Not one." Summer kept her eyes closed and hoped her friend couldn't tell she wasn't telling the whole truth. She hated being in the position of lying to her friends, but she hated the idea of her brother back behind bars even more.

"That has to be hard for her." Glory clucked sympathetically.

"None of it's easy," Summer agreed.

"On you either," Glory said. "All this has had to drag up the past for you as much as for your mama. Not only your brother being freed, but Trey Bouché being back in town…"

"You haven't heard the latest either," Summer glanced at her friend's profile. Glory couldn't let the non-existent relationship with Trey go. Summer was beginning to think Glory had a thing for him herself. "Jimmy Ray Hunt was murdered last night…oh, I forgot. You went out with him for a while, didn't you?"

Glory jerked her head once. "Don't remind me. I can't believe he's dead, though."

"Murdered," Summer said. "Trey came out to tell me. And also ask if I'd seen Jace."

"What? He thinks Jace had something to do with Jimmy Ray?" Glory swerved, one tire dropping into the bar ditch. She corrected, driving to the other side of the road. Finally, she got the car straightened out. "Why?"

Summer forced herself to let go of the door handle. "Trey thinks Lindy might be responsible for killing him. He believes Jace is now holding Lindy hostage. The Chief is all for this half-baked theory. I think they're both reaching." Summer's heartbeat jumped, whether from Glory's wild driving, or knowing her brother was loose, she couldn't tell.

"What do you think happened to Lindy?" Glory asked. "Could she have killed Jimmy Ray? If she got messed up in one of his bad deals, I feel for her. I saw more of that when I dated Jimmy Ray than I care to talk about."

Summer shrugged. "I have no idea what happened to Lindy. She was with Jimmy Ray the night before last and no one's seen her since. Now he's dead. Nothing adds up. I refuse to see how Jace ties into any of this, though." He couldn't be responsible for Lindy's mysterious departure. If he was, and she'd been defending him all this time…She didn't want to think about it.

"Yeah, I think Trey's looking for reasons to see you," Glory commented.

"If that's true, he's wasting his time." Summer declared, wondering if Glory was right.

• • •

Summer couldn't concentrate on the sermon. The inside of the old church seemed extra hot and she longed for the service to be over. Preacher Finn's voice droned on and on and on. She couldn't have repeated a word he said if she tried. Her back and legs felt sticky and tendrils of hair stuck to the sides of her face. She must've sighed because Glory elbowed her in the ribs. Making an effort, she tried harder to pay attention.

Knowing Glory's sharp eyes were on her, Summer refused to allow her gaze to drift three rows up and two over. Trey stood there with Mary-Gray who was glued to his side. The girl smiled up at him and Summer fought waves of jealousy.

As her gaze rested on the back of Trey's tanned neck, she thought Preacher Finn would probably have a coronary if he ever found out how she longed to slap Mary-Gray Bennet senseless.

Before her mind went any further south, she attempted to change the direction of her thoughts. Church wasn't the place for her to take in Trey's neck, the width of his shoulders, or the way his waist tapered to long legs. If she allowed herself to continue thinking like this, she might remember the night she'd fallen in love with him. This certainly wasn't the proper time or place for daydreaming about making love.

Closing her eyes, she forced her lust away.

Glory jabbed her again and Summer realized the congregation was about to sing. Picking up her hymnal, she mouthed the words with everyone else. The simple task took all her concentration. Forcing herself to keep her eyes on her music, she refused to glance at Trey again until the service mercifully ended. Preacher Finn invited everyone to stay for a picnic on the lawn.

Summer and Glory made their way outside. Wanting only to escape so she didn't have to see Trey with his date, Summer didn't hear what Glory said. Tipping her head she asked, "What was that?"

Glory rolled her eyes. "Try to focus. Do you want to stay for supper?"

She didn't, but she could see Glory did. "If you want to."

"I brought fruit salad."

"I forgot all about bringing something." Summer had been so consumed with her brother she hadn't given any thought to the picnic.

"It's okay. I made enough for both of us, and I have extra plates in my picnic basket," Glory said.

"Then let's stay," Summer said, although all she wanted to do was get out there before she bumped into Trey. Or had to watch Mary-Gray hang on him anymore.

The church ladies set up the meal on several long tables brought out from the basement. Reluctantly, Summer followed Glory through the line. The choices overwhelmed her. She chose enough that no one would notice her lack of appetite.

Together, they settled themselves under an oak tree on a blanket Glory retrieved from her car trunk. In spite of her resolve not to look for him, Summer's gaze sought Trey. She found him with the Bennet family just across the lawn. Mary-Gray nestled next to him, chattering like a squirrel. Mr. and Mrs. Bennet smiled benevolently as their other three girls formed a semicircle around them. Trey looked completely at home with the Bennet family. Summer's stomach did a flip-flop and the smell of fried chicken and fruit salad suddenly made her ill.

"Careful, you're wearing your heart on your sleeve," Glory said low enough only Summer could hear.

Jerking her attention to her friend Summer asked, "What?"

"Your feelings are showing," Glory said matter-of-factly. "For a woman not interested in a certain man you're certainly fascinated by who he's with."

"I am not." Summer took a bite of whipped cream delight. "In fact, I'm not sure what you're talking about. I was just seeing who stayed for supper."

Glory snorted, very unladylike. "Sing it to the choir."

"Okay, say you win. Just suppose Trey Bouché has gotten under my skin. There's nothing I can do about it. If I breathe his name, Mama goes off the deep end. Not to mention the absolute conviction his family has that my brother is the root of all evil in this town."

"You have to bend, too," Glory said. "You're so caught up in the past, you can't see the future."

"What do you mean? Haven't you heard a word I just said?" Summer stabbed at a cherry buried in the frothy dessert.

"I hear you, but you don't listen to me." Glory motioned toward the Bennet family and Trey. "That man is going to slip away from you for good if you can't find a way to put all this bitterness behind you. Are you happy, Summer? Is your mama? And Jace? There's only one way for all of you to be truly at peace. You have to find a way to set things straight."

"You ought to take Preacher Finn's job," Summer said, "if you think that can ever happen."

"I know it can." Glory had a dreamy look. "You have to want it bad enough. I'm not saying forget. I'm saying move on."

"I know." Summer played with her food as she listened. She knew her friend was right, but how to go about letting all the anger and hurt go? Turning loose of those feelings wasn't like letting a bird out of a cage, just open the door and let it fly away. Even if she could find a way to forgive, where would that leave her with Mama and Jace? They never would.

If she chose forgiveness she'd lose her family; if she chose them she lost any chance with Trey.

• • •

"That man was nothing but white trash."

Trey bit into a piece of chicken to avoid answering Mrs. Bennet. For the last half hour, her family had been discussing Jimmy Ray Hunt's murder and the list of possible suspects. They had tossed around everyone in Juliet from the barmaids to half of city council. Trey was quite sure if he hadn't been there, they would've considered his dad a possibility, too. He wondered what they would say if they knew Lindy had been in Jimmy Ray's bar. Mary-Gray would probably turn up her pert little nose and say, "I knew it."

His patience was quickly coming to an end with their little personal game of Clue. When Mary-Gray had called and invited him to go to church with her family, he had accepted for the chance to mingle with Lindy's friends. He thought he might pick up a lead as to who had really killed Jimmy Ray, but all he'd heard so far was gossip and misguided guesses. Although the murder was the talk of the picnic, he hadn't picked up a single piece of useful information.

Without being obvious, he kept Summer in his sight. Although she had come into church later than him, he knew when she arrived as though she had gifted him with a breath of fresh air when he was suffocating.

Tuning out Mary-Gray's meant-to-be-charming chatter, he glanced again at Summer and Glory. They seemed to be having an intense discussion with their heads close together. He wondered what they could be talking about so seriously, looking so pretty. No one could miss Glory in her crazy dress that clashed with her vibrant hair. But it was Summer he couldn't take his gaze off. Like her name, she looked sunny and bright in her flowery pink dress. Her skirt flowed out around her like the petals of a flower.

Suddenly she smiled and he couldn't breathe. Nor could he hear Mary-Gray. "Would you excuse me?"

Without waiting to hear their answer, Trey walked toward Summer. She looked up and their gazes met and held. He didn't have a plan, he didn't have anything to talk to her about, all he knew was he had to speak to her before she left. "Hi."

"Hey, Trey. What's up?" Glory spoke to him. Summer did not.

"Not much." He squatted on his heels like a child trying to coax a kitten out of its hiding place. "Just thought I'd catch up."

"Starting with Mary-Gray Bennet, I see." Summer's voice dripped ice.

He hid a smile. She was jealous. "A pretty girl asked me out. Do you know some reason I should've turned her down?"

"Not a one."

He did smile this time at her tone. "Me either. Are you enjoying your picnic?"

"I was."

Glory coughed. "I think I'll go get some more punch. Do you want some?"

Trey smiled at her. "No, thanks."

"No," Summer said.

Touching her shoulder, Glory said, "Be right back. Remember what we talked about."

"What were you having your heart-to-heart about?" He hoped it was him.

"I can't see where that's any of your business." She fiddled with the tiny gold heart she wore around her neck then sighed. "We were saying some things are hard to forget."

"Yeah." His smiled faded. "I know."

"Have you found Lindy yet?"

"No. Actually, that's why I'm here. I'm going to circulate and see if I hear anything." He frowned and picked at a strand of grass.

"You really think you're going to find someone here who knows where Lindy is?" She raised her eyebrows at him. "Honestly, do you think a kidnapper lurks among Juliet's churchgoing members?"

He studied the blade of grass. "Not really, but at this point I'll try anything."

Her frozen tone warmed a fraction. "You haven't found a clue?"

"No." He tossed the grass away, trying to think of a way to broach the other subject heavy on his mind.

As if she read his thoughts, she said, "Let me answer the question I know you're going to ask next. No, I haven't talked to Jace. He hasn't come home."

"Did I ask?" Why did he feel so crummy for wondering if Jace was behind Lindy's disappearing act?

"You wanted to."

He didn't attempt to deny it. "Where do you think he is?"

"Not with Lindy." She twisted the chain again. "I don't know, Trey. If I did, I'd tell you just to keep you from badgering me."

This wasn't going well. For once he didn't want to talk about Jace or even Lindy. He wished they could have one conversation without their siblings being the main focus. "I don't mean to hound you."

"And yet here you are."

"I'm sorry." He let his hands hang between his knees when all he wanted to do was reach out and take her face with his palms and kiss her until they both ached from it.

She tilted her head and stared at him like she had never seen him before. "If only you meant that."

"I do. More than you know." If he could just erase their history and make it all okay again, he would. But he had no magic, no way to pull down the invisible barrier between them.

"Words come so easily to you, Trey." She looked away. "Here comes Glory. And I see your date is looking for you. Good luck finding Lindy. I hope she's all right." She reached for her picnic basket.

He'd been dismissed. He handed it over, careful not to touch her, and stood. "Take care of yourself."

"You, too." Her big blue eyes glimmered and he hesitated. There had to be something to say to make them friends again. He knew what she wanted him to say—that he didn't think Jace had killed Soloman—and he couldn't do it. With a heavy sigh, he walked away.

Mary-Gray looped her arm through his and he managed to smile at her. Brunette hair glistening, a form-hugging dress that showed legs for miles and smelling like honeysuckle, she should've made the blood race to his cock. But she didn't pique his interest. "Re-introduce me around, will you?"

"With pleasure." She smiled at him and he faked one back.

As they moved from group to group, old friends greeted him warmly. All asked about his parents and many wanted to know about his time in Afghanistan. Although everyone went out of their way to make him welcome, this felt wrong to him. Without the Chief shooting the bull with his cronies, Trey's mother and MiLann sharing their secrets, and he and Jace off to play basketball, everything felt off kilter.

Spotting a group of men standing off by themselves, he asked Mary-Gray, "Would you excuse me for a minute? I'd like to chat with the guys."

"Of course. I'm sure my mother would like me to help clean up." With a show of dazzling white teeth, she let go of him. "Hurry back, okay?"

He nodded then joined the group of men, saying nothing, willing to listen. Buford Krebbs, a beefy barrel of a man, was speaking to his friends. "I don't care who killed Jimmy Ray. They did this community a favor getting rid of trash like that."

Several of them nodded in agreement.

Almost the exact sentiment expressed by Mary-Gray's mother and father. Trey wondered idly if the same kind of talk had gone around when Jace had been arrested for Soloman's death. He supposed so. Gossip was the nature of small towns.

"Kind of weird, though, don't you think? Jimmy Ray getting shot out of the blue like that? From what I hear, he's been a thorn in a few people's sides for a few years. Why do you think someone did him in now?" Trey asked.

"Darn right, he's been a sore spot." The speaker, a red-faced man Trey remembered as the grocer answered. "I don't know why your daddy didn't run him off the minute that establishment opened. Decent, God-fearing people don't want his kind around."

"You didn't mind stopping in there a time or two," one of them pointed out, "for a drink and a bit of titty-tat."

The grocer's face turned redder. "This isn't about me," he sputtered. When no one answered he stomped off.

Buford snapped his suspenders and rocked back on his heels, full of self-importance. "Tom's right. Samuel should've taken care of that lowlife a long time ago. Run him out of town like the snake he was. Shut him down on a business license violation or something."

"I guess Hunt probably had all his paperwork in order," Trey said mildly. "The Chief can't pick and choose who runs a business."

"That's right," Leroy Eaton said. "We can't have vigilante justice in this town. Look at what happened last time…"

"Leroy." Buford shut him up with one word.

Leroy shot a nervous glance at Trey.

"Go on," Trey urged. This is what he wanted, for the men to open up and speak of the past. "What happened that I don't know about? Something to do with Soloman's murder?"

"Naw, nothing about that old business. Why would you think that? All Leroy means is that we can't have folks shooting each other like we're cowboys out in the wild west." Buford put an arm around Leroy's thin shoulders and squeezed. "Right?"

"Yeah." Leroy kept his gaze on the ground. "That's what I meant."

"We have to let the Chief do his work. He knows what he's doing. We just have to trust him." Buford let go of Leroy's shoulders and slapped the skinny man's back, nearly knocking him down. "Like we always do."

Trey looked between the men, puzzled by their behavior. If he didn't know better, he'd swear Krebbs was warning Leroy to keep his mouth shut about something. Telling himself his imagination was working overtime, he tried to ignore his gut. These men were the Chief's cronies. They probably had a few tall tales they shared among themselves, not a cover-up of some kind.

Frustrated by the circle of silence, he bid them goodbye and went back to Mary-Gray. With a sky-bright smile, she threaded her arm through his. "I'm in the mood for ice cream. The ladies' society has some homemade. Will you get me a scoop?"

"Sure." Wanting only to get out of there, he tried to be patient. It wouldn't help his cause to annoy the Bennet family.

As they waited their turn, Trey nodded at the appropriate times but he couldn't have repeated a word the brunette girl had to say. His gaze wandered, hunting for Summer, but she wasn't with Glory. The redhead met his look with one of her own that was hard to read. He nodded and she gave a small wave. He turned his attention to Mary-Gray. "I'll walk you back to your folks, then I'd better get home. I promised my mother I'd spend some time with her."

A quick frown flitted across her perfectly made up face. "Okay, I understand. But, don't be a stranger."

After thanking her family and making Mary-Gray no promises, he looked for Leroy, but the man didn't seem to still be around. Curious what Leroy would say if prodded, Trey decided to go find out.

Chapter Twelve

Summer gathered the last of their picnic, anxious to go home. She wouldn't confess for the world, but watching Trey with Mary-Gray had made the evening seem endless. Just as she added the last item to Glory's picnic basket, a shadow fell across her and she looked up. Jody stood there, feet spread wide. As her gaze traveled upward, a shiver ran down her back. He didn't smile even a fraction.

"What is it, Jody?"

"You need to come with me." His tone, normally a soft lilt, was somber. He wouldn't meet her eyes, studying something near her chin instead.

Her heart skipped a beat. "Why? What is it? Has something happened to Mama? Did you find Jace? Oh, God, did someone shoot him?"

"No. No. Nothing like that." He shifted his weight. "The Chief wants to talk to you."

"I don't have anything to say to him. So go tell him to leave me alone. This is my day off." She continued to pack.

"He told me you'd say that. He said to come in or he'd come to your house." Jody's grave expression told her the Chief meant what he said.

Shooting Glory a trapped look, Summer said, "Fine. Glory's coming with me. We'll meet you there."

"No, just you. I'll drive you home." Jody waited as the put the rest of their things in the basket.

Glory shrugged. "I have things to do. I'll see you later."

Shaking with fury, Summer marched to his car, got in and slammed the door behind her. "The nerve of that man! Who does he think he is, God?"

Jody tightened his lips and didn't answer.

Within a couple of minutes, they pulled in front of the police station. "I'll walk you up," Jody said.

"I'm not going to cut and run." Summer climbed out and slammed the door behind her. "Let's get this thing over with."

"Okay."

Jody joined her on the curb. "The Chief just wants to ask you a few questions."

"I don't know anything."

"Tell him that," Jody suggested.

"Let's just get this over with." She marched in the building like a soldier going to battle.

Chief Bouché looked up from behind a scarred metal desk as they came into his office. "That'll be all, officer. Thank you."

Jody backed out of the room. "Yes, sir."

Not much had changed, Summer thought as her gaze roamed over the stuffed bookshelves and rows of file cabinets. For a moment, she allowed a rush of nostalgia to overtake her. She'd visited here many times as a child. Unsure where to direct her attention, she looked out the window. From this vantage point, she could see most of Juliet's main street. Regret for all they had lost filled her and she blinked back unexpected tears.

"It's been a long time," the Chief said quietly.

"Yes." She refused to look at him.

"Sit down, please." A request.

Summer hesitated for a minute then moved and sat across from him, spine straight, hands folded in her lap. She studied his face. He hadn't aged well. Creases had etched lines of time around his mouth and eyes. Gray shaded his formerly blonde hair. She met his gaze and held it. "What did you want to see me about?"

"I think you know."

"Like I've told Trey over and over again, I have no idea where my brother went." She made an effort to relax her stiff body.

"He hasn't been home? Made some contact?" His blue eyes bored into hers, but she didn't look away.

Summer held her voice steady. "No."

The Chief didn't blink and she was sure he knew she lied. "I hope you're telling me the truth. If I find out you've seen him and didn't tell me, I'll charge you with obstruction of justice. Understand?"

Not trusting her voice, she nodded.

"Are you aware Lindy is missing? I have reason to believe she might be with your brother."

"Do you have any evidence to support this theory?" Summer cleared her throat. "Or is this just a stab in the dark?"

His eyes turned a cooler shade of blue. "I don't make wild assumptions, despite what you may or may not believe. The evidence always supports me."

Summer wasn't going to argue with him about it. They both had their perspective and they would never see eye-to-eye. "Why do you think Jace would have anything to do with Lindy's disappearance? For all we know he may be in Mexico by now. Or maybe Canada. There's a million possibilities."

The Chief steepled his fingers. "Are you aware that Jimmy Ray Hunt was murdered?"

"I don't see…"

"One of the last people to see him alive was my daughter."

"And this involves Jace, how?" Summer, holding her temper in check began to lose it. "Is he to be held responsible for every dirty deed that happens in this town?"

"Not at all." He stood and went to the file cabinet farthest from him. Taking a key from his shirt pocket, he unlocked it and took some papers from it. Returning, he sat again and handed them to her. "But these lead me to believe your brother might be here and he might have taken Lindy."

With numb fingers, Summer took the sheaf of paper. Her heart filling with fear, she dropped her gaze. In her hand she held a letter from her brother. Without looking at the signature, she instantly recognized Jace's tiny scrawl. Forcing herself, she read her brother's words. The first were pleas—begging the Chief to find the real killer, to believe in him, to trust. The next set was full of theories to the real killer. And, finally, threats. Ugly menacing, promising revenge.

The handwriting was similar, but not precisely the same between the first and last ones. She couldn't put her finger on the exact difference, though. "These aren't the same," she said. She pointed to one. "Look, this one is tiny, almost impossible to read. And this one is a little easier. I'm not a cop, but these look like they weren't written by the same person."

"That's ridiculous," the Chief snapped.

Summer scanned the letters again. "I don't think some of these are in my brother's handwriting."

"Don't be melodramatic." The Chief snatched the letters out of Summer's hand. "Your brother is the one who wrote these. End of story. He's going to kill Lindy if I don't find him first."

"You believe Jace took Lindy to make you pay for not finding the real killer?" Summer's throat was so tight she could barely force the words out.

"He is the killer. Read these letters." The words fell like hammer blows on her.

"Even if he did write some of these, it doesn't mean Jace escaped, came here, and snatched Lindy," Summer said. "And what does any of this have to do with Jimmy Ray Hunt?"

"You tell me," the Chief shot back.

"I don't know." Her tense body trembled like a sapling in a storm.

"Did your brother ever give you any reason for disliking Hunt?" The Chief pressed her, almost as if he knew she had lied to him about seeing Jace.

She shook her head. Her fingers twisted in her skirt. "I don't think Jace even knew him. I can't remember."

"There's the possibility Jace murdered Hunt to throw us off his trail. Maybe he knew Hunt wasn't exactly a shining example of citizenry."

"You're reaching." Summer's fingers tightened until they ached.

"Am I?" His intense gaze pinned down like a rat in a trap. She knew how the rodent must feel. Both terrified and mad.

"Yes. As far as I know, there isn't a shred of evidence my brother even came this direction." She knew she should've, but felt no guilt for her lie. If it weren't for this man's incompetence, her mother's rapist would be behind bars and not her brother. Besides, there was no way her brother would've killed Hunt. He had no motive. Maybe Lindy was with Jace, but if so, how? The only person who could answer that question was dead. In her heart, she knew Jace hadn't murdered Hunt yesterday any more than he had offed Deke Soloman five years ago. "May I leave now?" She began to stand.

"There's one more thing." His voice grew icy.

"Yes?"

"We need to have an understanding about my son."

"What kind of understanding?" She did not want to have this conversation. Trey was the last person on the planet she cared to discuss with the Chief. Not sure how she felt about the younger Bouché, she didn't feel like examining her feelings in the privacy of her own head, much less with his father.

"Don't be coy, Summer. It's unbecoming. You know what I'm talking about. A relationship between you isn't wise. Not any more than it was five years ago," he said. "When you were twenty-two and he was just eighteen."

Guilty heat flooded her face. "I don't…"

He smiled, but it was more of a grimace. "Please do not insult my intelligence by denying that you and my son were intimate before he left."

The hot blush that started at her chest burned up her neck and face. For the first time, she couldn't meet his eyes directly. "There's nothing between Trey and me."

"I know there is not. I'm telling you it can go nowhere." He drummed his fingers on his desk. "You can only bring each other misery."

She stood on shaking legs. "I think you're the one who's guilty of bringing misery to everyone. But for the record, I don't want to see Trey. He seeks me out, not the other way around. If you think you need to interfere then talk to him, not me. Now, if you'll excuse me?"

Before she could flee, the door was flung open and Jody burst in. "Chief. You're needed downstairs. The coroner needs you in the morgue."

He stood. "He got something on Hunt?"

"No, sir. He said it was urgent." Jody moved aside and the Chief went by him, apparently forgetting Summer. Jody was hot on his heels and his voice carried in the hall. "Leroy Eaton hung himself."

Too shocked to move for a moment, Summer sat there staring after them. She'd just seen Leroy not more than an hour or so ago at the picnic. He'd seemed fine. What on God's earth had possessed him to commit suicide?

Summer didn't know what to do.

Jody was supposed to take her home.

Her gaze landed on the pile of letters. As she did so, she noticed a brown five by seven manila envelope on the bottom of the pile. Curious, she picked it up to see if it was another letter from Jace.

A black and white photo spilled out of the envelope.

A group of people smiled at the lens. Mama, Trey's mother, Buford Krebbs, and Leroy Eaton. Emily sat on the lap of a dark-haired, handsome man. All toasted the camera.

She studied the background trying to tell where they could be, but she didn't recognize anything. Where had the photo been taken? And who had been behind the camera? The Chief? Or Viola Krebbs? Summer's frown deepened. She couldn't fathom Mrs. Krebbs partying. A pain ripped through her as she studied the people in the pictures. They looked like they were having a great time. What she wouldn't give to for her mother to have fun like that again. Instead, she had a life of loneliness and pain. And Emily Bouché wasn't any better off. She lay dying.

Someone was coming!

Hurriedly, Summer dropped the letters back on the desk, stuffed the picture in her bag, and tried to look innocent.

The chief came in, his expression distracted. He started when he saw her. "You're still here?"

"I wasn't sure if you were done talking to me." She shifted her handbag, hoping he didn't think she acted guilty. "And I need a ride."

"I'll have Officer Marvell drop you off on his way to Leroy's place."

Summer bit her tongue. She badly wanted to ask him about Leroy. And the picture in her purse. Questions burst through her mind, but she held them in check. There was no way she could let on she'd been snooping. He already thought poorly of her. "Thank you."

Without answering, he picked up his phone and dialed. "Yes, I'd like you to take Miss Hill home. Drop her off, then go to the scene."

They didn't speak in the few moments it took Jody to come back. In his patrol car, Summer fastened her seatbelt. Her mind was on the smuggled booty in her purse. Her fingers itched to take it out and study the people again. She especially wanted to know about the man her mother had her arms around. She racked her memory trying to come up with a party her mother had been invited to, but nothing came to mind.

Had the rumors been true?

Violently, Summer pushed the thought away. No, her mother had always been decent. She wouldn't do anything to compromise her good name. There was no way she'd been doing anything wrong in that photo. Someone had caught a group of friends having a nice time, nothing more. Then why did Summer feel so odd about it?

One thing was for certain, she couldn't ask Mama. One look at her past, and she'd have a spell that would put her in bed for a week. Of all the people in the photo, there were none she could speak to. Not Mama, or Emily. Leroy had just committed suicide. And then there was Buford Krebbs. For a reason she couldn't name, Summer hesitated. He was nice enough when she saw him around town, but she didn't trust him and she really didn't respect his wife. Viola had never made any secret of disliking Mama. Now Summer wondered about it. Had Buford been a little too friendly toward a woman other than his wife?

That left the stranger. Summer tried, but couldn't recall ever seeing the man before. Where had he come from, and more importantly, where had he gone? Who else would know? Summer knew all her mother's friends. Maybe Jace would have an idea if he ever got the chance to look at the photo. Trey would. Like her, he would recognize his mother's friends. Summer rejected the idea. But it stuck with her like a burr she couldn't shake loose.

Jody turned into the empty church parking lot. "What are you thinking about so hard?"

"Leroy. Can you tell me what happened?"

"I don't know much, only someone found him hanging in his barn. I shouldn't talk about it."

Summer shook her head. "God."

He gave his head a sad shake. "Yeah."

"I also can't believe someone killed Jimmy Ray." She touched his arm. "Please tell me you don't think Jace had anything to do with it."

His somber eyes met hers. "No. I don't."

Unaware she'd been holding her breath, she exhaled. "Thank you, Jody." That means a lot to me."

"I can't see Jace coming here and killing anybody else. Not unless he's changed a whole lot. Even if prison has made him mean, what would be his reason? Far as I know Jace didn't even know Hunt." Jody shook his head. "It just doesn't fit."

"That's what I told the Chief." Summer's temper began to simmer. "He can't go around pinning every bad thing that happens in this town on my brother. He's not even here."

Jody shot her a look and she avoided his sharp gaze. "How do you know that?"

"I don't." She was becoming better by the minute at lying. If this kept up she might as well not even try to be honest any more.

"If you know something, Summer, tell me. You can trust me." He started the engine and pulled out on Main.

"I wish I could."

They drove in silence for a few minutes.

"Lilah told me she went out to your place for supper," Jody commented.

Summer's stomach plunged toward her toes. She studied her fingernails. Funny, she hadn't noticed that she'd bitten them to the quick. Maybe she could get Glory to give her a manicure. "Yeah. We were just trying to cheer up Mama."

"Is that all it amounted to?"

She shrugged, trying for nonchalant. "What else?"

"A welcome home party, maybe?"

By his tone, she knew he was fishing. Although she hated telling yet another fib, Summer wasn't about to give up her brother to any lawman. No matter how good a friend Jody once was, his duty came first. The past had taught her well to avoid that trap. "No. Nothing like that."

"If you do hear from him, talk to me," he said. "I'll make sure he gets a fair shake."

"I know." He would have a hard time of it with his loyalties split between an old friend and his job.

"How's Trey?"

She shrugged as a flood of confusion filled her. "How would I know?"

"I hoped you might give the guy another chance."

What was this, a conspiracy? First Glory, then Lilah, now Jody. What, had they all gotten together and decided to try and reunite her and Trey? "That's not likely," she said. "Since we don't have anything to build on except hurt and bitterness. That isn't a good foundation for anything."

"Do you still care about him?"

Summer thought about it for a long time before she answered. "It really doesn't matter how I feel, does it? My mama means more to me than anything. I can't risk what's left of her sanity by even saying his name. His family isn't any different. The Chief warned me away today."

"The old man can be pretty harsh at times," Jody said.

"That's the understatement of the year," Summer agreed.

Chapter Thirteen

At the little grocery store near Granny's house, Lindy used the pay phone to call Candy's cell. "Hey, it's me. They are? Thanks. Don't tell them you talked to me if they ask again, okay? I'll tell you why later. I need a favor. Yeah, another one."

Jace bounced from one foot to another. His expression was murderous.

"Listen, Candy, I need you to talk to your mom for me. Can you try and find which one of her girls was at Mugs-n-Jugs the night Deke Soloman was killed? It happened five years ago. One of the ladies who works for your mom was hanging all over Soloman. Would you ask your mom if she remembers who that was? It's important." She met Jace's angry eyes. "You can't call me back. I left my cell phone in your purse. Remember that time we stayed at my Grandma's house out in the woods? Come out there when you find out, okay? Don't let anyone follow you. And one more thing…bring me some clothes and makeup?"

Before the receiver even clicked off Jace snarled, "Clothes and makeup? This isn't a little girls' sleepover. And why the hell did you tell her where we're at? Are you trying to get your daddy to come down on me?"

"Maybe you like being grimy, but I don't," Lindy said calmly. "And we can trust Candy. Trey and Jody already talked to her about me. They're trying to find out where I am and she didn't tell them anything."

"I think you've just made a hell of a mistake." He slapped the wall with his palm. "Ah, damn."

She tried to touch his arm, but he twisted away. "I know it'll be okay."

"I can't take any chances."

"You're not," she said. Again, she reached for him and this time he allowed her to touch him.

"Wish you would've told her to bring a steak. I'm hungry," he muttered to himself more than her.

"How can you think about food in a time like this?" she asked, incredulous that he was worried about going back to prison in one minute and talking about food the next.

He gestured to the store. "We're here. I'm thinking it only makes sense to shop."

"But they're closed." Darting a glance around, she couldn't see a way in.

"So?" He smirked at her. "I'm a con, remember?"

"I'm not going to let you rob this old man," she protested. "We're trying to prove you're not a criminal, remember? If you do this it'll just prove the Chief right."

"Who said anything about robbing?" He patted his jeans pocket. "I have money, courtesy of Summer."

"But there's no one here to pay." She wanted to shake him. He was acting like such a dumb jerk.

"I'll leave the money on the register." Ignoring her protests, he went to the window. Placing his palms on the ledge, he jumped. His body slid halfway through the opening. He wiggled through the tiny opening like a snake going in a hole. "Meet me out front," he called.

Doing as he asked, although she was still tempted to get in the Jeep and leave him here, Lindy ran around front. There wasn't a soul in sight, probably nobody for miles. Dark had fallen and she wondered how he could find anything without any light.

The front door opened with a screech. He handed her a sack. "Take this."

"What's in here," she asked as he came outside, his arms full.

"Lots of stuff. Food, pop, a book or two—"

"Books?" She made a face at him. "We're not on vacation or in school."

"I like to read. Sue me." He frowned at her.

She followed him to the Jeep, bemused. This man was full of surprises. Who would've guessed that he liked to read for fun? What else did he like to do? Sit in a rocking chair and watch the sunset? She got in the driver's seat still thinking how little she knew of Jace. Though she knew in her heart he hadn't killed Deke Soloman. If he had he was the best actor she'd ever met.

Jace carried the sacks into Granny's house. He'd picked out lunchmeat, cheese, chips, and soda. There was also a cooked chicken, eggs, bread, and a few cans of soup. Oranges, bananas, milk, and cereal rounded out the supplies in two bags. She indicated the third. "What's in there?"

"See for yourself," he answered, busy stowing the food in the old-fashioned fridge.

She found hand soap, shampoo and conditioner, disposable razors, two paperbacks and a few scented candles. "Looks like you're planning on a nice long soak," she teased.

"You're the one who said they didn't like to be grimy." He faced her, his expression unreadable.

"You got this for me?" Pleased more than she ought to be by the simple gesture she impulsively threw her arms around him. "Thank you."

He submitted to her embrace, but didn't hug her back. Lifting her chin, she froze as their gazes collided. As if in slow motion, he cupped the back of her neck with one hand. Too shocked to react, she didn't respond as his lips moved over hers in a gentle path.

"We could share that soap." The words whispered against her lips.

"I'll save you some," she replied in a normal tone, although her pulse rocketed through her veins with mach force.

Abruptly he released both her mouth and head. "You do that. I'm going to fix my last supper."

Fleeing, Lindy grabbed the toiletries and went in the bathroom. She locked the door safely behind her. With trembling hands, she lit the candles and turned on the faucet. When the room began to steam and the scent of jasmine filled the air, she stripped out of the too-big clothes she'd put on the night before.

As she sank into the heavenly warm water, she moaned. Her injuries hurt like crazy, but the scratches were beginning to scab over.

Slowly, as her sore body relaxed, she wondered what had made her turn down Jace. Although Candy knew the truth—that Lindy hadn't made love yet—most everyone else assumed she got around. Although she'd sooner die than admit the reason to anyone, Lindy saved her virginity, hoping to find that one special person who would understand her like no one ever had. She desired what her parents had—a love so unique no one else would ever do. She ached for the same, but so far no one had fit the bill.

Jace did, her little voice mocked her. He got her like no one else. But he was all wrong. Older, an ex-convict, a family enemy. Was he worth throwing away all family ties?

Hadn't she already done that by being alone with him for the last few days? No matter what she said, the Chief and Mother would believe there had been an intimate relationship. By spending the night, not to mention two, in Jace's company, she had defied everything she had been raised to believe. A proper young woman of her station didn't run away to spend time with a criminal without her name being tarnished forever.

Although much cheaper than her usual brand, the shampoo Jace bought smelled like green apples. The scent reminded her of Granny's special fruit salad. Unwelcome grief caught her—for all the things that she didn't have any more. Granny would've understood, but she was gone now. Lindy couldn't talk to her mother, even when Emily had been well they hadn't been able to communicate very easily. Soon, she'd be gone too. Trey was home now, but they had grown apart in the last five years. Confiding in him would be next to impossible.

The water began to cool and although she wanted to add some more, she had promised Jace a turn. Reluctantly, she pulled the plug and stepped out of the tub. Wrapping herself in one of Granny's big fluffy towels, she realized she didn't have anything to change into. Looking at the dirty clothes on the floor with distaste, she debated whether to put them back on or stay in the towel. When she picked up the bloodstained T-shirt the towel won.

She fluffed her hair with her fingers, hoping Granny's silver hairbrush was still here somewhere. With no makeup, she felt naked, but there was nothing to do about it now. Making sure her temporary dress was secure, she took a deep breath and opened the door.

Lindy's stomach growled, and she went through the door. "Smells good."

"You hungry?" Jace eyed her outfit with a raised eyebrow before turning his attention to the food in front of him.

She blushed a bit at the look in his eye and glanced at the meal he'd prepared. Bowls of steaming chicken, corn, and biscuits sat in the center of the table. "Starving. You bought all this?"

"Yeah, and I found home canned pickles and jam in the pantry. There's no reason they shouldn't be good." His hot gaze roamed over her skimpy cover. She almost wished she'd put back on the bloodstained clothes thrown all over the bathroom floor.

"Mother said we'd leave that stuff here and eat it when we came." That would never happen now. Forcing back the lump in her throat, she popped one of Granny's sweet and sour pickles in her mouth. "Yum. Yeah, Mother was right."

"Is that what you're wearing?" Jace scanned her bare arms, legs and barely covered body with an intensity that frightened her.

Resisting the urge to cover her chest with her arms, she lifted her chin. "My clothes are dirty. Candy's going to bring me some clean ones. Until then, I'm staying like this." She knew how to act tough; she'd been doing it for the last year. Even when her insides shook with fear and something else she could pretend indifference. She did it now.

"Suit yourself." He shrugged and pulled up a chair. Dishing himself he said, "Let's eat."

Lindy stared at him without speaking until he looked at her.

"What?" He looked so innocent, she would've believed anything he said.

"Did your mother raise you in a barn?" She folded her arms and tapped her foot. "I don't think she did."

Without answering, he stood, pulled out her chair and indicated it. As delicately as she could, wrapped in a towel, she perched on the edge and he pushed her back in. "Thank you."

"My pleasure, princess." He sat again and this time waited for her to serve herself before he finished filling his plate.

When he lifted her fork she said, "Don't you say grace?"

"You do it." He took a deliberate bite and chewed.

She bowed her head and gave a short prayer.

"Does that do you any good?" He took another large bite.

"What? Praying?" She reached for a bowl.

He swallowed. "Yeah. Praying."

Lindy thought about it for a minute. "I guess it depends on the occasion."

"It never helped me. Not even once." He took another piece of chicken. "And I doubt it ever did much for you either."

She didn't answer, but praying as hard as she could hadn't taken her mother's cancer away no matter how much she wished it. She stirred her potatoes, appetite disappearing. "I guess not."

Jace filled his plate and emptied it three times without any more conversation.

Lindy ate a little and almost moaned when he got up and retrieved a pre-cooked pie from the counter. "How do you have room?"

"I could eat a bear. Prison food makes you sick, but you eat it anyway." Cutting the pie in half, he placed a piece on his plate and dug in.

Lindy studied his bent head. How had the boy she'd known stood it inside the walls of Angola? He had been the life of the party, always cracking jokes and playing pranks. Now he was so serious, so angry, she doubted he had a laugh in him.

"I cooked, you clean," he said. "Assuming the princess knows how to clean, that is."

"I know how," she said, miffed at the insinuation she didn't.

"Don't you have a maid to do all your chores?" His tone mocked her.

"Etta's family, not a maid." Why was he digging at her? So what, they hired a housekeeper. Big deal. A lot of families in Juliet had hired help.

"She doesn't wait on you? Fix your food, wash your laundry, make your bed? Fits my definition of a maid." He stuffed more pie in his mouth. "You're spoiled."

"I guess," Lindy mumbled, her already slim appetite gone. She got up and washed the dishes and stacked them while he sat at the table and watched. "If you'll excuse me, I'm going to lie down."

She went in the living room and flopped on the couch. Why was she bothering with Jace anyway? He was going to go back to prison, and nothing she could do would prevent that. Before she got too bogged down in her morose thoughts, someone knocked.

Before she opened the door, she checked and made sure Candy was on the other side. Lindy opened the door. "Get in here."

Candy bustled in carrying an enormous suitcase. "I brought you so much stuff. Clothes, a whole stash of makeup, fashion magazines…"

"Great. C'mon, let's go in the bedroom and I'll put on some of those clothes." Lindy glanced at Candy's tube top, skintight jeans, and high heels. "Did you bring shorts and T-shirts?"

Candy gave her a hurt look. "You asked me to, didn't you?"

They moved into the bedroom, lugging the stash between them.

Digging through the suitcase like it was a clearance rack at Dillard's, Lindy chose a pair of white satin panties with the tag still attached, low-rise denim shorts, and a lavender spaghetti-strap top. She slipped them on gratefully. Candy had also brought a pair of tennies.

"I brought stuff I never wear," she confided. She held up a bag of cosmetics. "Makeup, too."

"Thanks so much," Lindy sighed, feeling like herself as she sat in front of Granny's cracked mirror and applied her usual dark layers of makeup.

"No thanks needed." Candy licked her bright red lips and grinned. "But I want the scoop. Why are you on the run? What happened with Hunt and why are cops and your brother coming out to Mom's place asking all these questions?"

"Wait a minute and I'll tell you everything."

Candy handed her a tube of Scarlette Fire lipstick. "Here. Who are you here with?"

"Me." Jace stood framed in the doorway. Lindy's heart skipped a beat. He'd showered, droplets of water still clinging to his hair. He didn't have on a shirt either. Lindy's gaze locked on the defined muscles across his stomach. She swallowed. Hard.

Candy elbowed her and giggled. "Oh, I get it."

"No, that's not it." Lindy managed to drag her gaze off Jace's magnificent chest and faced Candy. "This isn't a little getaway for two. This is serious."

"Sex always is." She shrugged and dug around in the makeup case.

Lindy laid down the brush. "Listen, Candy, this is Jace Hill."

Candy's heavily made up eyes opened dramatically. "Oh."

"He needs help figuring out who really killed Deke Soloman a few years ago. Jimmy Ray Hunt tried to rape me but Jace saved me. I owe him a lot." Lindy paused for a breath.

"Jimmy Ray did what?" Candy's mouth fell open. Then she looked at Jace. "You were in prison for murder, right?"

He glowered at her. "Yeah."

"It wasn't his fault." For some reason it was important to Lindy that her best friend and Jace like and understand each other. "Please help us."

"So, what can I do?" Candy wanted to know. "But tell me about Jimmy Ray first."

Lindy avoided eye contact. "He didn't want to stop when I told him to. I fought him off and ran away. I went to the Chief's boat and Jace was there."

Candy couldn't seem to find her tongue. "Wow."

"Did your mom remember anything about the night Soloman was murdered?" Jace asked, bringing them all back to present.

"Carlene wasn't a fountain of information. She had a date last night, so she was still asleep late today. I woke her up and she was grumpier than usual, but even so, she clammed up tighter than a year-old mayo jar when I asked her if she remembered anyone getting mur…" Candy blushed. "Dying."

"For the record, I didn't kill Soloman even though I took the rap for it," Jace told her. "Did your mom know anything?"

"She told me a girl named Marie Lennox had a date with Soloman before he was killed. Marie got sick and Mom went instead. That's when she got weird. Asked me why I was asking all these questions and to leave her alone." Candy sighed. "When my mom says to scatter, you better do as she says."

"Does Marie still live out at the river?" Lindy crossed her fingers. "Maybe she'd know more."

Candy shook her head. "Mom said a john strangled her not long after this Soloman guy died. The cops didn't care. No one even looked into it." She gave Lindy an apologetic glance. "Sorry."

"It's okay." Lindy was learning some things she didn't like about the Chief. She wouldn't have believed them herself a year ago. The man she'd always admired for his morals wasn't the man she'd always thought he was.

Jace's fingers wrapped around the doorframe turned white. He hung his head and stared at the floor. "Damn."

"Did your mom tell you anything else that might help?" Lindy almost pleaded.

"No. Sorry." Candy looked between them. "I can try again when she's in a better mood."

"No. Don't. If she isn't suspicious already, asking her more questions will make her that way." Jace stepped in the room and leaned against the dresser. "We're keeping a low profile. Trying to figure out who's really responsible for Soloman's death. If whoever really did it finds out we're on his trail he'll cover his tracks more than they already are."

"What are you going to do?" Candy asked.

"I don't know." Jace frowned, a line forming between his eyes. "Maybe I'm going down a road that has no end. There's the possibility that I have to live with this on me the rest of my life. Maybe it's time to just face it. I'm not going back to that hole, though. I'll die first."

"No, you won't go back," Lindy protested. "There's got to be a way to prove your innocence."

"If there is I can't see it."

Candy looked between them. She told Lindy, "Your brother is worried about you. Why didn't you tell me Trey is so hot? He's come out to the river twice to see Carlene. He brought that black cop the second time. The copper wasn't too bad either."

"What did you tell them?" Lindy ignored the comments about Trey. Her friends had always chased him.

"Nothing. Just that you went with Hunt last night and that was the last time I saw you. He's pretty worried. They think he might have killed you since you haven't come home."

"Oh, God." Lindy covered her face with her hands. She had never considered that possibility.

"Leave now. Go home with Candy," Jace ordered, his voice guttural.

"No." Lindy looked up and their eyes met. Deep in his she saw fear—fear that she would go and leave him to fight alone. "Not until we prove you didn't kill Soloman. I'm not going anywhere until you're clear."

"That may never happen," he shot back. "You've got the chance to go. Take it."

"I said I'm not going." Lindy read the relief he didn't want to show her in his eyes.

"What can I do?" Candy asked. "I want to help."

"Just keep our secret," Lindy pleaded. "No matter what Trey or the Chief or anyone else says or does."

"No problem." Candy stood up. "I'm going to get out of here. I'll go to Mugs-n-Jugs and see what's going on there. Maybe I'll see someone who knows something."

"That's impossible," Lindy told her. "We went there last night to talk to Jimmy Ray. We found him dead."

"What?" Candy gaped at her. "Are you kidding?"

"Not in the least. It was horrible." She shuddered, remembering.

"Did anyone see you?" Candy looked around as if she were hiding from someone.

"Not that we know of. Jody Marvell came in and we hid in the closet. When he went to talk to the barmaids, we got the heck out of Dodge." Lindy waved her hands in front of her face. "I have never been so scared in my whole life."

"This is the craziest thing I've ever heard," Candy declared.

"You better get out of here before you get dragged in any further." Lindy hugged her friend. "Thanks for everything."

"I have one more thing." Candy handed Lindy her own purse. "You left this in my car last night. You might need it. Your phone is in there, right? If you need anything call me."

"You're the best." Lindy blinked back sudden tears and hugged her again. "I'll let you know if anything turns up."

"Me, too. If your dad's guys or that hottie brother of yours comes out again I'll shout it right out to you. After I distract him for awhile, that is." She smiled at Jace on her way by. "Hang in there."

He gave her a rare smile back. "I'm working on it."

Lindy smiled at Candy, too, forcing herself to swallow the unexpected wave of jealously that filled her mouth with a bad taste. She had no right to be jealous of Jace. He didn't belong to her. There was nothing between them but one short kiss. He hadn't asked her for her help. In fact he'd told her to go home not once, but twice. If Candy was his type, that was his business. After Candy left, Lindy went into the living room and stared out the window into the inky night. She didn't turn around when she heard Jace sit on the couch behind her. Her thoughts and emotions tangled in a jumbled mess and she didn't want him to read any of them.

"Want a Coke?" he asked finally.

"No."

"What's your problem?"

"Nothing." She folded her arms across her middle. She wasn't going to let him know how jealousy was eating a hole in her stomach.

"Something's bugging you," he insisted.

"No, it's not."

"Why didn't you take your last chance and go home with your friend?"

Still facing the window, she shrugged. "I don't know. Do you want me to leave so you could call Candy back? You sure were friendly with her for only knowing her less than an hour."

She could feel him move directly behind her. "Me and Candy, we're the same kind. Losers. You, on the other hand, have it all. You're ruining your life by staying here with me. I don't have much chance of making anything of myself, but you've got the whole world open to you and you're blowing it by staying with me. Your folks are never going to get over it."

She turned to look at him. "You don't get it, do you? I don't care." Silently, she willed him to see her heart. To understand the things she couldn't say. That his approval meant so much more to her than her than she could admit.

"Don't you?" He stared into her eyes.

"No."

"Liar." The whispered word feathered across her face.

She looked away. "I am not."

"You're bad at it, too." A small smile pulled at the corner of his mouth. He brushed her cheek with his knuckles. "Remind me to play poker with you sometime."

She froze as his touch went across her face. "You aren't getting rid of me."

"She can't hold a candle to you, you know." His eyes were half shut, his mouth a fraction from hers. She ached for him to kiss her.

"Who?" She had to force herself to keep from leaning into his palm.

"Candy. She's just a kid. But you're a woman made to stand by a man." He touched her lips with his fingers. She parted them slightly, breathless. Her heart jumped like it had been touched by an electric current and her body dampened, reacting instinctively.

"You liked her." She didn't recognize her own voice.

"She's sweet enough." His lips nearly touched hers. "But I like my women a little bit sour."

"I am not." Her voice croaked like a frog.

His fingers wrapped in a tendril of hair. "No, you're not. Anybody who doesn't see how good you are has to be blind."

Lindy couldn't have moved if a hurricane blew through and swept her away. How could this man, this convict, make her feel valued for the first time in her life? How did he know all the things she needed to hear? She blinked as if coming out a trance. "Stop it."

"What? Telling the truth?" He tugged gently on her hair. "Why?"

"Because you don't mean it."

"Every word."

"Stop teasing me." The words nearly strangled her.

"I'd never tease you." His eyes bore into hers, and mesmerized by their dark blue depths, she couldn't look away if she tried. This moment reminded her of one time she'd gone to the coast with her family. She'd lain on her stomach, floating on a boat, staring into the endless waters of the gulf. Nameless mysteries had been hidden there, too.

"Why are you saying this?" she managed.

"Someone has to." His gaze never wavered.

"Not you."

"Then who?"

She couldn't answer that, so she remained silent.

"You want to know one thing I like better on Candy than you?" His mouth moved so close to her she could feel his lips on hers.

She shook her head mutely. He was too close. *Danger! Danger!*

He lifted the piece of hair wrapped around his fist. "This God-awful color. You used to have the most beautiful sunny hair. And your face. What's with all this junk on it? Candy might need all that crap, but you're too pretty to do that to yourself."

Not sure if she was flattered or insulted, she didn't answer.

He dropped her hair, leaving her trembling and breathless.

Chapter Fourteen

Trey left the church picnic, headed home.

His mother was asleep, so he decided to search Lindy's room. Maybe there would be a clue there. Some of her clothes might be missing. Or maybe she kept a journal.

Etta would know.

He found her in the kitchen sipping a cup of tea.

"Can you help me for a minute?" he asked. "I need to see if any of Lindy's things are missing and I wouldn't know what to look for."

"Yes sir, Mr. Trey. I'll do it right now." She set her cup aside and wiped her hands on her apron.

"I can wait until you're done," he offered.

"No, sir, you can't. My missy is gone. That's most important." She led the way upstairs and they entered Lindy's room together. Trey glanced around. Large, on the northwest corner, a canopy bed made with a pink chenille comforter dominated the room. A discarded blue graduation cap and gown were flung across a chair. Some of the stuffed animals resting on the floor he recognized. Shelves full of riding and dance trophies covered one wall. He picked one up and read the inscription. Over a year old.

While he watched, Etta opened the door to the walk in closet and went through it. "Nothin' gone here."

"Does she have a duffle bag?" He looked on the top shelf. A sports bag with the logo 'Juliet Gators' sat there. Opening it, he found a blue and white soccer uniform. On the opposite shelf he saw a matching set of Coach luggage. Trey wasn't sure if he should be more or less worried. Obviously, she hadn't packed to run away.

"What about her dresser?" He opened the top drawer of her Queen Anne bureau. Lots of scanty underwear. Uncomfortable, he moved aside and Etta glanced through it. She shook her head. Each drawer was the same. When they had searched the last one, he asked, "Anything?"

"Nots so I could tell." She pursed her lips. "Laundry's done up, too."

"What about her makeup?" Trey suggested, although he wondered how anyone could tell, there was so much of it. He opened a bottle of expensive looking perfume and sniffed. Too sweet. He closed it.

They looked at the small vanity table covered with perfumes, lotions, and makeup. Etta again shook her head. "Everything seems to be here."

"You sure?" He already knew the answer.

Her head bobbed. "Uh-huh."

"Okay, thanks."

Although disappointed, Trey wasn't surprised. He glanced around. Pictures were taped along the edges of the mirror above the vanity. He leaned forward and studied them. Most were of Lindy and her friends. Many showed her at prom or homecoming. None of those were with one certain boy. Apparently, she didn't have a steady boyfriend. He continued to scan them. Several poses were of her at dance recitals and horse shows. He recognized most of the people. Mary-Gray and Becca were in many of them, but no one jumped out at him. No shots of Candy anywhere.

Turning away, he knelt and peered under her bed. Nothing but a few pairs of ballet shoes and riding boots. He felt between the mattresses. Nothing. Swallowing his disappointment, he stood. He'd hoped to find a journal. Maybe there was one in the desk by the window. One by one, he opened drawers, but found nothing of interest except her yearbook in the bottom left one. He glanced through it. Not one signature. Quite a bit different from his own senior annual. He had so many good wishes in his, people had written over the top of one another.

Did Lindy have any jewelry? She'd been wearing a pair of diamond studs in her ears and a pink sapphire necklace when he'd given her the bracelet he'd brought from Afghanistan. He searched for a jewelry box and found it on her vanity. He opened it and found an assortment of expensive jewelry. Two ruby rings and a charm bracelet looked especially valuable, but there didn't seem to be any empty slots.

Trey couldn't be positive, but he didn't think Lindy had left the house with the intention of running away. His fear growing, he took one last glance around. Nothing jumped out at him. Not sure what he had hoped to find, he closed the door behind him with a heavy heart. Why couldn't she have left out a clue like a brochure or a bus ticket stub?

The phone rang and he picked up.

"Hey, man, it's Jody. I'm out at the lake. Get out here quick." He hung up before Trey could ask any questions.

Trey raced downstairs and jumped in the Mustang. Dust billowed up behind him as he sped up the driveway. His heart pounded like a drum line. Had Jody found Lindy? Or Jace? Telling himself not to jump to conclusions, he made it to the lake in a few minutes.

Jody met him at the car. "Come on, I found something."

Tongue dry as a cotton patch in August, Trey followed him to the lake's edge. Jody pointed to an orange cooler resting at an angle in the weeds. "Recognize that?"

"Not offhand." Trey's fear was replaced by annoyance. Jody had called him out here to look at an ordinary cooler that anyone could've bought in a store? "What's so special about it?"

"Look closer." Jody pushed down some of the weeds.

Trey saw what he did. Nearly hidden by the angle and the mud it was buried in, he almost missed the large block letters on the side: THE EMILY. The cooler had come from the Chief's boat. "Have you touched it?"

"Not yet. I wanted you to see it first." Jody pulled on a pair of latex gloves. He waded waist deep and tugged the box out of the mud. Struggling to carry it to shore, he set it down with a thud. "Here's hoping this is nothing."

Trey moved so he could see the contents and braced himself.

Jody undid the bungee cord tied securely around the outside and lifted the lid. "Oh, man. Jackpot."

"Yeah." Trey breathed a sigh of relief. He'd halfway expected to find Lindy stuffed in the ice chest. Instead, the remnants of an orange jumpsuit, handcuffs and leg shackles laid there. "Jace's?"

"If I were a betting man, I'd have to say yeah." Carefully, Jody lifted one piece of jagged metal. "I'll have to check, but I'm guessing these came off him. I need to radio the Chief."

While he waited, Trey's mind raced. His gaze roamed the area. Somehow Jace had made it to the boat. Where had he gone from here? How had he managed to find Lindy and kidnap her? Trey didn't want to face it, but the truth was he didn't see how Jace had done all that. He feared Jimmy Ray had killed her and stashed her Jeep somewhere. Now there was no way to ask him.

Jody came back. "I have to take this in to the station, but I want to search the boat first."

"You think they're together?" Jace had apparently taken his little sister hostage, but it didn't make it any easier to admit. If only there was some other explanation. No matter how he tried, he couldn't find one. Trey waited to see what Jody had to say. He had known Jace all his life, too. The three of them had played football and baseball from elementary through high school and run around together. If Jody believed Jace capable of kidnapping for revenge, then Trey knew he wasn't crazy.

"I don't know what to think. All the evidence points that way. But we might be jumping to conclusions. I just can't see the guy I used to know hurting your sister. But I couldn't see him killing anyone either, even though he always was a hothead."

"What happened to his mama just pushed him over the edge, I guess. Who's to say if that had been you or I, we might have done the same." A shudder ripped down Trey's back at the thought of his mother in the condition MiLann had been left in. She'd been beaten so badly, she couldn't function for days, raped and tortured, left to die alone in a downpour. Her mind had protected itself the only way it could and snapped. Only a miracle had kept her alive.

"If someone did something like that to my mama, they wouldn't live to talk about it," Jody agreed. "And I'm a lawman."

"Yeah, so was my dad. I know it killed him he couldn't get enough on Soloman to put him away. When the Chief had to turn a rapist loose he about died inside." Trey had glimpsed a side of his dad most people didn't, the night the Chief had come home after freeing Soloman. He'd been sick at heart. He blamed himself, although there wasn't anything he could do. The evidence just didn't stack up to make the case.

"I don't doubt it," Jody agreed. "Your old man isn't always a hardass. He has a heart. He just keeps it well-hidden most of the time. Right now, for instance, he's so worried about Lindy, he can't stand himself."

"I know it. Which brings me back to Jace. Do you honestly think the guy has run off with my sister at gunpoint? And if he has, where did they go?" He swept his hand toward the lake and the forest surrounding it. "There's a million places they could be."

"We're watching her credit cards. If Jace has her, he's smart enough to not let her use them. He wouldn't have had any money. Cons don't make enough to spend and he didn't walk out of the front door with a state issued check. He ran from a bus wreck, so he couldn't have had a dime on him. In other words, he can't have gotten far on his own. And if Lindy is with him, no one has spotted her Jeep."

"He's got a great hiding spot, I'd say. Lindy's Jeep is bright yellow, not easy to camouflage. The military teaches us to hide right out in the open sometimes. I think that's it. I bet Jace is right under our noses and we're just overlooking him." Trey hitched a thumb behind him. "I think I'm right. Look where he landed. The Chief's boat."

"So where else is a possibility?" Jody pinched the bridge of his nose.

"Somewhere he would figure no one would go," Trey said.

Jody leaned against the railing, his hands under his butt. "He was your best friend. You tell me."

Trey searched his memory. "You know how much time we put into sports. Almost every day after school. When we weren't practicing, we spent a lot of time in the garage working on the Mustang. Hours and hours."

"What about school vacations? We came here to fish or ride around on this boat, remember?" Jody took a few steps away and stared into the lake. "I remember those days like they were yesterday."

"Yeah, we came here. Both of the families did, too. We used to spend a whole day out on the water, and then we'd picnic up on the shore in the evening. Sometimes, we'd grill the catfish we caught." Those days were only six years ago, but it felt like a lifetime.

Jody said, "We know Jace came here. Is there anywhere else that means something to him? Another location where he'd feel safe?"

Trey shook his head. "Not that I can think of."

"Keep studying on it." Jody lifted the jumpsuit with a gloved hand. "Yeah, this is Jace's all right. Angola will confirm it."

Glancing around Trey said, "I wonder how long Jace was here and how he found Lindy."

"Maybe he didn't."

Trey paused. They had staked everything they had on Jace kidnapping Lindy, but now he wasn't so sure. "I've been thinking. I just don't see Jace having a way to get from here to wherever Jimmy Ray was with Lindy and stealing her away from him. How would Jace know where to look, for one thing? I'm afraid we're going the wrong direction."

"I agree." Jody wiped his brow. "If I could've taken Jimmy Ray in for more questioning, I think I would've found out where your sister is. I don't think Jace had time to plan a kidnapping and carry it out. The bus turning over was a freak thing, not planned."

"You know what this means?" Trey didn't want to say it.

Jody wouldn't meet his eyes. "Jimmy Ray killed her and hid the body."

Trey swallowed around the knot in his throat. "Yeah."

"We better get some more manpower," Jody said grimly. "I need to search the boat first."

His stomach rolling, Trey followed him through *The Emily*. He knew the odds of finding a missing person in this neck of the woods. The possibilities were endless. There was the lake itself, miles and miles of deep water. Surrounding it was the forest. Thousands of acres of trees. A million places to hide a body. Only Jimmy Ray could lead them to Lindy and he couldn't.

"Looks like he stocked up and got out of Dodge," Trey commented.

All the food was missing.

"Seems like it." Jody headed for the door. "I'm going to take the new evidence to the station and get some more people hunting for your sister."

• • •

Summer used her key on the front door. A long time ago, they had left their house unlocked. No one else in the county bolted up but them. "Mama? Are you up?"

Getting no answer, her heart raced. Mama always met her at the door or in the kitchen. Had she suffered another breakdown worrying about Jace? With hurried steps, Summer checked the kitchen. Only the tick-tock of the clock on the wall met her. Biting her bottom lip, she looked in Mama's bedroom. She was asleep, snoring softly.

Relieved, Summer backed out and went into the kitchen for a glass of iced tea. A frosted raisin-apple cake sat on the counter. She cut a healthy piece and took it to the porch. Setting her food on the table, she went back in the house and dug the mysterious photo out of her bag. Holding it carefully by the edge, she took it outside and sat.

She chewed on a piece of cake and stared at the picture, trying to figure out where it had been taken. The background was dark; a flash had lit up the faces of the people but not much else. Mama and Emily Bouché wore dresses and both Buford and Leroy were in dress shirts and slacks. They all held drinks. Where had they been drinking? A party of some sort? Or a bar?

Summer's stomach clenched, her appetite fled. She'd heard whispers about her mother her whole life. There had always been insinuations that Mama was trampy, but Summer hadn't ever seen any evidence of it. Her memory flashed back to an ugly scene when she was in high school.

Patty Jane Myers had taken her daughter out of Mama's class at school and moved her into a different room. Another memory forced its way to the surface. When Summer had been in the seventh grade, Bess Crowley had been Summer's best friend. Suddenly, with no explanation, Bess had been forbidden to speak to Summer. She still didn't know why. Had it been more than pre-teen drama? She'd gone out of her way to make sure people didn't talk bad about her.

A tiny voice of doubt nagged her. In photographic evidence Mama was sitting on a lap of a man, her arms wrapped around his neck.

Had the talk been more than idle gossip?

Was Mama guilty of the things people said about her?

She was wild.

She chased married men.

She brought the rape on herself.

Summer's mind refused to wrap around the possibility. Even if a kernel of the gossip was true, and Mama had been wild, Emily Bouché certainly wasn't. She was the Chief's wife, someone who had a position to uphold in the community. Summer had never seen her behave with anything but perfect decorum. The idea of Emily even drinking beer out of a bottle was unfathomable. No matter how much she tried, Summer couldn't make herself believe her mother and Emily had gone out on the town partying. But by the truth in the photo, they had done something out of character.

Summer wished she could ask her mother about the picture, but she didn't dare. Who knew how she'd react. Mama's fits were almost unbearable and Summer didn't fancy triggering another one so soon. She tried to tell herself she was making too much out of a simple photo. So what if Mama had a night out with her best friend? Everyone did that sometimes. Summer had gone out with Glory and Lilah a few times. Something here just felt wrong, though.

Who could she could ask about it? Leroy Eaton had committed suicide. Not Emily. Buford Krebbs wasn't a possibility; if Viola got wind of this, she'd shred what little was left of Mama's reputation His image snuck in and stayed like an unwanted guest who wouldn't go home. He might know something she didn't. This puzzle was going to drive her crazy if she didn't solve it.

Guilt nipped at her, but she ignored it and dialed Trey. He answered immediately, his husky voice cutting across her raw nerves like a blade. "It's Summer. Can you meet me somewhere?"

There was a pause then he asked, "When?"

"Now." Her pulse jump-roped in her neck and she took a deep breath to steady it.

"Where?" Was it her imagination, or did his voice grow deeper?

"Somewhere we can talk." A million butterflies in her stomach collided head-on. "In private."

"Sounds serious." His husky tone did drop an octave.

"Yes, it is." She steadied her own trembling voice. "I'll tell you about it when I see you. Where would work?"

"What about *the Emily?* I'm here."

"I'll be there in about half an hour." She hung up.

Summer could barely focus on the road. Going to meet Trey like this was probably a mistake, but if she didn't hear the story behind the picture she would go crazy. There wasn't any other reason she wanted to see him. None whatsoever.

She followed the twisty dirt lane leading to Mystic Lake. Her heart pounded in her chest and ears like an out-of-control jackhammer. She took a deep breath and tried to calm herself. This was just an opportunity to ask Trey about the picture, nothing more. Her nerves were just on edge with everything that had been going on.

The Chief's warning rang in her head. *Stay away from Trey.* The Chief could just go stuff himself. She had quit caring what he thought five years ago. If her own mama wasn't just as adamant, she would've naturally gravitated to Trey, just like she always had.

Chapter Fifteen

Trey was waiting at the boat dock.

Wiping her hands on her khaki shorts, Summer stepped out and her gaze locked on Trey leaning against his bright red car, muscled arms folded across a wide chest, long legs crossed at the ankles. With the beams from a full moon framing him, he looked like a model in a jeans ad. All man, all sex appeal. She hoped he couldn't sense how an involuntary quiver low in her belly made it nearly impossible to move for a moment. She steadied herself and walked toward him. "I have to show you something. It's probably nothing. I mean it's something. Just no idea how important."

He nodded, but didn't smile. "Slow down."

Stung by his unfriendly tone, she hesitated. Had the Chief given Trey a warning, too? She fumbled around in her purse, found the photo and handed it to him. "This."

He hesitated a moment before he took the picture from her. "What is it?"

"I was hoping you could tell me, or at least have an idea about it." She watched his face as he studied the images in the photo. His eyes widened as they went over the familiar faces.

"My God," he breathed. "I don't believe this."

"What?" She knew the picture was weird. "Tell me."

"Where'd you get this?" His face was ashen, his mouth pinched.

"Why? Trey, you're scaring me." Her voice raised a notch. "What is it?" He was acting so strange. What was in that picture that had him so freaked out?

He pointed to the stranger in the picture. The one Mama had her arms around. "Don't you know who that is?"

"No. Should I? Tell me." Her mouth felt like she'd stuffed a rag in it. Dry and foul tasting.

His eyes when his gaze raised to meet hers were bleak. "Deke Soloman."

Summer shook her head so hard her ears rang. "No, that's not possible. He was a stranger. Mama said so—"

"Apparently not." He reached to steady her and fire shot through her when he grabbed her elbow. "Let's go sort this out."

Summer forced herself to climb aboard the boat. She sat on the bench and again studied the dark background trying to make something out. "I wonder who was behind the camera? Do you have any idea where this might've been? They're all drinking beer."

"That doesn't mean anything special," he said. "They could've been at a bar, home, or even here."

"Do you remember your mother ever saying anything about a birthday party or an anniversary or a wedding that she and Mama went to together?" Her fingers went numb and the picture floated to the ground. "Trey! That's it!"

He bent to retrieve it. "What?"

"Your graduation." She took the picture from him. "Look at what they're wearing. That's the dress Mama wore to your party. I remember because we went down to Jackson to go shopping for it together. We went to all the department stores, but nothing worked until we went to this place on Martinique. That's a side street with all these little dress shops…"

"Are you sure?" He peered at the picture as if he expected the people in it to speak to him.

She'd never been so sure of anything in her life. "Absolutely positive. And this is the outfit your mother wore, too. See?"

"I guess."

"Trust me, I know it." She jumped up. "Don't you see? Mama never wore this dress before your graduation and she never wore it after."

"You think they went partying that evening?" He gave his head a slight shake and frowned. "We've always thought MiLann was alone when she was attacked. But this looks like they all went out to celebrate."

She nodded vigorously. "I know it's hard to believe, but yes, I do. We don't know—"

"Because we were together," he finished.

Ignoring the fire in her belly the thought of that night ignited she nodded. "Yes."

"Soloman wouldn't have had any reason to come to *LeFleur*. So our mothers had to go somewhere he would've been." He glanced at her, his expression as puzzled as her own.

"Apparently they left *LeFleur* to party." She bit her lip. "But where? And why?"

"Where was the Chief?" Trey got up and leaned against the deck, stuffing his hands in his front pockets. "He wouldn't have just hung around the house while my mother and his friends all went out without him."

"Maybe there was an emergency that called him away?" Summer suggested.

"It's possible," he conceded, "but who would know after all this time?" A frown flitted across his face. "Besides him? And MiLann. Quizzing her is impossible. But…"

"What?" Had he remembered something?

He wouldn't meet her eyes. "It's nothing."

"Come on, Trey. What is it?" She stood and went to stand in front of him, forcing him to look her in the face.

"They fought that day." His words were forced.

"Who?" He wasn't making sense. "I'm not following you."

"Mother and the Chief. I heard their argument."

"About what?"

His frown deepened. "Not what. Who."

He wasn't going to say unless she pressed him. "Tell me. Please?"

"I came downstairs to talk to Mother about the party. I wanted something, I can't remember what exactly, but she and the Chief were shouting at each other…"

"What was the fight about?" Summer whispered. After all this time was Jace going to be cleared? Did Trey hold the key?

"Another woman." He took a deep breath. "Mother was accusing him of having an affair." He gave his head a little shake as if he could erase the memory.

Summer's mouth gaped open. "The Chief? No way. With who?"

He shrugged. "I don't know. I didn't stick around to find out. No one ever mentioned it again."

Grabbing his wrist, her arm brushing the denim of his pocket, Summer said, "Don't you see? That might've been the reason our mothers were drinking. Maybe the photo was taken at *LeFleur*. What if the Chief left, instead of the other way around? There was a bar at *LeFleur* that night, remember?"

"Yeah, but how did Soloman hook up with them?"

"We would've known if he was an invited guest, but maybe he was hired to set up or take down the bar."

Trey shook his head. "That would've come out at Jace's trial."

"Yeah, you're right." She was clutching at straws. "Who else would know if that man showed up after we left?"

"I don't know."

"What about Lindy? Maybe she was home that night." She hated to upset him more by bringing up his missing sister, but she was the only one Summer could think of who might have been there.

"Probably. But it's kind of hard to ask her right now." His tone resonated with worry.

"Still no word?" Realizing she had dug furrows into his inner arm, she dropped her hand.

"No." He sat next to her and looked at the picture again. "I can't believe this. Somehow your mama knew Soloman. Why didn't this surface at the trial?"

"Mama didn't go to Jace's trial. She couldn't. She was barely functioning at that point." Through blurry eyes, she stared at him. "I hope you're not saying Mama somehow led Soloman on, or that she deserved what happened to her."

"What?" Genuine shock raced across his face. "Of course not. No woman deserves that kind of abuse. I just can't believe this never came out before. Where did you find this?"

"In the Chief's filing cabinet. He pulled me in today to show me some letters from Jace…I went to put them away…and I found…this. I…took it."

"The Chief had to know." He crumpled the photo in his fist. "He had to."

"What are you saying?" Her breath came in short gasps and her heart felt like it was going to jump out of her chest. "Tell me what you mean."

"Don't you see? The Chief surely knew MiLann was somehow acquainted with Soloman." He flipped the photo against his palm. "Here's the evidence."

"You're not saying that the Chief knew Mama was out partying with Soloman before he raped her, are you?" Summer knew that was what he was saying, but she couldn't believe it.

"There's only one way to find out. Ask him," Trey said.

"You don't think he found out when Mama went to him for help after the rape?" The idea shook Summer to the core. If the Chief realized Mama was acquainted with Soloman before the rape, then had he known something that made him refuse to put Soloman in custody? But what?

"Why would it matter?" Trey asked. "Why wouldn't he still arrest that creep? Even if MiLann had been out with Soloman prior to what he did to her? Just because a woman parties with a man doesn't make it okay to violate her. The Chief doesn't believe otherwise."

Summer shoved the picture under his nose and tapped his mother's face. "Look who else is there. Your mother."

"What are you driving at?" He avoided her gaze.

"You know where I'm going, Trey. I don't want to have to spell it out." Why was he being so stubborn? Refusing to see the obvious right in front of him? If she could see it, why wouldn't he? She scanned the picture again. "There are five people in this picture besides Mama. Every one of them knew Soloman before the rape. Why didn't that come out at Jace's trial?"

"It wouldn't have made any difference." Trey got up and walked a few feet away and leaned on the railing. She refused to follow him. "Jace still killed Soloman for what he did to your mama. Just because those people knew him doesn't change anything."

"Wouldn't it?" Her voice could've frozen the North Pole. "I think it might've. I have a sneaking suspicion the Chief knew his wife and friends had been drinking with the man who hurt my mama all along. I think he kept his mouth shut when Jace was tried and convicted for murdering this man because maybe, just maybe, one of these people had a reason to kill Soloman. If Jace went to prison, none of these people had to."

"What would any one of them have to gain by murdering Soloman?" Trey asked. "Jace is the only one with a motive."

"That's the part I can't figure out," Summer said. "But I intend to get to the bottom of this. I'm going to prove my brother is innocent if it's the last thing I do."

"How?" Trey frowned. "If we go marching into the Chief's office looking for a fight, he'll clam up tighter than an old maid's knees. There's got to be another way to find out what we want to know. Asking either your mama or mine is out of the question. Leroy Eaton might tell me. If I handle it right. I was going to see him anyway."

He didn't know. "Oh, God, Trey. Leroy Eaton hung himself tonight."

"What?" The shock on his face registered just as her own must have when she'd heard the news. "Why?"

"I have no idea. Jody burst into the Chief's office and gave him the word when Glory and I were there."

"Man, that sucks. I still want to help. If what you're saying is true, then I want to know, too. If there's one secret there might be more." He came and sat next to her. "Look, I have reason to believe Jace doesn't have Lindy after all."

Hope thawed her a bit. Was she hearing him right? "What changed your mind?"

His words came slowly. "The evidence was pretty convincing that Jace had Lindy, but I don't think he does any more. It looks like Jimmy Ray may have done something to her."

For a minute, nothing in the world seemed to move. Even the waves of the lake seemed to still. Her heart soared. "Do you mean it? You don't think Jace took your sister?"

"No."

The single word she'd waited for. She wanted to wrap her arms around him. Instead she touched his arm. "Do you honestly believe Jimmy Ray hurt Lindy? Not Jace?"

"I'm afraid Jimmy Ray killed her."

The pain in his eyes gnashed at her heart. Without thinking, without reason, Summer wrapped her arms around him.

Slipping into his embrace felt as natural to her as breathing.

Wrapping her arms around his waist, she leaned her cheek against his solid chest. His heart beat against her face and she stood absorbing the sensation. She felt his lips brush over her hair and she moved closer until her breasts were crushed against him, her legs pressed into his. He circled her with his arms, his hands cupping her behind.

"Summer." The word was low, guttural. "Don't offer something you can't give."

She tipped her head back and met his eyes. The heat there seared her soul, but she met it evenly. No other man had ever made her feel the way he did. For five long years, she'd tried to put him out of her head and her heart, but he wouldn't leave. Being in his arms had always been right. She had loved him all her life.

"Do you know what you're doing to me?" His arms tightened around her.

"Yes," she whispered. Nothing else mattered. Not his father, not her mother. Not Jace, not Lindy. The only people who counted at that moment were the two of them.

He closed his eyes and groaned before his lips sought hers. He kissed her until any lingering doubts vanished.

He led her inside and they fell on the couch, her across his lap, his mouth on hers. Her denim shorts rode high, exposing her thighs, rubbing against her sensitive center. She wasn't the only one reaching overdrive with little prompting. Trey's erection pressed against her leg, reminding her of a time she had tried so hard to forget. She refused to think about what tomorrow would bring them. The only thing that mattered now was them.

His lips left hers, tasting her collarbone, dipping lower to the swell of her breast. Her nipples pebbled, rubbing against her satin bra, dying for his mouth. Pushing away all the ghosts whispering doubts in her ear, she angled her torso so his lips could more easily access her breast. Answering her prompt, he slid his hand under the hem of her shirt, edging it along her ribs, resting it at the bottom of her bra. A small whimper of encouragement escaped her when he stilled his lips.

Edging his thumb under the satin barrier, he ran it repeatedly over the underside of her breast. Summer had never felt anything so erotic in her entire life. Her back arched, pushing her against his devilish thumb. If he didn't move it another half inch up, she was going to scream. She turned her head and her nose bumped the side of his head. He smelled like sandalwood or cedar. Something masculine, something wonderful. Moving her head a fraction, she touched his ear with the tip of her tongue. He shuddered.

Her whole being seemed to depend on him. Her body was like liquid silver, uncontrollable, jumpy, ready to explode. With his thumb, he raked her bra over her taut nipple, making her jump. He tugged her tee up toward her neck and dipped his mouth toward her breast. Taking it in his mouth, he pulled deep. A silent scream fought for a way out of her throat. To silence it, she did what she'd been dying to do; she tasted the side of his neck with her tongue.

He groaned.

She couldn't decide what he tasted like exactly. But the sensation of his slick, warm skin on her tongue made her reel. Maybe it was just being in Trey's arms again after such a long time, but whatever the reason she didn't want to be anywhere else. They belonged together. They always had. She didn't care if she marked him, didn't care who saw. The thought made her suck harder, determined to show the world it didn't matter what anyone thought.

"Summer."

Gradually, she became aware that he had released her breast. Disappointed, she gave him a light nip and maneuvered her damp, erect nipple under his wonderful, sinful mouth again. But he sat up, nearly unseating her.

"Summer."

"What?" she grumped, wrapping her arms tightly about his neck.

Reluctantly, she opened her eyes. At first, nothing came into focus, but she gradually gained control and realized she had her tee tangled around her waist, her bra who knew where. With trembling fingers, she tugged her shirt back into place and scooted off his lap. God, what had she been thinking? She stole a glance at his neck. A dark red mark proved her lips had been there moments before. If the boat tipped over with her on it and sank to the bottom, it wouldn't be good enough to hide her from the Chief. And if Mama got wind of this, all hell would break loose.

She didn't care.

"Take me to bed," she ordered.

He picked her up and carried her to the bedroom. She wrapped her legs around his waist for the short trip.

She helped him lift her tee over her head. His mouth dipped to her breast again and she cupped the back of his neck with her hand. A powerful force built within her, making her ache so badly she burned with it.

One time had not been enough.

She reached between them and unbuttoned her own shorts. Somewhat shocked by her forwardness, she pushed her khaki shorts and undies over her hips and thighs. Trey rose up and shrugged his own T-shirt over his head. He unsnapped his jeans and slipped out of them and his undershorts. God, fully erect, he was beautiful.

Lowering himself onto her, he supported his weight with his elbows.

The hair on his chest brushed her nipples and they arched to attention. Desperate to feel him inside her, she spread her legs as wide as her shorts and panties wrapped around her thighs would allow. She pulled his mouth to hers and tangled their tongues together.

He reached between them and shoved her constricting garments out of the way. Then he pushed inside her in a powerful, hot rush.

She grabbed his arms and held on as he filled, stretched her.

Her breath rushed out of her in a shuddering gasp.

She hadn't expected this. He was too big, too much. Turning her head, she tasted him on the bicep. He wrapped his hands around her head, kissing her until she wanted him to take them both to heaven.

She lifted her hips and he shifted forward. A tiny spark deep within her lit.

Urging him on, she rocked and the flame leapt.

Heat from deep in her began to spread, warming her entire body. She licked his nipple and he pressed deeper. The fire burned hotter. She did it again. The flame leapt to a torch. She rocked under him, until together they burned. When she thought she could stand no more, he reached under her buttocks and lifted. Summer disintegrated into a pile of smoldering ashes.

Moments later, he too, came with a guttural moan.

She didn't know how long she lay there. When his weight became too much, she shifted. He rolled over, pulling her across his chest. Twisting her legs through his, Summer wished she could stay like this forever. If only they could forget the rest of the world. Impossible.

"What are you thinking?" he asked.

She traced a path from his collarbone to his bellybutton. "Just that we'd be fine if we could shut out everyone else."

"We can." His lips brushed over her hair. "Just don't think about them right now."

She moved to sit up. "I have to go."

He tightened his arms around her and kissed her forehead. "Not yet."

As much as she was tempted to stay in his arms, and forget her problems for a little while, she couldn't. "I've got to…Mama will worry."

He let her go with one last, lingering kiss that almost made her change her mind. She rolled away, looking for her clothes. "Do you see my bra?"

"It's right here." Trey's gaze was locked on something underneath the edge of the bed.

Reluctantly, she followed his line of sight. "Where?"

Instead of answering, he reached for something. "Here."

Before he had it shook open, she was suppressing a groan of dismay. A blue lycra mini skirt was in Trey's hands. Without being told, she instinctively knew it belonged to his sister. When she raised her gaze to meet Trey's dull recognition shined there. "If I were a betting man, I'd say Lindy has been here. Right under our noses all along. With Jace."

Numb, she nodded. She forced out a single word. "Why?"

He gave the torn garment a shake. "This is another piece of evidence that proves she was here with him. I can't keep quiet about this."

"What do you mean 'another piece of evidence'?" She managed to force the words out. They had just made love and he hadn't told her something about Jace? She tugged the sheet around her, wishing to get as far away from him as she could.

He met her eyes and his were troubled. "I wanted to tell you sooner…Jody found handcuffs, shackles, and a prison jumpsuit we believe are Jace's. They were in an ice chest out in the lake."

Summer couldn't find words.

"I need to let the Chief know about this." He reached for her as she twisted away. "I don't have a choice."

"No, you never do," she whispered through icy lips. Her stomach rolled and she fought to keep from throwing up. Little black spots swam in front of her eyes. Once again, Trey was going to testify against her brother. And send him straight back to prison before he could prove his innocence. "This doesn't prove anything except Jace was here." She grabbed at the first thing that came to her. "Not that Lindy was with him."

Trey ran a hand over the back of his neck. "I'm afraid it does prove exactly that."

"Please, Trey, I'm begging you, don't do this." Even as she pleaded with him, she knew he wouldn't do as she asked.

He clamped his lips together and didn't answer.

"That's what I thought. You're as stubborn as your pig-headed father. I don't know why I thought you were any different. I'm going home to Mama. Leave me and my family alone. I pray to God that Jace is halfway to Canada by now."

Without responding, he got up, dressed and went outside.

Too angry to react for a minute, Summer gasped like a fish out of water. Her fingers closed around a nubby pillow. Holding it over her head, she heaved it at the wall with a grunt. Livid, she chucked another one and then another until she had bared the bed of all pillows. Panting with rage, she laid down.

Tears streamed down her face and she swiped at them with trembling hands.

How could Trey have gone from saying he believed in Jace less than an hour ago to siccing the Chief on him in the next breath? She had been a fool to have faith in him. Trusting any member of the Bouché family was always wrong, wrong, wrong. Not a mistake she'd make again. In fact, the sooner she got out of here the better.

Her clothes had to be around here somewhere.

She gathered everything but her bra. When she didn't immediately find the missing underwear, she crawled along the bed and felt under the edge of it. She gasped when her middle finger bumped into something sharp. She realized she had run her finger into a carpet tack. She knew it wasn't going to stop trickling blood without a bandage of some sort. There should be a first aid kit in the bathroom.

Holding her bleeding finger, she went in search of a Band-Aid.

A large metal box had the first aid insignia across it. She opened it, but instead of Band-Aids and ointments there was a scrap of material inside. Curious, she pulled out a pink satin bra. If one wanted to call the scrap of shiny pink material a bra. A jagged rip ran up the seam, and on closer inspection she found tiny, dark spots that could only be one thing. Blood.

Lindy.

Summer's hand went numb. First Jace's prison uniform, now torn lingerie with blood on it. Emily Bouché wouldn't have ever been caught dead in something like this, and Summer doubted any other woman had been on the Chief's boat in recent years. Not any woman who would wear something like this anyway.

As soon as the Chief got word Jace had been here, he would either come himself or send someone to investigate. If Summer replaced the bra the police, like her, would conclude the only reasonable explanation was that Jace had hurt Lindy. The state of it suggested Lindy hadn't been a willing visitor. What to do? If Summer replaced the clothing, and the police found it, Jace would be in even more trouble. But if she hid it and Jace had done something to Lindy, then Summer would be guilty of aiding and abetting.

She had no choice. If the Chief found out Jace had hurt Lindy he would be even more relentless in finding and punishing him. Summer looked desperately for a place to hide the evidence. Wearing only a T-shirt and khaki shorts, she had no obvious place to smuggle anything. It might fit inside her pocket.

She folded the hot pink bra into a two-inch square and stuffed it in her back pocket. Feeling like a top CIA agent, she made her way back to the living room where, from this angle, she spotted her own bra stuffed in the back of the sofa. Jerking it on, she couldn't help but wonder how Lindy had come to lose her undergarment.

Chapter Sixteen

Trey watched Summer stomp by him, but he couldn't reason with her right then. The Chief was on the other end of the phone barking at him. Torn between chasing Summer and finding Lindy, Trey stayed on the phone. They had something that might lead them to Jace. If they knew for sure Jace didn't have her, they could concentrate somewhere else.

"Stay put. I'm going to send Jody right out there," the Chief ordered.

"Okay. I'll be here." Trey hung up and leaned against the boat railing and looked to the dusty lavender horizon. He hadn't taken any pleasure in telling the Chief he'd found a clue to Jace's whereabouts.

He didn't blame Summer for being mad, but she had to understand his position. If he did nothing, he would never forgive himself. He couldn't imagine Jace harming Lindy…but he had been convicted of killing Soloman in cold blood. If he was capable of that act, he could do anything. Trey had told Summer the truth, he did have doubts about Jace having Lindy, but it didn't change the past.

He knew Summer hoped the picture held a clue that would exonerate Jace, but Trey couldn't see how. He could at least look into the picture; see what he could find out. The Chief wouldn't tell him anything. But maybe his mother would—if she were up to it. He'd talk to her in the morning. Maybe she could answer Summer's questions. Although he didn't know if Summer would listen to anything he had to say now.

The sound of an approaching car interrupted his thoughts.

Jody drove up and parked. Then joined him on the deck, frowning. "Man, are you cursed or something? First of all you and I find Jimmy Ray's body, now you dig up Lindy's clothes."

Trey shook his head. "Coincidence."

Jody didn't look convinced. "Maybe."

Trey ran a hand over the back of his neck. Why was Jody giving him a hard time? "I just stumbled over the skirt."

"Where?"

"Under the bed." Trey parted with the information reluctantly.

Jody's eyebrows shot up. "Where's the evidence?"

Trey motioned toward the boat. He wasn't going to tell Jody he'd been here with Summer, or why. Until he had time to speak to his mother, he didn't want to share anything about the picture either. "It's below. I went below to look around and the skirt was crammed under the bed. I called the Chief as soon as I found it."

"The Chief put out an APB on Lindy. There was already one for Jace; she's included now. Anyone who resembles either one of them will be pulled over and searched," Jody said.

He took out his fingerprinting supplies and began to dust every flat surface with a fine black dust, then laid a wide strip of tape over it. "Some of these will be useless. The Chief's, yours, even those left by Lindy won't mean anything if she's been here before. You're going to have some explaining to do to explain Summer's though."

Trey jerked. "Summer? What does she have to do with anything?"

"Her prints are bound to show up." Jody lifted a piece of tape and placed it in a plastic bag. "Not to mention that dollar-sized hickey you're wearing is a pretty good clue she was here. Nobody else turns you on like she does, so I put two and two together."

Trey covered his neck. "Shit."

"Yeah. I've been waiting for you to tell me what she was doing out her with you, but I guess I know." Grinning, Jody said, "It's taken a while, but it's about time the two of you took a ride on the love machine."

"It's not like that." He wasn't going to discuss he and Summer's lovemaking with Jody or anyone else. He never had before; he wouldn't now.

Jody stared at him. "What is it with you? I never saw two people crazier about each other who just can't make it work. What's the problem with just shutting everyone else out?"

"I had to tell the Chief about that." Trey motioned to the incriminating scrap of material. "You can imagine how well that went over."

Jody squeezed Trey's shoulder. "Sorry, man."

"Yeah."

"I'm about done. Let's get out of here." Jody packed his supplies.

• • •

Summer floored her old car. Hot tears flooded her eyes. She wanted only to get home and try to prepare for the inevitable. Somehow, she had to figure out how to brace both herself and Mama for Jace's capture and subsequent return to Angola. Now that they had a clear clue the Chief and his men would be relentless in finding their quarry. Closing her eyes, she said a quick prayer for Jace's safety. She hoped he would keep his head and give himself up without a fight. If he didn't, he might be shot.

At the speed she was driving, the trip to town only took a few minutes. Slowing automatically as she approached the beauty shop, she glanced at the windows as she drove by. Although it was almost two A.M., the lights were on inside. Still steaming, and not wanting to go home, she pulled a U-turn and drove in beside Glory's aqua Taurus and parked. As she got out, a shadow fell across her door. Startled, she looked up into Galen's lopsided frown.

"Hello, Galen." She wasn't in the mood to visit with him tonight. The vacant, dull look in his eyes gave her a shiver. Still, she made an effort to be polite. "How are you?"

"Not very good." He lumbered out of the way when she opened her door and climbed out.

"What's wrong?" She stifled her impatience. He meant well and didn't deserve her wrath. A few minutes spent with him didn't hurt her and made him feel good.

He shuffled his big feet in the red dirt and a cloud of pink dirt flowed up around his ragged overall hems. His gaze was locked on the ground. "Miz Glory is mad at me."

"Why? What did she say?" Sometimes Galen earned a little money by hauling trash or supplies for the beauty shop or Bill, the owner of the Dairy Queen across the street. Afterward, Galen often hung around the Curl Up and Dye waiting for a chance to talk to Summer.

"She told me to go away and not come back." He did his little dance again. "I just want to help."

She patted his bare, grimy arm. "I'm sure she didn't mean anything by it. Why don't you come back tomorrow and see if there's something we need you to do then?"

A lopsided grin split his triple-chinned face. "Yeah. That is what I will do."

"Okay. See you then." Waiting until he trudged away, Summer turned to go inside. What was wrong with Glory that she had snapped at Galen? Not ever a big fan of his, Glory still wasn't normally short with him either.

When Summer stepped inside, there was no sign of Glory, but the washing machine in the back room was running and the radio played a Johnny Cash tune. The overwhelming scent of bleach filled the air. "Glory? Are you around?"

"Back here." She popped her head out of the door leading to the small room where they had a sink and a washer and dryer. "What're you doing out at this time of night?"

Summer poured them both a glass of iced tea and sat at her station. "Nothing."

In a minute, Glory joined her, carrying a red-stained towel. It looked like Glory had touched up her vibrant auburn color again. She hated dark roots. The red dye was next to impossible to get out of their towels. "What's up? Shouldn't you be with your mama?"

"I called and Mama's fine." Summer toyed with a brush. "I saw your car in the parking lot, and I didn't want to go home, so I thought I'd see what you were doing." Summer dropped the brush and spun her chair from side to side. She glanced at the back room. "What's up?"

"I couldn't sleep either and I was just catching up on the towels. They were stacking up and I want to be ready for tomorrow. We've got a very heavy day ahead of us. Lots of bookings." She sipped her tea. "Nothing interesting. What are you doing here?"

Summer avoided the question. "Did you yell at Galen about something? He was outside sulking. Said you told him to go away."

Surprise flitted across Glory's face for a second. "Oh, yeah. He was sitting on the step, mooning around as usual. I told him to go on home."

"Oh. Well, he took off." Summer didn't think Glory was telling the complete truth, but dropped it. Her mind was still on Trey and what had happened between them.

Glory eyed her. "You didn't stop to talk about Galen. What's on your mind? Your brother? Have you heard anything?"

Tears gathered at the corners of her eyes and Summer brushed them away. "Yeah, sorta. I went to the Chief's boat to meet Trey. He found a skirt that he's sure belongs to Lindy and a jumpsuit with Jace's number on it. Trey got all excited and called his dad…"

Glory held up her hand. "What? Wait. You lost me. You went to meet the hot guy? Why? Tell me about the suit, but I want all the juicy details about hunky Trey."

"It's a long story." Summer leaned back in her chair and glanced at her pale reflection in the mirror. She played with the ends of her hair. Anything to avoid Glory's knowing gaze.

"Well, spill it. I have all night." Glory's eager voice pierced her reluctance. "Why did you go to see Trey?"

"Because I have this picture that I wanted him to see…" Her voice trailed off. The picture. She didn't have it. Trey did. The last time she'd seen it, he had been picking it up from where she'd dropped it on the ground. Crap. Somehow, she'd have to get it back. That meant seeing him again.

"See what?" Glory prompted.

Summer didn't really want to get into any of this with Glory. But she should've known better. When she shot a glance Glory's direction, she had leaned forward, her freckled cleavage spilling out of her low-cut purple top. "Picture? Of what? Was it something naughty?" She licked her glossed lips and arched her penciled brows.

With a sigh, Summer said, "I found this picture with five people in it, including my mother, Trey's mother, Leroy Eaton, Buford Krebbs, and," she took a breath, "Deke Soloman."

Glory's mouth fell open. "What?"

"It gets worse," Summer said. "Trey's mother is sitting on that nasty man's lap and they're drinking. They look like they're having one big, happy party. It makes me sick when I think about it. And it doesn't end there. What if the Chief somehow knew his sainted wife and my mama were partying before the rape? Do you think it might've colored his response to her? I don't want to believe he'd be so awful, but it makes me wonder."

"My God," Glory breathed. "Do you know when this was, or where it happened? It opens a whole suitcase full of worms and questions, doesn't it?"

Summer shrugged helplessly. "Not a clue when or where. That's what I wanted to see Trey about. I couldn't think of anyone else to ask. Mama's out of the question; so is Emily Bouché. I just can't talk to Buford Krebbs. He's so nasty toward me and if his wife gets wind of this, she'll spread it all over town. Trey seemed like the logical person to talk to about it. I thought if we put our heads together we might be able to help Jace."

"How could you help him by knowing where the picture was taken?" Glory asked.

"Not so much where, but when. I think it was the night Trey and Jace graduated from high school. Mama is wearing the dress she had on when she was raped. She never wore it before or after. But that isn't the important thing. What matters is that all of those people were with Soloman. Maybe one of them had a reason to kill him. It's a long shot, but it's worth checking out." She took a long, shuddering breath.

"Did Trey come up with anything?" Glory's voice trembled. "Because if you did, justice has to be served. The real killer should be punished."

"No," Summer said miserably. "Trey found Lindy's skirt and the picture was kind of forgotten. And I won't ask again."

"Even if it means your brother's freedom?" Glory sat back and crossed her arms. "You don't exactly have a choice, do you?"

"I guess not," Summer said reluctantly. She didn't want to see Trey.

• • •

The scent of pine and black Mississippi dirt blew in the windows as Trey drove back toward Juliet. After Jody left, he'd spent the night on the boat, unwilling to go home. He inhaled, enjoying the clean scent. His mind turned in another direction. Summer.

His good feeling disappeared. Things always seemed to go wrong between them.

His mind drifted to the picture.

Leroy Eaton had been in it. His place wasn't far from here. Maybe Trey could sneak in and find something that would tie Leroy to his mother and the others. He slowed, checking mailbox addresses for Eaton. Trey realized Shantytown was less than a mile away, not that it mattered. He nearly missed the mailbox, hidden under an untrimmed mound of kudzu. The dirt road snaked off the narrow highway. Making a U-turn, he turned up the overgrown road, hoping he didn't tear the bottom out of the Mustang.

After a bone-jarring ride that seemed to go on forever, Trey pulled into a clearing. Leroy's place was filled with piles of junk, mostly twisted, rusted parts that took up every inch of available space. A few goats grazed in a weedy field. When a half-dozen tethered hounds began howling at his arrival, the goats scattered like buckshot. Trey spotted a dilapidated singlewide trailer on flat tires sitting back in the edge of the trees.

A pickup with a paint job that looked over a decade old sat in the yard. He parked next to it and stepped out. Taking care not to stumble over the stacks of odds and ends, he walked to the door and tried the doorknob. To his surprise, the house was locked. No one bolted their doors in Juliet. Not even at *LeFleur*.

Glancing around, he wondered where Leroy had killed himself. Maybe the barn, more of a shed really. Trey made his way through thigh-high weeds, hoping no snakes lurked there. He passed an old-fashioned hand pump, avoiding the mud puddle at its base.

At his approach, the goats surrounded him, nuzzling, looking for a treat. Pushing them out of the way, he went inside the barn. Not certain it wouldn't fall over on him, he stopped right inside the doorway and let his eyes adjust to the dim interior. When his pupils widened enough to focus, he cursed aloud.

A milking stool lay on its side.

Someone drove up as Trey was leaving the shed.

Jody. As he drew close he said, "What's up with you? Every time I turn around, you're tripping over a body or something. I'm beginning to think you're somehow involved in this whole thing."

Trey shook his head. "There's nothing that connects me to all of these incidents. Eaton has no links to me at all."

Jody didn't look convinced. "Why'd you come here?"

"Eaton and Buford Krebbs were arguing at the picnic. I thought I might find a clue as to what they were fighting about."

"Old men argue about the weather," Jody grumped. "But it is a bit suspicious that Eaton committed suicide the same day. What were they talking about?"

"I thought maybe what happened with Soloman and Jace." Trey parted with this reluctantly. He was reaching. Saying it out loud sounded ridiculous.

Jody's eyebrows shot up. "Why would those men have anything to add to that old story?"

"I don't know. The murder and everything that went on around it was the biggest thing that ever happened in Juliet. They were talking about Jimmy Ray and when Leroy said it was just like last time, it struck a chord with me. I knew it was a long shot, but I just wanted to see if there was anything to my theory." He kept the picture to himself. He wanted to figure out what it meant on his own.

"Did either of them act suicidal at the picnic?" Jody asked.

"Not particularly. But Leroy did act a little weird when Krebbs shut him up." Trey frowned trying to remember if Leroy had given any clues to how upset he actually was. Nothing came to mind.

"You didn't see any signs that he planned to go home and kill himself? What about Krebbs? Anything weird with him?" Jody waited while Trey thought about it.

"No, nothing." Nothing jumped out at him.

Jody sighed. "Juliet is turning into a regular crime bed."

Chapter Seventeen

Jace slept most of the day.

Lindy guessed his adrenaline had finally run down and exhaustion had set in. To occupy herself, she'd painted her fingernails and toenails with some of the supplies Candy had brought her. But when she'd reached for the makeup kit, Jace's words from the previous night rang in her ears *"This God-awful color. You used to have the most beautiful sunny hair. And your face. What's with all this junk on it? Candy might need all that crap, but you're too pretty to do that to yourself."*

She applied a touch of mascara and a light pink tint to her lips. Would he approve? No matter. Her opinion was the only one that counted.

If she weren't a strong-minded person, she wouldn't have been able to stand up to the Chief for the last year. If he had his way, she'd be enrolled in Ole Miss or Vanderbilt. She sure wouldn't have run with Candy and her crowd if she had any worries about what most of the town thought. And she wouldn't be in love with a convicted murderer.

In love?

She knew she was in her heart.

Although she had no doubts about Jace's innocence, she wished there was a way to prove it. Together, they had racked their brains but hadn't come up with anything viable. There had to be something they'd overlooked. A clue had to point to the real killer. But where? Lindy snapped her fingers. She spoke aloud. "That's it. The Chief's files. If there's something, that's where it'll be."

She almost danced to the bedroom door to tell Jace her idea. He lay sprawled across the bed his face pillowed in his arms. For a minute, she just stared at him awestruck. The muscles in his bare back mesmerized her. She longed to trace their path with her fingertips. Her gaze dropped to his magnificent ass. Encased in Levi's that had to be an old pair belonging to Trey, his ass begged to be caressed by a woman's hands. *Her hands.* She swallowed.

"See something you like?" Jace turned his head, lids hooded.

She shrugged. "I've seen better."

He rolled over and crossed his arms behind his head; his triceps pulling tight like rubber bands. The top button on his jeans was undone. A thin line of pale blonde hair beginning at his chest disappeared there. "Oh yeah? On skinny old Jimmy Ray? He wasn't exactly a muscle man."

"I don't know. His muscles didn't matter." She did her best to paste on a nonchalant look and pretend not to let on that Jace's flat, bare belly made her tingle in private places. "I'm not into jocks."

"What are you into then? Drug dealers with earrings and lotsa tattoos?" His grin went wicked. "Or cons who swear they're innocent?"

Yeah, I'm into you, brickhead. She wanted to scream it at him, but shrugged again. "I like guys who aren't afraid to be different. Who think for themselves."

He snorted. "Sure. I bet every guy you ever brought home was a perfect little clone of ole Daddy. Nice little college boys who only wanted to do the right thing. Bet you never even spoke to anybody Daddy wouldn't approve of before you got tangled up with Jimmy Ray."

Why was he pressing her? The truth was he hit too close to home for comfort. She hadn't dated much, and the boys she had gone out with had been safe. Even Candy's crowd had been under her spell. Jimmy Ray had been her one mistake. She'd underestimated him. All the others had been easy to control. "Why do you care?"

"I don't." He placed one foot on the other knee.

She pretended not to notice how the action pulled the denim jeans tight over his bulging crotch. "Then quit talking about this."

He grinned wickedly. "Why? You're the one who's started it."

Frustrated, she snapped her mouth shut. She wasn't going to win this battle.

"Wanna finish it?" His smile disappeared and the look in his eyes made her blood run fast, and her knees shake.

"What if I said yes?"

"I'd say you were trying to piss off your old man." The teasing was gone from his voice. He sounded bitter, mean. "I'd say you wanted to use me to get even."

"Then you're a bigger idiot than I thought you were." A wave of humiliation washed over her. She'd told him the truth in a moment of weakness and he threw it back in her face like a used hankie. She turned away to hide her embarrassment.

"Lindy." His voice slipped across her skin like a velvet robe.

Her back to him, she halted.

She didn't hear him move, but in the blink of an eye he stood at her back, his palms on her shoulders. The heat seared her and she flinched away from it. "What?"

"Wait." His word floated across her ears and she shivered.

"Why?" she managed. Every inch of her was on edge, ready to explode in every direction. The tiniest thing could shatter her. She stiffened her body in preparation for his next assault. He turned her around, gentler than she expected. The pupils dominated his dark blue eyes. She couldn't look away. It was if she stared into a magic glass reflecting her future. Desperately, she tried to read the message hidden there.

"I could stand being used by you."

Not the prettiest apology ever, but it would do. She slugged him in the stomach as hard as she could, but he didn't even flinch. "Don't say that again."

"Okay." The expression on his face frightened her, the look in his eye changed to one of something she'd never seen before. Her breath caught in her throat and she backed up until her spine was pressed against the doorjamb. With nowhere to run, she lifted her chin. She touched her dry lips with her tongue. What had she done? There was no going back this time.

Slowly, like a lion stalking its prey, he moved in for the kill. Cupping the back of her neck with his hand, he brought her mouth to his. He tasted her lips with a gentleness that surprised her. With tiny nibbles at the corner of her mouth he teased until she opened her lips and their tongues met in a tentative touch. Slowly at first, they tasted each other. Unclenching her fists, Lindy touched the flat, sculpted plane of his chest. Under her seeking hands his skin was warm; a light path of soft hair tickled her fingers.

He deepened the kiss.

Lindy drank in the sensation of his tongue and passion-warmed skin. She moved closer, mashing her hands between them. He allowed her to explore his chest, and she longed to search every inch of him. Her breasts, pressed into him, ached for attention. A damp heat beaded between her thighs and she instinctively spread her legs so that his jean-clad erection pushed against her belly.

He took his mouth from hers and brushed it across her forehead. "Do you want me?"

Yes! Yes! She couldn't have spoken then if the whole world waited. Instead, she nodded her head.

He tipped her chin up and their eyes met. "Say it."

She tried to look away, but he held her chin fast. "I…I want you."

"There's no one here, but you and me," he said. "Not your daddy or Jimmy Ray or anybody else."

"What are you saying?" She stared into his fathomless blue eyes. "I know what I'm doing."

He loosened his grip, but held her still. "You have to be ready. I can't deal with it if this is just one of your games to piss off your daddy."

He thought she used sex as a weapon. Why wouldn't he? He hadn't seen any evidence otherwise. She took a deep breath as heat burned up her cheeks. "I have to tell you something. I…well… um…have waited. For the right time, with the right person."

He dropped her chin like it burned him. "What?"

She felt a hot flush burn over her cheeks. Didn't he get that she was a virgin? "Come on. Don't make me spell it out. I'm saying I haven't slept around."

"Why now? Why me?" He reversed a step. If she hadn't been half offended, she would've laughed.

"I think you know the answer to that." She followed him so that their thighs touched.

He gave his head a quick shake and stepped away again so that the back of his knees bumped into the bed. "No. You don't want me."

"Yes." She stepped forward and touched his chest with one pink-polished nail. "You." She couldn't explain the reason she wanted only him. Weren't there animals that mated for life? She was like them; she'd instinctively chosen her partner. No way was she letting him get away.

"I can't." He sounded like he was drowning. Sweat misted his chest.

What was this? Every other guy she'd had to fight off tooth and nail, and now the one she wanted was saying no? Had prison turned him on to men or something? She frowned. "I don't understand."

He looked wildly for a way around her, but she stood between him and the door. "You don't get it."

"No, I don't. A minute ago you were hot and heavy. Now you're…" She let the sentence drop. She wanted to crawl under the bed and hide from embarrassment. "I'm chasing you around like a dog after a bone."

"Just let it go." He sounded desperate. He looked over her shoulder and she wondered if he was going to jump over her or something.

"What's wrong?" Her embarrassment turned to anger. What had she done to turn him off so suddenly? Maybe she shouldn't have told him she hadn't gone all the way before. Apparently she should've just gone along and pretended to be an old pro. She wasn't naïve. She knew what a man and a woman did in bed together. But it was important for some reason that he know he was the first. "Why won't you tell me?"

"I don't know how to make love to a…virgin." His face blazed bright, deep red. "Happy now?"

Lindy stopped dead. He couldn't have shocked her more if he had hit her in the face. "What? Are you joking? Haven't you done it before?"

"Yes," he ground out between clenched teeth, "I've been with a woman. And no, not any men if you're wondering. I didn't turn in prison. I haven't been with anyone who hasn't had a lot of experience."

"That's good," she said calmly. "So we figure it out together. That's what people who lov…want to be together do."

"I don't want to hurt you." His hand cupped her face and she leaned into it for a moment. "You deserve better. Someone who will be around…"

"There's nothing you can do to me that would hurt me." She turned her face and kissed his palm. "Except not make love to me right now."

She gave him a gentle shove that pushed him backward onto the bed. She landed on top of him, laughing. Her laughter faded at the look of desire on his face. A shiver of delight rocked her. This man was the one. The only one she'd ever wanted. Bending forward, she kissed him.

He wrapped his arms around her with a muffled groan.

Suddenly, all of Lindy's bravado fled.

She couldn't believe she'd been so bold as to tell this man she wanted to sleep with him. Straddling him, all she had to do was roll off and flee. His hands gripped her waist, although she knew he would let her go in an instant. But something held her still. She looked into Jace's eyes and delicious shivers rocked her body. This is where she wanted to be.

Leaning forward, she touched his lips with hers. The gentle kiss lasted only a second before she sat up and studied him. His eyes were closed, his lips parted slightly. Her hands roamed across his bare chest. Slipping her palms across his flat, brown nipples and the light trail of blonde hair trailing down the middle of his chest, she reveled in the sensation. His body, so different from hers, fascinated her.

His chest rose and fell faster, but his hands stayed motionless at her waist as she toured his bare upper half. Like a masseuse she gripped his shoulders, skimming her fingertips down his muscled arms until their hands met and intertwined at her middle. A kind of frustration was building in her. She longed for him to touch her, too. Her nipples pushed against the soft cotton T-shirt she wore and wet heat pooled between her legs. With a gentle tug, she guided his hands under the hem of her shirt, and then dropped them.

Her breath came in short, heavy rushes as his fingers splayed out over her ribs. And stopped. Stealing a glance at his face, she was surprised to find his dark eyes on her, a slight smile on his lips. As she stared, caught in his gaze, he removed his hands from her ribs and caught the back of her head with his palms bringing her down to kiss him again.

This time the kiss wasn't soft or short.

His mouth tore at hers like a starving animal. His tongue plunged in and out of her mouth like a preview of what his body would do with hers. Twist for turn, move for move, they met, retreated; their mouths arcing together like a current. Lindy felt his hands in her hair, holding her to him. Even if she could have, she wouldn't have pulled away. Her body needed to have him inside her, now, and she reached for the waistline of his jeans, her fingers curling around the denim material.

With a quick, seamless move, he rolled over, turning Lindy under him. Their mouths still locked in battle, he released her head and tugged the hem of her gray tee up over her belly and breasts, leaving it pooled under her arms and chin. Leaving go of her mouth, he moved to her right breast and breathed across her sores, now scabbed. His warm breath seemed to heal her. The sensation of him taking her nipple in his mouth was so remarkable she cried out and dug her nails into his belly.

"Did I hurt you?" Tenderly, he kissed the swell of her breast, where she was uninjured.

"No." It was all she could manage.

Somehow he fit his hands between them and slid her denim shorts over her thighs and legs and feet. With trembling fingers she unsnapped his Levi's. Then he took over, removing them himself. Only a tiny scrap of material—a lace thong—stood between them becoming one. Lindy curled her fingers around the edge of the lace and froze as his hand skimmed over hers.

So many sensations were bulleting through her, she couldn't begin to think. Breathing was an effort. His wonderful mouth, tugging at her breast, was making her arch her back. When his finger slid under the lace, across her soaked center, she nearly screamed. Instead, she bit him on the shoulder. His finger slipping inside her made her crazy…mad with a need she'd never had before. Her body began to pulsate, wanting something…more.

No one had ever been this far with her and no one else ever would. No matter what happened after this, she was with the man she wanted. Unaware how tightly she had been stretching the satin strap, she gasped when it snapped. She tasted a metallic, rust-like sensation in her mouth, and pulling back a fraction, she noticed she had drawn blood on his shoulder. Guilt grabbed her and she smoothed her palm over the bruised spot. Leaving it, she moved her hand over his back, to his hip, smearing a trace of blood as she went.

Taking her hand with his, he guided it to his penis. With uncertain movements she circled him with a quaking hand. When he took a harsh indrawn breath, she nearly released him. But if her hand on him felt as good as his did on her, she had to be doing something right. She stroked his soft, yet hard body and he moaned. She did it again. And smiled when he shuddered.

Shifting so that he was again poised over her, he looked into her eyes. His upper lip and brow were misted with a fine sheen of sweat and his arms holding him above her, shook. His erection pressed against the damp blonde curls between her legs. But he didn't enter her.

Her hands fell to her sides. "Jace?"

"You've got to be sure." He sounded like he could barely force the words out. The muscles in his neck corded like an athlete's. "It's not too late to stop."

"I don't want you to stop." Lindy moved her hips, instinctively trying to induce him to enter her. "Don't make me beg. Please?"

He closed his eyes and thrust into her.

Unprepared, Lindy screamed.

He froze.

A pain so intense it seared her insides threatened to tear her apart. Desperate for him to stop, she writhed and pushed at his chest. Tears ran down her cheeks. She tossed her head from side to side. "Can't."

"Shhh." His lips brushed at her tears. He moved a fraction and the pain sharpened.

She couldn't speak. It hurt to breathe. How could the pleasure he had been giving her just disappear? And why had no one ever told her it felt so bad to be united physically with a man? No wonder he said he didn't want to hurt her. He had meant it. God, how did women ever do this more than once? A great, bitter disappointment filled her. She wanted to curl up and cry.

Jace took her face in his hands and kissed her, gently, so tenderly she almost forgot he still had her pinned to the mattress. A slow awakening began in her. Although not comfortable, the ache wasn't as bad. He dipped his head and laved her breasts until her nipples hardened. As he took a pink tip in his damp, hot mouth, her back arched. His mouth loved her as if he had all the time in the world to please her. Tiny tingles began to build inside her. Involuntarily, her body lifted, pressing to his. He moved forward a millimeter and surprised her when it didn't hurt.

He tried again.

The tingles built to tremors.

He rocked his hips forward.

The tremors intensified.

He slid almost out, then back.

The tremors turned to waves.

He pressed deeper.

The waves boiled over, taking her to a crest...and left her hanging there.

Two more strokes and he shuddered and went still.

Slowly, her breathing returned to normal and she began to notice his weight.

"You okay?" he asked near her ear.

"Yeah." Too embarrassed to look at him, and disappointed more than she wanted to admit, she turned her face away and closed her eyes.

"Hey," he took her chin and turned her face toward him, "what's wrong?"

"Nothing." She wanted to be alone to process what had just happened.

"Are you…sorry?" His voice, barely more than a whisper, sounded scared.

She opened her eyes. "No…no."

"Disappointed?" His lips turned down.

She lied. "No. Are you?"

He bent and kissed her collarbone. "Baby, there's nothing you could do that would ever disappoint me."

A small shudder of delight skipped up her spine. The feelings she'd been holding in for years bubbled to the surface, and without thinking she blurted out, "I love you."

His face went stone still and his voice raked over her like a judge pronouncing sentence. "Don't confuse sex, even great sex, with love."

He sounded so much like Jimmy Ray, she wanted to hit him. For a moment she froze. Then she shoved him. "Get off me. And for the record, it wasn't that great. I said it was okay."

He rolled away and put his arm over his eyes as she sprang off the bed, hauling the blanket in her white-knuckled hands. If she let go, she knew she would strike him. "You are such an asshole."

"We agree on that." He sounded resigned. "I keep trying to tell you that, but you just won't listen."

"Well, I'm listening now. I got it. Until we figure out who set you up, you're stuck with me. Then you can go on about your life with no sign of me in your review mirror." She spun away, the blanket trailing behind her. SShe made it to the living room before the tears came, hot and fast.

Collapsing on the couch, she wrapped up in the blanket hoping it would cocoon her from Jace, from her humiliation. How could she have blurted out she loved him like that? She knew sex didn't mean everlasting love and marriage. She had been taken by the moment and blurted out the first thing that came to mind. Swiping at her nose with the edge of the blanket, she let her thoughts run rampant.

So stupid, stupid. A man like Jace wasn't going to fall in love just because he'd had sex. She'd reassured him she could handle it. Hah. She'd be lucky if he'd sit in the same room with her ever again, much less touch her. He probably thought she was planning the wedding right now. As if. The sooner they figured out who had set him up and he could go on about his business, and she hers, the better.

Wiping her tears, she sat up and wrapped her arms around her middle. She had turned her back on her family to be with him. There weren't a lot of options. She couldn't just walk in the front door of *LeFleur* and say, 'Hi, I'm home.' There was only one thing to do.

Put on a who-gives-a-shit face and stick it out until the truth was found.

Throwing off the blanket like a snake shedding its skin, she got up and strode bare as the day she was born into the bathroom and climbed into the bathtub. She lathered her hair then laid back to soak her sore body. Her muscles trembled, her woman's parts ached, but it was the pain in her heart that felt like it would never heal. It would, it had too, she vowed.

No one could live feeling this rotten.

Chapter Eighteen

As Trey entered the driveway at *LeFleur*, he spotted an ambulance and two patrol cars in the driveway. A lump of dread filled his stomach. Jumping out, he sprinted for the door. Had they found Lindy? Or had his mother taken a turn for the worse? Heart pounding, he skidded through the front door.

A flurry of activity at the door of his mother's room drew his attention. Two EMTs, guiding a sheet-draped gurney between them came out of the room, followed by a white-faced Chief.

Trey's gaze shot between the chief and the figure under the sheet. "Mother? No…" Trey took a step, and then faltered. "Chief?"

"Your mother, she…" The strong policeman stumbled a little, looked confused. He seemed incapable of speaking and fell onto the sofa with his hands hanging between his knees. His face had no color and his eyes seemed to have sunk into his head. He appeared to have aged ten years in one afternoon.

"What happened?" Trey didn't wait for an answer and moved toward his mother. His throat closed. He couldn't swallow the lump lodged there.

The EMTs were busy maneuvering the gurney out the sliding glass doors.

"Wait." Slowly, dreading what he would see, Trey approached the shrouded figure. As the EMTs stepped respectfully away, he reached to pull back the sheet. His finger closed around the cool material, his nerves seemed to be outside his skin. He couldn't think straight. When had his mother gotten so tiny?

"Don't." The Chief's voice cracked through the room. "Do not look at her like that."

Trey didn't lift the sheet, but he continued to stare at the shrouded figure, trying to remember his mother's face before she got sick. His heart clenched in a tight knot he didn't think would ever come undone. He had known her death was imminent, but he'd hoped to have more time with her. To be able to come to terms with all the things that would now forever be left unsaid.

He forced himself to nod at the attendants. He dropped the material. As he watched, they rolled the gurney out of the house and placed it in the waiting ambulance. After they closed the doors and drove away without lights, he turned toward the Chief. "Did you find her?"

The Chief's eyes were glazed over. Finally, he nodded.

"Where's Etta?" Trey walked to the bar and poured a bourbon—neat, the way the Chief liked it—and brought it to him.

Holding the drink with a shaking hand, but not raising it to his lips, the Chief said, "There's a note in the kitchen. She got called away. There was an emergency at her niece's house. Your mother was sleeping. Etta thought it would be okay to leave her alone for an hour or so."

"Mother passed while Etta was gone?" Trey sat next to the Chief, wanting to put his arm around his shoulders to comfort both of them somehow. But he knew his father wouldn't welcome it. "She died alone?"

He raised bleary eyes. "Your mother was murdered. Hill came in this house and smothered your mother with her own pillow."

"What?" Trey rocketed to his feet. This obsession was getting out of hand. Why wouldn't the Chief admit there might have been someone else who could have killed Soloman? And why would he think Jace would want to kill his wife? "You don't mean that. Who would want to murder Mother? She had a terminal illness. All this death has affected the way you're thinking. Leroy hung himself today. Jimmy Ray Hunt a day ago. That's it."

"I have proof." The Chief waved a trembling hand toward his wife's room. "See for yourself."

With disbelief in his heart, Trey trudged into his mother's sickroom. Normally dim, with low lights and the shades pulled, it now blazed with every light. The unpleasant scent of a stuffy hospital room and the lingering stench of her cancer assaulted his nose and he tried to ignore it. Nothing looked out of place. Her silver brush, comb, and mirror on the dresser looked exactly the same. He didn't touch the rows of medicine on the tray next to her bed. The closet stood empty, save several silk robes. Mother's clothes would be in the closet upstairs in the bedroom she'd shared with the Chief for twenty-five years.

What proof did the Chief think was here? Trey glanced at her unmade hospital bed and the pillow lying there. He averted his eyes then moved toward it. Glancing toward the door he saw the officers busy in the bathroom. They hadn't dusted in here yet. With a flick of his wrist he turned over the pillow.

Leaning close, he saw it.

A strand of dark hair.

He took a pair of clear plastic gloves Etta used off the nightstand and slipped one on. Then he picked up the hair and stuck it inside and empty medicine bottle. Jerking off the glove, he stuffed it and the bottle in his pocket.

The hair wasn't his mother's.

It was auburn.

He stuck his head in the bathroom door and froze. Two officers stood with their backs to him. One of them aimed a camera at the mirror and the resulting flash ricocheted off the surface, straight into Trey's face. Blinded for a moment, he wasn't sure he saw what his eyes were telling him when he could see again.

Etched across the mirror in bright, blood red lipstick were the words:

Two down

Two to go

Trey looked and looked again, not sure his eyes were seeing things correctly. Two down and two to go? Lindy and now his mother. Were the next two he and the Chief? Who had left the evil message? Had the writer killed his mother in cold blood? Why? One thing was certain—when he found out who had done this Trey would kill him with his bare hands.

The dark-haired policewoman saw him and frowned. "You can't be in here, sir. This is a crime scene."

Numbly, he nodded and backed out.

The Chief hadn't moved. He stared into the amber liquid within the glass held between his hands. Trey walked over and sat beside him, searching for healing words.

"Did you see the message?"

"Yes, sir, I did." He wanted to deny it, to push the awful image out of his head. But he couldn't. Someone had been in his mother's bathroom and left a note of hate scribbled across her mirror. "Why would someone want to hurt Mother and Lindy?"

"I'll tell you who. Jace Hill, that's who. He snuck in here and smothered your mother in her bed." Some of the bourbon in his glass splashed to the floor. "He took my daughter. She's probably laying dead in a swamp somewhere. He's out there laughing at us right now."

"How do you know Jace did these things?" Trey tried to remain the voice of reason. His mother's death had made the Chief's blind obsession worse.

"Did you see what he said?" the Chief asked. "'Two down'? That means your sister and your mother. He motioned between them. "'Two to go.' That means you and me. Half of our family is gone. If we don't hunt down Hill and put him back in a cage where he belongs, you'll be next. He'll save me for last to punish me."

"Sir, shouldn't we let the officers do their job? Maybe they'll come up with a whole different scenario." Trey wanted to distract the Chief from his vendetta. "For all we know, there might be a serial killer on the loose. Three people have died this weekend."

"It was Hill," the Chief insisted. "If you weren't packing a hard-on for his sister, you'd see it too. Your poor mother isn't even cold an hour and you're jumping to every excuse you can come up with to cover for that girl. Face it; Hill smothered Emily in her own bed."

Trey flinched at the image of his former best friend holding pillow over his frail, cancer-ridden mother's face as she fought for her life. If Jace had done this thing, Trey would pull the switch himself. Even Summer couldn't defend him. "Don't you find it odd that two other people have died this week, sir? Jimmy Ray Hunt and Leroy Eaton."

The Chief shifted his weight. "What are you suggesting? That your mother had some connection with a lowlife like Jimmy Ray Hunt? Emily didn't even realize white trash like that existed. And Leroy? He hung himself for one reason. He was a manic-depressive. I've known it for years."

"He seemed okay at the picnic yesterday, sir," Trey said mildly. Leroy had been a little odd, but he hadn't seemed so depressed that he would go home and hang himself in his barn within an hour.

"Leroy was a master of deception." The Chief sipped his drink and stared at the opposite wall. "Always pretending, always hiding from things that hurt him."

"Like what, sir?" Focusing on something but his mother kept Trey's grief at bay. If he stopped for a moment and let it knock him down he didn't know if he could get back up.

"He's been in love with my wife forever. I knew it all along, but he never acted disrespectful, so I left it alone. They died on the same day. Leroy would like that, if he knew."

Trey felt his mouth drop open. The quiet little barber had carried a torch for Emily? He'd hidden it well. "Leroy Eaton was in love with my mother?"

"Sure. We all were. Me, him, Tom down at the grocery store. Even old Buford Krebbs carried a torch for Miss Emily Devereaux." He snorted. "Course if I'd married old dog-faced Viola I'd be eyein' other women, too. Buford looked past Viola's shortcomings toward her daddy's money. But I was the lucky one, the man Emily picked. I won the prize. A fine lady, indeed. I didn't care a lick about her daddy's fortune. Never did understand why a sweet woman like her would pick a poor old goat like me, but she did."

"She loved you, sir." Trey's throat grew tight again. He'd never doubted their love for one another. They hadn't been great parents, but they had been good to one another. His father had always worshiped Emily, treated her like a china doll in a case. As if she were too good to be touched.

"Most men aren't so lucky." The Chief looked at him with hate-glazed eyes. "I'll hunt down the man who did this to her and see him fry. You better make a choice, boy, whose side you're standing on. If it's mine, or it's with the Hills. There isn't room for any ifs, ands, or maybes."

"Sir, Summer or MiLann can't be held responsible for something Jace may have done. We don't even know for sure he's the killer." Trey knew he was wasting his breath. The Chief had made up his mind and nothing Trey could say was going to change it. If he pursued a relationship with Summer, he could forget about his father. He reached out to touch the Chief then dropped his hand midway. "Mother wouldn't want us to blame them."

With unexpected violence, the Chief hurled his glass at the wall. "I don't want to think about anyone or anything except your mother right now."

Before Trey could answer, the front door swung open and Etta rushed in, tears streaming down her wrinkled cheeks. "Is it true? Oh, God in Heaven, tell me it isn't so. Say my Miss Emily isn't gone. Oh, Lordy. I just stepped out for a minute."

Trey rose and hugged her. "I'm sorry."

"Why'd you leave her at all?" The Chief's voice was freezer cold.

"It was Lilah," Etta explained through her tears. "I got a call from her house saying she was hurt and needed a ride to the hospital. I rushed over there fast as my ole bones could carry me. But when I got there, she was sittin' on the couch pretty as you please. Eatin' supper and watchin' her program. I was a little put out. I sure was."

"Who did you actually talk to?" Trey asked.

Etta moved out of his arms and blew her nose into a crumpled hankie. "I don't know for sure. I was in the kitchen, cookin' a nice roast…well, that don't matter does it? The phone rang and I took the call. Someone told me to rush right over to Lilah's place, that she was in trouble. I didn't do more than turn down my stove and drove straight over there."

"You didn't recognize the voice?" Trey asked.

Etta shook her head. "No, sir, I didn't. I was so afraid, I just took off. Miss Emily was sleepin'. I figured she'd be okay for a bit."

"You thought wrong." The Chief held not one ounce of compassion in his voice for the woman who'd been part of his family for three decades. "Dead wrong."

"Chief. Sir. It's not her fault." Trey understood his father's rage, but Etta wasn't to blame. If she had been here, she probably would've died, too. Someone had set her up, called her out of the house. He squeezed her upper arms then let her go.

"Sir? Chief?" The young policewoman stood at the door. "Will you come here, please? I need to show you something."

When Trey would've gone with him, the policewoman shook her head. "This is an investigation. You can't be in here."

The Chief plodded toward his wife's bedroom. At the door, he turned. "While I'm gone you best decide what matters to you.

•••

Trey was up at dawn.

In truth, he hadn't slept at all. The Chief had refused to tell him anything the police had found. He had left with them and still hadn't returned. Trey figured he had probably spent the night at his office. He stirred his coffee without really seeing it. He'd been sitting in the kitchen for an hour or more.

A small figure moved at the corner of his vision, and he started. *Lindy?*

"Didn't mean to scare you none," Etta said, slipping out of the shadows. She trudged to the fridge and got out orange juice and a bowl of eggs.

"Why are you up so early?" Trey swallowed his disappointment and straddled one of the barstools, watching Etta pour two glasses of juice.

She handed him one and turned to the stove. "I'm sure the Chief will be needing a meal. He's got a busy day ahead of him. Soon as word gets out about Miz Emily, peoples will be comin' in droves. Everyone sure loved her." Etta's small shoulders stooped forward.

Trey took two steps and enfolded her from behind. Sobs shook her small frame. He kissed the top of her cotton-white head. "Mother knew how much you cared for her." She nodded and wiped her eyes with the corner or her apron. "I'm sorry, too, for the way the Chief spoke to you last night."

It wasn't his job to apologize, but Trey knew how badly the Chief had wounded Etta. She had taken care of their family since the day Emily Devereaux married Samuel Bouché twenty-six years ago. This was her family. There wasn't anything she wouldn't do for any one of them.

"Oh, pshaw. He don't mean nothin' when he sounds off like that. He's just like an old hound who barks first and feels bad later." She slipped out of his arms and picked up the eggs. "I just let it be when he snaps. I know he don't mean it."

She was a better person than Trey was. The wounds the Chief had inflected on him would last a lifetime. The key was learning how to let go and not hold onto the bitterness. He watched Etta move about the kitchen, busy preparing a meal no one would have an appetite for. His mind was on Lindy. Somehow, he had to find her today. If she didn't hear about their mother and come home for the funeral, she might never get over it.

Etta set a steaming plate of scrambled eggs, ham, and toast in front of him and refreshed his dark chicory coffee. He had no appetite, but he picked at it to make her happy. He patted the chair next to him. "Sit with me. Please?"

Pouring herself a cup of steaming coffee, she sat across from him. Her small, gnarled fingers curled around her mug. "I can't linger. Your daddy will be needing me to pick out something for Miz Emily to be wearing. She'll want to look nice to meet her maker. Yes, sirree, Miz Emily did love her fancy clothes."

"Yes." He couldn't remember a time his mother hadn't been pulled together and elegant. Even during this last week, she had worn satin nightgowns and robes. No hospital garb for Emily Bouché.

Etta's dark eyes searched his face. "Your mama was so happy to see you."

Tears formed in his eyes and he blinked them back. He'd almost been too late. For whatever force had guided him home, he was grateful. He couldn't wish his mother was still suffering, and he prayed she was at peace, but he couldn't help but wish he'd had more time with her. Whoever had stolen her life had also taken her family's last few days with her. A burning fury boiled in his belly. Whoever had done this would pay for their crime.

The Chief's words rang in his ears. *Jace Hill did it. He's the killer.* Trey couldn't believe it. The friend he had known would no more have murdered a helpless woman than cut off his right hand. A threat of revenge from prison was one thing, but to actually carry out a murder was something else all together. Trey was beginning to think the Chief had lost all rationality when it came to Jace. Why did the policeman hate his former family friend so much? Trey couldn't figure it out.

He wondered what the forensic evidence showed. Had the killer left fingerprints or other clues behind? Would the Chief tell him even if he knew? Maybe Jody would if Trey could catch him alone. He wanted to give Jody the hair he'd found, too. Although he wanted to know, to understand what had happened to his mother, it was more pressing to find Lindy.

The phone rang. Trey moved to get it, but Etta beat him to it. He listened as she answered "yes sir" a few times. When she hung up, he waited for her to tell him what the caller said.

"That was your daddy. He just left the coroner." Her voice broke. In a minute, she continued. "He wants you to meet him at his office in twenty minutes."

Trey nodded. He got up and kissed her cheek. "I'll see you later."

"Take care of your daddy. This is the worst day of his life." She swiped at the spotless counter with a dishrag. "Go on. Get. He needs you."

•••

Trey found the Chief in his office. He sat behind his desk, a pile of papers lying in front of him. He looked up with red-rimmed eyes when Trey entered, but didn't speak.

"Sir? You okay?" Trey moved toward the Chief, alarmed by his appearance.

"Sit down." His voice was rough, like he'd been smoking and drinking all night. Or maybe crying.

Trey continued to stand. "What are you doing here? Why don't you come home with me? Get something to eat, try to rest."

Ignoring the suggestion, the Chief said, "I'm going to get that motherfucker once and for all. I should've done it sooner." He waved a hand over the letters scattered in front of him. "I ignored the truth when it kicked me in the face. Hell, I ignored all of them. I thought it was just smoke and mirrors. Look what's happened. Emily's dead. Doc Conner's all set to cut her open like she's a side of beef. And it's all because of my foolishness. I was soft, too soft."

"Chief, slow down. I don't understand. What's your fault?" The image of his mother lying on the coroner's table made Trey's stomach churn. He wondered if the Chief had suffered some kind of breakdown from that same idea. He wasn't making sense.

"I didn't pay attention. That's what's wrong." He swept the pile of letters off the desk with one hand. "And it was the biggest mistake of my life. Believe me now?" The Chief's voice went flat. "Are you ready to admit that your buddy sneaked in during the middle of the night and smothered your mother in her own bed?"

Trey didn't know what to think. He just couldn't wrap his mind around the idea of his childhood friend taking his mother's life. "I don't know," he said finally.

"Believe it. I'm going to order my men to shoot on sight," the Chief said. "An eye for an eye."

Trying to distract him, to dissuade him from his crazy plan, Trey asked, "What did Doc Conner say?"

"He met me at the morgue last night. His first reaction was that the cancer finally beat Emily, but when I told him about the lipstick on the mirror he had a different idea. He's going to do," the Chief's throat worked, "an autopsy."

Trey forced away the picture of his mother's body being subjected to a postmortem examination. "Did the officers find any fingerprints or other evidence left behind?"

"Not a damn thing. Angola must have taught young Hill a few things about crime." He was back in control, his voice again lacking any show of emotion. "But it doesn't matter. I know the truth. I know why he did it and I won't make the mistake of underestimating him again."

"There might be another explanation for Mother's death than automatically assuming Jace did it," Trey said.

"There isn't."

"Have you heard any word on his location? Or anything about Lindy?"

The Chief shook his head. "Not yet. But with every lawman in the South on the lookout, I'm pretty certain we'll tree him any minute. When we do, we'll find your sister. I pray to God he didn't make her suffer too much. If we can recover her body, we can have a double funeral. Your mother would like that."

Trey stared at him like he was a stranger. The Chief talked about Lindy as if she weren't his daughter. Maybe it was how he coped, but his emotionless tone was eerie. Trey knew if he didn't keep his own feelings under a tight rein, he was going to lose it. He had a lot of practice at forcing down emotions, and he fell back on the years of training he'd received now. Just get the job done, think about it later. He couldn't allow himself to hurt. He had to remain in control and find Lindy. The Chief didn't seem capable of making a rational decision right now.

Trey didn't have a lot of practice with planning funerals, but he knew there was a lot of work ahead of them. There were a lot of decisions to be made. Where to hold the service, who to conduct it, what kind of music and on and on. "Do you want Etta to do anything about arrangements?"

The Chief stared blankly at him for a minute. Then he said, "Tell her to go see Preacher Finn. Tell her to tell him your mother died, not how, mind you, but let him know that much at least. On second thought, you go."

"No, sir." Trey stood. "I'm not going to leave you until you've thought this through.

"No time for that now. I have a man to find." The Chief's eyes glowed with a feverish glint.

"Make time." Trey knew the Chief was crazy with grief and not thinking straight. "Or at least let me go with you."

"No, I'm going alone. If you have something to say to me, you can radio me." He stood and went to the locked cabinet in the corner. Unlocking it, he withdrew a shotgun. "I'll be in the field until I find what I'm looking for. I'm going to skin Hill like a rabbit."

"Chief, you can't mean to go out and shoot Jace Hill in cold blood. That makes you no better than he is." Trey didn't believe Jace had killed his mother, but if he had, he deserved all the law would do to him. But not vigilante justice. Jace had been wrong to deal it out, and this was just as wrong now. The Chief had tipped over the edge where Jace was concerned. Why?

Busy loading shells in the gun, the Chief didn't look up. "Don't you see? It's the only way. He has to pay."

There wasn't a soul alive who could stop the Chief when he was rational, much less like this. Still, Trey tried. "No, sir, I don't see. What I see is a dangerous obsession with a man who has been paying his debt to society. You have no proof he killed Mother or took Lindy."

"I have all the proof I need." He hoisted the gun to his shoulder and aimed at the wall.

Trey changed tactics. "You're needed here. When word gets out about Mother, folks will want to see you, talk to you."

"There'll be plenty of time for talking later." He stood and carrying the gun, moved around the desk. "Go on, get now. I'm not going to sit around and wait for that boy to come to me. I'm going to set things straight myself. I've waited too long."

Angling in front of him, Trey said, "I'm not going to let you do this. It's wrong."

A grim smile covered the Chief's face. "I'm finally making things right. You don't have anything to say about it."

"You're wrong. I'm not a kid anymore who you can send out of the country because it's not convenient to answer questions or dig deeper for the truth. I'm not going to be set aside again. Until I know the truth of what has happened, I'm going to stand right here. It's time you answered some of my questions."

The Chief tried to shoulder past him. "Get out of my way."

Trey spread his feet and dug in his heels. "No, sir."

"Move, boy."

"Why are you so set on Jace as the killer?" Trey wasn't going to budge an inch until he had some answers.

"Because he did it." His face turned red and the vein in his forehead throbbed. He pointed to the pile of papers on the floor. "You saw the letters with your own eyes. That's proof enough."

"They're no proof at all," Trey shot back. "All they are is a bunch of threats. There's got to be another reason you want Jace so bad. What is it? Since the day he escaped, you've been determined to prove that he's the one whose wrecked havoc around here. What's behind your reasoning?"

"Are you stupid?" the Chief continued, "or just led by your dick? You're just as determined to prove that boy didn't kill your mother, to get Summer Hill's attention, that you'll turn your back on your own flesh and blood."

"You're the one who turned your back on me," Trey shouted back. "Leave Summer out of this. None of this has anything to do with her." He calmed his voice. He wouldn't give into the anger. If he did, he would lose control and no one would win.

"You're spitting on your mother's grave," the Chief insisted. "Every time you bring up that girl, stick up for her brother, you drive another knife wound into my Emily's back."

"I just want the truth," Trey said. "And, I think Mother would, too."

"The last thing your mother would want is for you to be standing between me and her killer. I'm done with you." He brought the gun in an upward arc, crashing it into Trey's face.

Chapter Nineteen

Trey blinked and groaned.

His head felt like one of the watermelons the kids smashed for fun in the park on the Fourth of July. He didn't know how long he'd been out. A minute or an hour? He started to stand and a wave of nausea rolled over him. Struggling, holding onto the edge of the desk, he pulled to his feet. He felt like he might spin off into space and he fell into the chair.

"What the hell?" Jody was kneeling beside him. How long had he been there? "What happened to you?"

"My old man was a little pissed." It hurt to talk.

"You're bleeding. Did the Chief hit you?" Jody looked as if he couldn't imagine asking such a question.

Trey nodded and his stomach rolled. "Yeah."

"Why? Never mind. I'm going to get you over to the hospital and get that looked after." Jody reached for the phone. "You need some stitches."

"No." Trey forced himself to his feet, ignoring the dancing multicolored stars in front of his eyes accompanying the pain shooting through his temple. He touched his forehead with his fingertips and came away with blood on them. He swayed and held onto the desk with both hands. "You've got to find the Chief…he's going to kill Jace. I need you to keep him from doing something he'll regret the rest of his life."

Jody's mouth fell open. "What? Why?"

"You heard my mother was murdered last night?" Jody nodded and Trey ignored the way his heart twisted. He didn't have time for pain right now. "The Chief is convinced Jace did it. I'm not as sure."

"Man, that's too bad about your mama." Jody patted Trey's shoulder awkwardly. "Why does the Chief think Jace did it?"

"He's blinded by some kind of rage I can't figure out. He's determined to pin this on Jace, refusing to look at any other suspects. The killer left a message on the mirror written in lipstick. I can't see Jace doing that."

"What did it say?" Jody handed Trey a tissue from a box on the desk.

"It said, 'Two down, two to go'." Trey shook his aching head at the memory and shooting stars rocketed through his brain. "Lindy, Mother, the Chief, me." He ticked off each one on his fingers as he named each of them.

"Do you think Jace is going to kill you and the Chief?" Jody looked skeptical. "I thought we were past believing Jace took Lindy."

"I don't know what to think at this point," Trey said. "Three people have died in the last few days in this town. I'd lay odds against something like that, unless a serial killer was on the loose. And the MO doesn't add up. Jimmy Ray was shot, Leroy hung himself, and my mother was suffocated."

"Not only are the deaths different, the three people have nothing in common," Jody agreed. "If the three of them had something that linked them, something to tie them together, it might be more assumable the same person was behind it. But it doesn't seem likely that Miz Emily, Leroy, and Jimmy Ray had any common denominator. I can't imagine Miz Emily knowing Jimmy Ray. And Leroy hung himself."

"Jace wouldn't have any reason to hurt Jimmy Ray that I can think of," Trey said, "or Leroy. Even if he did kill my mother, he wouldn't have had a reason to harm either of the others. And if

Leroy died by his own hand, that leaves just Jimmy Ray. No link at all." His head hurt so much he couldn't think straight.

"I better find the Chief," Jody said. "I'll keep working this over in my head and see if I can figure it out. What are you going to do? Where can I reach you?"

"You can get me on my cell phone. I'm going to ask Summer one more time if she knows where her brother is hiding," Trey answered. "And if she does, I pray she tells me before it's too late."

Jody turned to go and Trey stopped him. There's one more thing."

"What?"

"This." Trey handed him the bottle with the red hair in it.

...

Summer, Glory, and Lilah stood talking at the desk.

They were gearing up for the day ahead when the front door burst open and Trey barreled through it. Before any of them could speak, he grabbed Summer's arm and half-dragged her toward the back room. "I need to talk to you. Now."

She dug in her heels. "Let go of me. What are you, some kind of cave man?"

"Just come with me," he insisted, propelling her forward. He slammed the door shut behind them, closing them in the storage closet. Barely big enough for the two of them, it squeezed them together like the bottles on the shelves around them. His thigh brushed her hip and she tried to move away, but there was nowhere to go.

"What's this about? I thought I made it clear the last time we spoke that we didn't have anything left to say to one another." Summer crossed her arms over her chest. Trey was much, much too close. She could smell his musky aftershave. Her body tingled in response to the heady scent. Unnerved, she reached for the door handle. "Start talking."

"Did you hear about my mother?"

"What about her?" Summer glared at him. He had a lot of nerve bursting into her work like this. For the first time, she looked squarely at him. He looked like he'd been through the ringer. He had a big lump and a trickle of blood on his forehead, and black rings rimmed his eyes. She handed him a red towel. "Here. Your head is bleeding."

"She died last night." He didn't sugarcoat it or try to soften the message.

The anger went out of her like air rushing out of a flat tire. She touched his hand. "I'm so sorry."

"Thanks. She didn't just die, Summer." He took a breath. "Someone murdered her."

It didn't take a genius to figure out where he was going. She wanted to scream. "Oh, I get it now. You came tearing in here because you think my brother, who no one has seen in days, did it." The sympathy she'd felt for him seconds before was replaced by rage. "My God, you just don't quit."

"There was a message scrawled across the mirror in red lipstick. It said 'two down, two to go.' The obvious conclusion is that someone meant Lindy, and now Mother. The Chief and me next. I was just with the Chief. He left the office with a shotgun, convinced Jace killed my mother. If the Chief finds him before anyone else does, he'll shoot first and ask questions later. I'm asking you one more time, Summer, if you know where your brother is, if you even have a clue, then you need to tell me now."

"So you can send him back to Angola," she cried. "You're trying to trick me. Make me sell out my brother."

He grabbed her arms and gave her a quick shake. "Damn it, why can't you get it through your thick head that Jace killed a man? Why can't you face it? Do you think I like this any better than you do?"

"No," she sobbed, twisting away. "I can't do this. I will not, cannot, believe my little brother stabbed someone to death."

He dropped her arms like she burned him. His voice growled like sandpaper across a fresh piece of wood. "Do you think I like it any better than you do? My God, I was the one who found my best friend standing over Soloman's body with a bloody knife in his hands. If I hadn't seen it with my own eyes, do you think I could believe it either? But I did see it, Summer. I've never forgotten how he looked. Like a crazy person."

She closed her eyes and shook her head. Trying to block his words, the images. "Stop this."

"Open your eyes." Once again, he grasped her arms, but not as fiercely. "Look at me."

Reluctantly, she did. His face, inches from hers, was set in harsh lines. His eyes and lips were narrow slits. "We can't go back and change what happened, but we can shape the future. Tell me now if you know where Jace is hiding. If the Chief finds him first there'll be blood on your hands next."

"I don't know," she cried.

"Tell me." His eyes bored holes into her soul.

She couldn't lie any more. If something happened to Jace and she could prevent it, she wouldn't be able to stand it. Maybe if he was found or turned himself in, he'd have a chance to prove his innocence. If he was killed, that would be the end of him. She looked Trey in the eye. "He came to our house that first night. He took my tip money and left. I don't know where he went. I swear."

He stepped back a step as if she were repugnant to him. "So, you have been lying to me. How many times have I asked you if you had seen your brother and you looked me in the face and told me you hadn't? Do you know anything about Lindy? So help me God, if you do I'll…"

"What, Trey? You'll do what? What more could you do to me?" She ignored the tears on her cheeks. His disdain shouldn't hurt this much. She pointed at him. "I don't care what you think of me. But for the record, I have no idea where Lindy could be. She wasn't with Jace when he came to see me."

"I'm supposed to trust you?" He looked at her like she was a stranger. "How?"

"Because I'm telling you the truth," she insisted, the fight going out of her. "I asked Jace to stay. To see Mama, to turn himself in. But he refused. I had to protect him."

"Like you're doing now?" he asked, his disbelief obvious.

"No. If I knew where he was, I'd go to him myself and tell him to hide, or to go back to Angola. Don't you see? I can't bear it if anything happens to my brother." She rubbed her eyes with the back of her hands.

"While you've been protecting your brother, my sister is likely lying dead somewhere. If you had only trusted me enough to tell me this sooner, we could've been hunting for her. You have no defense for what you've done." He sounded so cold, so distant, she barely recognized him.

His scorn burned more than she could've imagined. She stepped back again, and bumped into the shelves. There was nowhere to hide. "You aren't convinced he did it, then? Kidnapped Lindy and killed your mother?" She searched his face hoping for some sign, some crack. Just one iota of belief Jace hadn't done these horrendous acts.

His silence rang louder than words.

"I can't help you," she whispered. "Just leave."

Without replying, he turned and went out the door, leaving it open.

Blinded by a fresh rush of tears, Summer couldn't see him walk through the front door without a backward glance.

Glory and Lilah rushed in with her.

"My gosh, Trey looked like a thundercloud," Lilah said. "I wouldn't want to be the next person he bumps into. They might not survive his mood."

"Looks like he did plenty of damage here," Glory commented as she dampened a washcloth in the utility sink and dabbed at Summer's face with it. "You okay, hon?"

Summer nodded, too choked up to speak. She had hoped somewhere down deep that Trey didn't think the worst of Jace, but it turned out he did after all. The grim reality was Trey thought Jace was not only a cold-blooded killer of anyone who got in his way, but also a kidnapper. She didn't know what she expected Trey to do when he found out she had seen her brother and lied about it, but look at her like he'd never seen her before hadn't been it. "I'm okay," she managed.

"What's wrong?" Lilah took Summer's cold hands and held them in her own, warming them. Her amber eyes were filled with compassion.

Summer shook her head, unable to trust her own voice.

"What set him off?" Glory lifted a strand of Summer's hair and tucked it behind her ear. "He tore out of here like the seam in a fat lady's dress. Never said a word."

Summer took a long, shuddering breath. "His mother died last night."

"Oh, no," Lilah cried.

"That's too bad," Glory murmured. "The cancer finally beat her?"

"No, that's just it. It didn't." She pulled her hands away from Lilah and twisted them. She looked between her friends, and seeing compassion there, blurted out the rest. "Someone apparently murdered Emily in her bed last night. Trey believes Jace did it."

Her friends' mouths fell open in shock.

"That's not all," Summer told them. "The Chief has taken a shotgun and gone looking for Jace. He's going to shoot on sight."

"You're the one who should be mad," Lilah said loyally.

"I also told Trey I saw Jace the night he came home." Summer looked into her friends' faces. She didn't see condemnation there. "Please understand. I only saw him for a few minutes and I don't know where he went. I have no idea if Lindy Bouché is with him or not. I couldn't tell anyone."

"It's okay, honey. We understand," Lilah hugged Summer. "We forgive you."

"Yeah, sure," Glory said. "But I can see now why your boy stormed out of here like a hurricane. If you didn't tell him about seeing Jace he probably thinks you're holding back on everything."

"Exactly." Misery filled Summer. She didn't want to admit to herself how much she had hoped Trey would come around to her way of thinking. Now she knew that was never going to happen. It hurt worse than she'd imagined.

"Who says Miz Emily was murdered?" Lilah asked. "Maybe that's a mistake."

Summer drew a shaky breath. "Apparently the killer wrote a message on the bathroom mirror in lipstick."

"Oh my God." Lilah's eyes grew enormous. "That's horrible."

Glory, too, looked like she might be sick. Her pale skin went a shade lighter. "That's insane."

"Yes, it is." Summer held her hands out, palms up. "Who would want to murder a dying woman? It just makes no sense. No more than pinning her death on my brother does."

Glory frowned. "I hate to ask this, but do you think there's a chance he did do it? I mean he might've snapped or something."

"Of course he didn't do it," Summer declared. "How could you ask that?"

"Sorry, sorry," Glory said. "I had to ask. I mean who else would have any reason to knock off the Chief's wife? From what everyone says about her, she was a saint or something. Never a hair out of place, not even a chipped nail."

Summer pinned her with a look. "Think what you just said. I bet The Chief has tons of enemies. Not everyone in this town likes him all that well. My brother can't be the only one wrongly accused. Cops aren't always the most popular people because of the work they do."

"That's true. Jody was a lot more liked when he played football than when he became a cop," Lilah said. "Why not go after the Chief then? I mean it doesn't seem like someone mad at him would kill his wife instead of him. They had to be some kind of sicko to do that to a poor, helpless woman."

"Unless they wanted to make The Chief pay even more than Miss Emily," Glory mused. "The living suffer much more than the dead."

"That's true," Summer said, thinking of Mama, "the world can be a living hell sometimes."

"What is Trey going to do?" Lilah asked.

"He said he's going to try and stop the Chief from doing anything crazy, but I don't know if he can," Summer told her. "From what he said, the Chief has gone off his rocker, swearing revenge, and nothing is going to stop him. I pray Jace is nowhere around here. If the Chief finds him before Trey does Jace will be killed for sure."

"Do you need to go home?" Glory's emerald green eyes looked so kind, so caring that Summer wanted to cry again.

She shook her head. "No. I'll just upset Mama if I'm there. She'll know something is wrong and I don't want her getting all up in the air. Besides we're busy today and you need me here. If I keep my mind on other things, I won't have so much time to worry."

"You better comb your hair then," Glory said with a grin, "because the way you look right now, the only customer who'd let you work on her is the Bride of Frankenstein. You're face is a mess, too. Get fixed up then take Nora Lee Johnson. She's coming in at eleven o'clock for a style."

"Thanks a lot," Summer said. "I needed that."

"Let's get busy," Glory said. "Hard work can make a lot of things better."

Chapter Twenty

Trey drove without seeing the road.

He had known the truth all along, but still felt betrayed. He didn't think he and Summer had ever lied to each other before, but her trust in him had been shattered the day he sat on the witness stand and told the jury he'd found her brother with blood on his hands. Trey supposed he couldn't blame her, but he didn't want to believe the bond they'd shared was gone forever.

Would he do any different if it was Lindy? He didn't know. To find her, he had sacrificed the most important relationship he'd ever had. Would he lie to Summer to protect his sister? He told himself he wouldn't, but a little voice in his head said he might. The big difference was Lindy might be a pain in the ass, but she wasn't a killer. If she were, he wouldn't try to stand between her and justice. Apparently Summer didn't have the same ethics.

Bitter disappointment filled him.

Before he could dwell on it any further, his cell phone rang. He barked into it. "What is it?"

On the other end, Etta timidly asked for him.

"I'm sorry, Etta. What can I do for you?" He felt rotten for yelling at her.

"The funeral director phoned. He would like to speak to your daddy, but I can't get him to answer the radio and no one at the office knows where he is. People are coming by to pay their respects, too. Your daddy should be here to greet them."

Trey gritted his teeth. If the Chief were thinking clearly, he would be taking care of this. "I'll try to find him, but I have no idea where he went."

"Try Miz Clara's house. Maybe Samuel went to his Mama's place to get away to think. If you do go there, look for that sparkly blue brooch your granny always wore. I know Miz Emily would like to wear it now. She always favored that piece of jewelry."

"Yes, ma'am. I will." Trey hung up, his mind on Granny Clara. He had spent many summers with her. They all had. She had made simple things like fishing in the creek, picking berries, and canning jam fun. All his friends had loved to go there. Lindy used to fight them when it was time to go home.

He slammed on the brakes and almost threw himself through the windshield when he realized the implications. He picked up the phone and called Etta back. "Is there anything in Granny's house? Could someone stay there?"

"Sure they could. Your mama didn't want the place closed up. She said it meant too much to the family. She wanted to use it as a vacation house, but she got sick before that happened." She sniffled and paused. "Why all the questions, Mr. Trey?"

"If I'm right, Lindy's been hiding at Granny Bouché's house." His heart and pulse pounded at the thought. If his sister had been hiding—safe and sound—in plain sight all this time he would ring her neck. Then hug her. Then ring her neck.

"Oh, Lordy, I hope so." Etta's fervent hope came clearly through the phone.

"Me, too, Etta. Me, too." He sent up a quick prayer of his own. "I'll call you when I know something."

. . .

Lindy had spent the night on the couch.

Jace tried to talk to her twice, but she hadn't wanted to dissect their lovemaking—*sex*—with him. More determined than ever to dig for the truth, she hit the shower, dressed in a pair of jeans and tank top, and did her makeup, a little lighter than normal.

It would be impossible to sneak in the police station in broad daylight, but nothing would stop her tonight.

Jace came to the doorway. He leaned on the doorway, one arm above his head. His expression was unreadable. He had no shirt, the top button of his jeans undone again. Her mouth went dry and she turned away. She sniffed. If he thought she was going to fall for pure animal lust and attack him again, he'd better have another think. Plus, she didn't want to examine her feelings for him right now. Some time and distance would put her emotions in perspective.

A sound caught her attention. "What is that?"

Jace whirled toward the door. "Someone's coming."

Panic filled her and she couldn't move. Like a deer in a spotlight, she froze. "What do we do?"

"Cover for me." He spun around and disappeared into the bedroom.

Desperately seeking her mind for what to do, she looked around the room for signs Jace had been there. There were none. Her makeup was spread out across the table and the blankets she'd slept in fell across the couch, but a casual glance wouldn't give his presence away. Briefly, she thought of running out the back door and hiding in the woods, but her Jeep parked in the garage would give her away to anyone who bothered to look there.

Squaring her shoulders, she lifted her chin and faced the door.

As the knob turned, she held her breath.

The door swung open and she exhaled.

Trey stepped through the opening.

Neither spoke for a moment.

Somehow she kept from darting a glance toward the bedroom door. *Where was Jace? Had he run?* She hoped so. If he went back to Angola now, all would be lost. He'd never have another chance to find the truth behind Soloman's murder if he were caught now. "What are you doing here?"

"I could ask you the same question." Trey looked mad enough to do her bodily harm.

"You found me." Pretending indifference, she shrugged.

"We've been looking for you." His voice went deeper. "Everyone's worried sick about you."

"Why?" she asked. "I go off by myself all the time and no one cares."

"You're wrong. We all care." He looked around. "Gather your stuff. You need to come with me right now."

"I don't have to do anything, Trey. You're not my keeper." She glared at him, defying him to move her.

"I could shake you," he said. "While you've been out here doing God knows what, the Chief, Mother, and I have been worrying ourselves crazy over you. Things you don't know about are going on. We know you were with Jimmy Ray Hunt. When you didn't come home, we thought you'd been raped and murdered, your body dumped in the lake or the swamp."

She rolled her eyes. "And everyone calls me the drama queen? Please."

"Like I said, things have happened you don't know about." He reached for her and she avoided his touch.

"What? Did a meteor fall on Juliet? No, wait, I know. We got TV." She laughed. "Maybe even color?"

"Shut up and listen," he roared. "This is serious."

Shocked, she snapped her mouth shut. He'd never spoken to her like that in his whole life.

He motioned toward the sofa. "Sit down."

She narrowed her eyes at him, but perched on the edge of the couch. "What is so all mighty important?"

"Plenty has happened in the last few days. Jimmy Ray's been killed."

Lindy knew she'd better make it good if he was going to believe that she didn't already know. She widened her eyes and managed to gasp. "What? How? Why tell me? Do you think I did it?"

"Don't be ridiculous," Trey said. "No one thinks that. But you do have some explaining to do, like how your bracelet ended up in his office."

Lindy didn't have to pretend this time. Her startled gaze shot to her arm. The gold band with the red stones he'd given her was missing. When had she misplaced it? Obviously when she and Jace had found Jimmy Ray. She wanted to curse her stupidity. One more time she'd screwed up.

"It's not important right now." He looked so solemn she wanted to scream. "I have to tell you something else. I don't know how to say this, exactly, so I'll just do it. Mother died last night."

For a long minute, Lindy stared at her brother. Then she shook her head. "No. That's not possible."

"I'm sorry, Lindy, but it's true." His soft tone confirmed his words.

Tears formed and her throat knotted up. Mad at her mother so long for being sick, Lindy almost couldn't process that she was gone.

This time, Trey did touch her. His hand gripped hers. "Lindy. You've got to be strong. This isn't easy to tell you either."

"Tell me," she managed through a wave of tears.

"Mother was murdered. The killer left a message on the mirror." Trey's hand nearly squeezed hers in two.

"What?" Lindy stared at him through streaming eyes. "Who would do something like that?"

"The Chief thinks it was Jace." Trey swallowed. "In fact, he's out looking for him right now with a gun. If the Chief finds Jace, he's going to shoot on sight. Jody's tracking Jace, too. I pray he finds him in time."

Her gaze shot to the bedroom door. Could Jace hear this? "Jace didn't kill Mother," Lindy choked. She jerked her hand away from Trey's. "We've got to stop this lie before it's too late."

"I know," Trey said soothingly. "We will."

"The Chief can't kill Jace." Lindy was near hysteria. "He didn't murder Mother."

"There's a lot of circumstantial evidence," Trey said. "Although I have a hard time believing it myself, Jace does have the best motive."

"You don't understand," Lindy said on a sob. "Jace couldn't have done it."

"I wish it wasn't so, too," Trey said.

"Listen to me," she shouted through her tears. "I'm telling you Jace didn't do it."

"How are you so sure?" Trey frowned.

"Because I was right here."

Both Trey and Lindy whirled toward the voice.

Jace stood in the bedroom door, his expression defiant. "I've been here the whole time. I never left this house," he said. "Ask her."

Trey looked between them. He hadn't expected to find Jace here, but he wasn't surprised either. "Is this true?"

Lindy nodded. "That's what I was trying to tell you. Jace has been with me the whole time. He never left."

"How long have you two been playing house?" Trey's voice had a deadly tone. He advanced toward Jace. "If you've touched her, I'll kill you."

"Be careful what you say," Jace snarled back. His hands curled into fists. "Someone might overhear and testify against you in court."

"I only told the jury what I saw. You were standing over Soloman's body with a bloody knife in your hands." Trey moved a few feet closer. "Should I have lied? Maybe said you didn't do it?"

"I didn't." Jace's gaze never wavered. "But I'm wasting my breath with the almighty Trey, aren't I?"

"If you didn't kill Soloman," Trey said, ignoring the dig, "then who did?"

"I don't know," Jace admitted, "but it wasn't me."

"Every criminal in the world says they didn't do it," Trey said. "Show me some proof. A theory, even. Something besides this infernal cry of innocence. Maybe you might've been justified in what you did. But just admit the truth."

Lindy darted between them and wrapped her arms around Jace's waist. "What if he is telling the truth? Did you ever think of that?"

"He's not." Trey waved his hand in a disgusted gesture.

"That's right, I wanted to throw away everything," Jace said. "I wanted to rot behind bars for the rest of my life. Don't you get it? If I knew who offed Soloman, I'd be shouting it from the rooftops."

"Trey." Lindy moved forward and grabbed his shirt. "Just listen. I know he's telling the truth. He wouldn't lie to me."

Trey looked into her eyes and what he saw there stilled him. She was in love with Jace. Trey lifted his gaze to Jace's face. "You bastard. I ought to kill you where you stand for touching her."

"Yeah, you should." Jace looked him in the eye. "The way I should've kicked your ass when you slept with my sister five years ago."

"That was a little different," Trey said, staggered. How did Jace know? "I didn't know you knew."

"Of course I knew." Jace curled his lip into a mocking sneer. "You were hot for her your whole life. More people than you think saw you two go off alone on grad night."

"Your sister was an adult, not a kid." Trey hands balled into fists. "Not a little girl. I wasn't a convict."

"Hey, I'm standing here. I'm not a kid and it wasn't his fault." Lindy spread her palms over Trey's chest and held him there. "Jace didn't do anything that I didn't want him to. Don't you get that?"

God help him, he did. He knew how it felt to love someone so blindly it hurt. To feel so deeply all others no longer mattered.

The way he'd felt about Summer his whole life. This moment was the turning point. If he turned his back on her brother, did what his heart told him was right, she would never forgive him. If he held his tongue, Trey didn't know how he could live with himself. He didn't agree with Lindy's choice, but it was hers to make. He looked at Jace. "You can't run. There's nowhere to hide."

"Then help us," Lindy begged. Her big brown eyes again swam in tears. "The person who killed Soloman is still out there. With your help, we can find out who it was and free Jace."

He hesitated. He'd never doubted what he saw. Jace standing over the body. Maybe he'd been telling the truth all the time. Maybe, just maybe, there was someone else who wanted Soloman dead. But who? "We don't have much time."

Lindy squealed and threw her arms around his neck. "Thank you, Trey. Thanks so much."

"You're welcome." He unwound her arms from his neck and said, "Let's talk it through. Maybe we can come up with something if we all put our heads together."

Lindy turned toward Jace. "Did you hear that? Trey's going to help you."

"What's the catch?" Jace looked like he'd swallowed a lemon peel.

"No catch." Trey looked him the eye. He took a breath. Admitting the possibility of Jace's innocence wasn't easy. "Maybe because I do owe you one."

"Maybe you do and maybe you don't. How do I know you don't plan on running straight to your old man and turning me in all over again? I trusted you once before and you sold me out."

"Think what you want, but my sister thinks she's in love with you. I'm doing this for her." *And Summer.* "Take it or leave it."

Jace watched him warily. "I don't have a choice, do I?"

"No."

Lindy smiled at both of them. "I knew you two would be friends again someday."

They were far from friends, but Trey didn't correct her. "Let's start at the beginning and see what we can come up with."

"There's coffee in the kitchen." Lindy motioned toward the doorway. "Let's go in there."

The three of them sat in awkward silence around the table.

Trey studied his old friend's face. There was little resemblance to the fresh-faced kid who'd been his buddy since pre-school. Harsh planes had replaced babyish features, the lanky limbs replaced by muscles that rippled under his clothes. But it was the bitterness covering the old sparkle that seemed the biggest change of all.

Lindy kept darting glances at Jace, her expression unreadable. But she was unmistakably head over heels.

"Besides you, who would've had a motive to make Soloman pay?" Trey figured there wasn't any reason to beat around the bush and asked the hardest question first.

Jace shrugged, his hands wrapped around his mug. "I don't know. Mama was so out of it, she's not a possibility. Summer? Not in her personality."

"I saw a car leave the motel," Jace said, "just as I walked up. But I didn't get a good look at the plates."

"What about the make or model?" As well as Jace knew cars, he'd remember it if he saw clearly enough.

Jace shook his head. "No. A sedan. Light color."

"That doesn't help much," Trey said. "But it's a start. Let's go back even further. How did you hear Soloman was going to be released?"

"Your old man called my house to tell us. He wanted us to know there wasn't enough evidence to arrest Soloman. I couldn't believe that bastard could do that to my mother and get away with it. I tore down to the station to yell at your old man. He told me he couldn't help it. The physical evidence disappeared and Mama wasn't lucid enough to finger Soloman in a lineup. I shouted at him, told him he was a piece of shit. I swore I'd kill Soloman."

"I remember," Trey said with a nod. "I had come to the station to talk to the Chief and I heard you from the hall. You stormed by me. I tried to stop you, but you weren't going to be deterred. But I didn't think you meant to really kill someone."

"I went to Soloman's room," Jace said, a faraway look on his face. "The door was unlocked. I opened it and went inside. I saw his feet. I moved closer and saw the bed and the wall covered in blood. Soloman was stuck, facedown. I turned him over to check his pulse and saw the knife. I grabbed it, that's when I got blood on my hands. He was already dead."

"I showed up right about then," Trey said. "You looked at me like you didn't see me and you said he got what he deserved."

"Yeah." Jace looked at him. "I did."

"He died from the stab wound," Trey said. "If you didn't stab him, who did?"

"Not me." Jace stared back, unblinking.

"No one else had the motive that we know of." Trey took a sip of tepid coffee.

Lindy, sitting silently between them, spoke up. "Soloman was a stranger in town. No one knew him or had seen him before."

The picture.

Trey almost rocketed out of his chair. "That's not true. Soloman knew MiLann. He also knew our mother and a couple other people in town. Hold on."

Racing to the car, he retrieved the photo Summer had stolen from the Chief's locked file cabinet. Coming back, he showed it to the other two. "Look. Summer took this from the Chief. He had it hidden in a locked drawer. How do you suppose these five people knew each other?"

"My mother knew her rapist?" Jace dropped the photo as though it had acid on it.

"Apparently." Trey picked it up. "Where was this? Who took it? Summer says it's the night of our graduation because that's the dress MiLann wore that night. She has never worn it again."

"Yes, that's the dress Mother wore to your graduation party, too." Excitement showed in Lindy's face. "What do you think this means?"

Trey shrugged. "Do you know if the Chief and Mother went somewhere that night? After the party, I mean. Maybe they went out and took MiLann with them. The rapist waited in her car, and when she left the party he made her pull over and he attacked her. But what if this group went out somewhere and that's where Soloman found her?"

"I don't know," Lindy said. "They were still at home when I went to bed."

Frustrated by the message he knew was hidden in the picture, Trey stared at it. "If we could only see the background. Maybe we could tell something else."

"I didn't realize Mama and Emily were so friendly with Buford Krebbs and Leroy Eaton," Jace said. "I don't remember either of them ever coming to the house. Another thing is strange here. Viola's not in the picture. Isn't she Buford's wife?"

"Maybe she was the photographer," Lindy suggested. "Maybe a few couples went out after your graduation for a drink."

"Where's the Chief if that's the case? And Leroy didn't have a wife. According to the Chief, Leroy was in love with our mother and carried a torch for her for years." Something nagged at Trey. At the edge of his mind like an itch he couldn't scratch, it was bugging him to death. "He hung himself yesterday after church. The Chief said Leroy's been fighting a deep depression for years."

"Oh, poor Mr. Eaton. That's weird, him dying so close to Mother." Lindy wiped her eyes. "If he was really in love with her all those years it's like, what do you call it, poetry something?"

"Poetic justice," Trey answered absently, his mind elsewhere. "Maybe the Chief didn't want his picture taken. You know how he always hides when the camera comes out."

"What's weird is that a group of friends would take a picture with a stranger," Jace said. "Why would they let Soloman get in it with them?"

"Were they all drunk?" Lindy wiped her red nose with a Kleenex.

"Not likely," Trey said. "We're getting off the subject. We need a motive for someone to kill Soloman."

"Maybe he did something to one of them." Jace pointed to the picture. "Insulted someone somehow. Hell, maybe your old man killed him for making a lewd comment to the missus."

"You're stretching," Trey said. "Be serious."

"We could ask them if so many of them weren't dead," Lindy said. "But three of these people have died, and out of the other two, one isn't exactly an accurate source of information." She shot Jace an apologetic look. "Sorry to say that about your mama."

Trey sat up like he'd been stung. "Let me see that again."

With a puzzled look, Lindy handed him the picture. "What?"

"Don't you see? Two of the people in this picture are dead besides Soloman. Mother and Leroy. Two down, two to go. Someone is going to kill MiLann Hill and Buford Krebbs. We have to warn them."

"What the hell are you talking about?" Jace grabbed the picture and looked at it like it was a magic mirror that would answer him.

"Mother's killer left a message on the mirror. It said 'two down, two to go'. We assumed that meant Mother and Lindy, but, God help them, it meant Leroy and Mother. The other two are MiLann and Buford Krebbs. I've got to warn them." Trey jumped up.

"But who would kill them?" Lindy wailed. "And why?"

"Figure that out and we'll know who killed Soloman," Trey said. "If only we could retrace his steps that night."

"He was at Jimmy Ray's bar a few nights before he was killed." At Trey's incredulous look, she explained. "My friend Candy told me he was with one of the woman who lives at the river. Candy's mother is…"

"I know who she is," Trey interrupted. He waved the picture at her. "Do you realize what you just said?"

Lindy shrugged. "No."

Trey's voice throbbed with excitement. "Think about it. If Soloman was at Mugs-n-Jugs before he died, that's probably where this picture was taken. A group of people drinking beer, Soloman included in the group, MiLann raped that night. I need to talk to this woman. She might've even been the photographer."

"She's dead," Jace said. "Candy told us that, too."

Trey's euphoria faded. "Another fizzled lead."

"Maybe Carlene knows more than she told Candy," Jace suggested. "It's worth a try to ask her."

"I'll see if she knows anything else." Trey jumped up. "Lindy, come with me. You're needed at home. Jace, stay here out of sight. Keep a low profile. If you see any sign of the Chief hide and hide well. We'll come back as soon as we can. It might be a few days."

"But…" Jace began.

"Just do it. I think I've got an idea how to prove you didn't kill Soloman." Trey grabbed Lindy's hand and dragged her toward the door.

Chapter Twenty-One

There was little conversation between Trey and Lindy on the way home. When had Lindy grown up? She was a woman now, in love with Jace Hill, for better and most likely worse.

Finally, Lindy spoke. "Do you really believe Jace is innocent now? After all this time, you've changed your mind?"

Trey glanced at her. He could hardly believe it himself. "Yeah. I think he took the rap for someone who got off scot-free."

"I'm glad." She sighed and leaned back into the seat.

"Lindy," he began. "Do you think a relationship with Jace is smart? He's twisted by prison, bitter, and mean."

"Don't." She wagged a finger at him. "I know what I'm doing."

"I hope so. I don't want to see you get hurt." Trey's heart ached at the thought of his little sister in love with a man who might never gain his freedom. If they couldn't figure out a way to prove his innocence, they would all pay for it.

"I won't," she said. "What about you and Summer?"

"What about us?" he hedged. "There is no me and Summer."

"There could be. Tell her that you believe in Jace. It'll mean the world to her." Lindy punched him in the arm. "So there, big brother."

He grinned at her wondering when she'd gotten so smart.

His smile faded as they turned into *LeFleur's* driveway. He glanced at Lindy, her face etched by sadness. A few cars sat in the lane, but not the Chief's big Cadillac. Trey hoped Jody had found the Chief. Trey would check in with him as soon as he saw Lindy safely inside. He led her in the house.

A few people stood in the front room, gathered around talking among themselves. Trey skirted them, his hand on Lindy's lower back. "Let's find Etta and let her know you're home. I want to ask her if she's heard from the Chief."

In the kitchen, Etta looked up from a cake she was cutting. Her knife clattered to the floor. She flew to Lindy and took her in her arms. "Oh, my baby." She reached for Trey. "Both of you. You're home."

Trey submitted to her tight embrace for a moment. Then he pulled away. "Any word from the Chief or Jody?"

Etta shook her head. "Not a thing."

He reached for a piece of cake. "I'm going to call Jody. Then I have something I need to do."

"Let me go with you." Lindy's big, brown eyes pleaded with him.

"You need to stay here," he said. "I'll be back soon and let you know what I find out."

"Promise?" Her voice cracked.

"I swear." He hugged her and Etta again and went to the den. He picked up the phone and dialed Jody. He answered on the second ring. "Have you found the Chief?"

"Not yet. No one's seen him. I've looked everywhere I can think of," Jody said. "But he's faded like fog on a hot day."

"I need to talk to you. Where are you?" Trey asked.

"Coming in from the lake. I thought the Chief might've gone to his boat, but it didn't look like he's been there anytime lately."

"Wait by the turnoff to Shantytown. I'll meet you there in fifteen minutes." Trey hung up and hurried to his car.

In a few minutes, he climbed out of his car and in with Jody. "Drive toward Shantytown and I'll tell what I found out today." As Jody drove, Trey filled him in on the day's events.

At the end of his spiel, Jody shook his head. "Man, I can't believe your sister's been with Jace all this time. You really think if we find out who killed Leroy and your mama, we'll know who killed Soloman, too?"

"I'm convinced of it," Trey told him. "It finally clicked what the message on Mother's mirror meant. Not my family, like the Chief thinks, but Mother, MiLann, Leroy, and Buford."

"What about Jimmy Ray? He makes five, not four." Jody waved his hand. "And Soloman's six."

"I don't think either of them counts in this equation. I believe the killer is referring to the four who are left now. If I could only figure out who wrote the message. It wasn't Jace. Lindy was with him and she swears to his whereabouts."

Jody lifted his eyebrows and said, "Do you mean they were getting busy?"

"Yeah." Trey didn't want to think about his sister and Jace in a sexual way. He blinked away the image. "Someone has to have a motive."

"Why are we going to Shantytown? Shouldn't we be warning Miz Hill and Krebbs?"

"Lindy said Candy told her one of the girls from out here was with Soloman at Jimmy Ray's place partying right before he died. I think Carlene might've heard something about who he was with from her girl. Maybe even something about the person who killed him. If she does, we can head off the killer before they try to get the last two."

"Maybe this hooker did him in," Jody suggested. "We'll question her, too."

"We can't. She's dead."

Jody shot him a look, raising his eyebrows. "There are a lot of people dying around here all of a sudden."

"Do you think her death is related to this mess, too?" Trey asked his friend. "I understand this woman died a few years ago. But maybe she died because she knew too much?"

"We're going to find out." Jody's expression was grim. "I'm thinking Jimmy Ray ties in too. If it's true the picture was taken at Mugs-n-Jugs, then that brings him into this in a big way. Maybe it explains why he died now when he's made so many enemies over the years."

"We also need to question Buford Krebbs," Trey said. "Trying to talk to MiLann will be a waste of time. I don't think she's well enough to know what day it is."

"We'll go there next." Jody parked the cruiser. "But first, let's find out what Carlene can tell us."

•••

When no one came to Carlene's door, they opened it.

She raced toward the river in a scarlet camisole and a pair of tap pants that barely covered her ass.

They chased her and Jody grabbed her around the waist, spinning her around.

Panting, she winked and licked her full lips. "You boys just can't stay away, can you?"

"We need to ask you a few questions," Trey said. "Why'd you run?"

"We've already been down this road," she said with a pout. "I can't think of a thing to tell you that I haven't already."

"I can." Trey was sick of her runaround. "What can you tell us about a woman named Marie Lennox? A few years ago she went to party in town with a man named Deke Soloman. He raped MiLann Hill and was later killed himself."

Carlene's features became guarded. "I don't know nothin' about that business."

"Let's take this down to the station." Jody handcuffed her and led her to his patrol car.

• • •

Carlene glared at them. "I don't have nothin' to tell you."

"Sure you do." Jody flipped open a small notepad and scanned a page within. "Marie Lennox was one of your girls. They don't make dates without your say-so. Marie wouldn't have gone into town without your knowledge and consent. So, the question is, what do you remember about her arrangement with Deke Soloman?"

With a heavy sigh, Carlene looked off into the distance. "Maybe it's time this all came out."

"What?" Jody looked at her coolly.

She let out a long sigh. "Marie told me she had a date with a man in town. I usually don't agree to that. The girls can get into trouble when they're not at their own place, but she insisted. Said he'd pay her well." Carlene shrugged one pale shoulder. "I said what the hell, she could do what she liked. A few hours later, she came down with the flu or some bug. She couldn't go, so I took her place. Soloman didn't give a damn. He just wanted a woman, and he was willing to pay well."

Jody made a note in his notebook. "Did you tell him who you were?"

"Nope. I just went. The girls don't make money, I don't make money." She waved her hand in the air. "I have to keep my place running somehow."

"When was this?" Trey asked, the edges of a memory playing on one corner of his mind.

She leaned back and crossed her legs. "Honey, I think you know the answer to that don't you?"

"Don't play games with us," Jody warned. "Just answer the question."

"Make me, sugar." She ran one finger along the strap of her satiny top, sliding it down her arm. Half of her freckled breast was exposed.

"Pull up your shirt," Jody said coldly. "Or I'll do it for you."

"What happened to Marie Lennox?" Trey asked.

"Nothin'." Carlene tugged up the strap of her top and focused her cinnamon eyes on him. "I already told you."

"How did Marie Lennox die?" He leaned close and stared intently at her.

Staring blankly over his shoulder, Carlene said, "A john killed her, strangled her."

"When?" Trey pushed.

"'Bout three years ago." Carlene's hands shook. Whether she really felt something or was pretending, he couldn't say. "Why are you bringin' up all that bad business?"

"We think her death has something to do with all these deaths that have happened in the last few days. Somehow, someway, that night with Soloman ties into the rest of it. Can you remember anything about the night you went to town and met him? It would've been the end of May, around the twenty-eighth to be exact. On the weekend." The day of his graduation had been a Saturday.

"I know when it was," she said impatiently. Her face took on a faraway look. "I saw him."

"Did he think you were Marie?" Trey stared at her, riveted. He knew what she was going to say. He held his breath.

"Probably. Customers don't care what a girl's name is long as they get what they pay for."

"How do you know the date?" Jody asked. "What was so special about it that you can recall it now?"

"I had to do something." Her voice took on a bitter tone. "Tell him."

"Who?" Trey choked out, but he knew. The memory grew, came into sharp focus like a picture lifting out of developing fluid.

Carlene looked at him and smiled gently. "Your daddy, of course."

"What the hell are you rambling about?" Jody said. "Quit talking in riddles."

His gaze locked on her face Trey said, "She's telling the truth."

"What the hell are you saying?" Jody shifted his weight. His expression suggested Trey had lost his mind.

Without taking his eyes off her Trey said, "That night, graduation. I went in the house and heard them fighting. It was over her."

"Who, man?" Jody's voice held an edge of impatience.

The years rolled away and Trey replayed the scene in his mind. "The Chief and Mother were in the den. The door was closed. I could hear their voices, but not all the words. I heard enough to know the Chief had been seeing another woman."

"Who?" Jody looked at Carlene. "You? No way."

She smirked. "Uh-huh."

"That explains why a hard-ass like the Chief never shut down your place," Jody said.

"It makes perfect sense now," Trey said. "My mother waited until after the party then she went out to get even. She knew how to make the Chief pay. By slumming and taking his closest friends with her. Leroy was in love with her, he would've gone just to be near her. Who knows why Buford tagged along? They all went to Mugs-n-Jugs, the sleaziest joint in town. The place my father would hate her going the most." Trey licked dry lips. "You have no idea what you set in motion that night, lady."

"Samuel had it coming," she defended herself. "For more years than I could count he promised me the moon, the stars, everything. I just wanted what he offered so freely, but never gave."

"And when you heard about my graduation party plans, you realized he was blowing hot air? You went to see him, to threaten him with telling my mother the truth?" Trey forced himself to breathe, to not lunge at her and strangle her. "Why that day?"

She narrowed her eyes at him. "Deke Soloman, that's why."

"What did he have to do with you?" Trey asked, puzzled.

She looked away and clamped her lips shut.

"Ma'am? What happened with Soloman that you went to the Chief?" Jody asked.

She shook her head.

"Oh my God." Trey knew what had made her go to the Chief. "Soloman did it to you, too."

She looked at him without answering. The pain in her face confirmed his suspicions.

"What did he do?" Jody tapped his pencil on a pad of paper. "Miss Carter? What happened between you and Soloman?"

"The no-good bastard raped her," Trey answered for her. He moved to touch her, to offer solace, but she lifted a hand and held him away.

"That's why you went to the Chief?" Jody asked. "To tell him about it?"

"Yeah." A bitter, broken laugh escaped her. "He said I wanted attention, to make him leave Emily. He said I was just a slut, that rough sex didn't mean rape. I threatened to tell Emily about us. He said I was a whore and no one, including his wife, would ever believe a story like that from me."

"That son-of-a-bitch." At that moment, Trey would've wrapped his hands around the Chief's throat and choked him until he died. Because he had not listened to Carlene, and taken Soloman into custody, he had been free to rape again. Trey's mother and MiLann Hill moved in his path also because the Chief hadn't locked him up. His stomach boiled, and Trey fought the urge to vomit. "Somehow my mother overheard your conversation and she went out partying to get even. That night Soloman raped MiLann Hill."

Carlene nodded. "It all adds up."

"Man, this is twisted," Jody commented. "If only the Chief had listened to you, none of this would've happened."

"The stubborn, stupid old man," Trey said almost to himself. Then louder, "But we still don't know who killed Soloman, or why."

"I do." Jody took a pair of handcuffs off his belt. "Carlene Carter, I'm placing you under arrest for the murder of Deke Soloman and Emily Bouché. You have the right to remain silent…"

"Are you out of your ever-loving mind?" Trey asked. "What in the hell are you doing?"

Pinning a cold stare on him, Jody said, "Here's your killer. I'm taking her into custody."

Carlene jumped up. "I didn't kill Soloman, Emily, or anyone else."

"She's got no motive," Trey said.

"Didn't you hear her story?" Jody asked. "She as much as said it was the Chief's fault she was raped for not arresting Soloman all those years ago. The reason she offed Soloman is obvious."

"Why would I kill his wife now?" Her voice rose in hysteria. "I wouldn't have a reason."

"There are no other suspects." Jody snapped one cuff on her wrist. "But you just gave me your reason. The oldest one in the book as a matter of fact. Jealousy. It's been eating at you all these years. You saw your chance to kill Emily and you took it."

"You're insane." She struggled to free herself from his iron bracelet. "I didn't do anything."

"Jody, let her go. She's not the killer," Trey said. "You're forgetting 'two down, two to go.' Even if Carlene wanted my mother out of the picture after all this time, who are the other three?"

"You, Lindy, and the Chief," Jody insisted, holding the twisting woman with both hands. "Sometimes revenge is sweet no matter how long you have to wait."

"Let go of me, you nutcase," Carlene shrieked, flopping like a bass on the end of a line. "I didn't kill anyone."

"Lindy's not dead," Trey said. "So, she's not one of the two down."

"Carlene didn't know that," Jody grunted. "We told her ourselves a couple days back we thought Lindy was a goner. I think this lady saw an opportunity to get even with your daddy and jumped for it. What better way to throw us off the trail than to lay a false lead? You saw her leaving Leroy's place and she left a strand of red hair at the scene of your mother's death."

"Why now?" Trey wondered if his lifelong friend had gone off the deep end. He was reaching, really reaching to make Carlene the culprit. If she wanted revenge this badly, wouldn't she have exacted it five years ago when the Chief had turned his back on her?

"Simple. You're back in town." Jody sounded so sure, and he had a point. "Until now, she hasn't been able to get all of you."

"What about Leroy?" Even as he asked, Trey remembered the Chief saying Leroy suffered from depression and there was no forensic evidence to suggest he had been murdered.

"He hung himself because of his depression," Jody said. "End of his story."

"If you're even halfway right, and I don't think you are, what made her snap now?" Trey looked at the flopping woman and had to admit she did look a bit off her rocker with her long auburn hair flying around her angry face.

"Simple. Your daddy hasn't just turned his back on her. This time he turned his back on his baby girl."

"Lindy? He hasn't shown much interest in her I'll admit, but turn his back on her? I don't think…"

"Trey, man, I'm not talking about Lindy. I mean your old man's other baby girl." Jody snagged Carlene around the middle. "I mean her little girl. The Chief's other daughter. Candy."

Trey's jaw hit his chest. "What?"

"I saw the resemblance the other day when I was here, but it didn't click until just now. When the lady here was talking about her affair with the Chief, I realized she'd had a child by him." Jody brushed her hair out of her face. "Am I right? I know I am."

With a jerk of her head she confirmed his story.

"But why would that make you want to kill us?" Trey could hardly believe any of this. He had a half-sister he never knew about. "Why not sue for child support or go public or something? Isn't murder a little drastic?"

"I didn't kill nobody." Carlene aimed a kick at Jody's crotch. He dodged her foot.

"Not when the Chief would move heaven and earth to find his legitimate daughter. He turned his back on Carlene when she went to him to report a rape. But she thought he would do anything to find Lindy. When you and I came out here combing the woods for Lindy, she snapped. Isn't that right?" Jody continued, "What she doesn't know is the Chief isn't that worried about his legitimate daughter any more than he worried about his mistress's child."

"Is this true?" Trey's entire body ached. Because she had been disbelieved, this woman had taken his mother's life. He wanted to hate her, but all he felt was sorrow for all of them. So many lives ruined because the Chief hadn't made the right choice.

"No," she spat, "but you got it all figured out, don't you?"

"You killed Soloman, too, for what he did to you, didn't you?" Trey looked at Carlene, but saw Jace. He saw his mother. He saw MiLann. He saw Summer. And finally himself.

Bile rose in his throat.

He forced it down with Herculean effort.

A series of events had been set in motion one night five years ago that had stolen so much from so many.

Now it was over.

Chapter Twenty-Two

Lindy stared in the mirror, but not really seeing herself. She toyed with the dozens of bottles of nail polish, makeup, and hairbrushes scattered across her vanity. She couldn't get Jace off of her mind. Was he okay? Was Trey having any luck finding the true killer? Even if he did, it didn't mean Jace would want to be with her. He hadn't made any promises. She reached for a brush, but stood instead.

Over Etta's protests Lindy said, "I have to run an errand. Don't worry. I'll be back by dinnertime."

A few minutes later, she pulled into the parking lot of the Curl Up and Dye. Taking a deep breath, Lindy hoped Summer would see her. She jumped up the steps and went inside. Glory and Lilah were both with customers. Lindy didn't see Summer anywhere.

Glory looked up, her mouth full of bobby pins. "Can I help you?"

"Is Summer here?" Lindy twisted the ring on her right hand. Would she throw her out?

Glory removed the pins. "She's in back. Can I do something for you?"

"Um, no thanks. I really need Summer." Lindy perched on the edge of one of the chairs. She didn't know what she was going to say exactly, but she knew she had to let her know Jace was safe.

Summer came out of the back room, wiping her hands on a towel. When she spotted Lindy, she stopped mid-step. A small frown played around her mouth.

Lindy stood. "Hi, I um, need a haircut. Can you fit me in?"

Summer gave her a jerky nod. "Come back here and let me shampoo you out."

Lindy followed her to the farthest corner of the room where a row of sinks lined the wall. Waiting until Summer wrapped a bib around her neck and she'd leaned back into the sink Lindy whispered, "Jace is safe."

Summer's hands stilled and their eyes met. "How do you know?" She poured a capful of peach scented shampoo into her palm and rubbed it into Lindy's hair.

"I was with him."

"Did he…force you to go?" Lindy could feel the other woman's hands trembling against her scalp.

"No. I wanted to be with him." She took a deep breath. "I love him."

Summer gasped and her hands stilled for a millisecond. "Does the Chief know this?"

Lindy shook her head. "No."

"Thank God," Summer whispered. "Where's Jace?"

"At my Granny's. Safe." Lindy looked up at Jace's sister then closed her eyes for a minute. "Have you heard about my mother?"

"Yes, and I'm sorry." Summer had turned off the water and toweled her dry.

"Thank you." Lindy sat up and squeezed the water from her hair. "But that isn't why I'm here. I wanted to let you know about Jace and I want to tell you Trey knows, too."

Summer swayed and grabbed the chair. "Oh, no."

"Listen," Lindy said, "Trey knows Jace didn't kill that awful man who raped your mama. He's helping us now."

"Helping to send Jace straight back to Angola." Summer's voice rose. She took a breath when Lilah and Glory looked her way. "Trey has always believed my brother killed Soloman. He came back here to prove it."

"That might've been true before, Summer, but it isn't now. I trust Trey to help." Lindy bit her lip. How to convince Summer, Trey was on the up and up?

"If you truly love my brother, then go to him and tell him to run before it's too late," Summer insisted. "Trey betrayed him before, he'll do it again. If Trey knows where Jace is, he'll be arrested and returned to prison before the sun goes down."

Lindy bit back an angry reply. It wouldn't do Jace any good for her to fight with Summer. Trey probably wouldn't appreciate her interference either. Still she said, "There's one more thing. I love your brother with my whole heart. And my brother loves you the same way. If you feel half of what I feel for Jace, then you'll try to give Trey another chance. Jace has."

"What would you like me do to your hair?" Summer avoided her gaze.

"Dye it a couple shades darker than yours." Lindy thought of how Jace had said he liked her blonde. She probably had just messed up things worse between Summer and Trey, but at least she'd tried to help.

As Summer applied the pre-color to Lindy's hair, she asked, "When is your mother's funeral? And where?"

"Wednesday at St. Francis Chapel," Lindy answered. "It would mean a lot to Trey if you could come."

"I'll think about it." Summer was unwilling to make a commitment. Her mind was on what Lindy had just told her. It had taken a lot of guts for her to come here and voice her opinion. But she couldn't be right. Trey wouldn't just throw away five years of conviction and help Jace now. Would he?

About an hour later, Summer guided Lindy back to the main area, ignoring Lilah and Glory's stares, and held up a medium blonde dye. "How's this one?"

"A little lighter, please." Lindy touched one end of her damp hair. "My real color is pretty light. Not quite as pale as yours, but light. Mother always loved my hair."

"Okay, how about Butterblonde?" Summer suggested. "It'll flatter your complexion."

"Sounds good."

Acting as if she were concentrating on the job at hand, Summer didn't talk for a while. Glory and Lilah were busy with their own clients, not paying her any attention. Finally she said, "You had the most beautiful hair when you were a little girl."

"I always wanted yours." Lindy looked into her lap.

Summer chuckled. "We looked like sisters."

"We were close enough," Lindy said.

Her good feelings disappeared and Summer snapped her lips together.

About the same time, both the other two clients left.

"We're going to get a sandwich at the Dairy Queen," Lilah said, "do you want us to pick up something for you?"

"A turkey on wheat, no mayo for both of us," Summer said, "and thanks."

"We'll be back in a bit," Glory said as they went through the door.

After a minute, Lindy asked, "How's your mama? Is she any better?"

"Some, not much." Summer sighed. "She still won't go outside. I keep hoping, but no luck yet."

"She will sometime." Lindy met Summer's eyes in the mirror. "Does she know about Mother?"

"No," Summer admitted. "I didn't think it was a good idea to tell her. You never know how she'll react to things."

"What about Jace? Will you let her know he's okay?"

"Of course," Summer said. "That'll make her happy."

"And me? What about that? What will your mama think of the way Jace and I feel about each other?" Lindy's soft brown eyes followed her in the mirror. Hope filled them.

Summer smiled a little. "I think my mama knows how you feel. I think she's known her whole life."

Lindy laughed, a twinkly sound. "Yes, I believe you're right."

"Can I ask you something?" Summer asked. "How did you know loving Jace was the right thing to do? Surely the Chief wouldn't be too pleased. He might turn his back on you if he finds out."

"I don't care. Jace is the most important thing." Lindy's voice and gaze never wavered.

"Does he love you, too?"

Lindy looked to her lap. "He hasn't said so. It doesn't matter. I love him enough for both of us."

"You're willing to give up your entire family for a man who isn't sure he loves you in return?" By turns, amazement and shame filled Summer. Amazement that this girl-child was willing to walk away from everything she'd ever known for love. Shame that she didn't have the same conviction.

"He's the one."

Not sure what to say about that, Summer said, "Time to wash this out."

Surprisingly, she was enjoying Lindy's company. She'd always been fond of the younger girl. After she rinsed the extra color out and steered Lindy back to her seat, Summer turned her away from the mirror. Retrieving her scissors from the drawer, she expertly cut Lindy's hair. Then she dried it. Summer spun her around toward the mirror. "Ready?"

Lindy didn't speak as she faced her reflection. Her eyes widened and she lifted a hand to touch her pale blonde hair. Tears filled her eyes and she blinked furiously. "It's awesome."

"I think so, too." Summer lifted her hair and dropped it a few times. The horrible black had been replaced by a sunny blonde, the dead ends gone, a shoulder-length blunt cut now in place that showed off her angled jaw and big eyes to their best advantage.

"Thank you, Summer. Thanks so much." Lindy stood up and hugged her. "Don't forget what I said."

Summer nodded. "Take care of my brother and give him my love." She escorted Lindy to the door and watched her drive away.

In a heartbeat, Glory and Lilah were through the door. Glory was all over Summer. "What was that all about? When did the princess come home? Where's Jace? Did he kidnap her?"

"I don't know," Summer evaded. "But she's been with Jace, and no, he didn't make her go. He's safe for now."

"Where were they?" Glory dug sandwiches out of a sack.

For some reason, Summer didn't want to answer. She took the sandwich and turned away. "I don't know. She didn't say, only that he's safely hidden. Another thing she wanted me to know was that Trey has had a change of heart. He no longer thinks Jace killed Soloman."

"What?" Glory's mouth fell open. "Why not? And who does he suspect?"

Summer sat at her station and unwrapped her meal. She shrugged. "I don't know."

"I wonder if Jace gave him a lead?" Lilah took her meal to her workstation and sat. "Maybe Jace knew something that Trey's checking on while Jace stays out of sight."

Glory placed her uneaten sandwich on the desk. "Like what? If Jace knew something, wouldn't he have said so a long time ago?"

"No one was listening back then," Summer said. "Now they are."

• • •

After two straight hours, Jody came out of the interrogation room.

Trey met him at the door. "Did she say anything more?" He held his breath. Maybe Carlene confessed and exonerated Jace.

"Nothing. She swears she didn't kill Soloman, but she's got no alibi."

"Do you still think she did it?" Trey asked.

"Yeah," Jody said with a deep sigh. "I do. The DA will charge her in the morning, after he sees all the evidence."

Trey moved toward the door. "I need to find the Chief and talk to him. He needs to hear this and start things in motion to exonerate Jace. Summer needs to know, too."

"Don't forget to tell Jace," Jody called. "And Lindy."

Trey waved, but didn't slow down. The person he had to talk to first was Summer.

• • •

Summer swept the floor, singing along with the radio. Lilah had gone to help her Aunt Etta prepare for Emily's funeral. Glory had left early, saying she didn't feel well. Nearly six, the day had passed in a blur since Lindy had been there. All afternoon, Summer had played their conversation over in her head.

Still marveling that such a young girl knew her own mind so well, Summer wished she were as strong. If she admitted how she felt about Trey, that she'd loved him always, her mama might never speak to her again. Although, apparently Jace would. Searching deep in her heart Summer knew she'd forgiven Trey a long time ago for the part he played in sending Jace to prison. He hadn't committed the crime. He had been honor-bound to tell the jury what he'd seen.

What she still had a hard time with was that he was so sure Jace had killed Soloman. There had never been a moment's doubt, and that's what hurt. Why had Trey had so little faith in his friend? When Jace cried out that he was innocent, why hadn't Trey at least listened? Maybe, just maybe, if he had Jace would've had a plausible explanation. No one had slowed down long enough to find out if he had really only touched Soloman to find out if he were breathing or not.

The bell over the front door chimed and Summer looked up, startled.

Trey walked through and their eyes met, but neither spoke for a long moment.

"Hi," he said.

"Hi." She gripped the broom with both hands. "If you're here to tell me Jace is all right, I already know. Lindy came by earlier and let me know." Summer swiped at a spot on the floor with the broom. "So you can go."

He grabbed the broom handle. "Don't you want to know the rest?"

Their eyes met and held. "I can't think of much more I'd want to know. Unless you're here to tell me you've already informed the Chief where Jace is and he's been arrested." She tugged on the broom, but he held fast.

"Will you let go of this and listen for a minute?" He pried the broom from her and leaned it in the corner. Motioning to her chair he said, "Sit down."

Seeing he wasn't going to leave until she did as he asked, she obeyed. "What is it?"

"I have so much to say to you. I don't even know where to begin." He took a deep breath. "Jace didn't kill Soloman."

She stared at him without reacting for a moment. Then she doubled up her fist and slugged him in the belly. He didn't flinch. "What do you expect me to do, Trey? Fall down weeping because the great Trey Bouché proclaims my brother's innocence? You're a little too late."

"I'm telling you I was wrong. It was confirmed today, but I've known it for a while now. The problem is there was no way to prove he didn't do it until now." His dark eyes bored into hers.

"What happened now?" she asked warily.

"Jody found the person who killed Soloman." He didn't pad the words or try to sugarcoat them.

"Who?" Summer couldn't breathe. Her chest felt too tight to draw a breath. "Why?"

"The picture you found? It was taken at Mugs-n-Jugs. My mother and yours and also Buford and Leroy went there the night we graduated. My mother found out the Chief was having an affair with Carlene Carter. Mother was furious and she went to blow off some steam. Soloman was there, too. He hooked up with your mother and raped her. But she wasn't his first victim."

"What do you mean?" She wished she would've sat when he told her to.

"He did the exact thing to Carlene a few nights previously." Trey took her hands. "She went back and killed him when the Chief didn't listen to her."

As the implications of his words sank in, Summer began to cry. "Oh, God."

"I know." Trey took her in his arms and kissed her hair. "I'm so sorry."

She pulled back and looked into his face. "Are you sorry for what you did to Jace, too?"

"I did what I thought was right at the time."

"That's not an answer," she accused.

"It's not the answer you want," he corrected. "Yes, I regret what happened. I'm sorry Jace lost five years of his life, but I can't tell you I was wrong for testifying that I saw him standing over Soloman's body with bloody hands."

Summer looked down. Not exactly what she'd been hoping for, but somehow, it was enough. "I've been wrong, too."

He lifted her chin. "For what?"

"For wanting you to lie for Jace." Years of anger evaporated with her words. Summer felt like she'd just wiped the slate clean. "That was wrong."

"He's your brother. You had no choice but to stand up for him." His gravelly voice raised goose bumps on her arms.

"Yes, but you are…" She couldn't continue.

"What am I, Summer? Say it." His hands went to her arms; he lifted her to her feet and his mouth moved within a hairbreadth from hers. "Just tell me."

Lindy's courage flashed in Summer's head. "You're the man I've always wanted," she blurted. "Forever, it seems."

"That's good," he breathed across her lips, "because you're the only woman I've ever wanted, too." They both smiled at the way his words came out.

His mouth slanted across hers and she lost all thoughts.

Leading him into the supply closet, she reached around him to lock the door. "We've wasted so much time," she whispered as he bent to claim her mouth again.

"No more." His kiss was hot and sweet and demanding.

Chapter Twenty-Three

Emily's funeral was scheduled for ten A.M.

Late at night, the Chief had come in and locked himself in his bedroom. Trey had tried to talk to him, to get him to discuss the developments with Carlene and Jace, but the Chief had not responded. Etta had left food for him at his door, but he hadn't touched it. Because he told them to go away and leave him alone, they knew he was alive.

There hadn't been any promises made between Trey and Summer, but the future looked good.

Lindy joined him in the kitchen. "Hi."

"How are you?" He searched her face for grief. Like him, Lindy missed their mother but knew she wasn't suffering now. "Your hair looks nice."

She touched a strand of her blonde hair. "Thanks. Yeah, I'm okay." She poured a cup of coffee and sat across from him.

"Does Jace know how lucky he is to have you?" Trey asked.

She grinned. "He'd better."

"It won't be easy to have a life with him," Trey warned. No matter how grown up she had become, Lindy was still his little sister and he felt compelled to try and help her.

"Do you think I don't know that? If you think getting around MiLann is going to be a piece of chocolate cake then you're living in dreamland," Lindy said.

"I know." He sipped his coffee trying to think of a way to phrase his next bit of news. Finally, he bit the bullet. "I have some things to tell you."

"Like?" She frowned at him.

"Jody caught Soloman's killer." He leaned back and smiled. "And it looks like we have a sister. Someone close to you."

For the next hour, he filled her in on all that had happened.

A big smile broke across her face. She leaped up and danced around on her toes. "This means Jace can go free?"

He nodded. "There'll be a lot of red tape, but yeah, he should be exonerated."

"What does the Chief have to say about all this?" Lindy slowed for a moment. "Has he admitted he made a mistake in arresting Jace?"

"He doesn't know. He won't come out of his room. We'll talk to him after the service." Trey got up and hugged her. "But see, miracles do happen."

•••

Summer stood toward the rear of the church as Preacher Finn eulogized Emily Devereaux Bouché. He spoke of her childhood in Louisiana, her marriage to Samuel Bouché, and the two children she loved so well, Trey and Lindy. Summer wiped away tears as the preacher talked about Emily's love of her family. Summer knew he spoke the truth. Emily had once been like a second mother to her.

Her gaze strayed to the flower-draped coffin. The casket was closed, for which Summer was grateful. Florists in three counties must've sold out for this service. Blooms of every description stood like sentinels at the front of the church. A cool breeze on her arm made her shiver. She rubbed her arms as her gaze went to the Chief, Lindy, and Trey seated together, heads bowed. There were no other family members, but Etta sat with them. Summer's heart ached for Trey. He looked so forlorn. Behind the Chief, Juliet's police force and many other city officials took two pews. Several policemen from other surrounding towns were also in attendance. They filled the rows on the other side of the aisle.

Jody stood almost directly behind Trey. Ida Barnes, the Chief's longtime secretary, at his back. Summer glanced around. She recognized nearly everyone. Lilah had come with her and they were seated together. But when Summer had asked Glory if she planned to attend she'd said no, someone had to keep the shop running. Oddly, Buford Krebbs must've had the same train of thought because his wife, Viola, stood without him two rows up from Summer, sandwiched between her friends.

As the service concluded, the family followed the casket out of the church. The Chief marched like a tin soldier, no apparent emotions on his face, his movements jerky. Etta trailed behind him, wiping her nose with a lace handkerchief. Lindy and Trey walked out next, holding hands. Lindy's eyes were bloodshot and her face puffy, but she looked like a lady, her newly blonde hair secured in a sedate twist, her dark gray dress, although figure hugging, was age appropriate.

But it was Trey who took Summer's breath. His features were strained, but he seemed composed. Wearing a dark suit with a dress shirt and tie, he was handsome enough to make her knees weak. As he drew near, he must've felt her gaze upon him because he glanced up and their eyes met for a second. A tiny smile played at the corner of his mouth for just an instant, then it was gone. She nodded at him. It was enough that he knew she was here for him. Summer closed her eyes and said a quick prayer for the family.

She felt as if someone were staring at her. Without being obvious, she glanced around. On the other side of the aisle, Mary-Gray Bennet shot her a glare. Summer met the other girl's hard look without flinching. She was sorry Mary-Gray had set her cap for Trey, but he wasn't available any more. As soon as they could, without upsetting everyone, they would publicly become a couple. A small shiver of delight danced up Summer's back.

An usher motioned for her to leave and she walked out of the church.

The sun blinded her for a minute. When she could see again, she saw groups of people standing in groups near the grave across the road. Her eyes searched for Trey. She found him near the open gravesite talking to the Chief and Lindy.

Near Summer's elbow, Lilah asked, "Do you see Jody?"

"I don't see him. Let's go toward the police cars. Maybe he's over there." They wove their way through the throngs of people heading the opposite direction, in search of him.

"There he is." Lilah pointed his direction.

Near his patrol unit, Jody spoke into his radio. His expression was grim.

"Something's wrong." Lilah broke into a quick jog. "I'd know that look anywhere."

"The interment is going to be very soon." Summer looked over her shoulder and saw the family take their seats at the edge of the grave. Preacher Finn bowed his head.

"I'm telling you, something's happened," Lilah insisted, dodging a minivan.

Jody looked up when they approached. He hung up his radio. Lilah was right; he looked as though he'd seen a ghost. "We've got a problem."

"What is it, baby?" Lilah wrapped her arms around his waist.

Gently, he removed himself. "We've got the wrong person in jail. Carlene Carter didn't kill Mrs. Bouché or anyone else. I just got a call. The hair Trey found on his mother's pillow isn't Carlene's."

"Who's then?" Summer asked.

He shook his head. "We don't know yet. There's more. Someone shot Buford Krebbs in the back today when he entered his store through the side door. He's in surgery, but not expected to live. Whoever did it tried to make it look like a burglary, but I think our killer is on the prowl again."

"Oh, God." Summer covered her mouth with her hands. Dropping them like lead weights, she said, "Mama. She's in danger."

"I'll send a unit out to check on her," Jody said.

"She won't let anyone but me inside." Summer looked around for a way to get out of the packed parking lot. Her old car was stuck between two pickups she didn't recognize.

"I'll take you," Jody said. "I'll send Carole Rasley to Krebbs's place."

"We should tell Trey," Summer said, uncertain if she should interrupt his mother's service. Extreme, yes. But her mama's funeral might be the next one if she didn't do something.

"You two go on. I'll tell Trey where you're at." Lilah shoved Jody. "Go! Hurry! Before it's too late."

He opened the door and ushered Summer in then ran around and jumped in the driver's seat. Picking up the radio, he called Officer Rasley and told her to stay at the Krebbs's scene until he could get there. Then he tore up the road, red and blue lights flashing, siren screaming.

• • •

Trey threw his handful of dirt on top of his mother's coffin and turned away. He scanned the crowd of mourners for Summer, but didn't see her. Lindy grabbed his hand and he glanced at her strained face. He hoped she could make it through the rest of the day without falling down. He hoped they all could. The Chief stood nearby. He hadn't broken down, but he acted as if he were somewhere else. His mind seemed to be a million miles away.

Someone touched Trey's arm. Lilah stood there, a fearful expression on her face. "I have to talk to you. Now."

Her tone convinced him and he let go of Lindy's hand with an apologetic glance. He walked a few feet with Lilah then stopped. "What's wrong?"

"Jody got a call on the radio. There was a break-in at Krebbs's store. He got shot in the back and they don't think he's going to live. Summer was with me. She thinks her mama is in danger and she and Jody tore up out of here like two cats with their tails on fire."

Trey began moving before she was done talking. "Thanks, Lilah."

He approached the Chief. "Sir? There's trouble brewing."

Lindy joined them. "What's going on?"

Trey didn't see any reason not to tell her. "Buford Krebbs was shot a little while ago. He's in surgery. Carlene Carter is being held for Mother's murder, so she couldn't have been the one who did it. I think MiLann Hill is in danger. I've got to go."

"Oh, no," Lindy cried. "Someone might go after Jace, too. Daddy, listen, Jace didn't kill Deke Soloman. Whoever did might be after him. I have to warn him."

"Call Jace on your cell," Trey ordered, not waiting for their father to say anything to her.

"Better yet, I'm going to him." Before either of the men could react, Lindy turned and sprinted across the lawn, her shoes flying off as she ran.

The Chief's mouth was white and pinched. He looked ill. "Hell no, Carlene didn't do anything like that." He turned to Ida. "Go to the jail now and turn Carlene loose right now. Tell her I'll talk to her later. Make sure she gets home all right."

"I've got to go to Summer," Trey said. "If something happens to MiLann…"

"We'll both go." The Chief shot Trey an impatient look. "Move."

As they climbed in the Mustang, Trey gave the Chief a puzzled glance. "Sir? You're leaving Mother's funeral. Are you sure you want to do that?"

"Got no choice." He grunted as he settled in the leather bucket seat and tethered the seatbelt around his big frame. "Damn cars are made for midgets."

Trey spun the car around and as he hit the road he asked, "What do you mean, you have 'no choice?'"

"I can't let anything happen to MiLann," the Chief said. "If I do, I'll have more rights to set wrong."

"What do you mean? Carlene?" Trey concentrated on the road, and didn't glance over. "If she didn't kill Soloman or Mother, then who did?"

He didn't answer.

•••

Lindy sped up the driveway to Granny's, her heart pounding in her chest. If anything happened to Jace, she'd never forgive herself. She loved him with her whole heart. No matter the cost, no matter the end, she would stand by him.

Skidding the Jeep to a halt, she jumped out and ran to the front door. She barreled through it, shouting, "Jace! Jace! Are you here?"

"Up here," he called. In a minute, the attic ladder dropped and he climbed down. As he approached, he said, "I wasn't sure you'd come back."

"I told you I would. You aren't going to believe this," Lindy cried, launching herself at him. "I have so much to tell you."

He caught her as she wrapped her arms and legs around him. "What do you have to tell me, little girl?"

"For one thing, Trey did what he said he would and found out who killed Soloman. You're going to be set free." She hugged him tight. "And, I'm not a little girl."

"No, you're not," he agreed, looking into her eyes with open desire. Still holding her, he said, "Tell me what happened. Start at the beginning."

"The Chief had an affair with Carlene Carter…Candy is her daughter, maybe my sister…we have to do DNA…Mother found out about it…she went to the bar with the Chief's friends… Soloman raped Carlene, too, and she killed him." She took a breath. "So you're going to be freed."

He shook his head. "I don't follow."

"It's complicated," she said. "But trust me; everyone will know you're innocent by the time I'm through. I'll shout it from the rooftops, from town square, from the water tower. You name it. If I can be heard, I'll be there."

"You'd do that for me?" His lips moved a mere fraction of an inch from hers.

"I'd do anything for you," she said, her voice as husky as Trey's. She giggled. "Even color my hair."

He gaze moved to her blonde color and his eyes widened. He reached to touch the one curl she'd left down with one finger. "It's gorgeous. Just like the rest of you."

"Flattery will get you everywhere." She tightened her legs around his waist.

He slipped one hand up her back and bare neck, cupping it. "Will it get me here?"

"Uh-huh." Her eyes locked on his.

"I'm crazy about this color," he whispered as his hand moved to the clip holding her French twist and releasing it. Her hair tumbled around her face.

"Keep talking," she ordered as she clasped her hands behind his head. Then she moved her mouth close to his ear. "Please."

"Have I told you how much I like you in my arms?" His free hand tangled in her hair.

"No," she said. She wasn't going to let him off easy.

"Have I told you how much I want to be inside you?" He reached for her dress and tugged it up over her hips. His fingers slipped along her belly, lower, resting at the top of her satin panties.

She shivered and a hot flash of desire flooded her. "No."

"I'm saying it now." His fingers slid lower, but not nearly far enough.

"Love me," she suggested.

"Whatever the lady desires." He carried her to the bed. Settling her gently on the covers, he stood above her and helped pull her tight, gray dress over her head.

Leaning back against the pillows on her granny's bed, Lindy lifted her chin and met his hot gaze. Her heart filled her chest and she was so taken by her love for him, she couldn't speak for fear the magic would end.

"You are so special." His hands hung by his sides.

With steady fingers, she reached for the front clasp of her bra and undid it. Shrugging her shoulders, the satin fell to the bed. Her nipples puckered in the warm air. Lifting her hips, she shimmied out of the scrap of satin and lace covering her womanly parts. Completely nude, except for the matching diamond bellybutton stud and earrings, she laid proudly before him. Already damp, she wanted him inside her *now*.

She reached for him, but he instead of pressing down on top of her as she expected, he knelt in front of her and touched the tip of his tongue to the diamond in her bellybutton. The move was so unexpected, she burst out in laughter. Against her stomach, she could feel his lips move into a smile.

But all laughter died a moment later when he pushed her legs apart and bent his head to her. His mouth brushed across the springy curls between her legs. A small gasp escaped her then another as his tongue dove into the opening of her body. Her fingers curled into the blankets and her head fell back. Tingles rushed over her, from head to toe. Every muscle tensed, tightened like a string on a kite lifting for the sky.

Lifting her bottom with his hands, he touched her clit with his tongue. It was enough. Her body convulsed in a series of shakes that seemed like they would never end. Lindy opened and closed her mouth, gasping for air, not hearing her own cries.

She hadn't recovered her breath or sense of equilibrium and he was over her, entering her. Instinctively, her hands went to his buttocks, her fingers digging in. He plunged deep and she met the thrust with an equally eager movement of her hips. Like two dancers, they rose and dipped and lifted each other to the place of pure pleasure. In her ear, he began to breathe in quick, jerky pants. His eyes closed and his mouth opened a fraction. Lindy's body tightened, encouraged him to spill his seed. Her own quivers built and built until she exploded in a million directions at once. As she shattered, he, too, found his limit and came, crying out into her hair.

For a few minutes neither moved.

Then Jace rolled to his back, pulling her across his chest. "Lady, you're amazing."

Her already speeding heart went into overdrive "Thank you."

He lifted her limp hand and kissed her palm. "I owe you so much."

She raised her head and looked at him. The flames he'd just lit began to die. Keeping her voice from shaking, she asked, "Is that what this was? Some kind of payment?"

"What do you want it to be?" His expression was guarded. "Some forever kind of thing?"

"Oh no, you're not going to get me to fall for that one again." She rested her chin on his chest and looked into his deep blue eyes. "I told you I loved you and you told me not to mistake great sex for love. The screwing was awesome, but you won't trick me twice."

"Don't say that," he said with a frown. "I don't want to hear my wife talk dirty about the way we make love."

Her eardrums pounded, but Lindy kept her expression blasé. "Wife? Lovemaking?"

"Yeah." He grinned and her heart did a few cartwheels. "Making love. What we have is too good to call it anything else."

"What are you saying? What's this about a wife?" She had to hear the words; he had to say it. She ran her fingers across the ridges of his stomach and back up to his flat, brown nipples. "I want to be sure I'm not hearing things."

"He rose up and took her face between his hands. "Lindy Bouché, I'm so lucky to have you. I want you and I need you."

She held her breath.

She didn't blink.

The moment seemed eons.

He said, "I love you."

She doubled her fist and slugged him in the stomach. "I knew it!"

He laughed and brought her mouth to his. Just before he kissed her he said, "Will you do me the honor of marrying me?"

"Yes, oh, yes. I'll be proud to marry you. I love you, too, Jace Hill. For the rest of our lives."

He rolled over her, his body once again ready to prove his devotion.

Chapter Twenty-Four

Summer hit the ground running.

Jody pounded after her. "Wait, Summer. There might be someone in there."

She disregarded his advice. Leaping up the steps, she saw her fears weren't unfounded. The screen door on the porch stood ajar, as did the kitchen door. Mama never would have left either open. With her heart in her throat, Summer moved across the porch, Jody at her back.

"Summer," he warned, "Don't go in there."

She ignored him.

Stepping into the kitchen, it took a moment for her brain to process what her eyes were telling her. Mama sat at the kitchen table, her eyes huge, her lips pressed tight. The angry red scar stood out in sharp contrast to her white face. In her shaking hands, she held a letter.

Seeing who was with her, Summer breathed easier. "Thank God you're here. Buford Krebbs was shot today and we thought whoever did it might come here…"

Mama whimpered.

"Summer," Jody said.

Then she saw the gun pressed to the back of Mama's head.

"Oh, God, what's going on?" Her knees shook and she felt as if she might fall to the floor. She took one step forward, and the gun was pointed at her.

"Stay where you are or I'll kill her in front of you. I didn't want it to be like this, but you gave me no choice." The gun didn't waver and neither did the owner holding it.

"Glory?" Summer shook her head to clear her vision—sure she was seeing things. But her boss, her friend, stood in front of her, pointing a gun at her chest. Her features were twisted with rage, her green eyes unfocused, her mouth a thin line. Even her hair looked angry—standing on end in tight, sharp spikes.

"Yeah, me." Glory chuckled and the hair on the back of Summer's neck stood on end. "Fooled you, didn't I?"

Summer felt Jody at her shoulder, but didn't look at him when he said, "Let Mrs. Hill go."

"Shut up, cop. Another word out of you and I'll waste her right here." Glory shoved the gun at Mama's head for emphasis.

He held up his hands in a gesture of surrender and backed away several steps.

Summer tried to send Mama a message, staring into her frozen blue eyes. "Yes, you got me. I don't understand. Why are you mad at me? Let Mama go, and I'll do anything you want."

"You'll do anything I want anyway." Glory cackled and the sound was that of a madwoman. She poked Mama in the back with the gun barrel. A small whimper was Mama's only response. "Shut up, you crazy old bitch."

"You're my friend, why are you doing this?" Summer balled her hands into fists. None of this made any sense. "Why do you want to hurt Mama? She's never done anything to you."

Glory's eerie laugh bounced off the walls. "You are so wrong, *friend.*"

Dumbfounded, Summer couldn't think what Glory meant. As far as she knew, Mama had always treated Glory well. In fact, she was one of the few people Mama trusted enough to allow inside her house. "Please let Mama go," Summer pleaded.

"Not until she pays for what she did." Glory's irritation grew and she moved around. "I can't let her get away with it."

Summer locked her gaze on the gun. "Surely you're mistaken. Mama couldn't have done anything to you. The only times you've seen her I've been right here with you, and I can't think of a thing she could've done to make you so angry."

"She took him away from me," Glory screamed. "They all did."

"Took who?" Certain her friend had lost her mind, Summer wondered if she could get through to her. If only someone would come and help.

Glory's lips turned into a sneer. "You're so stupid."

"Yes." Summer would say anything to get Glory to free Mama. "I am dumb. I don't know who you mean. Please tell me."

"Daddy, Daddy, Daddy," Glory sang in a babyish voice. Her eyes half closed and she began to rock from side to side. Her hand holding the gun slipped to her waist.

Seeing her chance, Summer took two quick steps. Glory's eyes flew open and she jerked the gun up at Summer's chest again. Her features looked normal. "Try that again and it'll be the last move you make."

"I'm sorry." Summer stepped back. "Forgive me." Out of the corner of her eye, she could see Jody, as helpless as she.

A car pulled into the driveway.

Glory pushed the pistol into the side of Mama's head. "Keep them back."

"Summer? Are you okay?" Trey's voice echoed through the kitchen. In a minute, he appeared in the doorway, the Chief behind him. "Oh, shit."

Mama's terror-glazed eyes went wider, but she didn't move. She resembled a wax figure, pale and frozen. Except for her hands, which shook like a tambourine player's.

Summer wanted to rush to Trey, to let him take over, to fix this. Instead, she motioned for him to stop. He nodded and both he and the Chief stood silent. In a normal tone she said, "Glory was just explaining to me why she's so angry with me."

Glory tipped her head back and howled. With her free hand, she slapped her thigh. "Oh, that's rich. You're so simple, you never knew I was the one who was making all of the bad ones pay for their sins. You couldn't even see it when it was right under your nose. Like when I was washing my bloody shirt at the beauty shop."

A shiver climbed up and back down Summer's spine. "You mean when you were at the shop the other night? When I stopped to talk to you?"

"Uh-huh." Glory's green eyes glittered. "Right under your nose and you didn't even know. Dumb."

"Whose blood was on your shirt?" Summer dreaded the answer.

For a long moment, Glory stared at the gun in her hand and Summer feared she would pull the trigger. As if in a trance she said, "He told me. All of it. I had to sleep with him to make him say, but he came clean. Don't you see? I had to make it right."

"Who?" Summer whispered. "Who told you something?"

Glory heaved a tremendous sigh. "Do I have to explain everything to you?"

With a vigorous nod Summer said, "Yes, please make me understand."

"I snuck in the back door and I held this gun to his head and I made him squirm like the worm he was." Glory looked at all of them by turns. "None of you even suspected I killed him. He had to die because he knew the whole story and he never said a thing. My Daddy was killed and he just sat there and never said a word. He laughed."

"Who laughed?" Summer whispered. Glory had lost her mind. Nothing she said made sense.

"Jimmy Ray." Trey's voice echoed in the kitchen like a cannon going off and they all jumped.

"Don't say that name," Glory screamed and swung the gun his direction. "Don't say it ever again."

"I'm sorry," Trey said. "He shouldn't have laughed at you."

Fat tears rolled down her face. "No, he shouldn't."

In a soft voice Trey asked, "Can you tell us what happened? What did he do to your daddy?"

Summer held her breath as he took a few steps toward Glory. She seemed unaware of his movement. "Daddy, Daddy, Daddy."

"Who's your daddy?" he asked. "Tell me."

"Her daddy was Deke Soloman," the Chief said. "Can't you see it?"

Everyone looked at her. For the first time, Summer recognized the red hair, the evil green eyes with the identical hate in them as the man in the picture. "My God."

"That's right, I'm Glory Soloman. I came to this godforsaken place to avenge him. I waited and waited until the time was right. Then I struck. One at a time, they went down like a house of cards. No one even looked at me." She glared at them. Then she poked Mama again. "If your devil spawn had just stayed in jail where he belonged, no one would've even thought to put it all together. Could've made them all pay for what they did. But no, he—" she pointed at Trey "—had to start nosing around."

Summer couldn't seem to connect the dots. "What does Jace have to do with anything?"

"I know." Trey looked at Glory. "May I explain?"

She snorted. "If you can."

"I think I figured it out." He looked at the Chief. "It all starts with you. You began to have an affair with Carlene Carter. It was all fun and games until she took Marie Lennox's place with a john at Mugs-n-Jugs one night in May. This john was Deke Soloman. How am I doing so far?"

The Chief gave a quick, sharp nod.

Trey continued. "For whatever reason, Soloman raped Carlene. She didn't tell him she was someone else when she took Marie's place. There wasn't any reason to."

MiLann made a strangled sound.

"I'm sorry, Mrs. Hill. If the Chief would've only listened to Carlene when she came to tell him about the rape, you wouldn't have been the next victim." Trey shot his dad a withering look.

"Daddy didn't rape anyone," Glory shouted. "Sluts teased him and he didn't like that. But he didn't have to force anyone to get what he wanted. All the women loved him. He had a new girl every week. And he had me. I was all he needed."

"I'm sorry," Trey said in a low voice. "May I go on?"

Glory gave a quick nod.

"Because the Chief chose not to act on her report, Carlene was furious. She went to my mother and told her about the affair. But she didn't stop there. She stalked Soloman and killed him…"

"That whore didn't kill my daddy," Glory screamed. She waved the gun at the Chief. "He knows the truth. Tell it."

Looking sick, the Chief looked around as if he wanted to escape. Seeing none, he said, "Hill did it."

"No, he didn't," Summer denied. "Stop lying."

"Chief," Trey said, "this is the time."

With another desperate look around, he realized he was trapped. He seemed to shrink before their eyes. "All right. I don't know all of what happened. Carlene came to me and when I told her to go home, she told Emily about us. Emily was furious with me, but it was the boys' graduation and she didn't want to upset them, so she agreed to wait until the next day to do anything else."

"I heard you fighting," Trey said. Their ugly words flashed in his head. "Then what happened? I think I know, but we'd like to hear it from you."

"At the party Emily got angrier and she had too much to drink. She was making threats, telling me she was going to leave me. I told her to go to bed. Sleep it off. Instead, she left the party with MiLann, Buford, and Leroy. Those were my friends and she knew it would hurt me if they took up for her. Hell, they were bound to. Both were half in love with her. Leroy was all the way gone. I went to bed, not knowing what to do."

"They made a fool of my daddy," Glory said, "tell that part."

The Chief looked helpless. "I can't."

Trey's gaze went to Summer. He hoped she could see how much he loved her in his eyes. If Glory snapped and something happened to her mother, he didn't think she would ever pick up the pieces. Somehow, they had to get Glory calmed down. He opened his mouth, praying for the right words.

"I can." MiLann's soft voice carried like a starling on a breeze.

"Mama?" Summer sounded like a little girl. "Are you sure you want to do this?"

Her eyes were clearer than they'd been in years. "I remember. Emily was so angry and she wanted to go to the bar. Somehow Mugs-n-Jugs was suggested. We all thought it would be fun. It was…at first. Jimmy Ray Hunt even got out his camera and snapped a photo. He said he would have something to blackmail the Chief if he tried to stop any illegal activities."

"The picture in your office?" Summer asked.

He jerked his head. "Yeah."

"Go on," Trey said gently. "If you can."

MiLann took a deep breath. "Soloman was there. He was fun and we invited him to join the party. He liked Emily a lot. He wanted to be with her…"

"But she was too good for him," Glory screamed. "The teasing bitch."

"That's my dead wife," the Chief shouted back. His face turned red and the vein in his forehead throbbed.

Everyone stared at Glory. She glared at the Chief. "Shut up. I want to know once and for all what happened."

"It's true," MiLann confirmed. "Emily teased him. And she led on Buford and Leroy, too. Finally, someone suggested we go to the motel, and we did. Emily told me on the way she had no intention of sleeping with Soloman or anyone else. She said that would make her no better than Samuel, and she was Catholic and she wouldn't betray her vows. When we got to the Blue Cat, she told Soloman she wouldn't lie down with white trash, said she had a reputation to maintain. Leroy and Buford laughed with her. Soloman took off, furious and hurt. I left them and went after him to try and apologize."

"That's when it happened," Trey said gently.

"He didn't rape her," Glory screamed. She jabbed MiLann with the gun again. "Don't you say it."

Half turning in her chair, MiLann faced her squarely. "I won't lie. Shoot me if you will. You can't make my life any worse. Kill me and put me out of my misery. Soloman went insane and hit me. I fell to the floor in a daze. He stomped on me with his feet, he screamed, he raved. Said I was a poor second. That Emily was a tease, a slut, and many other horrible things. I eventually passed out. I went in and out of consciousness. That's when he…"

"Mama, stop," Summer whispered.

"Raped me." Her voice rang strong.

No one spoke.

"You're lying." Glory sounded so sure. As if not a word MiLann had just said struck a chord with her.

Trey thought she must've been a wooden puppet if the woman in front of her hadn't touched her in some way. "Do you know who actually killed Soloman, Mrs. Hill?"

She took a deep breath. Her fingers curled around the paper in her hands. "Yes."

"Her son didn't," Glory said. "He was framed."

"Then who?" Summer's heart pounded so hard she feared it might jump out of her chest.

Glory looked at her with cold, dead eyes. "MiLann knows."

Trey looked at Summer for a long moment. "Tell us what you have there, Mrs. Hill. Is that a letter from Jace?"

"No," Summer said. "Mama doesn't know."

"Admit it," Trey ordered the Chief. "Mother felt guilty for what MiLann suffered because of her. She found Soloman and killed him. No one saw her and she got away with it. When Jace went off the deep end and vowed vengeance, she kept quiet."

When he didn't answer, MiLann whispered, "Yes. It's the truth. This is a letter Emily sent me. It's all in here. She wanted to clear her conscience before she died. She killed Soloman with a knife from her own house. When I was in the hospital, the Chief misplaced the rape kit."

The Chief said, "She was my wife. I had to protect her."

"Oh, God, no." Summer stumbled and Trey caught her in his arms. "You and Emily let Jace go to prison for a murder he didn't commit. Why? He was only a boy."

"She couldn't take it, he could." The Chief didn't look apologetic.

"You dirty son-of-a-bitch." Summer tried to squirm out of Trey's arms, but he held her fast. "You bastard. You let an innocent kid go to prison when you knew he didn't do it so your lily-white name wouldn't be dirtied."

"He's not worth it." Trey glared at his father. "He's got to live with what he's done."

"I didn't know for sure," the Chief said. "I had my ideas about what happened that night. But when Trey found Jace with Soloman's body, it was the thing I needed to hear to shut up my suspicions."

"Emily turned her back to save her own skin," Summer sobbed. "Mama was raped because of her. Jace has rotted away in prison. May God forgive her soul."

"But I made the rest of them pay," Glory crowed. "Every last one. Marie Lennox because Carlene told her he did the bad thing. I haven't gotten around to that slut Carlene yet. Leroy Eaton and Buford Krebs for laughing at him, and most of all, Emily Bouché for killing him. It was so easy. Nobody even put it all together. I've been planning my revenge all for years. There's only MiLann left."

"When Jace escaped and I came home, you had to put your plan in motion," Trey said. "Because we might've figured it all out. You wanted your justice. Someone might steal it if we put it all together, right?"

"You're not as dumb as some," she said. "Those letters from Jace? Half of them were from me. I've been tormenting the old Chief forever. Now that we all know the truth, it's time to finish it." She pressed the gun to MiLann's head.

Trey shoved Summer out of the way, leaped over the table, narrowly missing MiLann, and grabbed the gun. A shot rang out. Blood spread across his chest and the room went crazy.

• • •

Jace stopped on the steps of the courthouse. He turned and faced Lindy. "Are you sure you want to do this?"

She squeezed his hand. "I'm positive."

"It won't be easy," he warned. "I don't have much."

"I don't care." Her eyes glowed with happiness. "You're all I need."

He tugged her close and wrapped his arms around her. How he had gotten so lucky to find her? "Come on. Let's get married."

She smiled at him and they went inside.

In a matter of minutes, they were man and wife.

Jace kissed his bride. Although the future wasn't certain, he knew he had a great new start. He still had to be officially cleared by the state, but he didn't have to return to Angola. Better, they had settled a large sum of money on him, so he had some time to find what he wanted to do.

He shook the judge's hand and turned to his bride. "Ready?"

"Completely."

As they walked down the hall leading to the Chief's office, Lindy stumbled.

"You okay?" Jace asked, wrapping his arm around her shoulders.

She blinked rapidly and gave her head a quick jerk. "Yeah. I'll be all right. I'm so sorry for what the Chief did to you."

"He hurt you, too." Jace would do anything to take that pain away.

"Not so much," she said bravely. "You're the one who suffered the most."

"It's over now." He led her through the door into the sunshine. "And it's a brand new day."

• • •

"May I see Trey?" Summer held her breath, not sure if he still wanted to see her. She had been at the hospital the whole time he was in surgery and by his side every minute he was in the hospital. They hadn't talked much because he had been too doped up. The bullet had gone through into his shoulder, lodging there. The doctors had taken it out; assuring him he would have full use of his arm and hand.

Why she worried was because the Chief had gone to his office, spread out Jace's letters and shot himself in the head. She prayed Trey wouldn't blame her for the Chief's actions.

Etta waved a shaky hand. She appeared to have aged by at least a decade. "Hi, honey. Mister Trey is upstairs in his old room. Go up if you want."

Summer went toward the stairs. "How is he?"

"Mendin' fine."

Wrinkling her nose, she went up the wide staircase and down the hall to Trey's room. She knocked lightly and entered. In a big bed near the window, Trey lay still, apparently asleep. Moving across the room, she kicked off her sandals and sat in the chair nearby.

He opened his eyes. "I thought I was dreaming about an angel."

"Not today." She reached for his hand. "How are you feeling?"

"Been better, but pretty good now." A weak smile lit up his pale face.

"Do you need anything? A drink? Pain pills?" She glanced around for them.

He tugged her close. "Just you."

She blinked back sudden tears. "Being around me almost got you killed."

He struggled to a sitting position. "Are you kidding? That crazy woman was going to murder your mother. I couldn't let that happen. I've already done so much to your family."

Summer put her finger over his lips. "Hush. That's over now. You did what you had to do at the time. No rational person would've thought their own mother would kill someone."

He took hold of her hand and moved it. "I'm so sorry," he whispered. A deeper kind of pain than physical swam in his dark eyes. "If the Chief had only listened…"

"Trey, stop. There's no way any of that is your fault." She wasn't going to let him blame himself. He was a pawn in all this.

"Can you forgive me?" His husky voice grated like gravel in rattling around in a cement truck.

"There's nothing to forgive you for," she insisted. "You didn't know."

Her heart jumped a few beats. This man had always been the only one for her. So much lost time to make up for. She leaned forward and touched her lips to his. "I need you, Trey."

"Enough to put the past behind us?" His eyes filled with hope. "The Chief wouldn't say he was wrong or that he was sorry before he died. It's as if he couldn't make himself admit what he or Mother did. I hope he's found some kind of peace."

"Trey, don't. I love you. Not the Chief, you." She kissed him, trying to erase the image of the Chief's death out of his head. "You're not like him."

"No, but I can't help but feel responsible," he said. "If I hadn't been so stubborn and listened to you, a lot of this could've been prevented." Wrapping his good arm around her, he pulled her half on top of him.

Careful not to hurt him further, she said, "Trey, it's taken me all these years to admit that you did what you had to do. You're an honorable person and you had to tell the Chief you saw Jace with the knife. You did what was right. There was no way you could know what would happen. Besides, Mama's actually doing a lot better. She stepped outside, to the garden today. Facing her demons was the best thing that could've happened."

"Thank you for understanding." Trey brushed her hair back. "I hope MiLann makes a full recovery."

"It looks like we're going to be related by our siblings," Summer said. "Jace and Lindy got married."

"Lindy called me, too," Trey said. "She put Jace on the phone. I told him I'm happy for them."

"Yes, me too." Summer's eyes filled. She couldn't blink them back fast enough and a few slipped down her face. "Everything's good."

"Not everything." Trey wiped her cheeks with his thumb. "It must be quite a shock to find out all that about Glory. Did you have an inkling she was Soloman's daughter?"

"Never." She blinked back tears. It would take a long time before she felt better. "I'll miss her. I'm so sorry she was so damaged by her father."

"Jody did some checking. Turns out Soloman was a grifter. He stole from wealthy women all over the south. He knew who my mother was from the minute he set foot in the bar." Trey hugged her close. "Soloman dragged Glory around with him her whole life. She wasn't with him that night because she had stayed in New Orleans to work her own job. The police caught her and she spent the next two years in prison. The minute she was released, she made her way here to avenge her father."

Summer gave her head a little shake. "Your mother killed Soloman because of what he did to Mama. Glory killed her and the others for what she thought they did to him. Buford is going to be paralyzed from the waist down. We all paid. Jace, you, me. Even Glory. All because of our parents' decisions. So much death and destruction."

"We have a chance to pick up the pieces," he said against her hair.

"Lilah and I are going to try and keep the shop going, but it won't be easy. She told me Jody took over the Chief's job. The city council will have to approve him, but I don't know why they wouldn't go for it. Jody is a great guy." Summer lifted her chin and watched him to gauge his reaction.

"No matter what happens, we have each other," Trey whispered in her ear. "I love you, Summer. I will love you forever."

She sat up a little and said, "I love you, Trey."

"Prove it," he said. "Marry me?"

"Only if we can do it today," she replied. "Because I don't want us to lose another minute."

He kissed her.

"Can you do this?" She slipped her hand under his T-shirt.

His eyes drifted shut. "Uh-huh."

She moved her hand lower and slid it inside his pajama pants. Her hand circled his penis. "What about this?"

"Barely." A smile played around his lips.

After a few slow strokes, she asked, "Am I hurting you?"

"Terribly."

Her hand quit moving. "I can stop."

His eyes flew open. "Only if you do want me to die."

She stood and slipped out of her clothes. Then, carefully, she slid his pants past his hips. "Are you strong enough for this?" She dropped her own clothes on the floor.

"I'll force myself," he ground out.

Summer straddled him and guided his penis into her. Carefully, as so not to injure him, she leaned forward and touched his lips with hers. He circled her neck with his good arm and held her close. She rocked her hips.

He thrust up and she thought she was the one going to die.

Their bodies caught and held a rhythm.

She cried out as she came in a shuddering finale.

Moments later, he too came.

She slumped forward, breathing heavily, his good arm around her waist. In a minute she rolled off him. He held her snuggled next to him. "Don't go anywhere."

"I won't. Never again," she promised.

About the Author

Falling in love with romance novels the summer before sixth grade, D'Ann Lindun never thought about writing one until many years later when she took a how-to class at her local college. She was hooked! She began writing and never looked back. Romance appeals to her because there's just something so satisfying about writing a book guaranteed to have a happy ending. D'Ann's particular favorites usually feature cowboys and the women who love them. This is probably because she draws inspiration from the area where she lives, Western Colorado; her husband of twenty-nine years; and their daughter. Composites of their small farm, herd of horses, five Australian shepherds, a Queensland heeler, nine ducks, and cats of every shape and color often show up in her stories!

http://dlindunauthor.blogspot.com/

http://www.facebook.com/DLindunAuthor

I love to hear from readers, please contact me at dldauthor@frontier.net

A Sneak Peek from Crimson Romance

(From *The Right Combination* by Nancy Loyan)

Safes are as mysterious and alluring as a woman.
Strong yet gentle to the touch. Equally as tempting.

Yellow crime barrier tape billowed in the humid breeze as it surrounded Samuals Safe and Lock Company like an animal pen. Only demented animals, Rafe thought, would commit such a sordid murder. He had experienced many, far too many, in his ten-year career.

"Special Agent Costillo, FBI," Rafe announced, flashing the leather bi-fold containing his credentials.

"Yeah, we've been expecting you," answered the uniformed Miami policeman standing guard at the crime scene, swiping his sweaty brow.

When a federal crime involved safes, Rafe was often a part of the investigation. He was the FBI's top expert on safes and vaults. Connections at the FBI's Miami field office knew he was in town visiting his family and informed him of the crime scene.

He had been involved in mob-hit cases where the victim had been locked in a safe and tossed in a lake, a new take on cement shoes. Incidents where people were murdered for the contents of a safe or vault were not uncommon. Having three legendary safe technicians murdered and stuffed in safes in the span of three months was unusual. Having one occur in the city of his birth while he was visiting made him uneasy.

Homicide detectives met him as he crossed over the tape and entered their territory.

The front office of the safe and lock company was typical for the business. A service counter was equipped with key duplicating equipment and key blanks.

Fingerprinted glass display cases featured the newest in security gadgetry and brass door locks. Modern metal safes and safe cabinets of various heights lined the walls, cardboard placards displaying features and price tags. Everything was a bit dusty, the air a bit stale, and the plank floors scuffed and worn. The shop was not unlike his father's. The thought alone made the hair tingle on Rafe's neck. Knowing that the victim could have been his own father made his blood chill. These murders were in familiar territory, in a world where he grew up, in a business he knew all too well, with victims with whom he could personally identify. He swallowed hard to get the bitter taste of anger out of his mouth.

"Back here," a detective in a rumpled tan suit motioned. He led Rafe through a doorway toward the back warehouse.

Heavy metal safes in shrink-wrap sat on wood pallets awaiting shipment. A rusted yellow forklift was at the ready. Used safes, some ornately painted, and some cast iron stood forlorn in a dark corner. Others were stacked in boxes. Johnson bars were propped against the cinder block walls.

Rafe followed the detective toward the back wall of the warehouse where a six-foot tall, double-door Mosler stood. The safe's chipped army green paint revealed its 1940s vintage; the drop handles its make. Its thick doors were open. Nickel alloy compression bars glimmered as the detective flashed his Mag Lite in the safe.

Though empty, and devoid of shelves, the compartment above an open money chest revealed puddles of blood. Streaks of burnished red smeared against the sides, back, and inner doors of the large safe.

"The body's at the coroner's," the detective said without emotion. "Forensics have been out and have taken samples."

"What were the signs of trauma?" Rafe asked, noting the blood and powdered residue from fingerprinting.

The detective shook his balding head. "No visible signs of gunshot or punctures. Only one weird thing."

"What's that?"

The detective looked at him, steely gray eyes turning to glass. "Three of the fingers on his right hand are missing."

"What three fingers?" Rafe asked, though he knew the answer from reports on the New York and LA murders.

"Thumb, forefinger, and middle finger," the detective answered. "Severed clean and nowhere to be found."

"The fingers a safeman uses to manipulate safes open," Rafe muttered. "I gather Mr. Samuals was right-handed?"

"We questioned his employees. Yes."

Rafe sighed.

"Since you guys have been called in, this isn't an isolated incident, is it?" the detective asked, staring at him.

Rafe met his gaze. "I'll have to review the coroner's report and forensics before making a judgment." From experience, he knew the answer.

• • •

After returning to his assigned FBI field office in Los Angeles and reviewing reports on the three "safeman murders," there was no doubt that a serial killer was on the loose. A definite pattern, a signature, had emerged. The crime scenes were organized with little evidence to work with, revealing a killer who went at great lengths to avoid detection. The murders appeared preplanned, deliberate, and calculated. Rafe also knew that he was dealing with a "trophy taker." The killer removed body parts creating a crime signature, a pattern connecting the crimes. The motive, though, was as mysterious as the individual committing the murders. The question of who, when, where the killer was going to strike next infiltrated his head like a bad headache. Rafe reviewed the facts in his mind.

There were more similarities than differences between the three murders. All of the victims had been safemen of great renown within the business.

Irving Samuals was a safe tech with a big ego. Some said it was as big as his Budweiser belly. Boastful of his skills, he was featured frequently on television, in newspapers, and in magazines. Touted as the best in Dade County, Irv's colleagues, including Rafe's father, had questioned his true ability. If not for the New York and LA murders, his death would have easily been considered a direct result of his flamboyant personality and lifestyle. The way he flaunted his skills, gold jewelry, and money would have left little speculation as to his murder.

No money or goods, though, had been taken from his shop or home. He was rendered unconscious and strangled to death and stuffed into one of his safes. Three fingers, those he used to manipulate safes were severed and missing. The calling card of a deranged killer. A mouse luring cats.

Johnny Pennetto, the Brooklyn victim, was as quiet and unassuming as wallpaper. Unlike Irv Samuals, he had guarded his privacy. With an unlisted telephone number, caller ID, a post office box, and frequent moves, he was a vagabond always looking over his shoulder. If not for his being a bonded independent contractor and a safe tech for reputable locksmiths, one could have easily assumed him to be a crook. Unfortunately, with all of his suspicions and precautions he had been hunted and murdered, stashed in a safe in one of his locksmith client's warehouses.

Georgie "Sticky Fingers" Martin was another story. A reformed criminal, he had found God and redemption and had given up his skill at opening safes as well as adding to his rap sheet. A legend in criminal and law enforcement circles, Georgie had retreated from life as an underworld safecracker to preach the Gospel. He made it to heaven earlier than expected, his casket a safe he had stored in his home office.

Rafe sat perched on the corner of his metal desk sipping strong black coffee. He stared at the reports stacked on his desktop and shook his head. Though he specialized in crimes relating to safes and vaults, including murder, this was his first experience with a serial killer and the first such case assigned to him as the designated agent in charge. His undergraduate degree in psychology, the courses he took with the FBI's behavioral science unit, and field experience in criminal profiling would come in handy.

"Serial killers have a disease," he had been told by one of the experts in the field.

"This one has an addiction to safes," Rafe thought aloud.

An addiction to safes was something he could relate to. After all, he had grown up amidst safes and safemen. His father was one of the best in the business and was determined that his son possess the same skills. From the time he could walk and talk, Raphael Costillo spent hours in his father's shop and out on service calls. The first word he ever uttered was "safe" and he had memorized the manufacturers and characteristics of safes before he knew the states and their capitals. He could see a safe, rattle off its make, model, and age and know how to logically proceed in opening it. When other parents were fearful of their children getting locked in a safe and suffocating, the Costillo's beamed with pride because their son could open them. He had kept a yellowed newspaper article and photograph of himself at age five beside a small Alpine he had manipulated open.

Safes had been good to him. By being a safe and vault technician, he had worked his way through college and law school. The profession even helped to finance a comfortable apartment and a shiny red Corvette, luxuries for most college students. Yet, his schoolmates thought the luxuries came from some secret life of crime. After all, how could a Hispanic boy from Little Havana finance such an upscale lifestyle? There wasn't enough challenge in working in his father's small shop and he needed to escape from the old neighborhood. He needed more. More stimulation. More demands. More knowledge that he was doing something to benefit society as well as his family and himself. He needed to prove that he was an equal and not a minority. To his father's shock, he joined the FBI.

Thinking about his father at Costillo Safe and Lock in Little Havana made him shudder. The "safeman murders" were hitting too close to home. The victims were people he understood. Some he had even met at safe and lock conferences and conventions. His father was the victims' contemporary. Luis Costillo was as legendary in the safe business as the victims. Rafe couldn't imagine his father murdered and stuffed into a safe. The thought made him flush with anger. He had to do everything within his ability to uncover the killer because his father could have been and could become a victim.

"Yo, *amigo*. Don't you have anything better to do than sit around and drink coffee?"

One didn't have to see Anthony DeGrasso to know he was around. The tangy pungent Aqua Velva after-shave and cologne he favored preceded him. Rafe rubbed his nose to suppress a sneeze. Though in the LA office the past two years, Tony retained that brash Brooklyn accent and attitude. A fellow FBI Special Agent, Tony grated on him but Rafe and he had formed an amicable, almost friendly working relationship.

"At least I drink real coffee, not that rotgut espresso you thrive on," Rafe answered with a chuckle.

"Heard you've been assigned to the 'safeman murders' case," Tony said.

"Yep." Rafe took another sip of his coffee.

"Hot Fingers Costillo to the rescue."

"You got it." Rafe winked though he hated the nickname given to him as a teen and perpetuated through the years.

"Seriously, how's it going?"

"It's going. My fear is that we have a serial killer on our hands. The faster we nab the guy the better."

"Who would wanna kill safe techs?" Tony asked, shoving his hands in his pants' pockets. "Not for Rice Krispies, eh? You know, *cereal*, serial?"

"Who would want to kill anyone?" Rafe didn't find humor in murder.

"Got a motive?"

Rafe stroked his chin. "First things first. Enough about me, what are you working on?"

"A bank fraud."

"Could be interesting."

Tony shrugged his sloped shoulders. "You get the high profile cases. I get the crumbs."

"But I get the stress and the danger, not to mention the nightmares. I'm sure you sleep well at night."

"With Bertha?" Tony's bushy black brows shot up.

"Hey buddy, you married her."

Tony winked. "That's not what I meant."

"Viagra works, doesn't it?" Rafe teased. With Tony it was difficult staying serious for long.

"You know, that's what you need, a good woman. You wouldn't be needing all that strong coffee."

"Here we go again. Have you been talking to my sister and my mother?"

A knock rattled Rafe's office door.

"Come in," Rafe called.

In strolled a bespectacled young woman, his more efficient than pretty administrative assistant.

"What's up, Jamie?" Rafe asked, eyeing the padded envelope she gingerly held.

"This came for you. Priority Mail," she answered, handing him the envelope.

"Who's it from?" Rafe asked, cocking an eyebrow as he perused the front of the envelope.

"I don't know."

"Hmm," Rafe mumbled. He hated envelopes and packages that arrived without return addresses. In his field, though, they were common. Informants and witnesses often wanted to shield their true identities.

"It's been checked with a wand," Jamie said.

"That's reassuring," Rafe said, casting a glance at the girl who was too smart and too plain for her own good.

Tony cleared his throat. "Surprise package?"

Without comment, Rafe ripped open an end. Inside was another smaller padded envelope with a sticker. Printed in red were the words, "Caution: Dry Ice."

After tearing open the end of the small envelope, Rafe spilled the contents on his desk.

A finger, cleanly severed, lay atop a mountain of papers.

"Holy shit!" Tony yelled.

Jamie, covering her mouth with her hands, raced out of the office.

Rafe stared at the finger, speechless.